Hesperus Or Forty-Five Dog-Post-Days
A Biography Vol. I

by

Jean Paul Friedrich Richter

Double9
BOOKS

Hesperus Or Forty-Five Dog-Post-Days
A Biography Vol. I
by Jean Paul Friedrich Richter

Copyright © 2024

All Rights reserved.

ISBN: 978-93-62761-20-0

Published by

DOUBLE 9 BOOKS

2/13-B, Ansari Road
Daryaganj, New Delhi – 110002
info@double9books.com
www.double9books.com
Tel. 011-40042856

ABOUT THE AUTHOR

Jean Paul, a prominent German Romantic writer, is renowned for his masterpiece "Hesperus; or, Forty-Five Dog-Post-Days," subtitled "A Biography." This literary work, published in 1795, intertwines elements of satire, humor, and philosophical depth to create a unique narrative experience. In "Hesperus," Jean Paul explores the life of the protagonist, Hesperus, through a series of whimsical and introspective episodes. The subtitle, "A Biography," suggests a deep dive into the inner workings of the character's psyche, presenting a vivid portrait of Hesperus' experiences, thoughts, and emotions. Jean Paul's distinctive writing style, characterized by elaborate prose and imaginative storytelling, captivates readers as they journey through Hesperus' adventures and encounters. Through witty observations and profound reflections, the author offers insights into the complexities of human nature and the pursuit of happiness. "Hesperus; or, Forty-Five Dog-Post-Days" stands as a testament to Jean Paul's literary genius, earning him acclaim as one of the foremost writers of the Romantic era. With its blend of humor, philosophy, and vivid characterization, this work continues to resonate with readers, inviting them to ponder life's mysteries and marvel at the beauty of storytelling.

CONTENTS

PREFACE TO THE THIRD EDITION

Two long Prefaces follow on the heels of this third,—the first that of the second edition, and the next that of the first. Now, if I make this third again a long one,—and perhaps also, in fact, the many remaining ones of future editions,—I do not see how a reader of these latter can get through the lane of antechambers to the historical picture-gallery: he will die on his way to the book.

I report, then, briefly. In this edition such amendments have been made as were most needed and easiest. In the first place, I have frequently translated myself into German out of the Greek, Latin, French, and Italian, and in fact in every instance where the speech-cleanser, with proper respect for the subject itself, demanded it. Once for all, we writers must all accommodate ourselves to the verbal-alien-bill, or decree for exiling foreigners, of Campe, Kolbe, and others; and even our beloved Goethe, however much he too "emergiert" and "eminiert," will at last, in some future edition or other, have, for example, to throw both of these very words, which in the latest[1] he brings forward in the same line, out of the book. Is it not time, now that we have ejected the foreign peoples which had been long enough encamped in Germany, that we should send after them what has still longer remained behind,—their echo, or words?

Only let Kolbe, or any other Purist, be a reasonable man, and not exhort us to change the technical words which are the common property of cultivated Europe—e. g. of music, of philosophy—into vernacular ones which will not be understood, especially in cases where the hand of the interpreter would snatch and pluck away the butterfly-dust of variegated allusions. For example, the name Purist itself may serve as an example. Supposing one should call Arndt a *political Purist* of Germany, and Kolbe should substitute political *speech-purifier*, or pure of speech, this small conceit would give up in the translation the little bit of ghost that it haply possessed.

Even if the author, however, has not turned out such things,—as some philological anchorites do, who, like the windpipe, eject all foreign matter with disagreeable coughing and spitting, and only retain their native air,— still he has at least sought to imitate the glaciers, which from year to year gradually shove down foreign bodies, such as stone and wood, from their sides. How diligently I have done this in the present edition of Hesperus, on every side, may be seen by the old printed copy interlined with the new emendations, and I could well wish Herr Kolbe would just travel to Berlin and inspect the copy. At least I will beseech the German Society there, which some years ago made me a member, to go to the bookstore and see for themselves what their colleague has done, what erasions and substitutions he has made.

The ones who have properly sinned the most against the German language, and against those who understand no other, are the natural-historians, who—e. g. Alexander von Humboldt—import the whole Latin Linnæus into the midst of our language, without any other German signs of distinction than the final flourishes of German terminations, or tail-feathers, wherewith, however, they are as little intelligible to the mere speaker of German as a man would be to a stranger behind him through his mere queue. Has not our inexhaustible language already shown its capability of creating a German Linnæus when we read a Wilhelmi, and still more that true German in heart and speech, Oken?

For the rest, the German language will, in general, never shrink up and grow impoverished, even by the greatest hospitality towards strangers. For it steadily produces (as all dictionaries show) out of its ever fresh stems a hundred times as many children and grandchildren and great-grandchildren as the foreign birth it adopts in the place of children; so that after centuries the thicket that has sprung from our prolific radical words must overshadow and choke up the strange words which have shot up only as flying seed, and finally rear itself into a true banian forest, whose twigs grow down to roots, and whose upward-planted roots strike out into summits. How entangled and wild with foreign growth will, on the contrary, after some centuries, the English language be, for instance, with its native but powerless stem full of engrafted word-shrubbery, capable only of inoculation, and fetching back from its duplicate, America, more new words than wares!

The second, but easier thing which has been done for this third, improved edition of Hesperus, of course is, that I have gone slowly through the whole Evening Star with weeder in hand, and carefully eradicated all the fungous weeds of genitives, or Es's, in compound words, wherever I found them, which on the very title-page of the *Dog's*-Post-days was unfortunately the case. I had, however, much to endure in this work. Of the old actions of our over-rich language against itself, too many are attachments upon its real estate, and I was compelled, therefore, to leave many a nested crew of Es's where it had too long been settled, and appealed to witnesses and ear-witnesses for right of possession.

Even up to the hour of this Preface, the author of the "*Morgen-Blatt letters on compound words*" has been waiting, not so much for a thorough-going *examination*, (it were, perhaps, too soon for that,) but first of all for a comprehensive *reading* of them, which, to be sure, the scattering archipelago of sheets, like islands lying apart from one another, will make difficult so long as the periodical has not yet run through its circle of numbers. But then I shall hope from the speech-investigator, when he has them complete in his house and hands before his judgment-seat, a thorough refutation or approbation.

Finally, in the third place, after the double amendment of two editions, (for the first received great improvements, and in fact *before* it was printed,) a third was undertaken which had for its object to let fly at harshnesses, obscurities, mistakes, and other over-lengthenings and overshortenings of dress.

But, heavens! how often must not a writing-man have to improve upon himself, who is hardly over half a century old! Were he to live, in fact, into a Methusalem's millennium, and continue to write, the Methusalem would have to append so many volumes of emendations that the work itself would have to be annexed to them as mere preliminary matter, appendix, or supplementary sheet.

For several years the author has found in his earlier works, in a high degree, a fault which he has met with in Ernst Wagner, Fouqué, and others, frequently repeated or imitated, namely, the passion for enacting, in his authorial person, the trumpeter, or usher, of the emotions, which the subject himself should have and show, but not the poet. E. g. "With sublime calmness Dahore replied." Why add *sublime*, when it is superfluous, presumptuous, and premature, provided the answer really exalts, or, if it does not so, the result is still more pitiful? The poet who, in this way, is the *fore-echo* of his personages, takes for his model certain modern tragic poets, like Werner, Müllner, &c., who prefix to every speech for the actor the bookbinder's directions: "With touching emotion," — "with a sigh of painful remembrance out of the depths of sorrow," — mere sentences of intensity, or rather of impotence, which only a pantomimic dance needs or can follow, but which no piece of Shakespeare's, of Schiller's, or of Goethe's needs, because, indeed, the speech itself teaches how to speak it.

For the rest, I have not the courage, now that I am a quarter of a century older and more aged, to give the first youthful outstreamings of the heart a different channel, and a weaker fall and course. Man in later life too easily regards every change in his junior as an improvement; but as no man can take the place of another, so, too, cannot the same man act as his own substitute in his different periods of life, least of all the poet.

The best *wedded* love is not what the *maidenly* was; and so, too, is there in inspiration and delineation a maiden muse. Ah, all first things in poesy, as in life, whatever else may be wanting to them, are so innocent and good; and all *blossoms* come so *pure-white* into the world, in which by and by,— as Goethe says,[2] even of material colors, "The sun tolerates no white." Therefore shall all the ardent words of my inspiration for Emanuel's dying and Victor's loving and weeping, and for Clotilda's sorrow and silence, stand evermore in Hesperus uncooled and unchanged. Even the Now shall take nothing from the Once. For although during these twenty-five years I have been made, by some imitations and echoes of the book, actually sick of myself, nevertheless I overcome the disgust of this self-surfeit by the hope that the youth who wrote will again, by and by, find young men and young women to read him, and that hereafter, even for older readers, more will survive of the thing imitated than of the imitations.

And so, then, may this Evening Star—which was once the morning star of my whole soul—run its *third* circuit around the reading world in the fuller light of a better position toward the sun and the earth!

JEAN PAUL FR. RICHTER.

Baireuth, January 1, 1819.

PREFACE TO THE SECOND EDITION

I have as yet completed nothing of this Preface beyond a tolerable sketch, which shall here be given to the leader unadorned. I may perhaps, by the gift of this sketch, also raise the curtain which continues to hang down before my literary workshop, and which hides from posterity how I labor therein as my own serving brother and as master of the Scottish chair. A plan is with me, however, no outline of a sermon in Hamburg, which the head pastor gives out on Saturday and fills out on Sunday. It is no automaton, no lay figure, no canon, after which I work; it is no skeleton for future flesh, but a plan is a leaf or sheet on which I make myself more comfortable and move more at ease, while I shake out upon it my whole brain-tree, in order afterwards to pick over and plant the windfalls, and cover—the paper with organic globules and layers of phœnix ashes, that whole brilliant pheasantries may rise out of it. In such a sketch I keep the most unlike and antagonistic things apart by mere dashes. In such sketches I address myself, and *thou* myself like a Quaker, and order myself about a great deal; nay, I frequently introduce therein conceits which I do not have printed at all, either because no connection can be contrived for them, or because they are of themselves good for nothing.

And now it will be time that I should really present the reader such a sketch, which happens to be this time the plan of the present Preface. It is headed:—

ARCHITECTURAL PLAN AND BUILDING MATERIAL FOR THE PREFACE TO THE SECOND EDITION OF HESPERUS.

"But make it short, because, as it is, the world will find it a long way through two antechambers into the passengers'-room of the Book.—Joke in the beginning.—Seldom does a man bowl all the Nine Muses on the literary ninepin-alley.—The conclusion from the reflection.—Bring out many resemblances between the title Hesperus and the Evening Star, or Venus, of which the following must be specimens: That mine, like the latter, is full of high, sharp mountains, and that both owe their greater splendor to their unevenness; further, that the one as well as the other, in its transit across the sun (of Apollo), appears only as a black spot.—(In your copy-book of letters you must have made numbers of such allusions.)—The world expects that the Evening Star in the second edition will come up from below, as Lucifer, or Morning Star, and that the glorified body of the paper will tabernacle a glorified soul: let it pass, and bring the world to its right bearings.—Regard pedants, who sustain and fodder themselves on words, not on things, as like the after-moths, which devour and digest wax cakes, but no honeycomb.—No one so very much resembles as pedants do the magpies, which are at once thievish and *garrulous*: they dilute and filch.— Into the critical hell precisely those classes of persons are not cast, which the Talmud also exempts from the Jewish, namely, the poor, those who cannot count, and those who are carried off by the diarrhœa.—Be a fox, and cajole the critical billiard-markers who announce loss and gain."—

This last I do not understand myself, because this sketch was written as long ago as the winter. I can rather confess, without irony, that the critical quarter-judges, or country-judges, have spared my life, and have not thrown over me either a Spanish mantle, or a cloak of humility, or a bloody shirt and hair-shirt. This indulgence of the critics for a writer of books, who, like a Catholic, performs more good works than he needs for salvation, is certainly not their worst characteristic, as they thereby exert such a beneficial influence on our empty days. For one must now be very glad if only four or five new similes are sent to the Easter fair, and if at Michaelmas only a few flowers, which are novelties, are offered for sale. Our literary kitchen-servants know how to play off on the table-cloth and into our mouths the same *goutée* over and over again, under the appearance of six different dishes, and entertain us twice a year with an imitation of the celebrated potato-banquet in Paris. At first came on merely a potato-soup; then potatoes again in another preparation; the third course, on the contrary, consisted of potatoes rehashed; so, too, the fourth. For the fifth, now, one could serve up potatoes again, when one had only announced for the sixth, potatoes cut into the novel form of brilliants,—and so it went on through fourteen dishes, of which, fortunately, one could still say, that at least bread, confectionery, and liquor comforted the stomach, and consisted of potatoes.—

Censure is an agreeable lemon-juice in praise; hence both are always bestowed by the world together, as if in the form of an oxymel; just as, according to the Talmud, a few fingerfuls of assafœtida were thrown with the other things upon the altar of burnt-offerings. The only thing, accordingly, which I will expose about the reviewers after the foregoing praise, and with which they really offend, is this, that they seldom (their heart is good) understand much of the subject or writing on which they pass judgment; and even this blame applies only to the greater part of them.—

"Weave it in (the sketch goes on) that you cannot make out what the unveiling and unshelling of women's arms,[3] bosoms, and backs at the present day can mean, just as, formerly, peacocks were served up on the game-dish with precisely the corresponding parts, necks, wings, and heads, unpicked.—It will be well, therefore, if you conjecture that the shell-less ladies are female Jesuits and Freemasons in disguise, because in both orders the mysteries and veilings begin with denudation; or lay these unfeathered limbs at the door of some starvation or other, as a chicken creeps forth from an egg, out of which one has only drawn off a few drops of the white, with featherless spots.—Threaten, at least, that ladies and crabs are best when caught and boiled in the moulting-season."—

This is one of the cases of which I said above, that in them I was obliged to give up and throw away conceits of the sketch, for want of connection with the main subject: for really the whole matter of the moulting of the limbs has nothing in common with the Preface, except the year of birth.

"You must deviate from other authors," the plan goes on, "and glide silently over the approbation you have reaped, so that the world may see just what you are.—One expects from the Preface to a second edition a little map of products, or a harvest register of all the after-bloom which exalts the second above the first: give them the register!—

With pleasure!—First, I have corrected all typographical errors,—then all slips of the pen,—then many cacophonies of language,—moreover, verbal and real blunders enough; but the conceits and the poetical tulips I have seldom rooted out. I saw that if I did so there would be left in the world not much more of the book (because I should strike out the whole style) than the binding and the list of errata. The theologian hates juristic allusions,—the jurist, theological ones,—the physician, both,— the mathematician, all of them. I love them all. What shall one leave out or retain?—The woman is displeased with satire, the man with softening warmth, (for *coldness* in *books*, as in *cakes of chocolate,* he holds to be proof of excellence,) and the public itself has forty-five opinions upon a chapter, as Cromwell dictated four contradictory letters to the same correspondent, merely for the sake of concealing from his scribes the purport of the one which he really despatched.—To which opinion shall an author adhere in such a disagreement?—Most properly to his own, as the world to its own.—

For the rest, my little[4] work can hardly see so many *printed* editions as I have arranged of *written* and improved ones in my study; and therefore great alterations in it are, if not less indispensable, at least more difficult. In the plan of the story itself, therefore,—even supposing I had forgotten that it is a true one,—there is little to change for the better, because the work is like my breeches, which were not made by a tailor, but by a stocking-loom, and in which the breaking of a single stitch of the right shank unravels the whole fabric of the left. For it is an essential, but undeniable, fault of the book,—which I easily explain by the want of episodes,—that the moment I take out from the first story (or volume) any defective stone whatever, immediately in the third all totters, and at last comes down. Of course I thereby fall far in the rear of the best new romances, where one can break out or build in considerable pieces without the least injury to the composition and fire-proof quality, simply because they resemble, not, like my book, a mere house, but a whole toy-city from Nuremberg, whose loose, unhitched houses the child piles away in his play-house, and whose mosaic of huts the dear little one easily puts together for his amusement, streetwise, just as he fancies. A true story always has the annoying thing about it, that in its case this cannot be done.

However, I sufficiently excuse my work on the score of artistic *changes* and *improvements* by true *enlargements* of it through historical additions. As I fortunately have for some years myself lived and been housed among the persons whom I have portrayed, accordingly I am perfectly in a position, as fly-wheel of this fair family circle, to supply, from the depositions of living witnesses, a thousand corrections and explanations which otherwise no man could learn, which however throw light on the somewhat dark history. Let the critic simply turn over the two nearest chapters of the book, or the remotest, or any others.

My critics would complacently persuade me that I should have avoided in the additions what they call superfluous wit, and skilfully watered the gleaming naphtha-soil of my Evening Star, which was neither to be quenched nor sunk, with fresh history.—Heaven grant it! I have slim hope of it; but I should be glad if the reviewers would assure me that I had— although not sold at auction or covered up the crowded images in my Pantheon-Pandemonium—still, however, at least hung them farther apart.

"On the whole," continues the sketch, "take in hand the historical *grafting-knife* rather than the *weeder*!"

I just said that I have done so.

"But as touching those dried-up, withered men, in whose eyes nothing is great but their own image, and whose stomach at the sight of a fairer movement of the exalted heart is taken with a *reverse* movement,—in short, whom everything nauseates (except what is nauseous),—make believe as if you did not perceive them; and so much more as they resemble patients who are gnawed by the tape-worm, and who, according to medical observations, sicken and vomit at all music, especially organs, think rather of the good souls whom thou knowest and lovest, and of the good ones whom thou only lovest,—and therefore at the end of the Preface be earnest and grateful and rejoice!"—

Verily that I should have done, even without the sketch!—How could I remain insensible to the indulgence with which, on the whole, the world has appropriated the Aphrodito-graphic[5] fragments of my Evening Star, which runs around the sun with such remarkable aberrations, or deflections, and in so little of a planetary ellipse, that it may easily, as often happens to the Hesperus in the sky, be taken for a hairy, bearded, and tailed comet?—And how hard and cold must the soul be which could remain without emotion and without joy at the thought of the shortest happy day, nay, even happy second, or *third,* into which it had been able to introduce suffering men; and at the wide-spread relationship of lofty wishes and holy hopes, and friendly feelings, and at the gracious concordat wherein the brawlers and wranglers in this first world of the prosaic life give each other their hands in the *second* world of poetry, in mutual recognitions, and become brothers?—

Once more, good Asterisk and secondary planet of the soft evening-star above me, I follow thee on thy way with the wishes of three years ago for every soul which thou canst gladden. Only never rise upon any eye as a rainy star,—only never lead one astray, so that it shall take the *moonlight* of poesy for the *morning* of truth, and dismiss too early its morning dreams!— But into the torture-chambers and through the prison-gratings of forsaken souls throw a cheering radiance; and for him whose blessed island has sunk away from him to the bottom of the sea of eternity, transfigure thou the low, dark region; and whoever looks round and looks up in vain in a dismantled Paradise, to him may a little ray from thee show, down on the ground, under the yellow leaves, some hidden sweet fruit or other of a former time; and if there is any eye to which thou canst show nothing, draw it softly upward to thy brother, and to the heaven in which he shines.—Nay, and if I ever grow too old, then comfort me also!

Hof, May 16, 1797.

PREFACE, SEVEN REQUESTS, AND CONCLUSION

PREFACE

I Was going to be indignant, in the beginning, at some hosts of readers with whom I know not what to do in this book, and I was about to station myself at the gate of Hesperus as porter, and with the greatest incivility send off particularly people who are good for nothing, for whom, as for a prosector, the heart is nothing but the thickest muscle, and who carry a brain and heart and interior parts generally as moulds of plaster statues do their stuffing of wood, hay, and clay, merely in order to turn out *hollow* from the casting. I was on the point, even, of scolding at honest business-people who, like Antoninus the Great, thank the gods that they never did much at poetry; and at those to whom the chapel-leader, Apollo, must discourse on a rebeck, or straw fiddle, and his nine soprano girls with the ale-house fiddle and corn-stalk bass-viol. Nay, even at the reading sisterhood of the Romances of Chivalry, who read as they marry, and who among books, as among gentlemen's faces, pick out, not the fair, feminine ones, but the wild, masculine ones. —

But an author should not be a child, and embitter for himself his Preface, when it is not every day that he has to make one. Why did I not rather in the first line address *those* readers, and take them by the hand, to whom I joyfully give my Hesperus, and whom I would present with a free copy of it if I knew where they lived? — Come, dear, weary soul, thou that hast anything to forget, either a sad day or a clouded year, or a human being that afflicts thee, or one that loves thee, or a dismantled youth, or a whole life of heaviness; and thou, crushed spirit, for whom the present is a wound and the past a scar, come into my *Evening-Star* and refresh thyself with its little glimmer; but, if the poetic illusion gives thee sweet, fugitive pains, be this thy conclusion from it: perhaps that, too, is an illusion which causes me the longer and deeper ones. — And as to thee, loftier man, who findest our life, which is passed only in a *glass*, darkly, less than thyself and death, and whose heart a veiled great spirit grinds brighter and purer in the dead dust of other mouldered human hearts, as one polishes the diamond with the dust of a diamond, I may call thee, too, down into my evening and night star to such eminence as I am able to throw up, that, when thou seest gliding around it at the foot, as around Vesuvius, *morganic fays* and mist groupings and dreamy worlds and shadowy lands, thou shalt perhaps say to thyself, "And so is all dream and shadow around me; but dreams imply spirits, and clouds countries, and the shadow of the earth a sun and a universe?" —

But to thee, noble spirit, who art weary of the age and of the after-winter of humanity, to whom sometimes, but not always, the human race, like the moon, seems to go backward, because thou mistakest the procession of clouds flying by below it for the course of the heavenly body, and who, full of exalted sighs, full of exalted wishes, and with silent resignation, hearest indeed beside thee a destroying hand and the falling of thy brothers, but yet castest not down thy eye, upraised to the ever serene, sunny face of Providence, and whom misfortune, as lightning does man, destroys, but not *disfigures*; to thee, noble spirit, I have, to be sure, not the courage to say, "Deign to look upon my play of shadows, that the Evening-Star which I usher before thee may make thee forget the earth on which thou standest, and which now with a thousand graves lays itself, like a vampyre, upon the human race, and sucks the blood of victims!" — And yet I have thought of thee all through the book, and the hope of bringing my little night and evening piece before wet, upraised, and steadfast eyes has been the sustaining maul-stick[6] of my weary hand.

As I have now written too seriously, I must, out of the seven promised petitions, among which only four are such, omit three. I therefore present only the

First Request. That the reader will pardon the title, "Dog-Post-Days," until the first chapter has explained and excused it; and the

Second. Always to read a whole chapter, and never half a one, because the great whole consists of little wholes, as, according to the Homoiomereia[7] of Anaxagoras, the human body consists of innumerable little human bodies; and the

Seventh Request, which flows partly from the second, but concerns the critics only, not to anticipate me in their *fugitive leaves*,[8] which they call Reviews, by the publication of my leading incidents, but to leave the reader some few surprises, which, to be sure, he can have only once. And finally the

Fifth Petition, which one knows already from the Lord's Prayer.[9]

CONCLUSION

And now, then, become visible, little peaceful Hesperus—Thou needest a little cloud to veil thee, and a little year, in order to have completed thy orbit!—Mayest thou stand nearer to Truth and Virtue, as thy image in heaven does to the sun, than the earth into which thou shinest does to either of the three; and mayest thou, like that star, never withdraw thyself from the sight of men, except by hiding thyself in the sun! May thy influence be fairer, warmer, and surer than that of the Almanac-Hesperus, which superstition places on the misty throne of *this* year!—Thou wouldst make me happy a second time if thou shouldst be an *Evening-Star* to some withered mortal, and to some blooming one a *morning star*. Sink with the former and rise with the latter; glow in the evening sky of the first between his clouds, and overspread his past life-road up the mountain with a soft lustre, that he may recognize again the far-off flowers of youth; and rejuvenate his antiquated recollections into hopes!—Cool off the fresh youth in the early hours of life, as a tranquillizing morning star, ere the sun falls hot upon him and the whirl of day sets in!—But for me, Hesperus, thou art now well set; thou hast hitherto journeyed on beside the earth, as my companion-planet, as my second world, on which my soul disembarked as it left the body to the buffetings of earth; but to day my eye falls sadly and slowly off from thee and thy white flower-bed, which I planted around thy coasts, down upon the damp, cold ground where I stand, and I see how we are all encompassed with coolness and evening, torn far away from the stars, amused with glowworms, disquieted with *ignes fatui*, all veiled from each other, every one alone, and feeling his own life only through the warm, throbbing hand of a friend, which he holds in the dark.—

Yes, there will indeed come another age, when it will be light, and when man will awake out of sublime dreams and find—the dreams again, because he has lost nothing but sleep.—

The stones and rocks, which two veiled shapes, Necessity and Sin, like Deucalion and Pyrrha, throw behind them at the good, shall become new men.—

And on the western gate of this century stands written: Here is the road to Virtue and Wisdom; just as on the western gate of Cherson[10] stood the sublime inscription: Here leads the way to Byzantium.—

Infinite Providence, thou wilt make the day dawn. —

But still struggles the twelfth hour of the night; nocturnal birds of prey shoot through the darkness; spectres rattle; the dead play their antics; the living dream.

JEAN PAUL.

In the *Vernal Equinox,* 1794.

1
DOG-POST-DAY

In the house of the Court-Chaplain Eymann, in the bathing-village of St. Luna, there were two parties: the one was glad on the 30th of April that our hero, the young Englishman, Horion, would return from Göttingen the 1st of May to stay at the parsonage,—the other disliked it; they did not want him to arrive till the 4th of May.

The party of the 1st of May, or Tuesday, consisted of the Chaplain's son, Flamin, who had been educated with the Englishman till his twelfth year in London, and till his eighteenth in St. Luna, and whose heart with all its venous ramifications had grown into the Briton's, and in whose ardent breast during the long Göttingen separation there had been *one* heart too few; next, of the Chaplain's wife, a native Englishwoman, who loved in my hero a countryman, because the magnetic vortex of nationality reached her soul over land and sea; and, finally, of their eldest daughter, Agatha, who all day long laughed out at everything and doted on everything without knowing why, and who, with her polypus-arms, drew every one to herself who did not live quite too many houses off from her, as food for her heart.

The sect of the 4th of May could measure itself with its rival, for it also made out a college of three members. Its adherents were Appel (Apollonia, the youngest daughter), who acted as cook, and whose culinary reputation and certificate of good bakery would suffer by it, if the guest should come before the bread rose; she could well conceive what a soul must feel who should stand before a guest with her hands full of skewers and needles, beside the flat-iron of the window-curtains, and without having even the *frisure* of her hat, or of the head which was to be under it, so much as half ready. The second adherent of this sect, who ought to have had most to say against Tuesday,—although he said least, because he could not talk and had only recently been baptized,—was to be carried to church on Friday for the first time; this adherent was the godchild of the guest. The Chaplain knew, to be sure, that the moon sent round her godfather-bidder, Father Riccioli,[11] among the *savans* of earth, and got them into the church-book of heaven as godfathers to her spots; but he thought it was better for him to take a godfather within a circumference of not more than fifty miles. The

Apostles'-day of the churching and the Festival-day of the arrival of the distinguished godfather would then have beautifully coincided; but now the plaguy fine weather was bringing godfather along four days too soon!

The third disciple of Friday was, at bottom, the heresiarch of this party, the Court-Chaplain himself: the parsonage wherein Horion was to have his temporary court residence was all full of rats,—a regular ball-room and *plaza de armas* of the same,—and of these the Chaplain wanted first of all to clear his house. Few court-chaplains, with hectic in their bodies and rats in their houses, ever made so much stench on that account as did this one in St. Luna against the beasts. It would have taken very few clouds of it to smoke all the court-dames out of Europe. Did not our hectic patient burn as much of the hoof of his nag as he had sawed off from it? Didn't he even take one of the sharp-toothed creatures themselves prisoner, and smear him with gudgeon-grease and train-oil, and then let the arrested subject go, that he might as a pariah trot up and down through the holes, and constrain by his ointment rats of higher caste to emigrate? Did he not go to work by the wholesale, and actually take a buck to board, of which he wanted nothing except that he should stink and displease the tailed monks? And were not all these remedies as good as useless?... For the deuse take rats and Jesuits! Meanwhile, I will at least offer people here on the very third page the moral, that against both of these pests, as against toothache, mental troubles, and fleas, there are a thousand excellent recipes which have no effect.

We will now, in a body, make our way farther into the parsonage, and concern ourselves as minutely about the family history of the Eymanns as if we lived only three houses distant from them. Horion,—the accent must fall on the first syllable,—or Sebastian, by abbreviation *Bastian*, as the Eymanns called him,—or Victor, as Lord Horion, his father, called him, (for I give him now one name and now another, just as my prose-prosody requires,)— Horion had, through the Italian Tostato, who was a peripatetic Auerbach's court for that whole region, and was hurrying on to St. Luna, caused the little oral lie to be palmed upon his dear friends at the parsonage, that he was coming on Friday: he wanted, first, to give them a real surprise; and, secondly, he wanted modestly to tie the hands, which on his account *would* be scouring, brushing up and serving up; and, thirdly, he regarded an oral lie as at least more trivial than a written one. To his father, however, he wrote the truth, and fixed his entrance into the parsonage for the 1st of May, or Tuesday. His Lordship had his abode in the residence city of Flachsenfingen, where he applied to the Prince at once moral blinders and *eye-glasses*, and *guided* his vision while he *sharpened* it; but he was himself blind, though only physically. For that reason his son had to bring an oculist with him from Göttingen, who should operate upon him in the Chaplain's house on

Tuesday. When he caused his Victor to be made Doctor of Medicine, many Göttingen people, to my knowledge, wondered that so high-born a youth should put on the Doctor's head-piece,—that *Pluto's helmet*, which makes, not, like the mythological one, the wearer, but others indeed invisible,—and thrust on his finger the Doctor's ring,—that *ring-of—Gyges*, which only to others imparts invisibility: but was, then, the condition of his father's eyes unknown or an insufficient apology to the people of Göttingen?

His Lordship wrote to the Court-Chaplain that he and his son would come to-morrow. The Chaplain read over the Job's-post silently three times in succession, and thrust it back with comic resignation into the envelope, saying: "We have now ample hope that to-morrow our Doctor will certainly arrive with the rest;—fine tournaments and watering-place amusements do I anticipate, wife! when to-morrow comes in, and my rats in a body dance like children before him;—besides, we have nothing to eat; and then, too, I have nothing to put on, for not before Thursday can I extort from that Flachsenfingen wind-bag[12] a hair-bag,—and you laugh at it? Is not one of us in the very middle of April made an April-fool of?" But the Chaplain's lady fell on his shoulder with redoubled exclamations of delight, and ran right off to gather to this rose festival of her good soul the little brethren and sisters of the church of the children. The whole family circle now resolved itself into three terrified and three delighted faces.

We will seat ourselves only among the joyous ones, and listen while they, during the afternoon, work away as portrait-painters, drapery-painters, and gallery-inspectors, at the picture of the beloved Briton. All remembrances are made into hopes, and Victor is to bring nothing with him that is changed except his stature. Flamin, wild as an English garden, but more fruitful, refreshed himself and others with his delineation of Victor's gentle truthfulness and honesty, and of his head, and praised even his poetic fire, which he generally did not rate very high. Agatha called to mind his humorous knight's-leaps,—how he once took the drum of a passing dentist and drummed the village together for nothing before his theatre, because he had previously bought out the whole travelling apothecary's shop of this honest and true friend Hain,[13]—how he would often, after a child's baptism, post himself in the pulpit, and there be-preach two or three devout spectators in their work-day sward, till they laughed more than they wept,—and many another piece of waggery, whereby he would make no one ridiculous but himself, and set no one laughing but other people.

But women will never approve of it (only men can) when one, like Victor, belongs to the British subdivision of humorists;—for with them and courtiers wit itself is caprice;—they cannot approve that Victor should love to *descend* to carriers, clowns, and sailors, whereas a Frenchman would rather *creep upward* to people of *ton*. For women, who always respect the citizen more than the man, do not see that the humorist makes believe that all which these plebeians say he prompts them to, and that he intentionally exalts the involuntarily comic to what is artistically so,—folly to wisdom, the earth's madhouse to a national theatre. Quite as little does an official comprehend, or a cit, or a metropolitan, why Horion should so often make such a wretched choice of reading from among old prefaces, programmes, advertisements of travelling artists, all which he would peruse with indescribable gusto,—merely because he made believe to himself that all this intellectual sack of fodder, which belonged properly only to the rag-picker, he had himself prepared and filled, with satirical design. In fact, as the Germans seldom appreciate irony and seldom write it, one is forced to foist fictitiously a malicious irony upon many serious books and reviews, in order to get any of it at all. And that, indeed, is no more nor less than what I myself aim at, when in court-session I elevate in thought the court-house to a play-house, the advocate to a juristic Le Cain and Casperl, and the whole assembly to an old Greek comedy; for I never rest till I have made myself believe that I have caused the good people just to study out the whole case as a star-part, and am therefore really theatre poet and manager. Thus, in fact, do I merrily carry my dumb head as a comic pocket-theatre of the Germans through their most august institutions (e. g. the university, the administration), and exalt, in perfect silence—behind the dropped curtain of my face-skin—the comic of Nature to the comic of Art.

To return: the Chaplain's wife now related as much about Victor as all knew before. But this repetition of the old story is just the fairest charm of domestic discourse. If we can often repeat to *ourselves* sweet thoughts without *ennui*, why shall not another be suffered to awaken them within us still oftener? The good lady pictured to her children how gentle and tender, how delicate and womanly, her dear son was (for Victor always called her his mother),—how he relied upon her in all things,—how he was always sporting without ever teasing anybody, and always loved all human beings, even the greatest strangers,—and how she could open before him better than to any matron her oppressed heart, and how fondly he wept with her. A court-apothecary, with a heart of pumice-stone,—*Zeusel* he writes himself,—once even regarded this melting of the warmest soul as a case of *lachrymal fistula*, because he thought that no eyes could weep but diseased ones.... Dear reader, do you not feel now just as the biographer does, who can hardly wait for the entrance of this good Victor into the parsonage and the biography? Will you not offer to him the friendly hand, and say: "Welcome, unknown one! Lo, thy soft heart opens ours here on the very threshold! O thou man with eyes full of tears, dost thou, then, feel with us, that in a life whose banks are lined with affrighted ones clinging to the *twigs*, and despairing ones clinging to the *leaves*, that, in such a life, where not only follies, but woes also hedge us round, man must keep a wet eye for red ones, an aching heart for every bleeding one, and a gentle hand that shall, in sad sympathy, hold the thick, heavy chalice of sorrow for the poor man who must drain it, and shall slowly raise it to his lips? And if thou art such a one, then speak and laugh as thou wilt, for no one should laugh at men but he who right heartily loves them."

In the afternoon the Chief Chamberlain, Le Baut,—a fragrant leaf-skeleton,—sent his page, Seebass, to the Chaplain to beg that he would—for the palace lay near the parsonage across the way—remove the buck for a while, only until the wind should change, because his daughter was coming. "Esteemed Mr. Seebass!" answered the rat-controvertist, with emotion, "carry back my submissive compliments, and you see my distress. Tomorrow the Lord and his son and his oculist will gladden me with their presence, and the cataract is to be couched here. Now, at present, the whole house stinks, and the rats still carry on composedly their night-dance in the midst of the perfume; I assure you, Mr. Seebass, we can take assafœtida and stuff the parsonage with it up to the ridge-pole, not a tail shall we expel thereby; nay, it pleases them the more. I, for my part, am already preparing myself to see them to-morrow, during the operation, spring up on the very oculist and patient. Thus it fares with us all, please announce at the palace, but say that I was going to-day also to try an excellent rosewood-oil."

He fetched, therefore, a great sack of hops and dragged it up under the roof, in order there, in a literal sense, to lead the rats by the nose into the bag. Rats are notoriously as dead-set upon rosewood-oil as men are on anointing-oil, which, so soon as only six drops fall on the skull, makes one a king or bishop on the spot, which I see by the fact, that in the first case a golden hoop shoots round the hair, and in the second it actually falls off. The militia, that is, the Chaplain, sprinkled the sack with some oil, and laid it with its mouth stretched and fastened wide open to receive the enemy;—he himself stood in the background, concealed behind a similarly oiled stove-screen. His plan was, to start out when the beasts were once in the sack, and carry off the whole crew like bees in a swarming-bag. The few chamber-hunters who read me must have frequently used this kind of trap. But they may not have stumbled over it as the Chaplain did, who was caught with the fragrant stove-screen between his legs, and who lay unable to stir, while the enemy ran off. In such a situation a man is refreshed by the trill of a curse. So after the Chaplain had struck a few such trills and thrills, had betaken himself to the family, and said to them, *en passant*: If there were in the temperate zone a fellow who from his swaddling-clothes rode a mourning-steed, who was lodged in a second mouse-tower of Hatto, and in an Amsterdam house of correction, and in limbo,—if there were any such correctioner, in regard to whom the only wonder was how he continued alive,—he alone was the one, and no devil beside him ... after he had relieved himself of this, he left the rats in peace,—and was himself very much so.

In the night nothing memorable occurred, except that he kept awake and listened in every direction to hear if something with a tail might not be stirring, because he was minded to vex himself to his heart's content. As there was no sign of the beasts to be detected, not so much as a side-leap, he got out and sat on the floor, and pressed his spy's-ear to that. As good luck would have it, just then the movements of the enemy with their ballets and gallopades burst upon his ear. He started up, armed himself with a child's drum, and woke his wife up with the whisper: "Sweet! go to sleep again, and don't be frightened in your sleep; I'm only drumming a little against the rats; for the Zwickau Collection of Useful Observations for Housekeepers in Town and Country, 1785, recommends this course."

His first thunder-stroke gave his hereditary foes the repose which it snatched from his blood relations.... But as I have now put everybody into a condition to imagine the Chaplain in his shirt and with the cymbal of the soldiery, let us rather go to the bed of his son Flamin, and see what *he* is doing therein. Nothing,—but out of it he is at this moment taking a ride at this late hour, and that, too, without saddle or waistcoat. He, whose bosom was a cave of Æolus, full of pent-up storms—(any discreet prothonotary in Wetzlar would have scraped his fish-head or partridge's-wing cleaner or brushed his velvet-knee cleaner than he)—could not possibly lie longer on his pillow,—he to whom a drum came so near to-night, and to-morrow a friend. Anybody else, of course (at least the reader and myself), in the midst of the transparent night wherewith April was closing, the wide stillness on which the drum-sticks fell, the longing for a loved one with whom to-morrow would again make whole a desolate heart and a dismembered life, would have been filled by all this with tender emotions and dreams;—its only effect on the Chaplain's son was to fling him on his nag and out into the night: his inward earthquakes could only be allayed by a bodily gallop. He flew up and down the hill, on which he would to-morrow reunite himself to his Horion, ten times. He cursed and thundered at all his passions—to be sure *with* passion—which had hitherto laid the bone-saw to their hands linked in friendship. "Oh! when I once have thee again, Sebastian," he said, and twitched his nag round, "I will be so gentle, as gentle as thou, and never misconstrue thee; if I do, may the thunder—" Ashamed at his self-contradictory impetuosity, he rode merely at an ambling-pace home.

His longing for his returning friend he expressed in the stable by plucking out some hairs from the top of the horse's head, drawing the cue-hair like the fourth string of a fiddle, and twisting off the bit of the key to the fodder-chest. Only a man who languishes for a friend *exactly* as for a loved woman deserves either. But there are men who go out of the world without ever having been troubled or concerned at the fact that no one in it had loved them. He who knows nothing higher than the *commercial treaty* of self-interest, the *social contract* of civility, or even than the *boundary* and *barter agreement* of love, such a one,—but I wish he had never ordered me from the publisher!—whose withered heart knows nothing of the *Unitas Fratrum* of men joined in friendship, of the intertwining of their nobler vascular system, and of their sworn confederacy in strife and sorrow—But I see not why I should talk so long of this ninny, as he knows not how to enter into the least feeling of Flamin's yearning, who desired a loving, appreciative eye, because his faults and his virtues stood out in equal relief; for with other men, either at least the spots balance the rays, or the rays the spots.

Only in princely stables is there an earlier and louder din than there was in the parsonage on the blessed 1st of May. I ask any female reader at random, whether there can ever be more to polish and to boil than on a morning when a lord with a cataract is expected, and his son, too, and an eye-doctor? Men's resting-days always fall upon women's rasping-days; father and son went composedly to meet the doctor and the coucher.

The 1st of May began, like man and human history, with a mist. Spring, the Raphael of the northern earth, stood already out of doors and covered all apartments of our Vatican with his pictures. I love a mist whenever it glides off like a veil from the face of a fair day, and whenever it is created, not by the "four *faculties*," but by greater ones. When (as this one did on the 1st of May) it webs-over summits and streams like a drag-net,—when the clouds, pressed down by their weight, crawl along on our lawns and through wet bushes,—when in one quarter it soils the heavens with a pitchy vapor and lines the wood with a heavy, unclean fog-bank, while in the other, wiped off from the moist sapphire of the sky, it gilds with minute drops the flowers, and when this blue splendor and that dirty night pass over close by each other and exchange places,—who does not feel, then, as if he saw lands and nations lying before him, on which poisonous and mephitic mists move round in groups, now coming and now going? And when, further, this white night encompasses my melancholy eye with flying streams of vapor, with floating, fluttering particles of perfume-dust, then do I sadly see in the vapor human life pictured, with its two great clouds on our rising and setting, with its seemingly light space around us, and its blue opening over our heads....

The Doctor may have thought so too, but not father and son, who are going to meet him. Flamin is more powerfully affected by distant than by near nature, by the gross than by the detail, just as he has more feeling for the state than for the family room, and his inner man loves best to twine upward on pyramids, tempests, Alps. The Chaplain enjoys nothing about the whole thing except—May-butter, and from his mouth, amidst all this moral apparatus, issues nothing but—spittle, and both, because he is afraid of the damp's preying upon him and gnawing at his throat and stomach.

As they strode down from the hill which was the scene of the nocturnal gallop into a valley confused with patches of mist; there marched out from it to meet them three garrison regiments on the double-quick. Each regiment was four men strong and as many deep, without powder or shoes, but provided with fine openwork high-ruffles,—that is to say, with porous pantaloons, and with superfluous officers, because there were no privates for them at all. When I now go on in my description to add, that both staffs, as well the regimental as the general staff, had over six hundred cannon in their pockets, and in fact a whole siege-train of artillery, and that the first platoon had wholly new *yellow* balls,[14] unusual in war, which germinated sooner than the gunpowder sowed by the savages, and which they thrust with the tongue into the muskets,—I should (I fear) make my readers, especially my lady readers, a little too distressed (and the more as I have not yet hinted whether these were soldier-parents or soldier-children) if I were to dip my pen again, and actually append the annoying circumstance that the troops began to fire at the befogged Court-Chaplain,—unless I leaped forward instanter with the information beforehand that a man's voice from behind the army cried, "Halt!"

Forth came out of the rear ranks the general field-marshal, who was just as tall again as his lieutenant of artillery;—with a round hat, with flying arms and hair, he rushed impetuously upon Flamin, and attacked him with intent to destroy,—less from hatred than from love. It was the Doctor! The two friends hung trembling in each other's arms, face buried in face, breast pushed back from breast, with souls that had no words, but only tears of joy: the first embrace ended in a second,—the first utterances were their two names.

The Chaplain had volunteered as a private along with the army, and stood with tried feelings on his insulating-stool, with a bare neck, around which nothing clung. "Just hug each other a moment longer," said he, and turned half-way round: "I must station myself only just a minute or two at the hazel-bush yonder, but I will be back again directly, and then I, in my turn, will embrace Mr. Doctor with a thousand pleasures." But Horion understood the natural recoil of love; he flew from the son's arms into those of the father, and lingered long therein, and made all good again.

With appeased love, with dancing hearts, with overflowing eyes, under the full bloom of heaven and over the garniture of earth,—for Spring had opened her casket of brilliants, and flung blooming jewels into all the vales, and over all the hills, and even far up the mountains,—the two friends sauntered blissfully along, the British hand clasping the German. Sebastian Horion could not say anything to Flamin, but he talked with the father, and every indifferent sound made his bosom, laden with blood and love, breathe more freely.

The three regiments had gone out of every one's head; but they had themselves marched obediently after the general field-marshal. Sebastian, too humane to forget any one, turned round toward the escort of little Sansculottes, who came, however, not from Paris, but from Flachsenfingen, and had attended him as begging soldier-children. "My children," said he, and looked at nothing but his standing army, "to-day is for your generalissimo and you, the memorable day on which he does three things. In the first place, I discharge you; but my retrenchment shall not hinder you any more than a prince's would from begging; secondly, I pay each of you arrearage for three years; namely, to each officer an allowance of three seventeen-kreutzer-pieces, because we have in these days raised the wages; thirdly, run back again to-morrow, and I will have all the regiments measured for breeches."

He turned toward the Chaplain, and said: "It is much better to make presents in articles than in money, because gratitude for the latter is spent as soon as that is; but in a pair of presented pantaloons, gratitude lasts as long as the overhauls themselves."

The only bad thing about it will be, that the Prince of Flachsenfingen and his war-ministry will at last interfere in the matter of the trousers, since neither can possibly allow regular troops to have more *on* their bodies than *in* them, namely, anything at all. In our days it should at last enter the heads of the stupidest commissary of equipment and provisioning,—but in fact there are discreet ones,—first, that, of two soldiers, the hungry is always to be preferred to the well-fed one, because it is already known, by the case of whole peoples, that the less they have, so much the braver they are; secondly, that just as, in Blotzheim,[15] of two equally virtuous youths, the poorer is crowned, even so the poor subject is preferred to the rich, though they may be equally courageous, and is alone enlisted, because the poor devil is better acquainted with hunger and frost; and, thirdly, that now, when on all the steps of the throne, as on walls, cannon are placed (as the sun receives its brilliancy from thousands of vomiting volcanoes), and, as in a well-conditioned state, the rod of up-shooting manhood is forced into ramrods,—the people advantageously fall into two classes of paupers,—the protected and their protectors; and, fourthly, the Devil take him who grumbles!

When my three beloved *personæ* at length arrived in front of the parsonage, the whole disbanded army had secretly marched after them and demanded the breeches. But something still greater had travelled after them from Flachsenfingen,—the blind lord. Hardly had the Britoness smiled-in her young guest, not politely, but delightedly, hardly had Agatha, for the first time, seriously, hid herself behind her mother, and old Appel behind the pots and kettles, when Eymann, who was in the midst of his cleaning, made a long leap from the window at which four Englanders—not foreigners, but horses—came trotting up. Now for the first time the question occurred to every one, where the oculist was; and Sebastian had hardly time to reply, that there was no one else to come, for he himself was to operate on his father. Into the short interval which the father occupied in passing from the carriage-door to the room-door the son had to squeeze in the fib, or rather the entreaty *for* the fib, which the family was to put upon his Lordship, that his son had not yet arrived, but only the oculist, whom a recent apoplectic attack had deprived of his speech.

I and the reader stand amidst such a throng of people, that I have not yet been able even to tell him that Dr. Culpepper had as good as punched out the lord's left eye with the blunt couching-needle; in order, therefore, to save the right eye of his beloved father, Sebastian had applied himself to the cure of those impoverished beings, who, as regards their sight, already grope round in Orcus, and only with four of their senses stand any longer outside the grave.

When the son beheld the dear form veiled in such a long night, for whom there was no longer child or sunlight, he slid his hand, whose pulse trembled with pity, joy, and hope, under Eymann's, and hurriedly extended it, and pressed the father's under a strange name. But he had to go out of the house door again, till the trembling of his hand under the weight of the salvation it was bringing should subside, and he restrained out there his heart beating with hope by the thought that the operation might be unsuccessful; he looked with a smile up and down along the twelve-horse-team of the corps of cadets, that the emotion and yearning might pass from his excited breast. In-doors, meanwhile, the Chaplain's wife had made the blind man a still blinder one, and lied to him *quantum satis;* whenever a lie, a pious fraud, a *dolum bonum,* a poetic and legal fiction is to be gotten up, women offer themselves readily as business secretaries and court-printers, and help out their honest man. "I very much wish," said the father, as the son entered, "that the operation might at once proceed before my son arrives." The Chaplain's wife brought back the anxious son and disclosed to him the paternal wish. He stepped lightly forward amidst the embarrassed company. The room was shaded, the couching-lancet brought forth, and the diseased eye steadied. All stood with anxious attention around the composed patient. The Chaplain peered with a ludicrous anxiety and agony at the sleeping infant, prepared, at the least cry, to run with it immediately out of the couching-chamber. Agatha and Flamin kept themselves far from the patient, and both were equally serious. Flamin's noble mother drew near with her heart seized at once by joy and anxiety and love, and with her overflowing eyes, which obeyed her agitated heart. Victor wept for fear and for joy beside his dumb father, but he passionately smothered every drop that might disturb him. Thus does every operation, by the climax of preparation, communicate to the spectator heart-beating and trembling. Only the veiled Briton,—a man who lifted his head coldly and serenely, like a high mountain over a torrid zone,—he offered to the filial hand a face silent and motionless; he kept composed and mute before the fate which was now to decide whether his dreary night should reach even to the grave or no farther than this minute....

Fate said, Let there be light, and there was. The invisible destiny took a son's anxious hand and opened therewith an eye, which was worthy of a finer night than this starless one. Victor pressed the mature lens of the cataract—that smoke-ball[16] and cloud cast over creation—down into the bottom of the pupil; and so, when an atom had been sunk three lines deep, a man possessed immensity again, and a father his son. Oppressed mortal! thou that art at once a *son* and a *slave* of the dust, how slight is the thought, the moment, the drop of blood or tear-drop, that is required to overflow thy wide brain, thy wide heart! And if a couple of blood-globules can become, now thy Montgolfier's globes and now thy Belidor's percussion-balls,[17] ah, how little earth it takes to exalt or to crush thee!

"Victor! thou? Is it thou who hast cured me, my son?" said the delivered man, taking the hand that was still armed with the surgical instrument. "Lay it aside and bandage me again! I rejoice that I saw thee first of all." The son could not stir for emotion. "Bandage me, the light is painful! *Was* it thou? speak!" He bandaged in silence the open eye amidst the glad tears of his own. But when the bandage hid from that noble stoical soul everything, his blushing and his weeping, then was it impossible for the happy son to contain himself any longer;—he gave himself up to his heart, and clung with his tears upon the veiled countenance to which he had given back brighter days; and when he felt on his trembling breast the *quicker* beatings of his father's heart, and the *tighter* embrace of his gratitude,—then was the best child the happiest,—and all rejoiced at his joy, and congratulated the son more than the father....

Twelve cannon went off from that number of door-keys. They shot this History dead.

For now it is actually gone,—not a word, not a syllable of it do I know any longer. In fact I have never in my life seen or heard or dreamed of, or romantically invented, any Horion or any St. Luna;—the Devil and I know how it is; and I, on my part, have, besides, better things to do and to lay open now, namely,

THE OVERTURE AND SECRET INSTRUCTIONS

Another would have been stupid enough to begin at the very beginning; but I thought to myself, I can at any time tell where I live,—in fact, at the Equator, for I reside on the island of *St. John's*, which lies, as is well known, in the East Indian waters, which are entirely surrounded by the principality of *Scheerau*. For nothing can be less unknown to good houses, which keep their regular literary waste-book (the Fair-Catalogue) and their regular stock-book (the Literary Times), than my latest home product, the *Invisible Lodge*,—a work, the reading of which my sovereign should make still more obligatory on his children, and even on his vassals, (it would not expressly contradict the Recesses,) than the attending the national university. In this Lodge, now, I have placed the extraordinary pond better known by the name of the East Indian Ocean, and into which we, of Scheerau, have steered and moored the few Moluccas and other islands on which our productive business lies. While the invisible lodge was being transformed by the press into a visible one, we again prepared an island,—namely, the isle of *St. John's*, on which I now live and write.

The following digression ought to be attractive, because it discloses to the reader why I prefixed to this book the crazy title, Dog-post-days.

It was day before yesterday, on the 29th of April, that I was walking in the evening up and down my island. The evening had already spun itself into haze and shadow. I could hardly see over to Tidore Island,[18] that monument of fair, sunken spring-times, and my eye glanced round only on the near buddings of twig and blossom, those wing-casings of growing Spring,—the plain and coast around me looked like a tiring-room of the flower-goddess, and her finery lay scattered and hid in vales and bushes round about,—the moon lay as yet behind the earth, but the well-spring of her rays shot up already along the whole rim of heaven,—the blue sky was at length pierced with silver spangles, but the earth was still painted black by the night. I was looking only at the heavens,—when something plashed on the earth....

It was a little Pomeranian dog, who had leaped into the Indian Ocean, and was now heading full for St. John's. He crawled up on my coast and rained a shower of drops as he waggled near me. With a dog who is an utter stranger, it is still more disagreeable undertaking to spin a conversation than with an Englishman, because one knows neither the character nor the name of the animal. The dog had some business with me, and seemed to be a plenipotentiary. At last the moon opened her sluices of radiance, and brought me and the dog into full light.

> *"To his Well-Born,*
> *Superintendent of Mines,*[19] Mr. Jean Paul,
> *on*
>
> *Free.*
>
> St. John's."

This address to me hung down from the neck of the animal, and was pasted to a gourd-bottle which was tied to his collar. The dog consented to my taking off his iron collar, as the Alpine dogs do their portable refectory-table. I extracted from the bottle, which in sutlers' tents had often been filled with spirit, something which intoxicated me still better,—a package of letters. *Savans,* lovers, people of leisure, and maidens are passionately sharp-set upon letters; business-people, not at all.

The whole package (name and hand were strange to me) turned upon the one point, to wit, that I was a famous man, and had intercourse with kings and emperors;[20] and that there were few mining intendants of my stamp, etc. But enough! For I must needs not have an ounce of modesty left in me if, with the impudence which some really possess, I should go on excerpting and extracting from the letters, that I was the Gibbon and the Möser[21] of Scheerau, (to be sure only in the biographical department, but then what flattery!)—that every one who possessed a life, and would see it biographically delineated by me, should set about the matter at once, before I was pressed away by some royal house as its historiographer, and could absolutely no longer be had,—that it might occur in my case as in that of other mine-intendants, before whom often the deluded public never took off its hat, until they had already passed into another lane,[22] i. e. world, etc. Who apprehends this last more than myself? But even this apprehension does not bring a modest man to the point of lowering himself down to be the bellows-blower to the man that shall sound his eulogy; as I to be sure should have done, if I had gone on to lay myself entirely bare. To my feeling even those authors are odious, who, in their shamelessness, only *then* bring up the rear with the final flourish, that *modesty forbids them to say more*, when they have already said everything that modesty *can* forbid.

At length my correspondent ventures out with his design, namely, to make me the compiler of an unnamed family history. He begs, he intrigues, he defies. "He is able," —he writes more copiously, but I abridge all, and in fact I deliver this epistolary extract with uncommonly little understanding; for I have been this half-hour scratched and gnawed in an unusually exasperating manner by a cursed beast of a rat,—"to establish everything for me by documentary evidence, but is not allowed to communicate to me any other names of the personages in this history than fictitious ones, because I am not wholly to be trusted,—in time he will explain everything to me,—for this is a history upon which and its development destiny itself is still working, and what he hands over to me is only the snout thereof, but he will duly make over to me one member after another, just as it falls off from the lathe of time, until we get the tail;—accordingly the epistolary *Spitz* will regularly swim back and forth as a *poste aux ânes*,[23] but I must not on any account sail after the postman; and thus," concludes the correspondent, who signs himself *Knef*, "shall the dog, as a Pegasus, bring me so much nutritious sap, that, instead of the thin Forget-me-not of an annual, I may rear a thick cabbage-head or cauliflower of folios."

How successfully he has accomplished his purpose the reader knows, who is fresh from the first chapter of this story, which, from Eymann's rats to the cannonade complete, was all in Spitz's bottle.

I wrote back to Mr. Knef in the gourd only so much as this: "Anything nonsensical I seldom decline. Your flatteries would make me proud if I were not so already; hence, flatteries harm me little. I find the best world to be contained in the mere microcosm, and my Arcadia stretches not beyond the four chambers of my brain; the Present is made for nothing but the maw of man; the Past consists of history, which, again, is an aggregate present peopled by the dead, and a mere *Declinatorium* [24] of our perpetual *horizontal* deviations from the cold pole of truth, and an *Inclinatorium* [25] of our *vertical* ones from the sun of virtue. There is left, therefore, to man, who wants to be happier in than out of himself, nothing but the Future, or fancy, that is, romance. Now, as a biography is easily exalted into a romance by skilful hands, as we see by Voltaire's 'Charles' and his 'Peter,' and by autobiographies, I undertake the biographical work, on condition that in it the truth shall be only my maid of honor, but not my guide.

"In visiting-parlors one makes one's self odious by general satires, because every one can take them to himself; personal ones they set down as among the duties of *medisance*, and so pardon them, because they hope the satirist is attacking the person rather than the vice. In books, however, it is exactly the reverse, and to me, in case several or more knaves, as I hope, play parts in our biography, their *incognito* is a quite pleasing feature. A satirist is not so unfortunate herein as a physician. A lively medical author can describe few maladies which some lively reader shall not think he himself has; he inoculates the hypochondriac by his historical patients with their pains as thoroughly as if he put him to bed with a real attack of them; and I am firmly convinced that few people of rank can read living descriptions of the unclean disease without imagining they have it, so weak are their nerves and so strong their fancies, whereas a satirist can cherish the hope that a reader will seldom apply to himself his pictures of moral maladies, his anatomical tables of spiritual abortions; he can freely and cheerily depict despotism, imbecility, pride, and folly, without the least apprehension that any one will fancy himself to have anything of the kind; nay, I can charge the whole public, or all Germans, with an æsthetic lethargy, a political enervation, a politico-economical phlegma towards everything which does not go into the stomach or the purse; but I rely upon every one who reads me, that he at least will not reckon himself in the number, and if this letter were printed, I would appeal to every one's inner witness. The only performer whose true name I must have in this historical drama—especially as he plays only the prompter—is the—Dog. Jean Paul."

I have, as yet, got no answer, nor any second chapter; so now it depends wholly on the Dog whether he will present the sequel of this History to the learned world or not.

But is it possible that a biographical mining intendant, merely for the sake of a cursed rat, who, besides, is not working at any journal, but only in my house, must just run away from the public and thunder through all rooms, to worry the carrion to death?...

... *Spitzius Hofmann* is the name of the dog; *he* was the rat, and was scratching at the door with the second chapter in the flask. A whole crammed provisionship, which the learned world may nibble at have I taken off from Hofmann's neck; and now the reader, who loves to read wise things as well as stupid ones, shall have opened to him to-day—for henceforth it is certain that I shall go on with my writing—glad prospects which, from a certain feeling of modesty, I do not designate.... The reader sits now on his sofa, the fairest reading-Hours dance round him and hide from him his repeating-watch,—the Graces hold my book for him and hand to him the sheets,—the Muses turn over the leaves for him, or in fact read it all to him;—he has nothing to disturb him, but the Swiss or the children must say, "Papa is out." As life has on one foot a sock and on the other a buskin, he loves to have a biography laugh and weep in one breath; and as the fine writers always understand how to combine with the useful moral of their writings a something immoral which poisons, but charms,—like the apothecaries, who draw at once *medicines* and *aqua vitæ*,—so does he willingly forgive me, in consideration of the immoral which is prominent, the religious quality which I sometimes have, and *vice versâ*; and as this biography is set to music, because Ramler sets it beforehand into hexameter (which it certainly needs far more than Gessner's harmonious prose[26]), he can, when he has done reading, stand up and play or sing it.... I, too, am almost as happy as if I read the work;—the Indian Ocean flings up the peacock-wheels of its illuminated circle of waves before my island,—I stand on the best footing with all, the Reader, the Reviewer, and the Dog;—everything is ready to hand with each Dog-post-day: a recipe for ink from an alchemist; the gooseherd with quills was here day before yesterday; the bookbinder with gay writing-books only to-day: nature buds, my body blooms, my mind produces,—and so I hang my blossoms over the tan-bed and forcing-bed (i. e. over the island), send my root-fibres through the soil, unable (Hamadryad that I am) to guess from my foliage how much moss years may collect on my bark, how many woodchafers the future may gather upon the pith of my heart, and how many tree-lifters Death may lay under my roots,—nothing of all this do I surmise, but swing joyfully—thou good destiny!—my boughs in the wind, lay my suckling leaves to the bosom of a Nature filled with light and dew, and, with the breath of universal life fluttering through me, stir up as much articulate noise as is necessary, that one or another sad human heart, while contemplating these *leaves*, may forget, in short, gentle dreams, its stings, its throbbings, its stiflings—O, why is a man sometimes so happy?

For this reason: because he is sometimes a *littérateur*. As often as Fate, under its veil, dots off from the great world atlas to a special map the little life-stream of a *literatus*, which runs over some lecture-halls and bookshelves, it may possibly think and say thus: "Surely there is no cheaper or rarer way of making a creature happy than by making him a literary one: his goblet of joy is an inkhorn,—his feast of trumpets and carnival is (if he is a reviewer) the Easter-fair,—his whole Paphian grove is compressed into a bookcase,—and what else do his blue Mondays consist of than (written or read) Dog-post-days?" And so Fate itself leads me over to the

2
DOG-POST-DAY

At the gate of the First Chapter, the readers ask the incomers: "What is your name?—your character?—your business?"

The Dog answers for all: H. Januarius—i. e. Herr Januarius, not Holy Januarius; but the Prince of Flachsenfingen bore that name—had, in his younger years, made the grand tour or journey round the beautiful and the great world. He everywhere distributed gifts to strangers, which cost him but a single *don gratuit* from his subjects, and he succored and pitied many oppressed peasants in France, who fared as badly as his own did in Flachsenfingen. For the defenceless female sex, like all travelling princes, he did, if possible, still more; one may say of the greater number of them, that, like Titus, or like one sailing westward round the world, they, to be sure, sometimes lose a *day*, but seldom a *night*, without making others, and consequently being themselves, happy. In fact, the Regent must have foreseen the present depopulation of France; for he took measures betimes against it, and left behind him in three Gallic seaboard cities three sons, and on the so-called Seven Islands only one. The first was called the Welshman, the second the Brazilian, the third the Calabrian; the one on the Seven Islands, the Monsieur, or *Mosye*: these names were probably meant to allude to Princes of Wales, Brazil, and Asturias. He let his children grow up in no worse ignorance than ignorance of their rank: they were to be formed for future co-workers in his administration. Januarius was, to be sure, sensual and somewhat feeble, but—except where he *feared*—extremely philanthropic.

Lord Horion met Prince January twice on his journeys: the first time he cut across the princely planetary orbit as a comet, in the sense of a hairy star; the second, as a comet with a tail when in its perihelion. What I mean is this: it was just when Horion was in love with a scion of January's house, who lived in London, that he saw the Prince for the second time, and at his house in London entertained him and his court. Upon this very distant relative of the Prince my papers—from an excessive deference to political and domestic relations—throw an unseasonable veil. She was, at the time of marrying his Lordship, twenty-two years old, and her whole person was (if I may venture to adopt the bold expression of a London eulogist) nothing but a single, tender, still blue eye. That is all which is vouchsafed to the public.

The Prince willingly let himself be mastered and managed—by the lord, whom a singular mixture of coldness and genius constituted an unlimited monarch and commander of souls. The lord had, moreover, a beautiful niece in his house, whose charms in princes' eyes made such a spiritual Old Man of the Mountain as he at once *younger* and more *smooth*.

But the death-bell threw its discords into these harmonies of life. The beloved of his Lordship fled from the rough earth, and left behind her his first-born son as a memorial, and pledge of love; she died in her twenty-third year, as it were of the life of her child, some days after its birth, and the thin, tender twig broke down under the ripe fruit. Lord Horion bowed silently to fate. He had loved her terribly, without showing it: he mourned her in the same manner, without moistening his deep black eye.

The Prince found in the niece, i. e. in a true Englishwoman, something to his taste, for the reason that he *had* found what was still more so in the Frenchwomen; and on this ground he would, inversely, have loved them, had he previously known her. The subsequent Chief Chamberlain, Le Baut, had the same sentiments, and, what is still more, toward the same person; and as Indian courtiers imitate all wounds of their sovereign, so did Le Baut with an arrow of Cupid copy those of his master, and transferred to himself therewith one of the severest.

These London histories cannot last much longer, and then we shall happily get back again to our St. Luna.

A burning fever seized the Regent, which his physician, Dr. Culpepper, held to be merely zigzag dartings of fitful, gouty matter. I have been unable, hitherto, to ascertain whether this Culpepper has any tolerably near relationship to his well-known namesake and professional co-master in London. The fever hunted January so hard, and the Father Confessor instituted with his conscience, instead of extinguishing processes, so many incendiary ones, that in the agony of death he took a solemn oath never again at the sight of a maiden to think of Depopulation and Revolution. The same weakness which strengthened his superstition and childlike credulity ministered to his sensuality; when he was up again, he absolutely knew not what to do. The niece and his oath were next-door neighbors in the chambers of his brain. A clever ex-Jesuit from Ireland, who lived only for doubts of conscience, and had himself a *conscientia dubia*, flew to the help of the doubter, and gave him to understand that "his vow, especially before getting absolution from it, he must conscientiously keep, excepting the sinful and impossible point therein, that, namely, which, without the consent of his spouse, he had neither the right to promise nor the power to fulfil." In other words, the Jesuit failed not to show him, that he had in his fever sworn off only from the *unmarried* sex, and limited his celibacy merely to nuns, that accordingly his vow did not, to be sire, forbid him compound adultery, (which confession would do away) but it did with extreme strictness the simple kind. January was too religious not to refrain wholly from the simple form.

It is hard to investigate the relation in which his now *increased* love for his four grand dukes or *little* dukes in Gaul stood to the fulfilment of his vow; in short, he gave his Lordship the commission and full power to fetch the four little persons from Gaul to London, because he wanted to take his beloved anonymous little posterity with him to Germany. It was uncertain whether he loved the mothers so heartily for the children's sake, or the children for the sake of the mothers. His Lordship went gladly, like Kotzebue (but differently), after the death of his beloved, to France. At last there came, not from him, but from the tutors of the Welshman, the Brazilian, the Calabrian, the sad intelligence, that in one night, probably according to a concerted plan of conspired prince-stealers, the three children had been abducted; and not long after that the sorrowful post was not only confirmed by his Lordship, but aggravated by the new one, that the Monsieur or Mosye on the Seven Islands was no more—to be found there.

Fate often gives man the balsam before the wound: January received his fifth son, whom I shall never call anything but the Infante, still earlier than the tidings of his forfeited blessing of children. The chief Chamberlain, Von Le Baut, had wedded the mother of the Infante (his Lordship's niece); but he dated his marriage three quarter-days back, instead of announcing it one later. I have never been able to see the connection of this anachronism or misreckoning of time with the Prince's vow. For the rest, dangerous as January's *votum* made him to the *husbands* of his court, and harmless to the *fathers*, nevertheless, the virtuous confidence which the husbands reposed in the female virtue which they had appropriated to themselves by marriage was so unlimited, that they, without hesitation, led that virtue into the midst of his unbridled flames. Nay, they even disdained the fear of being suspected of doing so in order that, when he laid down his crown on the toilet-table of their spouses, they might play with the shining wall-crown (*corona muralis*) as with a *joujou*, and with its brilliancy throw a dazzling light into people's windows: for a courtier cares more to own his wife than to watch over her.[27]

It will come on presently, cry the puppet-players; it will be over presently, say I.

When, at length, his Lordship returned empty-handed, he was greatly surprised, not at the presence of the Infante, but at his adoption,—namely, at the marriage of Le Baut. But this High Chamberlain was—and no one minded it less than Horion—an ardent friend of the Prince; this rendered him capable of doing for him (as Cicero requires) even that which he would never have done for himself,—namely, a dishonorable action. In fact, it is an uncommon piece of good fortune for a courtier or a world's man, whose honor his high position exposes often to the worst of weather, that this honor, however sensitive to slight contusions,[28] easily gets over great ones, and can, if not by words, yet by deeds, be assailed without injury. Something similar is remarked by physicians in regard to madmen, or rather their skin, which to be sure feels the lightest touch, but on which no blister will draw. The Prince was knit to Le Baut by a threefold ligament,— by gratitude, son, and wife; his Lordship plucked the ligament asunder; that is to say, he laid bare to his niece the Chamberlain's heart, and discovered to her the poison-bag therein, and a dramatically carried out *plan*, which she had hitherto regarded as an *indulgent confidence*. All the nobility and pride of her nature flamed up in her with shame and wrath, and, pursued by crashing recollections, she flew with her child, and with the prospect of a second, out of the city to a country-seat of his Lordship's.

Now the Prince with his Lordship and his court (including even Dr. Culpepper) returned to Germany. Le Baut tarried awhile longer to appease the niece and persuade her to take the journey. But it was not only impossible to draw all her deeply sunk roots out of the land of freedom and go with the party to Germany, but she even separated herself, not only by seas, but by a bill of divorce, from the filthy favorite. She was obliged to leave with the Chamberlain her second child, his real daughter; but the first, the Infante, she clasped to her maternal breast. Le Baut was glad enough to let it be so, and thought that after the building-oration the scaffolding of the building should also go into the house-stove. But when he appeared under the German throne-canopy, his sun (January) stood at the summer solstice, which from decreasing warmth gradually passed over to cold storms. January's love could more easily rise and fall than stay still, and the greatest crime with him was absence. Le Baut, stripped of both wife and child, must needs lose now in comparison with his Lordship, because the latter came upon the stage, and under January's throne-canopy as treasurer and coast-warden of two treasures left behind in London. But there were deeper reasons. His Lordship easily governed the Regent, because he held him in neither by his own nor other people's vices, but by his own virtues. In the first place, he required nothing of him, not so much as diet and chastity. Secondly, he lifted no cousins into the saddle, but tipped bad men out of it; he bore him like a hawk on his gloved fist, but the falconer did it not for the purpose of darting the Prince upon doves and hares, but in order to make him at once *watchful* and *tame*. Thirdly, his firmness and his fineness mutually compensated each other: the best one to rule over changeable men is the unchangeable. Fourthly, he was not the favorite, but the associate, remained always a Briton and a lord and the country's beneficent bee-father (apiary), whereas January was the queen-bee and in the queen-bee's prison. Fifthly, he was one of the few men to whom one must be *equal* in order to resist their will; and any one who would play the juggler's trick of throwing a padlock on his mouth slyly, soon had one to fetters and manacles on his own soul. Sixthly, he had a good cheese. This last point needs no copious explanation. In Chester he had a farmer, who produced a cheese, the like of which was not to be found in Europe; but to princes generally an extraordinary cheese is more gratifying than an extraordinary address of thanks from the provincial syndic.

With such a conjunction of ill stars, of course our Chamberlain found the bill of divorce, which at first was written with sympathetic ink in January's face, gradually more and more legible. Still he read it through several times every week, in order to read it correctly; he could now no longer procure any lapdog a place, that is, a lap,—his letters of recommendation were Uriah's-letters,[29]—and now, when he actually succeeded in getting, through his Lordship, the charge of chief Chamberlain, he thought it high time to try, against the gout in his knee, bathing at his knightly seat of St. Luna year in and year out, and so he set off, having first been obliged to solemnly promise the whole court that he should come back well.

Properly, now, the preliminary history would be, according to promise, ended, so that I might get well on in the later history this work contains, were I not absolutely obliged on the Court-Chaplain's account to add this much more:—

The only place of which Le Baut had the presentation at court was the parish of St. Luna. He invested therewith, as its patron, the Rat-contradictor Eymann, who had begged from him in London the oral vocation to the

Court-Chaplaincy, and who could no longer obtain it. Hence the Dog-post-days always call him the Court-Chaplain, although in fact he is only a country pastor.

From the slight circumstance that Eymann, as travelling preacher, accompanied January's retinue, a great deal grew out. Eymann, at his Lordship's country-seat, offered to his present wife the neck- and breast-pendant of a heart hollowed with consumption, as a slight gift, which was accepted. To the couple while still in England their Flamin was born. Her Ladyship loved in the person of the Court-Chaplain's wife a worthy sister of her sex, and a worthy fellow-citizen of her native land; she urged her with fervent prayers to stay in England, and when all were refused, she begged and prevailed upon her at least to let her Flamin—in order to be at all events half a Briton—stay behind in the society of Victor and the Infante, till the friendly trio[30] should be transplanted simultaneously into German soil.

The Parson's wife was strong enough to sacrifice for the sake of her Flamin's finer education the enjoyment of his presence, and left him behind under the eyes of love and in the little arms of childish friendship. The same training hand—*Dahore* was the name of the teacher—reared and watered the three noble flowers, which sucked from one kind of bed and ether three kinds of color, and developed unlike stamens and honeycups. Dahore had the hearts of all children in his tender hand, simply because his own never boiled and blustered, and because an ideal beauty sat upon his youthful form and an ideal love dwelt in his pure breast. The three children loved and embraced each more warmly in his presence, as the Graces enfold each other before Venus Urania: they even bore all the same name, as the Otaheitans exchange names with those they love. When they had attained some ripeness of years, his Lordship came to put them all with Dahore on board ship for Germany. But before the embarkation the Infante caught the small-pox and was made blind, and Dahore was obliged to return with him to the distressed and weeping lady. Victor had long and speechlessly hung on the neck of his sick friend and clung around Dahore's knee, refusing to part from his two loved ones; but his Lordship parted them: Flamin and Victor were, from that time, educated in Flachsenfingen, the former for a jurist, the latter for a physician.

There are some improbabilities in Spitzius Hofmann's gourd-flask; but the Dog must be held responsible for what he delivers. Now the story goes straight forward again.

His Lordship, during the cannonading of the tattered or riddled garrison, withdrew with Victor into another apartment; and his first word was, "Unbandage me a moment, and leave thy hand in mine, that I may be sure of thy attention, for I have much to say to thee." Good man! we all remark that thou art more tender than thou art willing to appear, and we all praise it. Not *coldness*, but *cooling-off*, is the greater wisdom; and our inner man should, like a hot metal-casting in its mould, cool but slowly, in order that it may round itself out to a smoother form: for that very reason has Nature—just as they *warm* the mould for statuary metal—poured his soul into an *ardent* body.

He continued: "I have, my dear boy, in my blindness been able to dictate to thee only empty letters; I meant to save my secrets for thy arrival. I am watched by a small gunpowder-conspiracy." Victor interrupted him with the question, how he had so suddenly become blind. His Lordship answered, reluctantly, "One eye was probably so already before thy departure for Göttingen, but I did not know it."

"But the other?" said Victor.

Over his Lordship's face glanced the cold shadow of a buried pang; he looked on his son a long time, and answered, as if abstractedly and hurriedly, "Also! as I look on thee, thou seemest to me much taller and larger."

"That is, perhaps," replied he, for he guessed his thought, "an ocular illusion of the sensitive retina.[31] You spoke of a gunpowder-plot."

"They have found out," his Lordship continued, "that the Prince's son is not in London: they even assume that the disease was given to him at that time designedly; and the Prince daily speaks of the moment when I shall bring his son back to him. Perhaps he knows these suspicions. I was obliged to postpone my departure for London till my cure. Now I shall shortly start for England, where the son is not, to bring his mother; him I shall bring from otherwheres, and with just as good eyes as thou hast given me."

"Then," Victor broke out, "not the best of men, but his enemies, will be hurled down."

"No, I am to be *hurled down* first (to express myself in thy fashion),—but thou hast interrupted me: I have never had the courage to interrupt other people like fools,—for my absence is just what they want."

I, as installed historiographer, ask no leave of any one, and interrupt whom I will. One who is interrupted may jest, indeed, but he can no longer argue. The Socrates grafted upon Plato, who never let a sophist have his talk out, was therefore one himself. In England, where they tolerate systems even among the wine-cups, a man can spread himself out like a royal folio: in France, where the spectacles of wisdom are splintered into sharp, shiny bits, one must be as curt as a visiting-card. A hundred times is the wise man silent before the coxcomb, because he needs twenty-three sheets to express his opinion. Coxcombs need only lines; their opinions are upstarting islands, held together by nothing but emptiness.... I add the remark, that between the lord and his son a fine, courteous wariness reigned, which in the case of so near a relationship is to be justified only by their rank, their mental structure, and their frequent separation. —

"But my presence is, perhaps, still worse. The Princess —"

(The Prince's bride, since his first wife died early and without children, as Spitz says.)

"The Princess brings along with her a stream of diversions, in which he will no longer hear any voice but that which lures to pleasure. An interrupted influence is as good as lost. And then, too, I am, up to a certain point, so tired of this game, that I gladly flee from the new engagements in which this new arrival would involve me. Should she, as they say, not love him, she might so much the more easily govern him; and then my absence would be, again, not good. But, setting me aside, what dost thou propose to do during my absence?"

After a crotchet-rest, he answered himself, "Thou wilt be his Physician-in-ordinary, Victor." Victor's hand twitched in his father's. "Thou hast already been promised to him; and he longs for thee, simply because I have often named thee. He is impatient to see for himself how any one looks whose father he knows so well. As Physician-in-ordinary, thou canst, with thy art and thy fancy, keep him clear of strange fetters until I come again; then will I impose still softer ones on him, and go back forever. My engagement has had hitherto the design merely of averting strange ones, particularly a certain—" Then, with full heart and changed voice, "My beloved! it is hard in this world to win Virtue, Freedom, and Happiness, but still harder to diffuse them. The wise man gets everything from himself; the fool, from others. The freeman must release the slave, the philosopher think for the fool, the happy man labor for the unhappy."

He rose, and presupposed Victor's Yes. The latter had therefore to dribble out his rhetorical flood during the leave-taking. He began with compressed breath: "I detest most cordially the simoom of the court-atmosphere ..." (his Lordship has to answer for it with me, that the son leaves out here the concessive conjunction, "to be sure": whoever lets it be seen that he expects obedience, gets it at least in a prouder shape) "which sweeps over nothing but prostrate men, and turns him to powder who remains upright! I wish I could be in an antechamber on a court-day; I would say to all in my thoughts: 'How I hate you and your sour honey of pleasure- and plague-parties; the cursed watchman's- and rower's-bench of your card-tables; the gifts of full dishes of slaughtered provinces (I mean your gaming-plates and your meat-plates)!' But I know very well I can never express myself strongly enough upon the servile, tide-waiting court-oysters, who know not how to stir or open anything—not excepting their hearts—but only their shell, to draw something in ..."

"I have not *interrupted* thee yet," said his Lordship, and stood still for a moment.

"Meanwhile," the son continued, "I wade with the greatest pleasure down to the oyster-bank ... O, my dear father! how could I help going? Why have I not hitherto left your diseased eye unbandaged, that you might see in my face the absence of a single objection to your wishes? Ah! around every throne hang a thousand wet eyes, upturned by maimed men without hands; above sits iron Fate in the form of a prince, and stretches out no hand. Why shall not some tender-hearted man go up, and guide Fate's rigid hand, and with one hand dry, down below, a thousand eyes?"

Horion smiled, as one who should say, Young man!

"But I beg only for some legal postponements and delays, in order that I may get time to be more stoical and foolish,—foolish,—that is, I mean—contented. I should be glad to laugh and go on foot for two months longer among the good people around us, and by the side of my Flamin, particularly just now in the almanac spring and in that of my years, and before the ship of life freezes into the harbor of old age. Stoical I must be at any rate. Verily, did I not lay Epictetus's manual as a serpent-stone[32] to myself and my wounds, in order that the stone might suck out the moral poison; were I to go out of the house with a breast full of cancer-sores; what would the court think of me?... Ah! but I mean it seriously. The poor inner man—dried up by the intermittent fever of the passions, exhausted by the heart-palpitation of pleasure, burning with the wound-fever of love needs, like any other sick man, solitude and stillness and tranquillity, in order to get well."

Though he named the word "tranquillity," his inner being was agitated even to the dissolving-point, so much had the passions already stirred his blood and shaken his heart.

And now the two went back in a deepening silence of harmony to Eymann.

"I have a request for my Flamin."

"What is it?" said his Lordship.

"I do not yet know, but he wrote me he would soon name it."

"Mine to him is," said his Lordship, "that, if he will get a place, he must love the Pandects better than tactics, and, instead of the rapier, take the pen."

The son had been treated too politely by the father to have courage enough to ask for his secrets, especially that relating to the whereabouts of January's son. I treat the reader with the same delicacy, and hope he will have just as little courage; for, when any one explains himself guardedly, nothing is more uncivil than to put a new question.

His Lordship now travelled back, a cured man, to the Prince.

3
DOG-POST-DAY

The departure of his Lordship was the removal of the dam which had hitherto stood in the way of the flood of narrations, questions, and pleasures. The first investigation upon which the Parsonage entered was, to see whether it was really the old Bastian. And he it was, hide and hair; even the left side-lock he had still, as of old, shorter than the right. When the butcher's boy comes home from Hungary, he wonders that his kin are the same old pennies; they, however, wonder that he is no longer so. But in the present case there was mutual delight at the unchangedness on both sides. On every face lay the halo of joy, but on each composed of different rays. On a soft face, like Victor's, rapture looks like virtue. Old Appel, who had never, in all her life, turned over any leaves but those of David's Psalter and that in an ox's stomach,[33] expressed her pleasure all day long to the brass kettles by scouring them with unusual zest. The Vienna hospital for animals—consisting of an old pug and puss, who no longer hated each other, just as in the old man the good and bad souls are reconciled—and the bird-collection under the stove, which was one rusty-black bulfinch strong, took their full share of interest in the general uproar, and introduced themselves, and—which no ambassador would have done—waived the right of the first visit. Agatha expressed her joy only with her lips, by keeping silence with them, and pressing them to her brother's. To the Court-Chaplain's credit, it is reported that he took the invalid pug, who had the podagra in his hind-feet and the chiragra in his fore-paws, and shoved him quietly in his basket keeping-room and chamber under the stove again; restored the architectural order of the chairs without scolding; and rocked the little Bastian amidst the joyful confusion of tongues, that he might not wake up and aggravate it. But in the highly refined heart of Victor's countrywoman, the Chaplain's wife, the rays of joy from the whole family came to a focus, and diffused through her whole bosom the living glow of love. She smiled right into Victor's face to such a degree that she knew no way of escape but by bethinking herself of his destined chamber, which she directed to be opened and shown to him. Agatha flew forward with the jingling bunch of keys; and the guest, as he entered, was followed by only so many people as there were in the house, all eager to see what he would say to it.

He surrendered himself to all this friendly handling, not with the vain egotism of a cultivated stranger, but with a delighted, docile, almost child-like confusion; it gave him not the least concern that he looked like a child, so gentle, so glad, and so unpretending. In such hours it is hard to sit down, or to listen to a story, or to tell one.... Everybody began one, but the Chaplain interposed: "We have quite other things to talk about." But no *quite other things* came. Everybody wanted to enjoy the stranger where there were only four ears, but the six remaining ears could not be kept away. My description of his confusion is itself confused, but so it is with me always; for instance, when I describe haste, I do it, unconsciously, with the greatest. To a heart like his, that hung rocking in the feathers[34] of love, was there any need that it should see in every notched window-sill, in every smooth pavement-pebble, in every round hole drilled by the rain in the door-step, his boyhood's years mosaically pictured, and that he should enjoy in the same objects age and novelty? Those boyish years, which appeared to him out of a shadow, abiding on the lawns of St. Luna, between happy Sundays and among beloved faces,—those *boyish years* held a dark mirror in their hands, in which the glimmering perspective of his *childish years* ran backward; and in that remote magic-night stood, dimly gleaming, the form of *Dahore*, his never-to-be-forgotten teacher in London, who had so loved, so indulged, so improved him. "Ah!" thought he, "thou unrequited heart, too warm for this earth, where beatest thou now? why can I not unite my sighs with thine, and say to thee, Teacher, Beloved? O, man often perceives but late how much he was loved, how forgetful and ungrateful he was, and how great the heart he misunderstood." What nourished his still pleasure the most was the thought that he had earned it by his filial obedience to his father, and by his resolve to undertake the future labors-of-Hercules at court; for into every great joy of his the doubt would fall, like a bitter stomach-drop, whether he deserved it,—a doubt which reigning houses, palatines, patriarchs, and grand-masters have skilfully taken from them in childhood. The better sort of men find pleasure sweetest only after a good action,—the Easter-Festival after a Passion-Week.

My lady-readers will now want to hear what was cooked for dinner; but the documents of this Post-day, which reach me half by wheel and half by water, state, in the first place, that no one had any appetite,—which joy takes away more than grief,—except the three regiments, which slashed like veterans into the enemy,—that is, into the leavings of the table; secondly, that the meal was still leaner than the guest himself. We will, however, hereby invite all the reading-societies in a body to the *immovable* feast of the 4th of May, the Friday when, for the first time, Victor's arrival and his godson's churchgoing are suitably celebrated.

The Parson's wife extricated the beset darling in the afternoon from the musical circle of so many tones, and smuggled him away from under the eyes of her husband, whose Directress and Lady Mayoress she was, and led him to his chamber, that she might there, before him alone, distress and delight herself, and speak out her heart, like a mother. Long-suppressed sighs and antiquated tears now forced their way out of the opened motherly heart into another and tender one, which was, indeed, her son's best friend. She complained to him of Flamin's excitability, which Victor used always to allay; of his love for military life, while, after all, he was a scholar; and, finally, of the company he kept,—namely, he went roving round with a young page, one *Matthieu*, son of the Minister *Von Schleunes*, a dissolute, universally-beloved, universally-spoiled, bold, artful young scoffer, who, when his service allowed it, would spend his time either over yonder with the Chamberlain's people, or here with her son: "Heaven only knew what designs he had in his visits at a citizen's house." She rejoiced that Victor would bear off his old friend out of the traps and fangs of this rake. Victor pressed her hand with emotion, and said: "I could hardly think of sharing his heart with the best bond-fellow. Not so much as fall in love should he dare to, if it depended on me. Only me must he love, and one other person, who depicts him quite wrongly,—namely, yourself." He greatly mistrusted, also, her drawing of the sun-spots of Matthieu, because women seldom comprehend eccentric men, and because maidens, indeed, often love wild youths, but matrons (enlightened by marriage) always prefer gentle ones.

He easily drew the hearts of married women into his drag-net by a certain kindly gallantry towards them which a German saves for unmarried ones. Old ladies and old tobacco-pipes, however, easily cleave to men's lips. The younger pigeons he enticed to himself by his *comic salt*, as they catch turtle-doves by another kind. A *bon-mot* is to them a *dictum probans*; a *pasquin*, a *magister sententiarum*; and the critical calendar of scandal is to them a Kant's Critique of the Pure Reason, in an improved edition. With his medical doctor's ring, also, he fastened to himself female souls; as physician, he laid claim to corporeal mysteries, and then the spiritual easily follow these.

In the evening, when the woodland stream of the first jubilation had run out, three sober words were at length possible. The Parson, too, by this time, scolded less; for joy had made him rabid in the forenoon. Anger and the body are strengthened together, and therefore by pleasure. Hence in January and February, when dogs get the longer madness, men have the short one of wrath; hence convalescents grumble more at all about them, just as people do under strong mental excitements,—e. g. Dog-post scribes; hence, too, in the exhaustion following sick-headache, or a fit of intoxication, one is gentler than a lamb.

Towards evening, there already transpired something of consequence. Apollonia swept and dusted her blood-relationship and her guest with her whisks even sooner than the spiders and the dust. On the 4th of May was this day's arrival of the long-absent fugitive to be right properly celebrated. Flamin and Victor led the way through the Parsonage garden, whose *memorabilia* and *curiosa* are so edifying that the correferent[35] of these acts wishes he could, by the Dog-express, portray the garden to me more clearly. The Chaplain had stamped off many beds, not into rectangles, but had curved and twisted them into the shape of Latin characters, in double black-letter, to represent the initials of his family. His own (E) he had sowed with radishes; Apollonia's (A), with capuchin-lettuce;[36] Flamin's (F), with rape-cole; Sebastian's (S), with sweet-root, or *Glycyrrhiza vulgaris* (liquorice). Whoever was not present had left for him, at all events, a vacant place and *almanac royal* among squashes and Stettin-apples, round which was wrapped a perforated paper with the name cut out, which, after the peeling off of this wrappage, would appear green or red on the pale fruit. Victor, as he passed along by a C made of tulips, asked his Flamin the meaning of it. "Why dost thou ask?" he inquired; and the loquacious Parsonage-people, following after, drove away the answer.

Beyond the Parsonage-meadow stood—one had only to leap the brook—a hill, and thereon an old watchtower, in which there was nothing but a wooden staircase, and overhead nothing but a board covering instead of the Italian roof, both of which the Chamberlain had had made, that the people—not himself, for the unfeelingness of magnates labors for the feeling of minorites—might up there look round them a little. One could see from there the columnar architecture of the Creator, the Swiss mountains, standing, and the Rhine moving along with his ships. On the tower two linden-trees had grown aloft, twined together by nature, so as, sometimes, with their foliage, which had been hollowed out into a green niche and underlaid with a grassy bench, to fan, up there, a fevered islander. The loving party climbed the battlement, and carried up with them in their rural breasts a tranquillity which softly copied therein the still outer heaven that encircled these good hearts with its veiled suns. One lingering cloud gave a farewell glow, but it melted away before it burned out.

Now could the supplementary volumes of the Universal History of St. Luna be conveniently issued. Eymann could deliver his folio volumes of *gravamina* (grievances) upon the consistorial councils and the rats. All at once, Agatha, like her saintly namesake, was invoked down below by the organ-blower *loci*, who was *valet-de-place* of the village, and Parsonage-coachman. When certain authors say, "The coachman was blind, and the horse was deaf," they exactly reverse the case. The churl was deaf. He had in his *mouchoir de Vénus*—the handkerchief is, with the common people, at once letter-bag and envelope, because a letter is as important and rare a thing to them as a good one is to a reviewer—to-day discovered and unwrapped an epistle to Agatha, which he should have delivered yesterday with his Lordship's: but coachmen consider a master only as the mock-sun and second party to the horse, and the lady absolutely as no more than a parasite-growth of the stable; hence "immediately" means with them one or two or three days; and "to-morrow forenoon" meant, on the Ratisbon notification-programme of matters to be voted on, one or two or three years. Agatha, with more eagerness, hurried down, held the letter towards the lighter quarter of the west, and deciphered something, which, with sparkling eyes, she carried in a gallop up the stairs. "She is coming to-morrow!" she cried out to Flamin; for she seemed almost, in the person of every one of her friends, to love only the companion and friend of her other friends. The case was this: *Clotilda*, Le Baut's only daughter by his first wife (his Lordship's niece), was coming from the Girls' Institute in Maienthal, where she had been educated, back to her father.

"Do *you* take good care!" said the Chaplain's wife; "she is very beautiful."

"Then," said he, "I shall much rather take care *not* to take care."

"In fact," she continued, "all that is beautiful is now gathering around you" (here he tried to confuse and chastise her by a flattering look, but in vain). "The Italian Princess comes, too, on St. John's Day; and she is said to be as charming as if she were no princess at all, but only an Italian woman." There she did most princesses wrong; but a certain irony upon her own sex was the only fault of the Chaplain's wife, to whom, as to many other mothers, there were almost no step-sons and hardly anything but step-daughters.

He hoped, he replied, that very few princesses, even in America, had yet been married, in whose affections he could not have become completely entangled, and that merely from pity for such a poor, tender creature or heraldic beast, pressed under the seal-stamp and then on the contracts, which were often the only children of these marriages. "The young Mothers of the Country are really, like bee-mothers, set up for sale in their queen's prison, and wait to see into what hive the bee-father, or Father of the Country, will this year trade them off again."

A woman cannot possibly comprehend how a man whom she esteems can fall in love, except with her; and she can hardly wait to get sight of his beloved. Quite as curious is she about this man's style in his love,—that is, whether it is of the Flemish or French or Italian school. The Chaplain's wife questioned her confidential guest on this point also.

"My harem," he began, "reaches from this watchtower to the Cape, and away round the globe: Solomon is but a yellow straw-widower compared with me. I have in it even his wives; and, from Eve with her Sodom's Borsdorf-apple down to the latest Eve with an Imperial apple, and even to a marchioness with a mere fruit-piece, they are all in my hold and breast."

A lady excuses esteem for her sex on the ground that she is included therein. Women themselves have not so much as an idea of the peculiarities of their sex.

"But what says the favorite Sultana to this?" asked the Grand Inquisitress.

"She—" He paused, less from embarrassment than as one sunk in the fulness of glowing dreams. "*She*, of course—" he continued. "I pledge my head, meanwhile, that every youth has two periods, or, at least, moments. In the first, he stakes his head that he would sooner let his heart mould in his thorax or chest, and his *poples* or knee-joint grow lame, than that either should stir for any other woman than the very best of her sex,—for a real angel, a decided Quinterne.[37] He absolutely insists on the highest prize in the marriage Loto,—that is, in the first period; for the second comes, and cheats him out of so much. The female Quinterne would naturally require a *male* one; and, in case he were *that*,...

"I am a stupid drawing, an *ambe*, a double number, I say, and absolutely refuse to let the period have its talk out; but I shall still be on the look-out for the *Quinterne*.... And here let me ask, What would be the use of being a man if one were not a fool? Well, now, if I should draw the above-mentioned Quinterne,—which, to be sure, without any extravagant hope, I may well presuppose,—I should not be indifferent on the subject, but in raptures. Good heavens! I must instanter be frizzled, and have my profile taken. I should make verses and *pas*, and both with their traditional *pedes* (or feet); I should bend myself oftener than a devout monk, to make bows and (where there was anything to gather) bouquets; body, soul, and spirit I should have consist with me of so many finger-tips and feelers, that I should perceive at once (the Quinterne would perceive it still quicker) if our two shadows should come in collision. The touch of the smallest little end of a ribbon would be a good conductor to the electrical ether, which would shoot out from me in lightnings, as she would be charged negatively and I positively; and as to touching her hair, that could not create any less explosion than if a world should fall into the dishevelled[38] hair of a bearded comet....

"And yet what does it all amount to, if I have sense, and consider what she deserves, this good creature, this faithful, this undeserved one? What, in fact, were dull verses, sighs, shoes (boots I should put away), one or two hands pressed, a sacrificing heart, but a slight *gratial* and *don gratuit*, if thereby a creature was to be obtained who, as I see more and more, has everything belonging to the fairest angel that conducts man through life (invisibleness perhaps excepted); who has all virtues, and arrays them all in beauties; who gleams and gladdens like this spring evening, and yet, like it, conceals her flowers and all her stars, except the star of love; into whose all-powerful and yet gentle harmonica of the heart I would fain be so absorbed in listening; in whose eyes I would behold with such extraordinary delight the tear-drops of the tenderer soul, and the beamings of the loftier one; by whose side I could so fondly remain standing through the whole flying *opera buffa* and *seria* [39] of life,—so fondly, I say, that so the poor Sebastian might at least, when, in life's holy evening, his shadow grew longer and longer, and the landscape around—him melted away to a broad shadow, and he himself, too, that I might at least behold *both* shadowy hands," (one of them Flamin was just then holding,) "and exclaim—" (Checking himself:) "Here comes the-old bellows-blower, too, with something in one of his!"

As he could no longer either hide his emotion behind jest, nor the signs of it in his eyes behind some low-hanging linden-leaves, it was a real piece of good luck, that, just at the second when his voice was about to give way to it, he looked over the watch-tower, and saw the coachman come racing over again. The man cried from below, "he had got it from Seebass, but not till this moment." Agatha flew down passionately, and, after reading a billet below, darted off across the meadow. The bellows-blower ascended slowly, like a barometer before settled weather, and lifted himself and the billet he had brought back with him,—not a minute the sooner for all the beckoning overhead there,—with his levers, to the top of the tower. In the billet was written, in Clotilda's hand, "Come to thy bower, beloved friend!"

All eyes now ran after the runner, and fluttered with her through the clear-obscure of evening into the Parsonage, around whose arbor, however, no one could yet be seen. Hardly had Agatha caught sight of the opening of the latter, when her hurrying became flying; and when she was almost up to it, a white form flew out with widespread arms and into hers, but the arbor concealed the end of the embrace, and the eyes of all lingered long in vain expectation up in the cloister of love.

The Chaplain's wife, who generally would allow maidens only degradations and not elevations of rank, now imparted to Clotilda all the seven consecrations, and praised her so much—perhaps also because she was a countrywoman of hers on the mother's side—that Victor could have embraced the eulogist and her subject at once. The Chaplain added, as his mite to her praise, that he had printed the initial of her name (C) with tulips in red, like a title, and that the letter would shine out, when the bed bloomed, far and wide.

The husband and husbandman began now to break in more and more upon the sphere-music of night with the reed-stops of his cough; at last, he made off with Victor's enthusiastic female friend, and left the two friends alone, in the lovely night, with the two full hearts that panted to pour themselves out into each other.

Flamin had, during this whole day, shown a deepening silence of touching tenderness, which seldom found its way into his being, and which seemed to say, "I have something on my heart." When the watch-tower was comparatively deserted, Victor, who had become full of loving and softening dreams, could no longer conceal his tear-swimming eyes: he opened them freely before the oldest darling of his days, and showed him that open eye which says, "Look right through, if thou wilt, down to my very heart; there is nothing therein but clear love." ... Silently the vortices of love swept round the two, and drew them nearer together; they opened their arms for each other, and sank into each other's without a sound, and between the brother-hearts lay only two mortal bodies. Covered deep by the stream of love and ecstasy, they closed for a moment their enraptured eyes; and when they opened again, there stood the night sublimely before them, with its suns withdrawn into eternal depths; the milky-way ran, like the ring of eternity, around the immensity of space; the sharp sickle of the earthly moon glided, cutting, across the short days and joys of men.

But in that which stood under the suns, which the ring encircled, which the sickle smote, there was something higher, clearer, and more lasting than they: it was the imperishable friendship lodged in these perishable integuments.

Flamin, instead of being satisfied by this exhausting expression of our speechless love, became now a living, flying flame. "Victor! in this night give me thy friendship forever, and swear to me that thou wilt never disturb me in my love to thee."

"O thou good soul! I have given thee my heart long since, but I will gladly swear to thee again to-day."

"And swear to me that thou wilt never plunge me into misfortune and despair."

"Flamin! that distresses me too much."

"O, I beseech thee, swear it! and lift thy hand and promise me, even if thou hast made me unhappy, nevertheless that thou wilt not forsake me nor hate me." ... Victor pressed him to his bosom. "But we will come up hither when we can no longer be reconciled,—O, it pains me, too, Victor!— up hither, and embrace each other, and throw ourselves down and die!"

"Ay!" said Victor, in a low and exhausted voice. "O God! has anything happened, then?"

"I will tell thee all. Now let us live and die together."

"O Flamin! how inexpressibly I love thee to-day!"

"Now will I let thee see into my whole heart, Victor, and reveal to thee all."

But, before he could do it, he had to man himself by holding his peace; and they remained a long time silent, lost in the depths of the inner and outer heavens.

At last he was able to begin, and to tell him that that Clotilda, about whom he had jested to-day, had written herself in ineffaceable characters on his heart; that he could neither forget nor possess her; that the creeping fever of a frightful, frenzied jealousy burned, galling, within him; that he could not, to be sure, say a word to her about his love, according to her prohibition, until her brother (the Infante) should come back and be present; but that she, to judge by her demeanor, and according to Matthieu's assurances, had perhaps some regard for him; that her position must be an eternal wall of separation between them, so long as he took the *juristic* instead of the *military* road to promotion; and that on this last, if his Lordship would lend him a hand in the matter, he would attain to Clotilda more swiftly on similar steps; and that the request of which he had spoken in his letters to Victor was just this,—that he would repeat all to his Lordship, and beg his assistance. In fact, his wild arm could hold the sword better than the balance of justice. A frightful predisposition to jealousy, which even from future possibilities catches palpitations, was the chief reason.—Victor rejoiced that he could give his feelings the best language,—namely, action, and assented to all he required, with delight at his confidence, and at the absence from his communication of dreaded news; and so, newly attached to each other, they went to rest. And the Twins—that ever-burning, intertwined name of friendship—glimmered in the west, beckoning upward out of an *earthly* eternity; and the heart of the Lion blazed on their right....

There are men laid upon this earth, and bound to the soil, who never erect themselves to the contemplation of a friendship which winds around two souls, not earthy, metallic, and unclean bonds, but the spiritual ones that interweave this world itself with another and man with God. Such ones, degraded to the dust, it is, that, like travellers, regard from below the temple that hangs round the Alpine peaks as baseless and airy, because they do not themselves stand on the heights, and on the great floor of the temple,—because they know not that in friendship we revere and love something higher than self (which latter cannot at once be the *source* and the *object* of love),—something higher, namely, the embodiment and reflection of the virtue which in ourselves we only *approve*, and not till we see it in others can *love*.

Ah! can, then, higher beings judge severely the weaknesses of the shadowy groups that seek to hold fast to one another, driven apart as they are by north winds,—who would fain press to their bosoms the noble, invisible form of each other over which the thick and heavy earthly mask hangs,—and who fall, one after another, into graves into which the mourned draw their mourners?

4
DOG-POST-DAY

Clotilda, as Sebastian learned the next morning, had originally meant to stay at the seminary till after St. John's; but, as her best friend and schoolmate *Giulia* had gone beforehand, not to her parents, but to the long home, her distressed eyes must needs draw themselves away by a speedier departure from the grave-mound which lay like a ruin over her forlorn heart. Without packing up, she had fled from the flowerless Golgotha of her wounded soul; and a second contemplation of it, and a second departure, and a renewal of the old tears, still awaited her.

Never was a great beauty praised in a more unembarrassed manner by a little one than Clotilda was by Agatha. Generally, the only thing maidens appreciate about maidens is the heart; the evanescent charms of another's face have so little worth in their eyes, that they hardly care to mention them. Young men are justly reproached with selecting by preference beautiful youths for their friends. In the case of girls, on the contrary, their eulogists make much of the fact that they entirely despise female beauty, as a too loose and base cement-and-mortar of friendship, and that, therefore, to a beautiful woman, the *heart* of the very ugliest is more precious than the face of the handsomest on the five zones and scarfs of the earth. Agatha was otherwise: she ran over, the first thing in the morning, to the palace, to dress her friend.

Flamin behaved still worse. He could not wait for the reality itself to hang up Clotilda's Madonna-image in the chambers of Victor's brain: he anticipated it with the pen-and-ink sketch of a painter, which is, at least, not cold; for painters, in the *æsthetic* and in the *calligraphic sense*, seldom write well. The painter had, merely for the sake of seeing and sketching Clotilda, stretched himself, almost every Sunday morning, on a hill of Maienthal, where he transferred to his note-book the glittering landscape round the seminary; and the beautiful head which looked out of the eighth window he transferred into his heart. Even Flamin, who generally set even the vignettes of prose above the living oil-paintings of poetry, found, in the following Madonna or Clotilda of the artist, something to his taste:—

"When my conscious being is a single thought, and burns; and when, with the flames waving around me, I dip my hand into colors, to cool myself therein;—then, when the lofty beauty[41] that forever beams within me lets fall its image on the waves which tremulously picture heaven and earth, and sets on fire the clear stream; and then, when an image of Pallas, descending from heaven, rests upon the stream, a lily-casing and cast-off wing-wrappage of an up-flown angel,—a form whose unstained soul no body, but only the snow which lies around the throne of God, and out of which the angels weave their fleeting vehicular bodies,[42] encloses; and when the most delicate drapery is too coarse and hard, and becomes a wooden frame around that divine breath on the countenance, around that trembling flowered-velvet of flesh, around that skin of white roses transfused with a glow of red ones; when this reflection of my shining soul falls upon the colored surface,—then every one will turn round, and think Clotilda is lying asleep on the bank.... And here my art is over; for, ah! when she awakes, and when, for the first time, the soul shall move these charms like wings; when the fast-closed bud of the lips shall break into a smile, and the bosom breathes in half a sigh, and, from modesty, breathes it not out again; when the sighs, veiled in songs, steal from those lips,—which, like two souls, hover over without touching each other—as bees steal out of roses; when the eye stirs between gleams and tears;—then, when at length the goddess of heavenly love approaches her daughter, and electrically touches her still heart, and says, 'Do thou, too, love'; and now, when all charms tremble and bloom out, shrink and languish, hope and shudder, and the dreaming heart shuts itself up more deeply into its blossoms, and hides itself, trembling, behind a tear, from the happy one who has divined and deserves it;—then the happy one is mute, the happy one and the artist."

Victor saw beside him the happy one, who was his friend, looked upon him with moist eyes, and said, "Of that thou wast worthy!" But now twenty rowels spurred him to follow Agatha to the palace;—the pen-and-ink drawing of the artist; the arrangement of dresses; the relationship; the desire which every man has to see the Grace and Infanta of his friend; the desire which *not* every one has, but he had, to speak with any one for the first time (rather than for the eighth time); and, most of all, the evening of yesterday. Flamin's fire had yesterday burned Victor's bosom to a heap of tinder, through which nothing but sparks were running. He should have set all before him indifferently, because the contest *against* love differs in nothing from the contest *for* it, except in order of precedence. But let not the reader by any means imagine that now (as in one of your emasculated and emasculating romances) the Devil is to break loose in our biography, and the hero is to march into the palace and there fall down before Clotilda, and beg, on bended knee, "Be the heroine!" and go about to wrangle with her, out of love, and with the former *pastor fido* out of hatred, and actually play nothing else than the æsthetic, self-seeking, sensitive—scamp. If I should wish this last, I could excuse myself only on the ground that then I might perhaps come to some biographical murders and duels. I hope, however, I may still, without injury to morals or honesty, in the course of these pages make out a murder or homicide or two, at least in the last volume, where every æsthetic reaper thins out his characters, and throws half of them into the *oubliette* or family-vault of the inkstand.

Victor had too many years and acquaintances to allow himself, with so little regard to days of grace and double usance,[43] on the spot, before supper,—*cito citissime,*—what hast thou, what canst thou?—to fall in love. His optic nerve daily unravelled itself into finer and more delicate fibres, and touched all points of a new form, but the sore feelers curled back again more readily; every month the sight of a new face, like new music, made a *stronger* and *shorter* impression. He could only talk his way into love, not see it. Only words winged by virtue and sensibility are the bees which, in such cases, carry the pollen of love from one soul into another. But such a love, of the better kind, is annihilated by the least immoral alloy. How could it form and filter up in a defiled heart, filled with high-treason against a friend?

Victor would have gone to the palace as early as half past nine, but the Lady Chamberlain had not yet combed out her eyebrows and the King Charles's spaniel.

Seebass brought a billet to Flamin:—

I cannot see you, my dearest, to-day. Three Graces hold me fast, and the third you yourself have sent. Tell your British friend he must love me because I love you. Surgery may do without sympathy, but friendship cannot.

"Your Matthieu."

An absurd billet! When Victor heard that Agatha was the third Grace, there was a great hole torn in the curtain of the theatre in which Matthieu played Flamin's friend and Agatha's—first lover. Nothing is more annoying than a nest in which there sit none but brothers or none but sisters: the nest must be shaken up into a mixed and motley gradation,—that is to say, of brothers and sisters, packed in layers, so that an honest *pastor fido* can come and ask after the brother when he is only on the look-out for the sister; and so, too, must the girl who loves a brother absolutely and by stronger necessity have a sister whose friend she is, and who may be hook and handle to the brother. Our *Turkish* decorum required, therefore, that Matthieu should point his opera-glass at Flamin to see Agatha; and that Clotilda should visit the latter, since Flamin, as a man without ancestors, but of honor, could not possibly force his citizen's-visits upon the house of a chamberlain. Clotilda came often, and thereby involved herself in a contradiction, which I have till now been unable to solve, with the womanly refinement of her character.

Flamin dipped Matthieu's likeness into a quite different dyeing-copper from that the mother used: he was a jolly genius, and nothing worse. He personated everything in the world, and no one could personate him. He could imitate and travesty all the players of the Flachsenfingen troupe, and the boxes too. He understood more sciences than the whole court; yes, and more languages, even to the voices of the nightingale and the cockerel, which he mimicked so perfectly that Petrarch[44] and Peter would have run away. He could do with women what he chose, and every court dame excused herself by the example of her neighbor; for it used to be part of the *ton* in Flachsenfingen to have one's fidelity once put to the proof. They say love for him began to be knit, like a stocking, at the calf, but it is utterly false. It is therefore no wonder that, with such uninterrupted moderation in courtly pleasures, he grew stronger and *healthier* than the whole burnt-out, evaporated court, only he was too caustic, and too philosophic, and almost too roguish.

Victor and the reader and I have still, after all, only an indistinct, blurred crayon-drawing of Matthieu in our heads. My hero was somewhat pleased with him, as every eccentric man is with an eccentric one; it was a fault of his, that he pardoned too easily those of energy, even moral ones. With redoubled curiosity did he now take his way to the palace, or rather to its great garden, which joined thereto its semicircle of green beauties. He put in at the harbor of an embowered alley, and was delighted at the way in which the pierced shadow of the arbor, around whose iron skeleton tender twigs wound-like soft hair around hair-needles, glided dazzlingly over his body. Side by side with his arbor another parallel one passed along. He followed some scattered black paper snippings as way-marks. The fluttering of the morning wind tossed down from a twig a little leaf of fine paper, which he picked up to read. He was still on the first line, "Man has two minutes and a half, one in which to smile once, ..." when he ran against an almost horizontal queue, which was a black club of Hercules, compared with mine or the reader's plaited capillary tube. The queue was projected by a head crooked downward, which, peering in a listening attitude out of a niche in the arbor, was cutting a female profile, the original of which in a by-avenue was talking with Agatha. At the rustle of Victor's approach, the person, whose half-face was being stolen through the niche, turned round with surprise, and saw the proprietor of the Cyclops-queue with the profile-scissors, and also the hero of the Dog-post-days. The proprietor, without saying a word, thrust his artistic hand through the bush-work, and reached out to her her shadow or shadow-cutting.[45] Agatha took it, smiling; but the nameless one seemed to assume toward the cutter of forms and faces that seriousness which, on female faces, is nowise distinguished from contempt but in its ambiguousness, because his scissors awoke too strong a suspicion of his having been listening. Victor could perceive nothing of the nameless one yet except her stature, which, although bent forward a little, still surpassed the ordinary height. The face-cutter turned about with two flashing black eyes toward Victor, received him very politely, knew his name, told his own,—Matthieu,—and had, at his eighth pace, already had four good ideas. The fifth was, that he, unsolicited, introduced my hero to the couple in the side-arbor. The leafy nunnery-grating came to an end; a female form stepped forth, and Victor was so struck by it, that he, who knew little about embarrassments, or was made only more quick-witted by them, began his introductory sermon without the exordium, and that was—Clotilda. When she had said three words, he listened so to the melody instead of the text, that he understood not a word of what she was saying....

I have here, lying beside me, on the snow-white ground of vellum, the very *silhouette* which Matthieu had taken of her with the scissors. My correspondent will have me depict Clotilda as uncommonly beautiful. Otherwise, he says, a hundred things in this history are incomprehensible; and therefore he sends me (because he cannot trust my fancy) at least her profile. And that is to be, even during my writing, steadily looked at all the time,—so much the more, as it might seem actually to have been cut from the very face[46] of another loveliest female angel that ever flew out of an unknown paradise down to this earth: I mean the Fräulein von * * *, at present maid-of-honor in Scheerau; I am not sure whether all my readers know her.

Victor felt as if his blood had been driven outward, and with warm touches described its circles on the external skin. At last Clotilda's cold eye, of which not the intoxicated pride of beauty, but the sober, retiring pride of innocence belonging only to the female sex, was mistress, and her nose, which betrayed too much reflectiveness, brought his new Adam to his legs again, upon which the old Adam had already set himself up. He congratulated himself that he was Flamin's friend, and consequently had some claims upon her attention and her society. Nevertheless he continued to feel all the time as if everything she did occurred now for the first time in the world; and he watched her as one does a man who has been operated on for blindness from his birth, or an Omai,[47] or a Li-Bu. He kept thinking, "How could sitting down ever become her,—or the handing of a fruit-dish, or the eating of a cherry, or stooping down to read a note?" I am a still worse ninny beside the above-mentioned court dame.

At last came Le Baut into the garden, after the first toilet, and his wife after the second. The Chamberlain—a short, supple, bedizened thing, that will pull off its hat before the Devil in hell when it enters there—received the son of his hereditary enemy in an uncommonly complimentary manner, and yet with a dignity, for which, however, not his heart, but his rank, gave him strength. Victor, for the mere reason that he imagined him an injured person, cherished a predisposition of good-will towards him. Although Le Baut's tongue was almost, like his teeth, false and inserted, and consequently the words were so, too, which were made up of dentals and linguals, still his neither coarse nor uncourteous flatteries—among which his attitudes and intentions also are to be counted—pleased our honest Victor, who could not hate fine flatterers, as being weak persons. The Chamberlain's lady— who was already in the years which a coquette seeks to conceal, although she had still more reason to conceal the preceding ones—received our well-disposed hero with the sincerest voice that ever yet issued from a false Judas's bosom, and with the most artful face, on which it seemed impossible that the deceptions of love could ever have found room for a glance.

The new company took away Victor's embarrassment at once. He soon remarked, indeed, the peculiar fighting- and dancing-positions of the circle towards each other. Clotilda seemed reserved and indifferent towards all, except her father. The step-mother was refined towards the Chamberlain, haughty towards her step-daughter, obliging towards Victor, and bore herself with an easy and subservient coquetry towards Matthieu, who, on his part, was, toward the wedded pair, alternately complimentary and ironical; towards Clotilda, cold as ice; and towards my hero, as courteous as Le Baut was to all. Nevertheless Victor was more joyous and free than any of them, not merely because he was under the free heavens,—for a room always lay upon him like a blockhouse, and a chair was like the stocks,—but because he was among *fine* people, who, despite the most angular relations, give to conversation four butterflies'-wings, that it may—in contrast to the clinging caterpillar, who impales himself on every thorn—fly without noise and in little curves over all prickles, and alight only on blossoms. He was the greatest friend of fine people and fine turns of expression; hence it was that he took so much pleasure in the society of a Fontenelle, a Crébillon, a Marivaux,—of the entire female sex, and particularly of the decently coquettish portion of it. Do not mistake me. Ah! upon his Flamin, upon his Dahore, on all great men who were exalted above the refined, cowardly, vacant microcosmologists of the great world, his whole soul hung glowing; but for that very reason did he seek out, with a view to greater completeness, the smaller men, as fringe and corner-trimmings, with so much zeal.

Four persons had at this moment four telescopes pointed at once at his soul: for himself, he took nothing of the kind into his hand, because he was too good-natured and too happy to be the spy of a heart; and only after the lapse of some days did he observe the image which any one with whom he had been in company left behind in his brain. He did not conceal himself, and yet he was seen in a false light: good men can more easily see into bad ones than the latter can into the former. He guessed others better than they guessed him. Only Clotilda deserves a word of defence for having, even until after dinner,—during which Le Baut, the greatest story-teller of this story-telling century, carried through his part,—regarded him as too malicious and satirical. But she could hardly do otherwise: a woman easily discerns the human, but hardly the divine (or devilish), nature in a man, with difficulty his worth, but easily his intentions, and his inner complexion more so than his contour. Matthieu gave occasion for her error, but also (as I shall presently report) for its retraction. This Evangelist,[48] who was a much greater satirist than his namesake in the New Testament, placed almost all Flachsenfingen on his private pillory, from Prince and Court down to Zeusel;[49] only the Minister (his father) and his many sisters he was compelled, unfortunately, to leave out, and likewise those persons with whom he happened at the moment to be talking. What was called calumny in him was at bottom an exaggerated Moravianism. For, as St. Macarius commands that one shall, out of humility, add twenty ounces of evil when one has five, but with regard to good, the reverse,—accordingly ingenuous, courtly souls, seeing that no one will use this modest language, endeavor to speak it in every one's name, and always ascribe to him whose humility they wish to represent fifteen ounces more of evil and less of good than he really has. On the contrary, in the case of present company, they find this mediatorial system of satisfaction unnecessary: hence the life of such court-nobles is wholly dramatic; for as, according to Aristotle, comedy paints men as worse, and tragedy as better, than they are, so do the nobles referred to bring forward in the former only *absent*, in the latter only *present* persons. I do not know whether this perfection will go to the length of atoning for a real fault of the Evangelist,—namely, that, like the Romans on the Lupercalia, he—too often made thrusts at the female sex. Thus, for instance, he said to-day, maidens and raspberries were wormy before they were ripe; female virtue was the red-hot iron which a woman (as was also the case in the old ordeals) had to carry from the font (the baptismal-day) to the altar (the wedding-day), in order to maintain her innocence, &c. Nothing fell upon Clotilda—and the same I have always found the case with the best of her sex—more keenly than satire upon her whole sex; but Victor was astonished at her art—very peculiar to her sex and to worldly experience at once—of concealing the fact, that she both—endured and despised.

The Evangelist's example brought it about that Victor, too, began to phosphoresce at all points of his soul; the spark of wit ran round the whole circle of his ideas, which, like Graces, clasped each other by the hand, and his electrical chime of bells outdid the Page's discharges, which were lightnings, and stank of brimstone. Clotilda, who was very observing, mistrusted Sebastian's lips and heart.

The young nobleman held him to be one of his feather, and in love with Clotilda; and that, on the ground that "the gayer or more earnest tone into which a man fell in company was a sign that a female electrical-eel had struck at his bosom." I must confess it,—Victor's effervescent soul never allowed him to hit that expression of respect for women which does not run into untimely tenderness, and for which he often envied cultivated people of the world; his regard unfortunately always looked like a declaration of love. The Chamberlain's lady accounted him as false as her Cicisbeo.[50] People like her cannot comprehend any other kind attentions than polite or artful ones.

They kept our hero over there all day and half the evening.

Not once in the whole day was he able,—although the invisible eyes of his inner man stood full of tears at Clotilda's noble figure, at her secret grief for her cold, buried friend, at her thrilling voice when she merely spoke to Agatha,—for all that, he never found himself able to say so much as an earnest word: toward strangers his nature always impelled him in the beginning to make sundry satirical leaps and other caprioles. But in the evening, when they were in the festal garden, where his usual shudder at the emptiness of life was made more intense by merriment, as it always was,—whereas serious, sad, passionate conversations diminished it,—and when Clotilda granted him only a very cold civility, as if shown to him at a father's dictation, and did not divine in its full extent the difference between him and Matthieu, who assumed no second world, nor any inner man organically adapted to it: then was there a stifled feeling about his yearning heart; too many tears seemed to fill his whole breast and press for a passage; and as often as he looked up to the great, deep heavens, something whispered in his soul: Take not the least thought for the fine circle, but speak out!

But there was only *one* soul for him, to which Nature had attached those treadles, as to pedal-harps, which impart to every thought a higher tone of the spheres, to life a holy worth, and to the heart an echo from Eden: that soul was not his once so-loved Flamin, but his teacher, Dahore, in England, whom he had long ago lost from sight, but never from his dreams. The shadow of this great man stood, as it were, projected upon the night, hovering and erect before him, and saying, "Dear one, I see thy inward weeping, thy sacred longing, thy desolate heart, and thy outstretched, trembling arms; but all is in vain; thou wilt never find me, nor I thee." He gazed at the stars, whose exalting science his teacher had even then instilled into his youthful soul; he said to Clotilda: "The topography of the heavens should be a piece of our religion; a woman ought to learn the catechism and Fontenelle by heart." And then he described the astronomical lessons of his Dahore and the teacher himself.

From Clotilda's face there broke forth a great transfiguration, and she depicted with words and looks her own astronomical teacher at the Seminary,—how he was just as noble and just as quiet,—that he called himself *Emanuel,* and bore no surname, because he said, "With transitory man, with one whose genealogical tree so speedily sank into nothingness, the difference between family names and baptismal names was too slight";— that, unhappily, his noble soul inhabited a shattered body, which already bent low toward the grave,—that he was, according to the assurance of her Abbess, the gentlest and greatest man who had yet come from the East Indies (his native country), although there were some singularities of his way of life in Maienthal, which one had to overlook....

Matthieu, whose wit borrowed from the snake his line of beauty, his poisonous tooth, his leap, and his coldness, said, softly and composedly: "It is well for his withered body that he was not made astronomer and night-watchman here at once; he applied, several years ago, for a telescope and a horn."

Clotilda was, for the first time, suffused with a flush of angry redness, like the morning before the rain: "If," said she, quickly, "you know him merely from my portraiture, you cannot possibly seek this characteristic among his." But the Chamberlain came to the Page's assistance, and said that Emanuel had actually, five years before, been refused that application. Clotilda looked, as if for help, to the only one whose attentiveness was not ironical,—our Victor, on whom the reflection of her transfiguration threw its beauty,—and asked, more in the tone of hope than of assertion, "Should one expect anything like that of such a mind?" "Of mine sooner," he replied, by way of evasion; for he, who could have contradicted the Pope to his face, found it often impossible to gainsay fair lips, especially when they propounded a question with so much reliance on his negative. "As often as I walk through towns by night, I listen to the bodily night-watch with more pleasure than to the spiritual. In the silent, listening night, under the outspread starry heaven, there is something so sublime in the homiletic owl's-song or hoot of the night-watch, that I have a hundred times wished me a horn and six verses."

The Chamberlain and his *associé* took this for clumsy persiflage; the latter—perhaps for the sake of displeasing Clotilda, to the advantage of his heart's czarina, armed with false bosom and false rump—went on unshamed with his, and asserted that the best method of making the aforenamed anonymous person sad was a very merry one, a comedy;—to be sure, a farce moved him still more strongly, as he himself witnessed in him at Goethe's moral puppet-play or fair.

Then flashed upon the surprised Victor a new face and a new relation; for he was exactly like Emanuel. A fair, with its human streams running up and down,—with its flitting of figures to and fro, as in a clock with images,—with its perpetually buzzing air, in which fiddle-squeak and human janglings and lowing of cattle conspire in one deafening roar,—and with the booths, crammed with commodities, offering a mosaic picture of our little life, patched up of varied necessities.... a village-fair, by all these reminiscences of the great, frosty *New-Year's fair* of Life, made Victor's noble bosom at once heavy and full; he sank away, sweetly overpowered, into the din, and the human ranks around him absorbed his soul into its stiller fantasies. That was the reason why Goethe's Hogarthian *tail-piece* of a village-fair (like Shakespeare) always left him melancholy; just as he was most fond, indeed, of finding in the low-comic the highest earnest (women are capable only of a reverse discovery), and a comic book, without any nobler trait or hint (e. g. Blumauer's Æneid), he could endure as little as La Mettrie's[51] disgustingly laughing face, or the faces on the frontispieces of the Vade Mecum.

Like a true youth, he forgot himself and all around him, half-stretched out his arms, and said, with an eye in which one saw a soul longingly laboring at a portrait of Emanuel: "Now I know thee, thou nameless one! thou art the lofty man, who is so rare.... I assure you, Herr Von Schleunes, this Mr. Emanuel has something in him ... No, amidst this life on the wing, a thing which darts so *prestissimo* out of one rain-shower into another,[52] and from cloud to cloud, should not keep its bill open on the stretch for one continued peal of laughter.... I have read today somewhere: Man has only two and a half minutes, and only one for a smile...." He had quite lost himself in the thicket of his feelings, else he would have kept back more than he did, especially the last line of the leaf found in the garden. Clotilda was startled at something or other. He would now gladly have read the leaf through. She related to him now those characteristics of her teacher into which she knew better how to enter; that he was a Pythagorean, went only in white robes, had himself put to sleep and waked with flute-music, ate no leguminous fruits or animal food, and often walked half the night under the stars.

Lost in mute rapture over the teacher, he hung with enthusiastic eyes upon the friendly lips of the pupil, who was ennobled by her interest in a sublime and singular genius. She found here the first man whom she had ever put into an unfeigned enthusiasm for her Pythagorean favorite; and all her chasms turned themselves, blooming, towards Emanuel's image, like flowers toward the sun. Two fair souls discover their affinity first of all by the like love which binds them to a third. The full, inspired heart loves to hush and hide itself in a finery-room, which holds only heterogeneous persons, but when it finds therein its second, then in its joy at that its silence and secrecy and the finery-room are all forgotten.

The quicksilver of Victor's morning gayety had fallen ten degrees. In the twilight of his soul nothing peered forth but the paper which he wanted to read, and in fact presently read out in the avenue; and so he took an early leave.

The leaf had blown out of Clotilda's loose Album, and was written by— Emanuel.

"Man has here two and a half minutes,—one to smile, one to sigh, and half a one to love; for in the midst of this minute he dies.

"But the grave is not deep, it is the gleaming footmark of an angel who seeks us. When the unknown hand sends the last arrow at the head of man, he bends his head in anticipation, and the arrow merely takes off the crown of thorns from his wounds.[53]

"And with this hope, go forth from Maienthal, noble soul! but neither continents nor graves nor the second world can sunder or bind together two human beings: but only thoughts part or marry hearts.

"O, may thy life hang full of blossoms! From thy first Paradise may a second, as from the midst of one rose a second, be destined to bloom! May the Earth glow in thy sight, as if thou stoodest above it, and followedst with thine eye its path in heaven! And as Moses died because God kissed him, so be thy life a long kiss of the Eternal! And may thy death be mine!... EMANUEL."

"O thou good, good soul!" cried Victor, "I can now no more forget thee. Thou must—thou wilt—take an interest in my weak heart!" From his inner strings the drops of vapor that choked their music had now fallen off. His brain became a radiant landscape, in which there stood nothing but Emanuel's shining form. He arrived late at the parsonage, with a face expressive of blissful emotion; and in this glow he arrayed before his spectators the image of Clotilda, to whom he gave everything an angel has, even the wings that threatened a short stay. His friendship raised him so far above the suspicion of a suspicion, that he thought he could give his friend no warmer or tenderer proof of the same, than by the strongest sympathetic praise of Clotilda; Flamin's love for her passed over through this friendship into his soul. The feeling for the beloved of a friend carries with it an unspeakable sweetness and moral tenderness. For Victor I answer, in this matter, that he understood, indeed, how a friend can sacrifice his love to another, but not how the other can accept the offering; but for Flamin I cannot stand security that he is cool enough, and a sufficient connoisseur of men, to regard the prize-medals which Victor stamps upon Clotilda, and upon which he sets her beautiful face and his coat of arms, as only just so many coins *de confiance*, and as pledges of brotherly fidelity. He was too impetuous and too ambitious to see, or even to listen to, the truth; for his open-hearted friend had to suppress many a tender reproach, which would have tried him too much, because he had too much love of praise and fieriness of spirit, and too little self-confidence. Hence a flatterer like Matthieu fastened himself so much the more firmly with his ivy-hooks into the fissures of this rock. When he a little harshly called the nameless Emanuel an enthusiast, Victor said little more about him that day. Flamin—either because he was a Jurist, or because he was a Hotspur, or both—could endure anything better than poets, philosophers, courtiers, and enthusiasts,—one excepted, who was all these at once, namely, his Sebastian Victor.

5
DOG-POST-DAY

I must here—premise, once for all, that I should be very stupid if I did not notice the multitude of improbabilities in this history: I am well aware of them all; nay, I have observed some of them—e. g. in Clotilda's behavior, or those in my hero's medical doctorship—even sooner than the reader, because I have—read everything before he has. I therefore delayed no longer, but entreated my correspondent by to-day's Hofmann-mail to write me by the dog the next time, in his portrait-box, what we were all about. I told him flatly, that the devil a bit did he know, though I did, however, of the readers and their tyranny. I must tell him (I said) that they were people of sense, whom a Biographer, nay, even a Romance-architect, dared not approach with poetic deception, but they would say, like the Areopagus, "Give us the naked historical fact here, without any superfluous poetic dressing up." And in fact it was a marvel to me, I went on to say, that he should not yet know that they had so much, partly understanding and partly four-leaved clover[54] in them, that, if the greatest authors and tragic poets should undertake to be fine, and by æsthetic juggleries to excite in them fear, like cuppers, or pity, like beggars, they would cold-bloodedly let these men work till they were tired, and say, "We are not to be caught." That the Reviewers, however, were still more crazy and clever, and were perhaps the best *Skotometers* (measurers of darkness), at the same time that they were the wretchedest *Photometers* (light measurers) going. And finally, I said right out to my historical adjutant, that it was no injury to him, but very much to me, that I should be translated into several languages, and therein, for every improbability in the text, be dragged down into the scourging-cellar of a note, and there sorely lashed, without daring to open my mouth, if the interpreting scoundrel who translated (or transported) my gourd-bottle-case like a cask of wine, from one country to another, should, on the way, as all carriers do, outwardly besprinkle and inwardly fill up the wine with water.—He must, at least, (I entreated him) give me an answer, that I might show it to the readers, as an evidence that I had written to him.

By the next Dog-post-day, therefore, at all events, great things may be expected.—

Besides, the 4th of May comes into that also, with what should seem its two important Thanksgiving festivals for the arrival of the two Sebastians,—the little one into the world, the elder at the bathing-town.—Even Clotilda is to be there to-morrow, and Victor is very eager (and so am I) to see her in the sunshine of love beside Flamin; for over yonder all her charms seemed to bloom round a heart not yet smitten and ripened by love's ray, as flower-leaves hide the *white heart-leaves* from the sun.... Matthieu came to-day to take leave, because he was going back to-morrow to the city. Our hero was less and less pleased with him, and a Page's history, which he related of himself, renewed Victor's resolve to fulfil soon the entreaty of the Parson's wife by ridding himself of such a fellow.

Matthieu, as Page, rendered service to the chief Tutor's lady, I believe both the greater and the lesser service. Nevertheless, he had once to smuggle an Abbate and conscience-keeper into one of her cabinets, which was destined to be the confessional and holy place to a degree of which, to be sure, her stupid, jealous husband had no notion. Now there was in the next room a musical armchair, upon which, in fact, one played with no other instrument than the rump; so soon as one sat down in it, it began its overtures, and I myself once sat in such a one at Prince Esterhazy's. Our Mat,[55] as all the citizens of Flachsenfingen called him,—some government people called him even the Evangelist,—appointed the Abbate two hours too soon; but, lest the man with the shorn peruke should be tired of waiting, he first carried in the music-making chair as resting-bench and anchoring-ground for weary expectants. Toward three of the night, when the company was gone, except the chief Tutor, the counsellor of conscience, weary of standing, let his rump sink at last into the easy-chair stuffed out with favorite arias, and woke up with his breeches the whole wailing music therein with its thrilling passages, without the least possibility of stilling the cabinet-serenade of this alarmer. At last the husband darted like a herring at the final cadences (or falls), and dragged from his organ-stool the sedentary conscience-man in the midst of counterpoint and shakes, and spoiled his quail-call for him, I believe, by an administered cudgelling. The chief Tutor's lady easily guessed the master of the chair, Mat; but so very much a matter of course is pardon at court,—not merely *past* offences, but *future* ones being forgiven there by good, easy female souls,—that the chief Tutor's lady did not avenge herself upon Mat, although he *served* her two weeks and a half longer, till after just two weeks and a half....

Victor was indignant at Flamin's laughter; he loved drollery, but not bantering. His sweetened blood began gradually with this *mother of vinegar* to grow sour towards this Mat, whose cold, ironical gallantry toward the honest Agatha of itself exasperated him, though her phlegmatic, and, as it were, married pulse, beat in his absence and in his presence at the same rate. Still more heart-burning matter and acid collected in Victor's bosom, from the fact that he, who tolerated everything,—vain men, proud ones, atheists, enthusiasts,—could nevertheless not endure men who regard virtue as a kind of refined provision-bakery, wantonness as allowed, the spirit as an almsgatherer for the flesh, the heart as a blood-syringe, and our soul as a new shoot of the body. But this was what Matthieu did, who besides had a passion for philosophizing, and threatened to infect Victor's friend, who, in fact, was as cold toward the whole world of poets and spirits as a statesman, with his philosophical cancer-poison.

In the evening he endeavored to sound, a little nearer to Flamin's ear, a blast upon a second Trumpet of Fame against the departed pseudo-Evangelist. It was in the garden that he blew it. He took the hand of which Matthieu's was not worthy into his better one, and began, with the finest and heartiest forbearance,—which one must grant even to true friendship for a hollow friend,—his iconoclastic attack. For while he charged it upon the lady of the Chamberlain, that she threw down at Agatha from her high post looks nowise cleaner than what monkeys used to throw down from their high roosts at passers-by; and while he blamed the young Page, that, like many of the nobility, only among the nobility could he scent best (perhaps by the help of contrast) the heretical odor of one belonging to the burgher-class, and that his words and looks at the palace flew like icicles at the good, warm heart of Agatha; at the same time the reproach of this May-frost toward the sister was only a pretext behind which he veiled the observation, that the Page would not be Flamin's friend, if he were not Agatha's lover.

Flamin's silence (the sign of his indignation) gave the stream of his eloquence a new and swifter descent; in addition to this a nightingale, poetizing in Le Baut's garden, woke up all the echoes of love in his soul.— He therefore grasped, of course, both of Flamin's hands in that effervescence which always transformed his steps toward an object into springs, and thereby overshot the mark. Many plans miscarry, because the heart toils after the head, and because at the end of the execution one applies less caution than at its beginning. He looked upon his beloved, the fluting throat of the nightingale set the text of his love to music, and with indescribable emotion he said: "Best one, thy heart is too good not to be outwitted by those who cannot reach thee. O if, some day, the sharp edge of court *ton* should pass bloodily across the veins of thy breast (Flamin's looks seemed to ask, Art thou not then even satirical?)—O if he, who has no faith in virtue and disinterestedness, should one day himself cease to show any; if he should sorely betray thee; should the hand, which court-life had hardened, like a lemon-squeezer, wring blood and tears from thy heart, then, I beseech thee, despair not, only not of friendship,—for thy mother and I love thee far otherwise. O verily, at the time when thou art forced to say, Why did I not hearken to my friend who so warned me, and to my mother who so loved me?—then mayest thou come to me, to one who never changes, and who prizes thy error higher than self-interested vigilance; then would I lead thee weeping to thy mother, and say to her, take him wholly, thou only art worthy to love him." To all this Flamin said not a word. "Art thou sad, my Flamin?" "Tired!" "I am sad; the plaints of the nightingale strike upon my soul like echoes of *future* ones," said Victor. "Are you pleased with this nightingale, Victor?" "Indescribably, as if she were a friend of my innermost soul." "Thus are people imposed on; it is *Matthieu singing*," Flamin quickly answered. For the Evangelist differed from a nightingale in nothing except size. And then Flamin, somewhat irritated, and yet with a pressure of his friend's hand, took his departure.

6
DOG-POST-DAY

Knef's answer is wretched: "By your well-born's favor, dated the 6th instant, I see that the public has taste and some refinement, which does not surprise me, since the same is treated like gold-leaves, which are beaten out thin and fine, first within a book of parchment, and then between two of sheep-skin leaves, and thus, in like manner, by being passed from one book to another, and therein through the force of the press-bar, is made as fine as cavalier-paper.[56] If the public keeps on reading in this way a year or two, it may at last be more clever than Germany itself. Touching the improbabilities in our work, several such are of course desirable, because without them a biography or a romance gives miserable satisfaction, since it wants the charm by which the German hospital-ship and ship of fools, full of original romances, proves so attractive to us, ... which ship, as secretive-gland of disagreeable works, may justly be called the liver of the Republic of Letters, and the bookstore the gall-duct. But in reference to improbabilities, I am myself only too apprehensive that even the few on which we rely may in the end disappear. I am, &c."

The wag, as one may easily see, would fain pull the wool[57] over my eyes and those of the reader. For me, however, it is a magnificent document in evidence that I have done my part by writing to the rogue.

There are certain persons who, if in the evening they were very warm and friendly, the next morning are very gloomy and cold,—like Maupertuis's half-suns, which burn only on one side and disappear from us when they turn towards us the earthly half,—and if they were cold, the next time they are warm. Flamin forgot the next morning both the warm evening and the night-chill. Today is the festival of churching! Over there with Sebastian he launched out like a German police-puritan and purist, with fire-devils[58] and musketry against churching,—against infant-baptismal festivals,—against felling trees for Christmases and Whitsuntides,—against holidays, and against all the merry-makings of mankind.

Nothing in our century so enraged Victor as its haughty crusade-preachings against unfashionable follies, whereas with unfashionable vices it makes contracts of subsidy. He took a long breath to start with, and then showed that the good of a state, as of a man, consisted not in riches, but in the use of riches, not in its commercial, but in its moral worth, that the sweeping out of the ancient leaven and most of our institutions and pandects and edicts had for their object only to enhance princely incomes, not morality, and that one wanted to have vices and subjects, like the old Jews, bring their offerings only in one city, namely, the residence city,—that humanity, from time immemorial, had cut its nails only on its bare *hands*, not on its covered *feet*, which often themselves decayed on that account,—that economical and sumptuary laws were still more needful to princes themselves, at least to the highest classes, than to the lowest,—that Rome owed to her many holidays much of her patriotism.... Flamin had no eye for the little pearl-print of domestic joy, for infusory-flowerets of pleasure; on the contrary, his soul kept step with a Brutus when he strode majestically up to Pompey's statue, and with a sigh over fate drove the scissors of the Parcæ into the greatest heart of earth, which confounded its worth with its right. Victor had room in his heart for the most unlike feelings.

I cannot repeat often enough, that to-day is the churching. I will sketch it for posterity; not, however, with that curtness with which a newspaper-writer condenses the funeral of a king into three sheets, but a little more circumstantially. For the stately initial letters of this day the Parsonage had quite other reasons *in petto* than one has ever yet, to my knowledge, been pleased to disclose to our age: three interested parties wished to deceive each other,—at least, two did a third.

In the first place, the Lady of the Parsonage wished to deceive our hero, who did not know that to-day was the birthday of his father, and that that personage—whom she had taken the liberty of inviting—was coming today for the space of five minutes. In the morning, she set her two daughters to boiling yarn, in order that they might confess nothing to Victor,—at least, not the truth; for it is a well-known superstition that yarn boils whitest when one lies soundly over the operation. Hence we should be the more watchful when women lie, and inquire whether they mean, by their poetical deceptions, to *burn anything else white* except yarn. Her beloved Victor— that was her plan—should to-day present to her husband, whose cradle-festival[59] also fell on to-day, the usual congratulation, and afterward halve it, and carry it on to his Lordship, who was to arrive with his own birthday.

Secondly, Sebastian and she wished to deceive the old Chaplain, who had forgotten that he had been born, which absence of mind had already occurred to him at his first birthday. Mankind keep the run of another's life better than of their own; truly we make altogether too little account of a history which once was ours, and which is the shell of hours that have flown away, and yet the drops of time through which we swim do only in the distance of memory form the rainbow of enjoyment. Men know when all emperors were born and all philosophers died; women know, by reckoning time, only this, when their husbands, who are *their* regents and classic authors, underwent both. Victor, whose delicate feeling was seared by too great attentions to himself, was glad that Eymann's shoulders must bear half of to-day's honor.

Thirdly, the Lord of the Parsonage wanted to play his deception as well as any one else, and in fact upon everybody. As this Festival-day was to him—like the three High Festivals of the Cloisters—at the same time shaving-day, on which the wisest heads make the foolishest faces, the barber must needs cut with the razor-lancet upon the skin of the soul-keeper, as upon the bark of a birch-tree, a memorial of himself; but the little blood that flowed out suggested to the Parson a cleverer thought than what the cupper left therein, which, however, secreted the nervous sap, that, according to the merest sciolists, is the grease of our mental motions, the gold solution of our most significant ideas, and the spirit of our spirit. This cleverer thought which I so much praise was, to have a vein opened in his left arm, to conceal it from the whole household, in the evening to congratulate his Lordship and everybody, and, at last, to strip up his sleeve and show the wound, like a Roman, and say, "Congratulate me, I pray, on the bleeding!" He executed his idea, and the shaver was obliged, to his amazement, to hack something else beside the chin. The wounded man escorted him even to the outer door, not so much from politeness, as in order that he might not hold forth to the whole domestic company on the subject, but keep the occurrence absolutely to himself, except in houses where there was a beard and an ear. For let an historian be ever so much the *month-hand* of the age, and consequently the newspaper-compositor its *hour-hand*, and accordingly a woman its *second-hand*, still, after all, the beard-trimmer is both, woman and *second-hand*.

As Flamin and Victor passed down into the sitting-prinking-summer and winter-room, from amidst none but glad faces protruded one sullen one, which belonged to the Parson, who was plunging about like one possessed: there were two things which he could not possibly nose out,—his Bible and his powder-puff. Three minutes before he had thus lamented: "Am not I and my wretched life then singled out for a true Passion-history? Let an urn of fortune be given me, from which anybody else would claw out, as if he were crabbing, whole kingdoms. So soon as the Archfiend sees it to be me, he drops his dung in; and I claw that out instead of crabs and kingdoms, and nothing more. It would have gone finely to-day, the Devil saw,—we should have had until four o'clock in the afternoon no fun, but dog's-work; but then we should have broken loose; then would have come the dinner in the summer-house, the congratulation and salutation and real jollity.... And for you all this is still waiting; but to me, if the puff and the Bible do not appear, just send some of the soot and ashes (the leavings of the evening-feast) that I may brush therewith Fox's [his horse's] bit, and in the evening I can weed radishes by the summer-house."

At this moment, he had to salute, with the dipped flag of his poll, his tasselled cap, the Briton just entering,—when the gesture shook out of the cap a hair-tuft, which, to be sure, was not the long-sought Bible, but was the puff, which had been given up for lost. That is to say, the thinking and reading world, to which one does not often disclose the weightier facts, must at least come at this one,—that the Court Chaplain, just as men are snatched from among men to overtop and master the rest, precisely so bound up the hairs which his comb plucked out, into a skin-fascicle or hair-union, in order to powder therewith the others that were left standing,—which now could not, of course, by this most exalted spirit and pentameter,[60] be well christened anything else than a hair-puff. Nevertheless, Eymann's face was longer than his cap; he let this syringe of the coloring powder of his head lie and cool there, and said, "If I don't ferret out the Bible, then I don't see how this tuft alone is to get me out of the scrape."

As the Bible was sought before Luther's time, so now was the Canstein Bible, with its black beetle's-wing-shells. If anything could make this hard blow still more bitter, it was this,—that Eymann's band, like his reason, lay between the lost canonical leaves[61] as in a napkin-press; for the clergy, especially the Pope, love to make the Bible commentary a smoothing-press and finery-box to their outer man. Although he had eight other Bibles, even the simple Biblical Chrestomathy of Seiler, in the house, and to-day, at week-day church, did not need any at all, still it was certainly better and more human—that is, more foolish—that he should whistle the head of his vestry-beadle, the schoolmaster, to the window, and postpone divine service, like a reformation, by a quarter of an hour's interim, than that, instead of simply the hour of tolling, he should change nothing less than Bible and bands. Good heavens! how like exegetists and Kennicottists[62] they searched and smiled! "This hunting for the Bible," said Sebastian, "redounds to a clergyman's honor, especially as he seeks the truths in the Bible only by *daylight*, not by *funeral-torches*."

The monks, like the lighters of the street-lamps, have a *ladder* and much oil, but with the oil they *extinguish* the lamps and their own thirst, and with the ladder they conduct those who light them again up to the gallows.

As the Chaplain passed along before the quiet head of the six-weeks' child, which to-day's lace-cap already oppressed, he went back, from vexation at its indifference, lifted its bedizened head with his right hand, and thrust the left through the stratum of the cradle-straw, thinking there to exhume the Bible, which is usually the pillow and the supporting amulet of children (particularly of *Dauphins*), saying, meanwhile: "The miserable little brat would lie there through all our misery, perfectly cool, seeming to say, 'What's that to me?' if I didn't stir him up." And just at this moment something fell, not like a shot, but like a book, although it can be heard through my quill, even to the thirtieth century. Eymann flew, thoughtfully, into the second story, and found at his feet a smashed—mouse under his long-sought Bible. The Protestant imperial circles can never have been ignorant of the students' or Dr. Luther's mousetraps,[63] for which one needs only a book, and which are to mice what symbolical books were to candidates. Sebastian drew forth the corpse by the tail from under the Biblical vellum-mould, and Seiler's Bible-arrangement, swung the cadaver toward the light, and delivered extempore this funeral sermon: "Poor schismatic! the Old and New Testaments were the death of thee, but neither thou nor the Testaments are to blame! Only be glad that the Bible did not absolutely singe thee to ashes, like a Portuguese Israelite; but thy lines fell in enlightened times, where it takes away nothing but livings. It is genuine wit, if I ask, As the Bible used to extinguish conflagrations into which it was thrown, why not, then, *auto-da-fés* also?"

I have long been watching for an opportunity here to force the world to ask why the case of a mouse's death should interest it more than the shooting down of an army in general history,—the loss of another's hair-puff more than Christina's abdicated crown.[64] ... This interest arises from the source whence it comes with those to whom the case really occurs: because I relate it copiously, i. e. because the readers, like the heroes concerned in it, painfully live over one moment of childish history after another. Many little blows riddle the firmest man as surely as one great one; and it is all one whether fate does it or an author. And thus it comes that the modern man is placed so near to the index-finger of time, that he can see it move; hence a trifle, when it takes up *many* moments, becomes so great to us, and this short life, which, like the picture of our soul in the *Orbis Pictus*,[65] consists of points—of black and golden ones—seems so long. And hence, too, everywhere, as on this page, does our serious mood stand so near to our mirthful.

Except Flamin, all moved to church, godfather and godchild. It was a so-called week-day prayer-hour, such as will be set apart in every rational duchy and margravedom, where one still sees to it that the parson shall freeze once or twice a week, and that, as novices do for the exercise of obedience, they may be obliged to sprinkle dry sticks, to scatter the seed of the Divine word into empty pews, as Melancthon did into empty pots.[66] In German countries, mine and a few others excepted, it takes two centuries thoroughly to do away a folly,—one to recognize it, and one more to do it away. The *views* of a consistory always become rational a hundred years sooner than its orders (*circularia*) do.

In the latticed pew of the Eymanns, whose door made nearly a right angle with that of the vestry, Sebastian found all the flowers again, or at least the flower-skeletons, which had bloomed around his fair childhood's days,—figurative and literal ones; and the literal ones, which had crept away all soiled under the footstool of the choir-pew, opened out again into flowers of memory. He thought of his childish sorrows here,—among them the length of the sermon,—and of his childish pleasures, among which were to be reckoned the length of the voluntary and Eymann's kneeling on the middle of the pulpit-stairs. He pushed back the wooden lattice-window, and found in its wooden groove his initials, V. S. H., notched by his own hands. So far is it from the child to the youth! And man wonders at the distance. "Ah! then," said Horion,—and we will say it with him,—"all was to thee as yet infinite, and nothing little but thy heart. Ah! in that warm, quickening time, when a father is still God the Father, and a mother the mother of God, not yet did the bosom, oppressed with spirits, graves, and storms, press itself for comfort to a human one. All the four quarters of the world were installed in this church; all rivers were named Rhine, and all princes January. Ah! this tranquil and lovely day was set in a golden horizon of infinite hope and a ring of morning-red. Now the day is gone, and the horizon sunk, and only the skeleton remains there,—the latticed pew."

But if we now, even in the noonday hours of life, think and sigh thus, how much more at evening, when man folds up his flower-leaves, and becomes undistinguishable like other flowers,—at evening, when we stand low in the western horizon and go out,—then, when we turn round, and survey the short road strewed with trampled-out hopes,—oh! then, how much more sweetly will it not look upon us,—the garden of childhood, lying in the east, low down near the place of our rising, and still suffused with an old, pale redness,—how much more magically will it gleam on us, and yet how much more will it affect us to tenderness! And thereupon man lays himself down on the earth not far from the grave, and hopes here below no more.

To Eymann it must be a touching thought, that he, as he had for years given the benediction in this church to newly-delivered mothers only parishionally related to him, could, for once, give his wishes to a nearer one. Victor crept back into all his boyish Sundays and their illusions by this simple act, that he to-day, as in his tenth year, went, while the whole congregation were singing, into the vestry, to the Parson, and asked him for the page of the hymn. He enjoyed it with a real childish gusto to think that there were four *moving* creatures[67] in the temple,—the Parson, the Schoolmaster, the Exchequer-master of the poor's-box,[68] and himself. Is there anything more sublime, thought he, than a jingling alms-bag-father with a long, horizontal balance-pole, walking to and fro alone, among nothing but stiffened statues?

After church the festival began with mere preliminaries, as a treaty of peace does with articles about the neutral ground, about rank, &c. Only the world must not suppose that anything came on sooner than five o'clock in the afternoon, or that any one could earlier than that slip out of his prosaic week-day clothes into the poetic festal ones, or quietly settle down beside a neighbor; but, according to the order and programme of pleasure, all must now run up and down, obedient to Apollonia, that *majoress-domo*,—must carry away bean-poles and seed-cornucopias out of the summer-house,—fan out therefrom butterflies that had burst the cocoons and waked up bottle-flies,—tie back the twigs which had grown over the windows,—lug down the orangery, which consisted of a hundred blossoms of a pomegranate-tree, out of the parsonage into the garden alley, in like manner an invalid harpsichord, whose sounding-board had not sprung[69] so often as its strings.... The serious Flamin was compelled by the bustling Sebastian to take part in these puppet-plays,[70] and between them, in this preparatory chase of pleasure, the tormented visage of Eymann had to labor, to which Victor delivered the most essential exhortations: "Master Godfather, we cannot be earnest and busy enough,—this festival may yet be talked of in places where it will have influence; but a middle course between princely pomp and Belgian stinginess will, I think, throw upon us the most favorable light." All went well,—even the clouds dispersed,—Clotilda would come. The primate of the festival, in whose honor the church-going took place,— the little six-weeks'-man,—memorized his part aloud, which he had to perform after five o'clock, and which, as in the case of more than one hero of festivities, was to consist of nothing but going to sleep.

The memorizing consisted of his waking and screaming in one steady scream for the bosom in which the Creator had stored up for him the first manna in life's wilderness. But not till five o'clock did the mother still him with the maternal sleep-potion, and enable the little speaker to close his throat-lid[71] and eyelids at once. At first I had come near suppressing— from respect for the Parson's lady—the fact that she suckled, and so, like a whale as it were, still reckoned among the mammalia, nourished at her bosom another child than Cupid; but I flattered myself, upon reflection, that a person who is neither a theatre-princess nor a crown-princess would not be so strictly judged as others, if she *had* children or milk....

Before I say that Clotilda came, I will, inasmuch as she has eight residences,—although many a magnate who owns sixteen noble residences still seeks a seventeenth with walls in which he may sleep,—offer a slight excuse for her going into the house of a common citizen; but she needs after all no other justification than the fact that she was in the country, where often the oldest blood can avail itself of no better intercourse than that of citizens, unless perhaps it is that of cattle, which even some not uncultured cavaliers really prefer....

It strikes five o'clock,—the matchless beauty enters,—the moon hangs down towards her out of heaven like a white leaf newly budded,—the gay, innocent blood in St. Luna rises under her influence like the tide,—all is rehabilitated.

But the sixth chapter is run out.... And as Spitz is not yet on hand with the seventh, the reader and I can exchange with each other a rational word. I confess, he has long appreciated me and my doings; he sees clearly that all goes on in the finest biographical train,—the dog, my littleness, and the heroes of these dog-days. Nor have I ever denied that he will continue to be more and more dazzled by the splendor and sparkle of this foot-birth,[72] since I am so very busy, waxing, rubbing, and polishing at it,—more so than if it were a man's boot or a military horse's-hoof in Berlin. Nay, I need not wait to have it foretold to me from any cup of coffee-grounds (for I see it already from my knowledge of human nature and from the coffee which I drink) that this is saying the very least, and that the proper reading-rage will then, and not till then, come over the poor dear fellow, when, in the course of this work, at which, as in the low-warp tapestry,[73] two workmen weave sitting in one chair, the historic figures of this tapestry, together with their grouping, shall come forth from the ball of the foot to the seam of the skull. At present there is hardly a heel, a shin-bone, a stocking finished....

But when twenty or thirty ells of the work have been run off, then can I and my by-sitter expect what I will here portray: the reader will hurry as if the Devil were after him; to get through one Dog-post-day he will let six courses grow cold and the dessert warm. But what am I saying? An incarnate Romish king shall ride through the streets and a cannon-thunder bring up the rear,—he shall not hear it; his better half shall give in his library the best of suppers to a connubial excrescence,—he shall not see it; the excrescence itself shall hold assafœtida under his nose, shall give him in sport light blows with a woodman's axe,—he shall not feel it, so beside himself shall he be on my account, regularly out of his senses.

Now that is a misfortune, the certainty of which I seek vainly to hide from myself. When it once comes on, and I have unhappily brought him into that historical clairvoyance where he no longer hears or sees anything except my characters, which are put in *rapport* with him,—neither father nor cousin,—then I may be sure that he will hear a mining-superintendent still less,—for story is what he wants, and of *me* he knows absolutely nothing more,—nay, I will suppose, I should let off the motliest fire-works of wit, yes, that chains of philosophical conclusions should hang down in skeins out of my mouth, like ribbons from a juggler's,—what would it avail me?

Nevertheless, ribbons must hang down and fire-works play; but it shall be in this way: As from each year so many hours are left off that the remainder of four years makes out an intercalary day,—and as with me after four Dog-post-days there will always be so many Postscripts, so much wit and acuteness lying quite idle, as so much unsalable stuff,[74] that a regular *intercalary day* could well be made,—it shall be made as often as four dog-dynasties have gone by; only this is still requisite, that I first conclude and ratify with the reader the following boundary agreement and domestic contract, in form and manner to wit:—

I. On the part of the reader it is allowed and granted to the mining-superintendent on St. John's, him and his heirs and assigns, from this time forward, after every fourth Dog-post-day, to prepare and print a witty and learned intercalary day, in which there is no narrative.

II. On the part of the mining-superintendent permission is given the reader to skip over every intercalary day and read only the historical days, in consideration whereof both powers waive all *beneficia juris—restitutionem in integrum—exceptionem læsionis enormis et enormissimæ—-dispensationem—absolutionem, etc.* At the Congress of St. John's, May 4, 1793.

Thus reads the genuine instrument of the so-called Dog-contract between the mining-superintendent and the reader, and this Act of Renunciation may and must, in future misunderstandings between the two powers, be laid before an umpire or a confederate court,[75] as the single ground of decision.

7
DOG-POST-DAY

His Lordship excepted, all are now sitting and waiting for me in the parsonage-garden; but the garden itself not a mortal soul is yet acquainted with. It is a Chrestomathy[76] of all gardens, and yet no larger than the church. Many gardens resemble it in being at once kitchen-gardens, flower-gardens, and orchards; but it is also a *jardin des animaux*, as it contains in fact the whole Fauna of St. Luna, and a botanical garden, too; it is overgrown with the entire Flora of the village; and it is a garden of honey-bees and humble-bees also, as often as they happen to fly into it. Meanwhile such minor merits are really hardly worth naming, when a garden once has, like this, the merit of being the greatest English garden through which a man ever strode. It hides not only its end, — as every park, like every purse, must do, — but even its beginning, and seems to be merely the terrace from which one can see into that which one cannot see over, but, like Cook, may well circumnavigate. In the English parsonage-garden there are not single ruins, but whole broken-up cities, and the greatest princes have rivalled each other in their passion for furnishing it with romantic wildernesses and battle-fields and gallows-trees, to which (and that carries the illusion still higher) real rogues are tied, into the bargain, as fruit-pendants. The buildings and shrubs of different parts of the world are there, not huddled together into an absurd neighborhood, but neatly kept apart from each other by regular seas or water-scapes, which its size easily makes possible, since it contains over nine million square miles; and with what taste, in fact, these masses are brought together, the reader may estimate from the fact that all lords and all reviewers in the literary periodicals, and the readers themselves, are drawn into the garden and often stay therein sixty years. —

The Parson thinks also to get some credit from it as a Dutch garden, particularly by a peruke made of water, which hangs not on a wig-stand, but on a tin pipe, and which leaps so in curls that already several city-parsons have wished they could wear it. Butterfly-show-glasses kept off the night-chills from precocious roses of silk and early cucumbers of wax. Cucumbers which consisted of real cucumbers, he was the first among all pastors to put in, in order to worry himself with the fear that they might freeze; for this fear he must have, in order to rejoice whenever a glass bottle was broken in. his house: he could then carry this ice- or glass-mountain (which, in the case of wines, unfortunately heightens every year as our thirst does) into the garden, and with this manure-bell cover the heart-leaves. Round more important beds he ran a motley, mosaic border of crockery; his family was his verge-tool, — I mean, they had to break for him the few porcelain cups which he needed, in order with this motley powdered sugar to set off the more considerable patches, as a prince enchases and berings himself with the variegated order-ribbons drawn through the button-holes of his antechambers. As he could not set *whole* cups round the beds, but must first analyze them by his chemists, a reviewer who eats with him must avail himself of my hint to understand how it happens, if such a consumptive patient is not beside himself for rage, when some very valuable vessel is broken; for only when it happens to worthless ones is he no longer master of himself. Every housewife should set off such a bed as an Arndt's garden of Paradise, as a Golgotha for porcelain whereof the *fashion is changed*, for the good of her soul, in order that she may not lose her senses when a cup falls. "Dearest!" I would say, "bear up under this misfortune like a Christian woman; it, will turn out for thy advantage either in eternity yonder, or here in the garden."

Near a house, Dutch garden-ornaments, with their homely minuteness, make a better figure than thrilling Nature, with her eternal majesty. Eymann's clipped and carved parsonage-garden was in fact merely a continued family-room without roof or partition.

As the Parson twitched our Victor round through the garden, the guest almost forgot to praise the garden as a magazine of ideas, simply because he was looking forward too curiously and warmly to the arrival of Clotilda, and her demeanor towards his friend. Fortunately it occurred to him that the Parson counted upon incense-offerings and censers; he was so unwilling to defraud a laurel-hoping heart, that he for that very reason loved to attach himself to people of some merit, that so he might indulge his humane disposition to praise, without expense to the truth. Victor rejoiced at the prospect of Flamin's and Clotilda's meeting: how beautifully, he thought, will the moonlight of soft love fall upon his and her proud faces! And he held in store a rich tolerance and love for their love. For he not only had so much insight into the fleeting nature of our pleasures, that he could hardly be angry over the maddest, but he could even be present at the journeyman's greeting (or methodology) of—two lovers with real pleasure. "It is very foolish," —he said in Göttingen, — "every good-hearted man opens his arms in sympathy, when he sees friends, brothers and sisters, or parents embrace each other; but if a couple of monkeys in love dance round before us at the end of Cupid's string, and though it were on the stage, not a devil of us will take any interest in them, unless they dance in a romance. But why? Certainly not from selfishness, otherwise the wooden heart in the human block would also in the presence of friendship between others, or filial love, remain nailed fast; but, because the love of lovers is selfish, we are so too; and because in a romance it is not so, we are not so either. I, for my part, go on in my thinking, and make believe to myself in regard to every span of lovers I meet, that they were printed and bound, and I had them from the circulating library for paltry reading money. It belongs to the higher disinterestedness to sympathize even with its opposite. And by all means with you, poor women! Would you or I, then, oftentimes, with this life of yours so frittered away in sewing, cooking, washing, know that you had a soul, unless it fell in love? Many of you through long tearful years have never lifted your head except in the short, sunny day of love, and after it your bereft heart sank back again into the cool depths; so water-plants lie all the year drowned in water, only at the time of their bloom and love do their ascending leaves sit upon the water and sun themselves gloriously, and—then fall down again."

At last Clotilda entered, in conversation with the Parson's wife. She had on a crape hat, with a black lace portcullis, which at once beautified, divided, and concealed with a pierced shadow her beautiful face. But her eye avoided Flamin's eye, and only at times stole thoughtfully after it. He proved that precisely people of the greatest courage have the least with regard to beauty; he advanced not towards her one step. She asked our Victor eagerly about the arrival and the health of his Lordship. She then proposed to him, with the usual medical uncertainty of her sex, whether such an operation often transpired so easily, and whether he had already restored to many so much as he had to his father: he answered both questions in the negative, and she sighed openly. His respectful distance towards her would have increased by that at which his friend kept himself from her, had he not had something to hand her,—Emanuel's note. He could not steal it, as he had already repeated to her the first line; secondly, he must present it *under four eyes* (he could not through Agatha, for example), because he knew how she carried discretion to the extreme limits. Clotilda was one of those persons—troublesome to this biographer and his hero—who love to conceal all trifles: e. g. what they eat, where they are going to-morrow; who are furious with a friend if he blabs out how on St. Thomas's day last year they had a slight headache. With Clotilda it arose not from fear, but from a dark presentiment that he who babbled indifferent mysteries might at last tell weighty ones. He felt towards her, notwithstanding her pride, a mighty drawing to sincerity. He led her aside to the pomegranate-tree, and there—sparing her by his open-hearted lightness of manner the burdensome obligation she might feel with regard to a secret—handed her back the leaf. She was astonished, but said at once, her surprise related merely to her own negligence; i. e. she trusted him, but had some suspicion or other of her house-mates, and of the manner in which it got into the arbor. She took advantage of the orangery, and bent her inspired face close to the pomegranate blossoms. Victor could not possibly stand there alone so stupid; he, still a little struck with her astonishment, and at last with her almost too great pride, felt also a hankering after the pomegranate incense, and held his face down in it toward hers. He should have known, however, that any one who smells of anything does not look at the thing, but straight before him. Hardly, then, had he applied his olfactory nerves to the blossoms, when he opened his eyes, and Clotilda's large eyes stood opened full upon him; they were just at the highest and most effective elevation, of 45°, whether you speak of eyes or bow-shots. He turned his pupils forcibly down toward the leaves; she, still more prudently, stepped back from the bewildering orangery.

However, she was not embarrassed. He thought it unjust toward Flamin to observe her sentiments towards himself; but still he remarked this much,—that the observatory on which one would watch the occultations of her heart must be higher than is necessary in regard to other women. The custom of being admired had made her proof against that showing up, as in a glass, the impression of her charms with which men so often win to themselves the attention of woman's vanity. She was, as I have said, not embarrassed, but went on to tell her listener something further of Emanuel's character, which she lately, out of respect for her teacher, had not been willing to lay before such unholy ears,—namely, that he firmly believed he should die a year hence in the midnight of St. John's day.[77] Victor could easily guess that she herself believed it; but what he did not guess was, that this proud one, from pure tenderness of heart, had hastened her purpose of leaving Maienthal on St. John's day, in order not to meet the beloved man on the anniversary of the future day of his death. According to her account, this Emanuel had had a painfully exalted position among men; he was alone; he had had great friends on his bosom, but all had passed into the grave, and therefore he would also hide there his own head. Years give to stormy, over-vigorous men a finer harmony of the heart, but from refined, cold natures they take more than they give. Those strong hearts resemble English gardens, which age always makes greener, fuller, more leafy; whereas the man of the world, like a French one, is covered by years with dried-up and disfigured boughs.

Victor grew more troubled; every word which he won from her he regarded as a sacrilege upon his friend, the more so as the latter did not understand so well as he the art of opening a conversation with a lady. He had not the heart to shine, because he feared thereby to be a rival of his friend for her good graces. His Flamin seemed to him to-day taller, more beautiful, and better than ever, and he himself shorter and more stupid. He wished a thousand times his father had already come, that he might deliver to him with the greatest ardor Flamin's prayer for his aid in obtaining Clotilda.

At last he came, and Victor drew a full breath again. The good youth often seeks, by acts of sacrifice, to reconcile his conscience again with his *thoughts*. With heart-beatings of enthusiasm he awaited the moment of solitude. A garden detaches and draws together people in the easiest manner, and only in such a place should one impart secrets; Victor could soon, in an arbor which wove itself on four chestnut-trees with its blooming vein-work nest-wise over their heads, embrace his father with trembling emotion, and speak and glow for his friend with tongue and heart. His Lordship's surprise was greater than *his* emotion. "Here," said he, "is something which has long since fulfilled thy prayer in a different way; but I wished to reserve for thee the joy of bearing the message";—and therewith he gave him a most gracious autograph, wherein the Prince called the practising Advocate Flamin into the Administrative Council.

A most gracious autograph is the *Tetragrammaton* [78] and means of grace, which works supernatural effects and state-miracles; and the illustrious writing-thumb is the magic thief's-thumb,[79] as it were, by which the different wheels of the state-repeating-watch—the lever-wheel, the face-wheel, often merely the hand—is shoved forward or backward, according as it desires an hour earlier or later. Hence ministers often climb up and cut off for themselves such a thief's-thumb to carry in their pockets.

Sebastian is seized by joy, as by Habakkuk's angel, by the hair of the head, and carried through the garden, and driven with his news to the first he might meet, and that proved to be the Chaplain, who, with a comic face, swore it was all a fib of Victor's; but his restrained jubilation almost burst his compressed veins. Victor had no time for refutation, but hurried off with such a message to the heart to which it rightly belonged,—the mother's. The mother could not shape her mouth to anything but a blessed smile, into which the drops of joy overflowed from her eyes. No joy in nature is so sublimely affecting as the joy of a mother at the good fortune of a child. But the son, in whose soul, such as it was to-day, this sunbeam of fate was really needed, could not, in the surprise, be immediately found.

His Lordship, meanwhile, talked with Clotilda as with a daughter, and gave her a letter from her mother and the intelligence of his approaching departure. His manly kindness, guided by respect and graced by refinement, ennobled her attentiveness to his looks; and as she came forth from the affectionate and low-toned conversation with sparkling eyes, her tall form, which usually stooped a little, was raised by a certain inspiration to a noble stature, and she stood in the temple of Nature, as a priestess of the temple, infinitely beautiful. His Lordship separated from her. She found Flamin near the tulip-formed letter C, and the Goddess of Fortune appeared to him in the sweetest human incarnation, to deliver to him her gift. We need not say that the news and the news-bearer threw him into equal ecstasy.

Joy had shaken up the whole bee-garden in a swarming-bag and turned it into chaos. The foaming wine-fermentation could not work itself off till it ended in clear, tranquil rapture. His Lordship took himself out of the way of a gratitude swelled by so many ripieno[80] voices and off to his carriage, when the mother with her dumb heart-fulness overtook him; but nothing could she get from her blissfully burdened heart to her lips, save the modest words, that "to-day was his birthday, and his son did not know it, and ought *also* to have been surprised with a rapture." He tried to escape from her with a grateful smile, and said that he must hasten back to the Prince, who perhaps had taken as kind an interest in this very day as she; but Sebastian, with his friend whom he had found, overtook him at the garden-gate, and the hurrying lord was delayed a little longer by a swift embrace of his son. Not until he was off did the mother, who longed to unburden her love, clasp tenderly Victor's hand, and, forgetting the agreement, asked: "O dearest, why, then, did you not congratulate him on his birthday? For, indeed, *I* could not." Now for the first time he understood and felt the sudden embrace of his father, and stretched out his arms after him and would fain reciprocate it.

Here the old Parson, also coming out of the garden, struck in and said, as if talking nonsense, "I wish he were Administrative Councillor"; but his wife, without making any reply to that, said to him with overflowing voice and love, "Such a cradle-festival thou hast never yet lived to see as to-day's, Peter!" Agatha looked at her inquiringly and admonishingly. "Just out with it," said she, and enfolded the children and drew them both into the paternal embrace, "and wish your good father length of days and three more blessed children."

The father could not say anything, but stretched his hand toward the mother, to round the group of the loving Eden. Victor's sympathetic blood swelled up in his heart, to dissolve it in love, and he thought the silent prayer: "Never may any misfortune, All-gracious One, tear these entwined arms asunder!" But Flamin soon drew himself out of the concatenation, and said to Victor with a most grateful pressure of the hand, "Thou knowest not how I am always wronging thee." The Chaplain thought he should hide his emotion from all by saying: "I wish I had not deceived you. I have let myself be bled, but it was a stupid thing; if I had only known! only known! It is true; there, see for yourselves!" And finding that this mask was not adequate to cover the whole emotion of his soul, he called, in an overloud tone, to the poor forgotten Apollonia, who was rocking at the house door the awakened Bastian, to "come here!" But the poor girl, whose merely distant participation in the general mingling of hearts touched our Victor's tenderest feelings, shyly hesitated, till the mother came and indemnified her against any loss by all that for which mothers are never repaid. But not until the Parson's wife held her child in her arms and on her lips, did she feel that the imprisoned flames of her affections found vent, and her heart its alleviation.

Ah, that man should receive the fairest love precisely at the time when he does not yet understand it!—alas that not until late in life's year, as he contemplates with a sigh the love of other parents and children, he should say hopefully to himself, "Ah, thus did mine certainly love me too!"—alas that then the bosom to which thou wouldst hasten with thy thanks for half of a life, for a thousand unappreciated anxieties, for an inexpressible, never returning love, is already lying crushed under an old grave, and has lost the warm heart which so long loved thee!...

In domestic happiness the calm, cosey pleasures driven in between four narrow walls are only the most accidental constituent; its nervous and vital fluid is the blazing fire-fountains of love which spring out of kindred hearts into each other. The involuntary surprise had disconcerted the intentional ones. But the flood of joy had swept all parties together; and they still remained in the same confidential closeness to each other, when it had abated again. They sat down to the entertainment in the summer-house. Seldom are banquets spiced as this one was, by two extraordinary advantages,—want of food and want of room. Nothing whets the appetite so much as the fear of its not finding enough to satisfy it. It had been contrived by Sebastian, that for each guest only his favorite dish should be provided; for the Parson, stuffed crabs and potato cheese; for Flamin, ham; for the Hero, good Harry's beans. But in this case every one wanted another's favorite dish, and set his own up at auction.[81] Even the ladies, who generally eat and do not eat, like fishes, nibbled a little. The second intoxicating ingredient which they had, thrown into their cup of joy, was the table, together with the garden-house, of which the former would not hold the food nor the latter the feeders. Sebastian had betaken himself, with Agatha, to an affiliated table which had been adjoined outside to the window of the banquet-hall, merely for the purpose of screaming in from out there and whining, more than eating. This caprice was, at bottom, a covered modesty which feared being honored inside at the expense of the other guests, on his Lordship's account. His own solitude—perhaps in a painful sense—pictured to him the shy Appel, who, as vestal of the hearth, ate only the drawback toll of returning dishes, merely to try how they had tasted to others. He could not longer endure the thought of this separation, but took wine and the best of the dessert, and carried it in to her in her kitchen winter quarters. As, in doing so, he displayed upon his face, instead of his gayety towards girls, of which she might have made a too humble interpretation, the greatest seriousness of courtesy; he was so happy as to have given to a soul pinched up by nature itself—with no other flower-pot here to send its roots round in than a cooking-pot, and only the kitchen for its concert-hall and the spit for its music of the spheres—a golden evening and a long memory of pleasure. Let no one maliciously thrust his fist in the way of such a good snail-soul, and laugh to see how she wriggles over it; and let him who stands upright willingly stoop and gently lift her along over her little stone.

As to Clotilda, before dinner things went very well, but after dinner very ill. I speak of Sebastian, who, after the handing in of the petition to his Lordship, was happier and more light-hearted, and actually talked as frankly with Clotilda as if she were—a bride. For he had already said in Hanover, that "there was not a more tedious and holy thing than a bride, particularly if it were a friend's; sooner would he fritter away his time about the musty Pandects in Florence, or a holy body in a glass shrine at Vienna, than about her." In fact, it was hard to fall in love with Clotilda; I know the reader would not have done it, but would have gone coldly away again. "Her Grecian nose under the almost manly breadth of forehead," he would have said, "this sister-nose to all Madonnas and this frontier wild-game[82] so rare on German faces, her still but bright eyes, which seek nothing beyond themselves, this British gravity, this harmonious thoughtful soul, raise her above the rights of love. And even if this majestic form should incline to love, who could ever be so selfish as to pocket the present of a whole heaven, or so proud as to shoot his heart into hers like a smoke-ball, and becloud thereby this still, pensive serenity?" The reader will be glad to read his own words.

But after dinner things went differently. Under Victor's cerebral membrane, some hobgoblin had so thrown into pi all the letters of his ideas in the inner letter-case, that he was up to this time gay, but unsatisfied. He had tried to tie and untie Agatha's hair, to separate her double-bows into unequal, and for that very reason into equal halves again; but the operation had not pleased him as usual,—to-day's interludes of domestic love had put his mirthful spirit wholly out of joint,—and it seemed to him as if, withdrawn from the present joy, he should be happier, at least for a few minutes, in some quiet corner, and he particularly longed to see the sun set.

Add to all this the sight of Clotilda's increased love towards Agatha, — the sight of his friend, who, by the deepening silence of his tenderness, his mildening voice, and by a devotedness so irresistible in impassioned natures, commanded every heart, "Love me," — and, finally, the spectacle of night....

He had already been long sad, when he seemed still gay. Now the mother took the little hero of the forenoon out under the bland evening heaven. They all stood outside of the garden-tabernacle-of-the-covenant, in the first temple of man's devotion. The evening-blood of the sinking sun flowed into the clouds, as into the sea sinks the blood of its giants dying in its depths. The porous cloud did not avail to hide the heavens; it swam round about the moon, and let her pale silver glisten from amidst the slags.

The red clouds painted the infant. Every one took lightly his soft hands, which had already burst from the bud of pillows and the chrysalis of swaddling-bands. Clotilda — instead of lavishing on the little one carnally coquettish caresses, as many girls do *before* or *for* men — poured down a steadily streaming look full of hearty love on the new man, untied his too tight and cutting shirt-sleeve, screened from him the moon at which he was squinting, and said, playfully, "Smile this way and love me, *Sebastian!*" She could not possibly have meant to charge this line with metaphorical *ricochet*-shots; besides, the elder, unswaddled Sebastian knew full well that she could have anticipated no double sense; nay, he knew the rule, that the very anxiety wherewith some people banish certain subjects from their talk betrays the presence of the same in their thoughts. And yet, for all that, he had not the courage to smile like the rest, or to take the little hand which she had touched in his. She turned to him, and said, "But how does the child learn *our language, unless it has already a language it can master?*"

... I have, out of mere regard to the philosophers, had this printed in italics.

"Then it follows," he answered, "that the language of pantomime must signify just as much as articulate speech. As often as I see a deaf and dumb man go to sacrament, I think of this, — that all the instruction you can give imports nothing into man, but only indicates and arranges what is already there. The child's soul is its own drawing-master, the teacher is simply its colorist."

"What if this lovely evening," she continued, "should one day come up again to the memory of this little one? Why does the sixth year look more beautiful in remembrance than the twelfth, and the third still more beautiful?" A beautiful woman one cannot interrupt so easily as an ex-Dean; and so she was permitted to recur to this reminiscence: "Herr Emanuel once said, one should relate to children every year the story of their past years, in order that they might one day look back through all their years, even into the haze of the second." It is as if I heard the above-mentioned maid of honor personally speaking, under whose thin lace cap there lay more philosophy than under many a doctor's beaver, as quicksilver sticks in crape, and runs through leather.

Victor answered, with the usual sympathy of his good heart: "Emanuel stands near to man, and knows him. Two scene-painters lead man, beset by magic, through the whole stage,—*Memory* and *Hope*; in the present he is uncomfortable; enjoyment is poured out for him, as for Gulliver, only into a thousand Liliputian moments; how shall that intoxicate or satisfy? When we picture to ourselves a happy day, we compress it into a single happy thought; when we come upon it, this thought is diluted through: the twenty-four hours."

"I think of that," she replied, "as often as I walk through meadows; in the distance are flowers upon flowers, but, near at hand, they are all scattered apart, and separated by the grass. But yet, after all, *memory is enjoyed only in the present.*"

Victor continued to think only of the flowers, and said, abstractedly, "And in the *night* the flowers themselves look like grass,"—when it began suddenly to sprinkle.

They all stepped, in solemn mood, into the summerhouse, on whose roof the rain pattered down, while through the open windows the alternately shutting and opening moon's eye threw in like a glacier its snow-glances,—the tepid blossom-breath of the whole glistening landscape stole with healing balm on every human sigh, every burdened bosom. In this confined circle, separated from nature by the alternation of night and moonshine, one must needs take refuge in something near and familiar, in the old harpsichord. Clotilda's voice might make a flute-accompaniment to the whispering rain without. The Parson's wife begged—her to favor them, and with her favorite *aria* from Benda's Romeo,—"Perchance, my lost repose! perchance one day in the grave I may find thee!" &c.,—a song whose tones like fine dissolving perfumes penetrate the heart through a thousand entrances, and tremble there, and tremble more and more intensely, till at last they shiver it to atoms, and leave nothing of it behind in the harmonious annihilation but tears.

Clotilda without any hesitating vanity consented to sing. But for Sebastian, in whom all tones came in contact with naked, quivering feelers, and who could work himself into sadness at the very songs of the herdsmen in the fields—this, on such an evening, was too much for his heart; under cover of the general musical attentiveness, he had to steal out of the door....

But here, under the great night-heaven, amidst higher drops, his own can fall unseen. What a night! Here a splendor overwhelms him, which links night and sky and earth all together; magic Nature rushes with streams into his heart, and forcibly enlarges it. Overhead, Luna fills the floating cloud-fleeces with liquid silver, and the soaked silver-wool quivers downward, and glittering pearls trickle over smooth foliage, and are caught in blossoms, and the heavenly field pearls and glimmers. Through this Eden, over which a double snow-shower of sparks and of drops played and whirled through a misty rain of blossom-fragrances, and wherein Clotilda's tones, like angels that had got lost, went flying about, now sinking and now soaring through this magic-maze, Victor staggered, dazzled, overwhelmed, trembling and weeping, and sank down exhausted into the arbor where he had to-day fallen on his father's heart. He thought over the wintry life of that good father amidst mere strangers to the heart, and his solitary, sad celebration of today's festival, and the cold, empty room in the paternal bosom, which once the lost form of the beloved one had inhabited, and he yearned painfully for the heart of his invisible mother. He lifted his leaning head into the rain, and from the large open eyes fell not strange drops alone. He glowed through his whole being, and night-clouds must cool it. His finger-tips hung down, lightly folded in one another. Clotilda's tones dropped now like molten silver-points on his bosom, now they flowed like stray echoes from distant groves into this still garden. He spoke no name, he thought no thought, he neither acquitted himself nor accused himself; he saw it all as in a dream, when now a thick night glided across the garden, and now a sea of light swept after it.

But it seemed to him as if his bosom would burst, as if he should be blest could he at this moment embrace beloved persons, and crush in the closeness of that embrace in a blissful frenzy his bosom and his heart. It was to him as if he should be over-blessed, could he now before some being, before a mere shadow of the mind, pour out all his blood, his life, his being. It was to him as if he must scream into the midst of Clotilda's tones, and fold his arms around a rock, only to stifle the painful yearning.

He heard the leaves drip, and took it for a continuing rain. But the *Staub-bach* of the heavens had scattered itself in spray, and only Luna's fall of light any longer besprinkled the landscape. The sky was deep-blue. Agatha had been seeking him during the rain, and had only just found him. He woke up, obediently and silently went out with her, and met only cleared-up heavenly faces,—then all his nerves quivered, and he was compelled with a mute obeisance to take his painful and friendly leave. Each one had his own thoughts on the subject. But the Parson's wife told the company, he loved to hear music at a distance, only it always made him too melancholy.

Ah, when he reached his chamber, a happy and consoling thought embraced his soul. Clotilda's dirge, and all, fixed before his sight the form of the exalted Emanuel,—and it seemed to say: "In a year I shall be already under the ground, only come to me, poor child, I will love thee till I die!" Without desiring a light, he wrote with streaming eyes, which no light could have helped, this letter to Emanuel:—

"Emanuel!

"Say not to me, I know thee not! How can man, on this little grain of sun-dust called the earth, on which he warms himself, and during the swift moments which he counts off on his pulse between the flash of life and the stroke of death, still make a distinction between acquaintances and non-acquaintances? Why do not these little creatures, who have wounds of the same kind, and for whose coffins Time takes the same measure, fall without hesitation into each other's arms, and sigh, 'Ah, we are doubtless like each other and acquainted!' Why must first these fleshly statues into which our spirits are chained move towards and touch each other, before the beings disguised therein can imagine and love each other? And yet it is so human and so true a thought: what then does Death take from us except fleshly statues, what from our eyes but the loved countenance, what from our ears but the dear voice, and the warm bosom from our own? Ah, Emanuel! be to me no dead man! Accept me! Give me thy heart! I will love it!

"I am not very happy, my Emanuel! When my great teacher, Dahore,—that shining Swan of heaven, who, fastened to life by his broken wing-joint, looked up wistfully at other Swans, as they winged their way toward the warmer latitudes of the second life,—ceased to write to me, he did it in these words: 'Seek my duplicate! Thy breast will continue to bleed, until thou coverest its scar with another, and the earth will agitate thee more and more violently, if thou standest alone,—and only around the solitary do ghosts creep.'

"Emanuel, art thou not tranquil and gentle and indulgent? Does not thy soul yearn to love all men, and is not a single heart too narrow for it to shut itself up therein with its love, as a bee is shut up in a tulip when it folds itself to sleep? Hast thou not had enough of the repeating-work of our merry bells and mourning-bells, and art thou not weary of the family likeness of all evenings and times? Dost thou not look, out from this fleeting earth over the long way above thee, that thou mayst not grow nauseous and giddy, as one for the same reason looks out of a carriage into the road? Believest thou not in men around whom floats the mountain air of a higher position, and who up on their height stand in the midst of a still heaven, and look down into the thunders and rainbows near the earth? Believest thou not in a God, and seekest thou not his thoughts in the lineaments of nature, and his eternal love in thy breast? If thou art and thinkest all this, then thou art mine; for thou art better than I, and my soul would fain lift itself to a higher friend. Tree of the higher life, I embrace thee, I twine around thee with a thousand faculties and tendrils, that I may mount up out of the trampled mire around me! Ah, a great man might heal, tranquillize, quicken, exalt me,—me, poor creature, only rich in wishes, distracted by the war between my dreams and my senses,—flung sorely to and fro between systems, tears, and follies,— disgusted at the earth, which I cannot replace for myself, laughing merely from anguish at the tearful comedy, the most contradictory, saddest, and merriest shadow among all the shadows in the wide night.... O fair, good soul, love me!

"Horion."

Leaning his head on his hand, he let his tears flow, without thinking or looking, till nature was spent. Then he went to the harpsichord, and sang over to its accompaniment the most passionate passages of his letter; what strongly moved him always impelled him to singing, especially the emotion of longing. What can it matter to us that it was prose?

At the last line of his epistolary song the door slowly opened.

"Is it thou?" said a voice.

"Ah, come in, Flamin!" he answered.

"I only wanted to see whether you had come back," said Flamin, and went away.

I think it is necessary that I should here insert at least the following, namely, that Victor possessed too much fancy, humor, and thoughtfulness not to give out, when these three strings were violently struck at once, pure dissonances, which, with more harmonious intervals between these faculties,[84] would not have appeared; that he had, therefore, more *leaning* to enthusiasms and enthusiasts than *disposition* that way; that his negative-electrical philosophy had always to contend with his positive-electrical enthusiasm for the balance of power, and that from the effervescing of these two spirits came nothing but humor; that he wanted to have all his carnations of joy on the same bed, although one adulterated the colors of the rest (e. g. refinement and enthusiasm, exaltation above the world and familiarity with the tone of the world); that from all this, beside irony and the highest tolerance, must also result a heavy, immovable feeling of the nothingness of our inner moods, so fleeting and sketched with such a contrariety of colors; and that he, whom the bad man regards as two-sided and the well-disposed one as changeable, needs nothing, for the gracing and rounding off of his Adam or Palladium buried up in so much wood, but the scythe of Time. Time then be it.

8
DOG-POST-DAY

I wish the story were done, so that I might get it printed; for I have already too many subscribers to it among the common folk. An author in our days accepts advance payment for his book from the lowest fellow, — the tailor makes his pre-payment in clothes, the hair-dresser in powder, the landlord in rooms.

Every morning Victor gave himself a curtain lecture under the bed-quilt for the evening previous; the bed is a good confessional and audience-hall of conscience. He wished that yesterday's garden-club would take him for a veritable fool instead of a lover. "Ah, if Flamin himself should torment himself with jealousy, and if our hearts, once so long parted, should already come to be so again!" Here the bed-box, from a confessional, grew to be a fiery oven. But an angel laid himself in beside him, and blew away the blaze. "But what, then, have I done? Have I not with a thousand-fold pleasure spoken, acted, kept silence for his sake? Not a look, not a word, can be charged against me, — what else then?" The angel of light or fire had now to blow terribly against the shooting flame. "What else? Thoughts, perhaps, which however, like field-mice of the soul, leap under the feet, and stick like adders. But could the disciples of Kant impute to me then, that I took the little image of the loveliest and best form, which I hitherto vainly summoned up in the lands of three lords, and threw such a Raphael's head, such an antique of Paradise, out of the window of the *villa* of my brain, like apple-parings and plum-stones? I should wonder at the Kantians, if they did. And if it must stay there, am I to be an ox, ye Catechists, and coldly glower[85] at it? Not I. Nay, I will trust myself, and demand of the fairest heart even friendship, and yet leave to it its love!" Dear reader, during this whole summary process before the judicial commission of conscience, I have said to myself, over thirty times, "Neither of you, you nor the reader, is a hair more honest with your conscience!"

He drew himself slowly by the bed-cord out of the bed, which he used to quit with a spring; some wheel of his ideas stuck within him. He read his yesterday's letter, and found it too stormy. "That is just our insignificance," said he, "that everything which man holds to be eternal freezes over night;

not across our face do the most vehement gales pass more swift and traceless than across our heart. Why then am I not to-day what I was yesterday, and perhaps shall be to-morrow? What does man gain by this boiling up and down? And what has he then within himself to build upon?"

Meanwhile, the fire-wheel of our earthly time, the sun, had whirled up its revolving streams, and burned on the shore of the earth. He flung up the window, and was fain to bathe his naked breast in the fresh morning wind, and his hot eye in the Red Sea of Aurora; but something within him interposed itself like an after-taste between him and the enjoyment of the morning-land. The remorse of conscience for *future* actions spoils a good man utterly for enjoyment.

There rose slowly within him an overmastering emotion,—the former night passed by again before him with its flashing rain, and brought back to him his passionate heart and Emanuel's shadow,—he ran more and more vehemently, and in fact transversely, through the chamber,—tied his night-gown tighter, shook something from his eye, gave a perpendicular jump, jerked out a "No!" and said, with an inexpressibly serene smile, "No! I will not cheat my Flamin! I will neither seek nor shun her, nor will I desire her friendship till the time of his highest happiness. As I look upon thee[86] yonder, so will I upon her glorious, heavenly bust, without desiring that it take on warmth, and turn on me its cold plaster eye. But thou, my friend, be happy and all blessed, and never mayst thou once remark my conflict!"

Now, for the first time, did the church-attire of morning gladden him, and the morning air flowed like a cool necklace over his hot bosom, and threw back the playing hair and shirt-frill. He felt that now he was worthy to have written to Emanuel, and to have looked up at the heavens....

Flamin entered with some coldness, which was increased by the sight of the letter. Victor was not to be made cold; only when, down below, no one reminded him by a word of his yesterday's Dithyrambics, then did he, from fear of being betrayed, make an angry, covert oath, if *she* came, not to come,—which could be kept, too, for she did not come. She had still to bring away luggage from Maienthal, to besprinkle her friendships, and once more to set foot in the magic circle of her beloved teacher; and had, therefore, gone off.

The following weeks danced now like just so many hours in Anglaises and Cotillons before Sebastian. His forenoons hung full of fruits, his afternoons full of flowers; for in the morning his soul with its exertions lived in his head, towards evening in his heart. In the evening one loves cards, poems, confidential talk, woman, music, very much; in the morning, very little; in the spirit-hour is that love at its highest strength.

Except two other doubts that troubled him,—the first was, whether his Emanuel would write to him soon enough to enable him to visit him before he should be harnessed to the pole of the court and state-carriage; the second was the fear of being so too soon,—now he had hardly anything to do except to be happy or to make others so; for precisely in these weeks fell his holy or Sabbatical weeks...

I know not whether the reader is yet acquainted with them; they are not found in the improved almanac; but they occur regularly (with some men) either immediately after the vernal equinox or in the after-summer.

With Victor the first alternative was the one,—exactly in the middle of spring. I need not inquire whether it is the body, the weather, or who or what, that rings in this truce of God in our breast; but I must describe how they look, the Sabbatical weeks. Their form is precisely this: in a holy or Sabbatical week, many—e. g. I—are put off with mere Sabbatical days or hours. At first, one slumbers lightly, as on balanced clouds,—one awakes like a serene day. At evening one had made a firm resolve beforehand, and had therefore written it down in ciphers on the door, to grow better, and to apply the weeding-knife every day to one bed of weeds at least,—on awaking one is still so minded, and in fact carries it out. The gall, that excitable spirit, which usually, when it is poured, instead of into the duodenum, into the heart or heart's blood, sends up boiling and hissing clouds, is now in a few seconds absorbed or precipitated, and the exalted mind *feels calmly the bodily effervescence* without any of its own. In this lull of the wings of our lungs, one utters only soft, low words, one clasps lovingly the hand of every one with whom he speaks, and one thinks, with melting heart, "Ah! I could not begrudge it to one of you, if you were still happier than I." On the clean, healthy, tranquil heart, as on the Homeric gods, light wounds immediately close. "No!" thou keepest saying in the Sabbatical week, "I must for some days to come maintain this tranquillity." Thou requirest, as material for joy, hardly anything but existence; nay, the sun-sting of a rapture would condense this cool, magical, transparent morning haze into a tempest. Thou lookest up steadily into the blue, as if thou wouldst fain give thanks and weep, and around upon the earth as if thou wouldst say, "Wherever I might be to-day, there I should be happy!" and a heart full of sleeping storms thou carriest, as a mother does her child sunk into slumber, shyly and watchfully over the soft flowers of joy.... But the storms start up, nevertheless, and assail the heart!...

Ah, what must we not all already have lost, if the pictures of blissful days win from us nothing but sighs! O tranquillity, tranquillity, thou evening of the soul, thou still Hesper of the weary heart, which always abides beside the sun of virtue, if at thy very name our inner being is dissolved into tears, ah, is not that a sign that we seek thee, but have thee not?

Victor owed the *siesta* of his heart to the sciences,[87] particularly *Poetry* and *Philosophy*, which two move, as do *comets* and *planets*, around the *same sun* (that of Truth), and differ only in the *shape* of their orbits, as comets and poets have the *greater ellipse*. His training and talents had accustomed him to the vital air and oxygen of the study, which is also the only dormitory of our passions, and that only cloister and haven of bliss for men who would escape the broad whirlpool of the senses and fashions. The sciences are, more than virtue, their own reward, and they make one a partaker of happiness,—she only makes him worthy of it; and the prize-medals, pensions, and positive rewards, and the *patent* which many scholars would fain get for their studying, belong at most to the literary apprentice-brethren, who make it a penance and a torture, but not to the masters of the chair, who make it a pleasure and a delight. A scholar has no *ennui*; only a throne-incumbent has to prescribe for himself, against this nervous consumption, a hundred court-festivals, cavaliers of honor, whole countries, and human blood!

Good heavens! a reader who, in Victor's Sabbatical weeks, should have taken a ladder and climbed up to his window,—would he have espied anything there but a jubilant thing, that went gliding about over the fields of learning as among islands of the blest?—a thing which, in its ecstasy, knew not whether it should think or compose or read, and particularly *what* or *whom*, out of the whole *high* nobility of books ranged before it. In this bridal chamber of the mind (such are our study-chambers), in this concert-hall of the finest voices gathered from all times and places, the æsthetic and philosophical enjoyments almost overpowered his faculty of choice. Reading hurried him into writing, writing to reading, thinking to sentiment, and the latter to the former.

I could go on with more satisfaction in this description, if I had previously written how he studied; namely, that he never wrote without having read himself full[88] on the subject, and the reverse, that he never read without having first *thought* himself *hungry*. One should, he said, without an intense occasion and impulse from without, i. e. from within, not only not make verses, but even a philosophical paragraph; nor should any one set himself down and say: "Now, at three o'clock on this Bartholomew's day, I will go at it, and cleverly prove the following proposition." I can now proceed.

Now when, in this mental laboratory, which served less for analytic chemistry than for synthetic science, he ascended from the turmaline which attracts grains of ashes to the sun which attracts worlds, and even to the unknown sun toward which solar systems fly; or when the anatomical charts were to him the perspective sketch of a divine architecture, and the dissecting-knife became the gnomon of his favorite truth: that, in order to believe in a God, there was need of nothing more than two men, of whom the one might be dead, too, that the living one could study him, and turn over his leaves[89]; or when Poetry, as a second nature, as a second music, wafted him upward softly on her invisible ether, and he chose undecidedly between the pen and the keys, when he wanted to communicate aloft; ... when, in short, in his heavenly sphere, supported on a human cervical-vertebra, the nebula of ideas gradually resolved itself into bright and dark parts, and beneath an unseen sun filled itself more and more with ether,—when one cloud became conductor to another,—when at last the gleaming mass of cloud came together,—then did the inner heaven (as the outer one often does), by eleven o'clock in the forenoon, grow from all the flashes into one sun, from all the drops into one flood, and the whole heaven of the upper faculties came down to the earth of the lower ones, and ... some blue patches of the second world were for a flying moment open.

We cannot delineate our inner states more philosophically and clearly than by metaphors, i. e. by the colors of related states. The narrow defamers of metaphors, who, instead of the brush, would rather give us the black-lead, ascribe to the *coloring* the unrecognizableness of the *drawing*; but they ought to charge it merely on their non-acquaintance with the original subject. Verily, nonsense plays hide-and-seek more easily in the roomy, abstract, artificial words of the philosophers—since words, like Chinese shadows, increase with their circumference at once the obscurity and the emptiness of their contents—than in the narrow green hulls of the poets. From the Stoa and the Portico of thought one must have an outlook into the Epicurean gardens of poetry.

In three minutes I shall come back to my story. Victor said, he must have mountain-, garden-, and swamp-meadows, because he possessed *three* different whimsical souls, which he must drive to pasture on three sorts of grounds. He meant by that, not, as the scholastics do, the vegetative, animal, and intellectual souls, nor, as the fanatics do, the three parts of man, but something very like,—his *humorous, sentimental,* and *philosophical* souls. Whoever should take away from him one of these, he said, might as well strip him of the remaining ones. Nay, sometimes, when the humorous soul happened at the moment to be sitting uppermost on the revolving cross-bench, he carried his levity so far as to express the wish that a joke might be made even in Abraham's bosom, and that he might with his three souls sit down at once on the twelve thrones.

His afternoons he gave up now to a streaming humor which did not even find its proper hearers,—now to the people of the parsonage,—now to all the school-going youth of St. Luna, whose stomachs (to the vexation of every good schoolmaster) he provisioned more than their heads, because he thought that, in the short years when the bib expands to a napkin, enjoyment must find its way over the children's *serviette,* and had no other entrance than the mouth. He never went out without a whole military-chest full of small change in his waistcoat pocket. "I scatter it without thinking," said he; "but if from this metallic seed sowed broadcast whole evenings of joy spring up for the poor devils, and if just the innocent ones so seldom have them, why shall not one do something for the saved virtue and for pleasure at once?"

He said he had heard moral lectures, and desired for his extra-judicial donations and merciful endowments nothing but forgiveness. His Flamin, who pronounced him a careless sowing-machine on rocks, spent his little holidays before approaching the session-table in ardent hopes of being serviceable there, and in preparations for being able to be so; often, when the higher patriotism, with saintly halo and Moses'-glory, broke out on the beloved Flamin's face, tears of friendly gladness stood in Victor's eyes, and in the moment of a lyric philanthropy both swore on their hearts for the future a mutual support in well-doing and joint sacrifices for mankind. The difference between them was merely reciprocal exaggeration,— Flamin treated vice too intolerantly, Victor too tolerantly; the former, as administrative counsellor, rejected, like the Anabaptists, all festivals, and, like the first Christians, all flowers (in every sense); the latter, like the Greeks, loved both too much;—the former would have sacrificed to honor human victims; the latter knew no robber of honor but his own heart: he overleaped at the tea-table the paper half-nobility of our miserable points of honor, and, mocking at mockery, submitted himself only to the high nobility of virtue....

Victor sucked, with the feet of a green-frog, on every flower-leaf of joy,—at children, animals, village-Lupercalia, lessons; but dearest of all to him was Saturday. Then he made excursions through the glad unrest of the village, along by servant-men, hammering at their scythes, not to magnetize, but to sharpen them, and before the shop-door of the schoolmaster, at which his eye, like a Swiss, often stood for half an hour. For he could very well study the state of St. Luna's commerce in the little great-adventure-trade of the schoolmaster, who knew no smaller merchants' exchange than the one in his breeches' pocket. From this East India House he saw at a late hour people procuring the cheap pleasures of Sunday,—the wholesale dealer (the schoolmaster is meant), supported by his negro slaves, made the Sunday morning of St. Luna sweet with his syrup and hot with his coffee; and as well by the tobacco-culture of Germany was this tradesman enabled with spiral cables of pigtail to furnish the heads of the pipes, as through the silk culture the daughter's heads with Sabbath-streamers out of his Auerbach's court.... Our hero all knew. From every kennel a dog came wagging his tail to meet him to whom he had thrown in bread; from every window children screamed after him, whom he had bantered; and many boys, whom he passed, counted themselves happy if they had a cap on, — for then they could take it off before their master. For his first growing up in St. Luna was the history of St. Luna, which must have been drawn from the oral blue-books of the historic persons, and from the Imperial Postilion, the Parson's wife. This last, as a Mrs. Plutarch, always held up two characters, like pieces of cloth, side by side; and her husband read to him according to the best of his science and conscience upon the Church- and Reformation-history of his diocese. Victor devoted himself to this microcosmic world-history from two motives: first, in order — which is the object of professional students with the larger history — to dismiss it again clean from memory; secondly, in order to be as much at home in the village as the constable or the midwife, whence he hoped to derive the advantage of being grieved if a St. Lunite should die, and glad if he had previously married.

Now the story strides forward again, from one day to another, as if on the stones of the stream of time.

So sweetly then had the spring passed along before him with Sabbatical weeks, with Whitsuntides, with white blossoms, which fell gradually, like butterflies' wings, from the flying season. Victor had postponed the visit to Le Baut, thinking, "I shall have, at all events, to budge soon enough down out of the soft lap of Nature, and up to the court wire-bench and the object-holder (the throne) of the court-microscope"; — he had, to be sure, daily exhorted himself, now, soon, before Clotilda's arrival, to start so as not to draw any suspicion upon his intentions, but always in vain, ... when suddenly (for the day before it was the 13th of July) the 14th appeared, and with it Clotilda's luggage without her. Now he actually (according to the official dog-reports) crossed on the 15th the Brook of St. Luna,[90] passed the Alps of the Chamberlain's steps, and pitched his Cæsar's tent on Le Baut's sofa. He knew that to-day no one was there, not even Mat.

"Heaven keep our politeness safe and sound," said he; "without it there were not only no holding out among a set of knaves, but it pays also minute-tributes of pleasure, whereas benevolence pays only quarterly assessments and exchequer-instalments, and charitable contributions." Mr. and Mrs. Le Baut were as courteous as never before (I could swear, they had nosed out something of Victor's court-doctor's hat and Doctor's crown); only they knew not what sort of a mouth-piece they should screw on to such a whimsically twisted instrument as Victor was. Like all study-inhabiting crustacea, he would rather talk of things than of persons; Flamin, however, the reverse. For the married pair, there was nothing in any Messiad more sublime than that now, on St. John's day, the Italian Princess would be coming: of that no mortal could talk enough, especially in the village. I know not to what slip of Victor's it was owing, that he led most women into the notion that he loved them. Suffice it, the Chamberlain's wife, who at her years demanded no longer *love*, but the *show* of love, thought, "Perhaps!" Let no one mistake her, she, to be sure, always spent the first hour with a man on the *watch-tower* of observation; but the second, then, only on the *hunting-screen*, if the first had been fortunate, and she was cool enough not to hope more than she saw: she even made a jest of every one who, in view of her vanity—a womanly vanity, however—of too easily presuming upon conquests, should think to flatter her otherwise than openly. Suffice it, she judged our Victor to-day too favorably, in her sense, or too unfavorably in ours; as, in general, mere courtiers can see through only mere courtiers. Of Clotilda not a word was said, not even of the time of her return.

In fact, the Le Baut had a monstrous pride in herself to contend with towards her step-daughter,—of which my correspondent should have informed me what it rested upon, whether on relations or on merits; for of both there was an ample supply, inasmuch as the Chamberlain's wife had been the w—, that is, the mistress, of the present Prince's deceased father. I and a clever man have considered the question *pro* and *con*, whether she resembled Cæsar in love or in ambition. The clever man says, "In love," because a woman never forgets love, when a prince has been her teacher therein. The illustrious deceased father's heart had adored two beauties in her particularly, which aforetime the Scots[91] used to be so fond of eating, namely, the bosom and the rump. The great have their peculiar *grossièretés*, which the little dream not of. I would not print it, but it was known to the whole court, and therefore to many of my readers also. Well, the Devil brought along Time, who whetted his scythe and mowed away all of each of these charms which *hung over* in his territory. Now with women at courts—or in the courtyard[92] of a school, or a warehouse, or in a cow-yard—vanity, so soon as old Saturn (i. e. Time) attacks it with his scythe-chariot and with the small shot from his hour-glass, makes one of the most skilful retreats that I know of. Vanity lets itself be driven from one work or member after another; but at last it throws itself out of the weak parts into *strongholds*, e. g. into finger-nails, foreheads, feet, &c., and from there the Devil himself cannot dislodge it. The Chamberlain's wife had first to make herself such a part, namely, a *gorge de Paris* and a *cul de Paris*; these four *boundary hills* of her kingdom had daily to be restored, and raised, out of respect for property, against the shifting of boundaries produced by years. From this, now, my clever man concludes that her soul is always writing letters of marque to her body.

I am precisely the antipode of the clever man, and contend that Cupid is only her serving-brother, not the master of the lodge,—her adjutant, not her generalissimo; and this for the reason that she is still always applying either her own or Le Baut's hand to the restoration of the Solomon's Temple wherein she used to be adored as a goddess, side by side with the god,—because in marrying him she married nothing but the Chamberlain's key and his *assemblées* and his hopes of future influence,—because her hostility to Clotilda relates not to the face, but to the brain,—because her love is now without jealousy. That is to say, she stood in a certain amatory relation with the Evangelist Matthieu, which (according to our feeling as common citizens) differs from hatred in nothing but—duration. Persiflages of love were their declarations of love; their glances were epigrams; his hours of assignation he seasoned with comic accounts of his corresponding hours in other places; and at the time of day when a holy man usually prays off his psalm,[93] both were ironical. Such an *erotic* connection is nothing but the subdivision of a *political*.... But to return to the story.

The Chamberlain proposed now to show his guest something of more interest to a doctor and a scholar. To the chamber wherein the something was, they passed through the Chamberlain's wife's, and through Clotilda's. As they made a day of rest[94] in the former, Victor's eyes were fixed dreamily on Clotilda's profile, which Matthieu had lately cut out of nothing, and which the Chamberlain's wife, out of flattery to the profile-cutter, had hung up here under glass. Singularly—i. e. accidentally—the glass at this moment flew to pieces over the fair face, and Victor and the father were startled; for the latter was, like most great folk, for want of time, at once superstitious and sceptical; and it is well known that superstition regards the flying to pieces of a portrait-glass as a forerunner of the death of the original. The distressed father reproached himself with the permission he had given Clotilda to stay so long in Maienthal, since she would certainly injure her health there by unprofitable, youthful enthusiasms. He meant her mourning for her buried Giulia; for it was merely from sorrow for her, that, on the first of May, she had hurried hither without any baggage; and even the clothes of the beloved friend she had to-day sent among her own. He broke off in a cheerful tone, for Matthieu came, the brother of this Giulia, who only wanted to show and excuse himself, because, like several of the court church of half-brothers, he was going to meet the Princess.

Victor grew stiller and sadder; his bosom became at once a swelling flood of invisible tears, whose source he could not trace to his heart. And when next they had to pass through Clotilda's still and vacant chamber, where order and simplicity too intensely reminded him of the fair soul of the proprietor, his sudden and touching dumbness struck others also. He tore his eyes hurriedly away from some flower-drawings by her own hand, from her white inkstand, and from the beautiful landscape of the oil-tapestry, and stepped up hastily to that which Le Baut was unlocking. It was not any noble heart which the latter, with his golden key, although bored like a cannon, could fasten,[95]—the Titular Chamberlains in Vienna apply only an hermetically sealed one,—but what he opened was his *Cabinet d'histoire naturelle*. The cabinet contained rare copies and some *curiosa*;—a calculus taken from the bladder of a child, two seventeenths of an inch long and two seventeenths of an inch broad, or the reverse; the hardened *vena cava* of an old Minister; a pair of American feather-trousers; tolerable Fungites, and better specimens of *Strombi* (e. g. a staircase-shell, *not genuine*); the model of a midwife's chair and of a sowing-machine; species of gray marble from Hof in Voigtland; and a petrified bird's-nest,—duplicates not included.... Meanwhile I and the reader prefer to all this dead trumpery the living ape who was the cabinet's sole ornament and—owner. Camper should cut off from this living specimen the Chamberlain's head, and dissect it, if only to see how near the monkey borders upon man.

A great person has always some branch or other of science which he cares nothing about, and to which, therefore, he particularly devotes himself. To Le Baut's soul, hungering for knowledge, it was all one whether it were set in a cabinet of seals or of gems or of pistoles. Were I a great person, I would with the greatest zeal make buttons—or deliveries—or books—or Nuremberg wares—or wars—or right good institutions, merely from cursed ennui, that *mother of vinegar* to all vices and virtues which peep forth under ermine and stars of orders. Nothing is a greater proof of the general growth of refinement than the general growth of ennui. Even the ladies, out of mere flat ennui, a hundred times contrive pastimes for themselves; and the cleverest man utters his greatest number of platitudes, and the best his greatest number of slanders, merely to a circle that knows how to adequately bore him.

The court-page was the cicerone of the cabinet, perhaps for the sake of going about. Victor wronged him by the medical supposition that he affected a certain loose, unsteady, slouchy gait common to debauchees in high life; for he really had it, and for the reason that he, on quite other grounds than Victor's fine ones, never loved to—sit. But to proceed: Unless the Chamberlain's wife meant to tear aside the curtain from before Victor's soul, and spy out therein his sentiments toward herself and Clotilda by the fright which I am about to relate, then it can have been nothing but a very bad spirit which led the hand of the said Chamberlain's wife to a silver ingot. Behind the ingot lay, perhaps killed by crumbs of arsenic, a mouse. A female reader, who in similar dangers has suffered as a patient, can imagine how the Chamberlain's wife felt when she grasped, with the hard substance, something soft, and drew it forth, and then saw what it was. A *real* fainting-fit was inevitable. I confess I should myself hold her swoon merely as a feint, were the occasion less; e. g. had it been, not her senses, but her honor, that was assailed: but a mouse is a very different matter. In fact, before such malicious spectators as her husband and her Cicisbeo, she must long since have banished from her stage, as the French from theirs, this Fifth Act Murder; nay, I do not believe she could in any way have rendered herself so ridiculous in the eyes of a triumphant enemy of her virtue (except by a real swoon) as by a fictitious one. Terror at the trance[96] deprived the Evangelist of the use of his reason, and left him only the use of his wickedness and his hands, with which he instantly tore open the whole blind- and fence-work of her bosom, in short, the whole optical breast, to get air enough for the true one, on whose board he had a piece,[97] namely, her heart. But Victor pushed him away, and, sprinkling her with a few drops of ice-water, out of tender respect for her charms and her life, soon raised her up again. However, she forgave the page all that she guessed, and thanked the court-physician for all in which she was mistaken....

... Let me look away a moment from this black cobweb, and refresh myself with surveying the fairer world around me on my island, where there is no enemy,—and the flashing play of fishes and children on the shore,— and the playing mother who flings to them flowers and watchful glances,— and the great maple-trees which, softly murmuring with a thousand leaves and flies, bend downward to meet the foliage that glimmers in mimic dance under the waves,—and how the warm earth and the warm sky rest on each other in slumbering love, and bear one century after another....

Victor, before the end of his rural day, went sadly home. Saturday (the 16th of June[98]) sped softly by, and in its flight shook out a whole flower-head of winged seed for new flowers of joy.

The stars glided lightly over its night. A friendly, blue Sunday morning hung floating over the village in its finery, and held its breath lest it should snatch off a ripe, linden-blossom, or the down of a marsh-marigold. Victor could hear the forte-pianissimo sounding down from the palace over the reposing village, and must needs sigh with the asthma of blissful longing, "Ah, when shall I have to cease swimming upon this still, shining sea, over this fair anchorage of life?" ... When Fate answered, "To-day!" For this very day, on Sunday, there came from the residence-city of Flachsenfingen a light-headed fool (in fact, two) in a no less light-bodied Berlin, and took out of his package a letter to him from his Lordship.

"On the 21st of June (Thursday), the Italian Princess makes her entry into Kussewitz. On Wednesday, I leave here, and present thee in St. Luna to the Prince, who accompanies me to that place. I pray thee, however, to repair on the Saturday following to the *Island of Union*,[99] because the little which, for want of opportunity, I cannot say to thee in St. Luna, I shall reserve for the island. Thou wilt find me there. The bearer of this is our respected court-apothecary *Zeusel*, in whose house thou wilt, as court-physician, have thy future residence. Farewell!" H.

"Zeusel?" asks the reader, and ponders the matter. "I know not the Zeusels." No more do I; but I say to myself, Is not this carrying things too far? And is it not a regular imposition, that the correspondent of this work cannot, by all the representations made to him by me through the dog, be induced even to arrange things in this history in as orderly a manner as they are, indeed, in every wretched romance, and even in—a house of correction, where every new correctioner rehearses neatly to the old ones, in the very first hour, his total *Fata*, even to the introductory cudgelling on entering, from which the historian has freshly arrived. By Heaven! people actually rush and leap into my work, as into a passengers' room, and neither reader nor Devil knows who their dogs and cats are.

"I wish..." said Victor, and made six circumflexes upon it as apostrophes of the same number of omitted curses. For he was now to pass over from the Idyl of country life into the travestied Æneid of city life, and no road is surely more wretchedly paved than that from the study into the court smelting-houses and *chambres ardentes*,[100] from peace to turmoil. Besides, Emanuel had not yet written. Clotilda, the *Hesper* of those two fair evenings, was like the Hesperus in the sky, not to be seen over St. Luna. As we said, it was a wretched state for him. And now, in addition to all this, that Zeusel, his future landlord, the Court Apothecary, was, so to speak, a fool, full as light as his Berlin, or as the court-fourier, with whom he came, but fifty-three years older than the carriage, that is to say, fifty-four years old, and, taken for all in all, a human diminutive and vinegar-eel in body and soul, *peaked* in all respects, in chin, nose, wit, head, lips, and shoulder. This fine vinegar-eel—for the eel contends that he understands a certain refinement, which never could belong to any Roturier,[101] and he does not deny that his great ancestors wrote themselves, not Zeusels, but *Von Swobodas*—was travelling with the court-fourier, who administered the quartermastership in Kussewitz for the princely bride, toward that place, in order to remain there just so long as he was not wanted. Zeusel meant absolutely to have influence on the Flachsenfingen court by something beside his clyster-hydraulics, and to work upon the court household with something more than senna-leaves; therefore he bought up at a high price all private intelligence (he improved it forthwith into public) which he could collect of new meteorological phenomena in the court-atmosphere, and then, when certain people turned somersets down from the steps of the throne, he smiled finely enough, and remarked that he hoped such persons had regarded him as their friend, and not noticed the leg which he had thrust out of his shop-door by way of giving them a sly lift. He was, in spite of some good-heartedness, a liar from the beginning, not because he wanted to be malicious, but refined; and he evaporated his sound understanding, that it might drop in wit.

Towards Victor, as future courtier and patron, he knew not, for all that, how to assume the upright court-dignity which respects at once itself and others; but towards the people of the parsonage he amply observed the regular courtly contempt, and showed them well enough how little, without designs upon the Lord's son, he should have thought of even *looking* over their garden-wall or window-sill, to say nothing of *coming* over. Victor never hated anything else in his neighbor but hatred of other neighbors; and his respect for all classes, his contempt for all *eminent* fools, his disgust at ceremonies, and his inclination as a humorist for the little theatres of life, formed the greatest contrast to the pharmaceutic infusorium, and to its disgust with men and deference for grandees.

Victor gave his landlord thirty greetings to carry with him to the Italian *Tostato* in Kussewitz, who had travelled with him, laughing and dancing, a day and a half out of Göttingen. The Apothecary, at his departure, left behind in Victor an annoying, sour sediment; even at the organ-blower, who brought up the coffee every Sunday, he could not laugh as usual. I will explain why he used to laugh at him.

On that day the coachman was shaved, and, in fact, at first hand,— namely, by his own. Now the chin of this lazy box-incumbent had thrown up more mole-hills—so I euphoniously name warts—than are necessary for shaving and mowing. Among these the old man hacked and planed on Sunday morning,—for then it is that the common people put off at once the old Adam and the old shirt, and leave sins and beard to grow only on working-days,—boldly slipping his knife up and down among the warty *chagrin* and cutting away. Now the man would have looked pitifully, with his ploughed-up facial foreground,—so that one must needs have wept blood at that which ran in red lines down over the chin of this stone river-god,—if the Prosector, like a Roman, had, out of stupidity, exhibited his wounds. But he showed nothing,—he had more sense than that; he picked tobacco-spunk into small caps, and put the headpieces upon the sore warts, and so made his appearance.

"Let a Spener, a Cato the younger," said Victor, "just come into my study, and not laugh when a bellows-blower follows with coffee-cups, and with sixteen scalped warts and his chin bound up in spunk, looking like a garden-rockery overgrown with beautifully distributed moss,—let a Spener, I say, help laughing, if he can."

To-day he could help it himself. Weary of the day, he went out into the peaceful evening, and laid himself on his back on the summit of a steep hill; and when the sun, dissolved into a cloud of gold, tremulously flowed away over the liquid gloss of the flowers, and swam down on the grassy sea of the mountains, and as he lay nearer to the warm, throbbing heart of Nature, sunk down upon the soft earth as if in the repose of death, drawing down the clouds into him with sighs, fanned by winds coming from afar, lulled by bees and larks,—then did remembrance, that after-summer of human joy, steal into his soul, and a tear into his eye, and longing into his breast, and he wished that Emanuel might not reject him.—Suddenly slight steps drew nigh to his reclining ears; he started up, alarmed and causing alarm. A heavy travelling carriage came staggering lazily up the hill; behind, instead of servants, three pale foot-soldiers had thrust their hands into the footmen's straps, who had only a single leg among them which was of flesh, while they footed it on five wooden stilt-legs or boot-makers' signs, which, with something still longer, made of wood,—namely, three well-wrought beggar's staffs,—they had taken from the enemy; a coachman walked beside the carriage, and a gentlewoman, and close by Victor, as he sprang up, stood—Clotilda.

She came from Maienthal. This sudden illumination eclipsed all the tables of the law hung up in his soul, and he could not at once read the tables. She looked upon him with softer rays than ever, and the sun lent some too. With a smile, as if she anticipated his first questions, she gave him a—letter from Emanuel. A shrinking "Ah!" was his answer; and before he could accommodate himself to two ecstasies,[102] the carriage was already at the top of the hill, and she in it, and all had gone off.

He hesitated with trembling to gaze, absorbed, into the still, blue paradise of the fairest soul that ever overflowed. At last he looked upon the traces of a beloved human hand which he had not as yet touched, and read:—

"Horion!

"Man climbs a mountain, as the child does a chair, in order to stand nearer the face of the infinite Mother, and to reach her with his puny embrace. Around my height the earth lies sleeping, with all its eyes of flowers under the soft mist; but the heavens already lift themselves up with the sun under the eyelid; under the paled Arcturus mists begin to glow, and colors extricate themselves from colors; the globe of earth rolls, vast and full, to rapture, of blossoms and living creatures, into the burning lap of morning.

"So soon as the sun comes, I look into it, and my heart lifts itself up and swears to thee that it loves thee, Horion!... Glow, Aurora, through the human heart as through thy field of cloud, illuminate the human eye like thy dew-drops, and send up into the dark breast, as into thy heaven, a sun!...

"I have now sworn to thee, I give thee my whole soul and my little life, and the sun is the seal on the bond betwixt me and thee.

"I know thee, beloved; but knowest thou whose hand thou hast taken into thine? Lo, this hand has closed in Asia eight noble eyes,—no friend survives me,—in Europe I veil myself,—my sad history lies near the ashes of my parents, in the waters of the Ganges, and on the 24th of June of the coming year I go out of the world.... O Eternal One, I go; on the longest day the happy spirit wings its way out of this temple of the sun, and the green earth opens and closes with its flowers over my sinking chrysalis, and covers the heart that is gone with roses....

"Waft greater waves upon me, morning-air! Draw me into thy broad floods that stand over our lawns and woods, and bear me in clouds of blossoms over sparkling gardens and over glimmering streams; and dizzied between flying blossoms and butterflies, melting away under the sun with outspread arms, faintly floating over the earth, let me die, and let the bloody garment, dissolved into a red morning-vapor, like the ichor of the butterfly[103] just released, fall into the flowers, and let a hot sunbeam absorb the azure-bright spirit out of the rose-chalice of the heart up into the next world.... Ah, ye beloved, ye departed, are ye indeed departed? are ye, then, moving along as dark waves[104] in the quivering blue of heaven? even, now, in that abyss, full of veiled worlds, do your ethereal garments billow around the hidden suns? Ah, come back, sweep hitherward; in a year I melt and flow into your heart!

"—And thou, my friend, seek me soon! No one on earth can love thee so truly as a man who must soon die. Thou good heart, which these mild days press into my hands, even at this last moment, for a farewell, I will love and warm thee inexpressibly. During this year in which I am not yet taken away, I will stay with thee entirely; and when Death comes and demands my heart, he shall find it only on thy breast.

"I know my friend, his life and his future. In thy coming years stand open dark chambers of martyrdom; and when I die, and thou art with me, I shall sigh, Why can I not take him with me, before he sheds his tears?

"Ah, Horion! there lies in man a black Dead Sea, out of which only when it is agitated the blessed island of the next world lifts itself up with its clouds. But my lips will already lie under the earthly clod when the cold hour comes to thee in which thou wilt no longer see any God,—in which Death shall lie on his throne, and mow around him, and fling even to the domain of nothingness his frosty shadows and the lightnings of his scythe. O beloved, my grave-mound will then be already standing when thy *inner* midnight comes on; with anguish thou wilt mount upon it, and look sternly into the soft wreaths of the constellations, and cry:[105] 'Where is he whose heart crumbles beneath me? Where is eternity, the mask of time? Where is the Infinite One? The veiled self grasps after itself on all sides, and strikes against its cold form.... Gleam not upon me, broad starry field; thou art only the conglomerate *picture*, formed of colored earths, on an infinite *churchyard-gate*, that stands before the desert of a life buried under space.... Laugh me not to scorn, ye shapes on higher stars, for, if I melt away, ye melt away also. One, one thing, which man cannot name, glows forever in the immeasurable smoke, and a centre without limit calcines a circumference without limit.—Still I exist; the Vesuvius of death yet smokes above me, and its ashes envelop me; its flying rocks bore through suns, its lava-torrents move dissolved worlds, and in its crater the former world lies stretched out, and it sends up nothing but graves.... O Hope, where abidest thou?' ...

"Float enraptured around me, animated gold-dust, with thy thin wings,—I will not crush thy short flower-life; swell upward, giddy zephyr, and waft me down into thy blossom-cups. O thou immeasurable flood of radiance, fall from the sun over this narrow earth, and bear up on thy waves of splendor the heavy heart before the highest throne, that the eternal and infinite Heart may take the little ones which are nigh to ashes, and heal and warm them!

"Is, then, a poor son of this earth so unhappy that he can quail in the midst of the splendor of morning, so near to God on the hot steps of his throne?

"Fly not from me, my dear one, because a shadow always encompasses me, which daily grows darker, until at last it shall wall me in as a little night. I see the heavens and thee through the shadow, in the midnight I smile, and in the night-wind my breath goes forth full and warm. For, O man, my soul has stood erect toward the stars; man is an asthmatic, who suffocates if he lies down and does not lift up his breast.—But darest thou despise the earth, that forecourt of heaven, which the Eternal has thought worthy to move along as one in the bright host of his worlds? The great, the godlike, which thou hast in thy soul and lovest in another's,—seek it not in any sun-crater, on any planet-floor; the whole next world, the whole of Elysium, God himself, appear to thee in no other place than in the midst of thee. Be great enough to despise the earth; be greater, so as to respect it. To the mouth which is bent down to it, it seems a rich, flowery plain; to man in his *perigee*, a dark world; to man in his *apogee*, a glimmering moon. Then, and not till then, will the holy element, which from unknown heights is sent down into man, flow from the soul, mix itself with the earthly life, and quicken all that surrounds thee. So must the water, shed from heaven and its clouds, first run under the earth, and well up from it again, before it is purified into a fresh, clear draught. The whole earth is trembling now for rapture, till all rings and sings and shouts, as bells sound of themselves during an earthquake. And the soul of man is made greater and greater by its nearness to the Invisible....

"I love thee exceedingly!

"Emanuel."

Horion read through swimming eyes. "Ah," he wished, "were I only, this very day, near thee, with my disordered heart, thou glorified one!" and now, for the first time, occurred to him the nearness of St. John's day, and he proposed to himself on that day to see him. The sun had already vanished; the evening red fell like a ripe apple-blossom; he felt not the hot drops on his face, nor the icy dew of twilight on his hands; and with a bosom illuminated by dreams, and a heart tranquillized and reconciled to earth, he wandered back....

—By the way! is it, then, necessary that I should elaborate an apology for Emanuel as stylist and as *stylite* (in the higher sense)? And if such is necessary, need I therein bring forward anything more than this,—that his soul is still the echo of his Indian palms and the River Ganges; that the walk of the better sort of unfettered men, just as in dream, is always a flight; that he does not manure his life, like Europeans, with the blood of other animals, nor hatch it out of dead flesh, and this abstinence in eating (quite another effect than that of excess in drinking) makes the wings of fancy lighter and broader; that a few ideas, to which he guides with partial hand all the mental sap and nutriment (and this distinguishes not only madmen, but also extraordinary men; from ordinary ones), must in him obtain a disproportionate weight, because the fruits of a tree become so much thicker and sweeter when the rest have been plucked; and more of the same sort? For, to speak candidly, those readers who desire an apology, themselves need one, and Emanuel deserves something better than a— criminal defence.—

At this moment the consolation leaped up within my hero like a fountain, that he was to begin on Thursday his metempsychosis through nature,—his journey. "Deuse take it!" said he, skipping up; "what needs a Christian to coin money for the present distress,[106] and put on mourning-cloaks, when he can journey on Thursday to Kussewitz to see the handing-over of the Italian Princess, and on Saturday to the *Isle of Union*, and, what is more, on the same day, which is *one* day before St. John's, to Maienthal, to his dear one, his angel?"

O Heavens! I would that he and I were already about the journey,— really it may perhaps, unless all hopes deceive me, be quite tolerable!—

During the week-day prayer-hour of Wednesday, two carriages rolled along. Out of the full one stepped his Lordship and the Prince; out of the empty one, nobody. Old Appel had dressed herself up splendidly, and locked herself into the pantry. The Chaplain was happier,—he taught in the Temple. Seldom does one make a clever face when one is presented, or a stupid one when one presents. His Lordship led his son to the Prince's hand and heart, as a collateral security for his future loyalty, but with a dignity which won as much reverence as it showed. My good hero behaved himself like a—fool; he had far more wit than our deference for higher persons, or theirs towards us, allows. A talent which expresses itself outside the limits of feudal service may be regarded as high-treason.

His wit was only a covered embarrassment, into which he was thrown by two faces and a third cause. First, the Prince's....

—If the reading world complains that so gradually, as they observe, one new name and actor after another steals into this star Venus, and makes it so full, that, at last, the historical picture-gallery becomes a regular gallery of vocables, in which they must wander round with a directory in their hands, they have really only too much ground for the complaint, and I have myself already complained the most bitterly of the same thing; for, after all, the greatest load remains on my shoulders, inasmuch as every fresh ninny is a new organ-stop drawn out, which I have to take into my performance, and which makes the pressing down upon the keys more disagreeable to me; but my correspondent forwards to me in the gourd-flask, without leave asked, all these people to be quartered on me, and the rogue actually writes me I have only to tell the world, *There are still more people coming.*—

The Prince's face threw our hero into embarrassment, not from anything imposing about it, but because everything of that kind was discharged from it. It was a week-day and *current* face, that belonged on coins, but not on prize-medals,—with arabesque lines, which mean neither good nor evil,—tinged with a little dead gold of court-life,—anointed with a soft oil, which might stifle the strongest waves,—a sort of sweet wine, more drinkable for women than men. Of the finest turns, which Victor had intended to reciprocate, there was nothing to be heard or seen; but of apt and easy ones so much the more. Victor was embarrassed by the conflict and interchange of politeness and truth. Social embarrassments arise not from the uncertainty and impracticableness of the path, but from the crossways of choice and the perplexity of the scholastic ass between his two bundles of hay. Victor, whose politeness always sprang from philanthropy, must to-day let it spring from self-interest; but this was precisely what he could not get into him. Beside the paternal face, before which, with most children, the whole wheelwork of a free behavior grates and sticks, a third cause made him disconcerted and witty,—namely, that he was after something. I can tell by the look of every one,—except a courtier, whose life, like a Christian's, is a constant prayer for something,—the moment he enters the door, whether he calls as an alms-beggar and saint-by-works, or as merely a member of the joy-club.

Long before the people left the church, Victor already conceived a hearty love for the Prince,—the reason was, he was determined to love him, though the Devil himself stood before him there incarnate. He often said, Give me two days, or *one* night, and I will fall in love with whomsoever you propose. He was delighted to find on January's face no second-hands, no minute-hands, of those assignation-hours with which a good Cæsar generally seeks gladly to interleave, as with honeymoons, the tedious years of wedlock; but on his face nothing was displayed but continence, and Victor would rather swear by the face than by the reputation. He misses the mark; for on the male face—although it is made of mere printed characters of physiognomy, as certain pictures are of written letters—Nature has, nevertheless, written the *matres lectionis* [107] and signs of sensuality very small, but upon the female larger, which is really lucky for the former and stronger and less chaste sex. In fact, adultery is, with princes of the January stamp, nothing but a milder sort of ruling and conquering. And yet honest regents always return—with pleasure the wives, so soon as they have conquered them, to their former lords. This, however, is only the same greatness which led the Romans to deprive the greatest kings of their realms, in order afterward to present them with them again.

As princes are not, like jurists, bad Christians, but prefer to be none at all, January prepossessed our Victor by sundry sparks of religion, and by some hatred of the French Encyclopedists; although he saw that for a prince religion has indeed its good, but also its bad side, since only a crowned Atheist, but no Theist, possesses the invaluable *privilegium de non appellando*, which consists in this, that the accused party is not permitted (*per saltus* or by a *salto mortale*) to appeal to the highest jurisdiction beyond the pale of earth.

The conversation was indifferent and empty, as in such cases it always is. In fact, men deserve, for their conversation, to be dumb; their thoughts are always better than their talk; and it is a pity that one could not apply to good heads some barometrograph, or compositor's harpsichord, which should write off outwardly what is thought within. I would bet that every great head goes to the grave with a whole library of unprinted thoughts, and lets only some few book-shelves of printed ones go out to the world.

Victor submitted to the Prince the usual medical interrogatories, not merely as physician-in-ordinary, but also as a man, for the sake of loving him. Although people from the great world and the greatest have, like the sub-man, the orang-outang, lived out and died out in their twenty-fifth year,—for which reason, perhaps, in many countries kings are placed under guardianship as early as their fourteenth,—nevertheless January had not ante-dated his life so far, and was really older than many a youth. The Prince won the good, warm heart of Sebastian most by the unpretending simplicity which served neither vanity nor pride, and whose ingenuousness differed from the usual sort only in refinement. Victor had seen vassals stand in such a manner beside the mouth[108] of their liege-lord; that the latter looked like a shark carrying a man crosswise in his jaws; but January resembled a Peter-fish, which holds forth in *its* jaws a fine *stater*.

The Court-Chaplain, when he arrived, in his astonishment at a crowned guest, found it impossible to stir lip or foot; he remained immovable in the broad water-spout of the priestly frock, which was thrown around him like a sheet of royal paper round marchpane. The only thing in which he indulged, and on which he ventured, was—not to put away the Bible (the mouse-trap), but—to send his eyes secretly round the room, to spy out whether *it* had been properly stitched, folded, and superscribed by the registresses of rooms.

The Prince proceeded at once on his journey with his Lordship, who had to reserve his leave-taking of his son and his farewell sermons till the solitary day they were to spend on the Isle of Union. The son contracted a liking for the company of the Prince, when he thought over his demeanor towards his father; he had a double joy, a filial and a human, as that father transformed his own happiness into the happiness of the poor country, and only for the sake of doing good made foot-tracks for himself in the rock of the throne, as in Italy the footsteps of angels who have appeared and left a blessing are shown in the rocks. Other favorites resemble the executioner who hollows out for himself foot-holes in the sand, so as to stand steadier when he—beheads.

When the room was emptied, the first of Eymann's members to wake up—he still stood in the sentry-box of the priest's frock—was the index-finger, which stretched itself out, and pointed out to the family-circle the bed. "It would have been more satisfactory and serviceable to me," said he, "to have been strangled to death with that rag, than to have had his *Serenissimus* spy it out." He meant, however, his own soiled cravat, which he himself had thrown upon the nuptial bed,—that art-chamber and wareroom of his linen. Whenever one contradicted any tormenting notion of his, he argued it so long that at last he believed it himself; but if one admitted it, then he conjured up certain scruples, and adopted a different opinion. "His Highness must inevitably have seen the tattered thing through the bed-curtains," he replied. Finally he travelled over all the places where January had stood, and took observations at the torn neck-tie, and investigated its parallax. "We must adhere to the *blinding* of the windows, if we want to have any *peace*," he concluded, and—

So do I.

P. S. I shall always remark after an eighth chapter (because I get ready exactly two Dog-post-days in a week), that I have again worked for the space of a month. I therefore report that to-morrow June comes on.

FIRST INTERCALARY DAY

Must Treaties be kept, or is it enough that they are made?

The latter.—To-day the mining-superintendent exercises, for the first time, on the reader's ground and soil the right (*servitus oneris ferendi*, or I may say *servitus projiciendi*) which, according to the contract of May 4, he actually possesses. The main question now is, whether a dog-contract between two such great powers—inasmuch as the reader has all the quarters of the world, and I, in turn, have the reader—must, after being concluded, also be kept.

Frederick, the Antimachiavellist, answers us, and backs himself by Machiavelli: Certainly every one of us must keep his word so long as it—is for his advantage. So true is this, that such treaties would never be broken, if they were not once—concluded; and the Swiss, who, as late as 1715, swore one with France, might quite as well in all the Cantons have lifted their fingers and taken an oath they would every day regularly—make water.

But so soon as the advantage of contracts ceases, then is a regent entitled to break them in two cases,—those which he makes with other regents, and those he makes with his own step-children of the country,—his subjects.

While I was already at work in the cabinet, (not later than six o'clock, with the goose-wing, dusting the session-table, not with the pen,) I had under the latter a clever fugitive paper, wherein I proposed to show that the *ouverture* of treaties (*au nom de la Sainte Trinité* or *in nomine Sanctissimæ et individuæ Trinitatis*) was the cipher which ambassadors sometimes place over their reports, meaning that the opposite is to be understood. Nothing, however, came of the fugitive paper but a—manuscript. In this I was simple enough, and proposed first to advise princes, that, in regard to lies of necessity and truths of necessity, they must have, for every latitude and hour, *declinations* and *inclinations*. I proposed to whistle the state-chanceries to myself into a corner, and whisper in their ears, I would never suffer it, and, though I had only nine regiments in pay and starvation, that my hands and feet should be glued together with the sealing-wax of contracts, and my wings clogged with ink. That would I for the first time introduce into state-praxis; but the state-chanceries laughed at me, afar off in my foolish corner, and said, The whistler may believe, himself,—we do the thing otherwise.

In the works of Herr *Herkommen* [109]—the best German publicist, who, however, writes no *acta sanctorum* it is proved that a reigning prince need not observe at all any treaties, privileges, and concessions granted by his predecessor to his subjects; hence it follows that he is far less bound to keep his *own* covenants with them, since the enjoyment of the benefit of these covenants, which consists in nothing but the keeping or breaking, manifestly vests in him as proprietor. Mr. Herkommen says the same on every page, and absolutely swears to it. Nay, can there be a dean or rector magnificus who exercises so little reason—considering that, according to a general assumption, a king never dies, and consequently predecessors and successors grow together into one man—as not to draw from this the conclusion that the successor may regard his own covenants as those of his predecessor, and accordingly, since the two make only one man, may break them just as much as if they were transmitted ones?

Whoso chose to discourse philosophically about this might prove that, in fact, *no man whatever* needs keep his word, not merely no prince. According to physiology, the old body of a king (a reader, a superintendent of mines) in *three* years makes way for a new one. Hume carries it still farther with the soul, inasmuch as he considers that as a fleeting (not frozen) stream of phenomena. How much soever, then, the king (reader, author) may, at the moment of making a promise, be bound to keep it, still he cannot possibly be held thereto the next minute after, when he has already become his own successor and heir; so that, in fact, of us two contracting parties of the 4th of May, nothing more is extant than our mere *posthumi* and successors,— namely, ourselves. As now, fortunately, promising and fulfilling never enter into one and the same moment, herefrom may follow the conclusion, pleasant to all of us, that, in fact, no one at all is bound to keep his word, whether he is the top of a throne or only a chip thereof. Nor will courtiers (the corner-clips of the throne) oppose this proposition.

The public is requested to consider the Preface as the Second Intercalary Day, for the sake of symmetry.

9
DOG-POST-DAY

Ah, the poor miner, the delver in rock-salt pits, and the island-negro have in their calendar no such day as is here described or repeated! Sebastian stood on Thursday, as early as three o'clock, on the flying-board of his bee-hive, in order in one day to land in *Great Kussewitz* and be off again before people were up. A reader who has an atlas on the floor at his feet cannot possibly confound this market-town, where the presentation of the Princess takes place, with a namesake of a town, which the city of Rostock has annexed to its immovable property. Unfortunately, the whole house loved him so that it had already, for half an hour earlier, been out of the morning feathers of which the greatest wings of dream are made. Amidst the din of carriage-chains, dogs, and cockerels, he tore his tender heart away from eyes that were all love, and, as the beating of the former and the melting of the latter annoyed him, all grew still worse; for external noise stills the inner tumult of the soul.

Out of doors all the grass-pastures and grain-fields were bathing in the *shower-bath* of the dew and in the cold *air-bath* of the morning-wind. He hardened in it, like hot iron; a morning-land full of immeasurable hopes encircled him; he stripped his breast, threw himself all aglow into the dripping grass, washed (but not with any higher purpose than girls have) his firm face with liquid June-snow, and; strung with tenser fibres, stepped back from the shower-bath to his toilet,—only hair and breast he confined in no imprisonment.

He would certainly have started earlier, but he wanted to avoid the moon, whom he could no more marry to the sun than he could their respective children to each other,—namely, night-thoughts and morning-thoughts. For when the morning-clouds envelop man in their dew, when the loving birds dart noisily through the gleaming mist, when the sun looms forth out of the hazy glow, then does man, quickened in spirit, press his foot more deeply into the earth, and cling with new ivy-twigs of life more firmly to his planet.

Slowly he waded through a low avenue of hazel-bushes, and reluctantly swept off their chilled chafers; he held himself in, and stopped at last, in order to make himself late, that he might not reach the neighboring thicket just when the sun was entering his theatre. Already he heard the musical *mêlée* in the thicket; rosy clouds were spread like flowers in the sun's pathway; the watch-tower of the parsonage and village, that high altar whereon his first lovely evening had glowed, kindled again; the singing world of the air hung exulting in the hues of morning and the heavenly blue; sparks of clouds darted up from gold bars along the horizon; at last the flames of the sun streamed in over the earth....

Truly, were I every evening to depict sunrise, and every morning to see it, still I should cry, like the children, Once more, once more!

With benumbed nerves of vision, and with flakes of color swimming before him, he passed on slowly into the wood, as into a dark minster, and his heart swelled even to devotion....

—I will not assume that my reader has such a prosaic feeling in regard to morning as to deem this poetic one irreconcilable with Victor's character; nay, I venture to presume that his knowledge of human nature will find little trouble in discovering the *key-note* between two such distant tones in Victor as humor and sensibility. I will therefore commit myself unconcernedly to the happy contemplations of his feeling soul, and to my assurance of having all hearts in unison with mine.

The planet Venus and a grove show most beautifully in the morning and the evening; on both, at these hours, more rays of the sun fall than at any other. Hence our Victor felt, in the thicket, as if he went through the gate of a new life, as on this fiery morning he sauntered onward with the sun, which darted beside him from twig to twig, through the murmuring wood, away along under symphonious branches, which were so many music-barrels set in motion, over moss that lay in green sun-fire, and under evergreen bathed in heavenly blue. And this morning renewed in his heart the painful likeness of *four* things,—life, a day, a year, a journey, which resemble each other in their fresh, exultant beginning, in the oppressive interlude, in the weary, sated close.—

Outside in the copse, in the background of the woodland, Nature unrolled before him her altar-piece, miles long, with its chains of hills, with its dazzling country-houses, which had decked themselves with gardens as with festoons, and with the miniature-colors of the flowerets which played on the silver line of beauty traced by the brooks. And a cloud of enraptured, sporting, buzzing little creatures of silk-dust swept or hovered over the undulating picture.—What way should Victor take in the labyrinth of beauty?—All the sixty-four radii of the compass stretched themselves out as so many fingerposts, and he had sense enough not to propose to himself any particular hour of arriving. He therefore slipped off everywhere, to the right and to the left; he climbed over into every vale that hid itself behind a hill; he visited the pierced shadow-projection of every row of trees; he laid himself down at the feet of a more than commonly beautiful flower, and refreshed himself with pure love by its spirit, without breaking its body; he was the travelling-companion of the powdered butterfly, and observed his burying himself in his flower, and the hedge-sparrow he followed through the bushes to her brooding-cell and nursery; he let himself be spell-bound in the circle which a bee drew around him, and quietly suffered himself to be immured in the shaft of his own nosegay; he exercised upon every village which the motley landscape held up to him the right of way, and loved best to meet the children, whose days played even like his hours—

But men he avoided....

And yet there leaped from his heart a high fountain of love, which penetrated even to the remotest brother; and yet was he so entirely free from egotism, from that *sensitive* intolerance, which has its degree and source in common with the *Moravian.*—-The reason, however, was this: the first day of a journey was wholly different from the second, third, eightieth; for on the second, third, eightieth, he was prosaic, humoristic, social,—i. e. his heart adhered everywhere like hooked seed, and sent the roots of its happiness into every other being's lot. But on the first day came veiled spirits from all hours into his soul, who vanished if a third spoke,—a soft intoxication, which the atmosphere of nature, like that of a wine-store, communicated to him, spread itself, like an enchanted solitude, around his soul.... But why shall I depict the first day before I depict him?

In the first hours of the journey, he was to-day fresh, glad, happy, but not blissful; he drank as yet, only he was not drunken. But when he had thus for some hours wandered on, with drinking eye and absorbing heart, through pearl-strings of bedewed web-work, through humming vales, over singing hills, and when the violet-blue sky peacefully joined itself to the smoking heights and to the dark woods, rising like garden-walls behind each other,—when Nature opened all the pipes of the stream of life, and when all her fountains leaped up, and, flashing, played into each other, painted over by the sun,—then was Victor, who went through these flying streams with a rising and thirsty heart, lifted and softened by them; then did his heart swim, trembling like the sun's image in the infinite ocean, as the salient point of the wheel-animal[110] swims in the fluttering water-globule of the mountain stream.—

Then did flower, meadow, and grove dissolve into a dim immensity, and the color-grains of Nature melted away into a single broad flood, and *over* the glimmering flood stood the Infinite One as a sun, and *in* it, as a reflected sun, the human heart.—

All was one; all hearts grew to one greatest heart; a single life throbbed; the blooming pictures, the growing statues, the dusty clod of earth, and the infinite blue vault became the beholding face of an immeasurable soul.—

He might shut his eyes as much as he pleased, still there lingered in his dark breast this blooming immensity.

Ah, if he could have plunged up into the clouds, so as to sweep thereon through the undulating heavens over the boundless earth!—ah, if he could have floated with the flower-fragrance over the flowers,—could have streamed with the wind over the summits, through the woods!—O now would he rather have fallen on the heart of a great man, and sunk, enraptured and weeping, into his bosom, to stammer out, "How happy is man!"

He must needs weep, without knowing why; he sang words without sense, but their tone went to his heart—he ran, he stopped—he dipped his glowing face into the cloud of blossoming bushes, and would fain lose himself in the humming world between the leaves; he pressed the scratched face into the deep, cooling grass, and hung delirious on the breast of the immortal mother of Spring.

Whoever saw him from a distance took him for a madman; perhaps many a one does so still, who has never himself experienced how, through the cleared-up, blissful breast, as through the serenest sky, storm-winds may sweep, which in both dissolve in rain.

In this hour of his regeneration-day, his genius gave his heart the fiery baptism of a love, which clasped all men and all creatures into its flames. There are certain precious minutes of rapture—ah, why not years?—when an inexpressible love towards all human creatures flows through thy whole life, and opens thy arms softly to every brother. The least that Victor could do, whose heart was on the sunny side of love, was, if any one met him near a mountain, to turn out for him toward the steep side,—not to pass by any one who was fishing, for fear of throwing a frightening shadow on the water,—to wander slowly through a flock of sheep, and, if a child was shy of him, to make a long circuit aside. Nothing could surpass the soft voice with which he wished every pilgrim more than *this* good morning; nothing the look of anticipating emotion with which in every village he sought to spy out any poor body whose calluses and scars and gashes required a sponge or pain-killing drops. "Ah, I know as well as an amanuensis[111] to a Professor of Morals," he said to himself, "that it is no virtue, but only a luxury, to take away the crown of thorns from a lacerated brow, the prickly girdle from sore nerves; but this innocent pleasure will still be begrudged me, and when on so many roads mangled men are lying, why on mine does no one stretch out his hand that I might place in it some compensation for this undeserved heaven in my breast?"

He would fain carry his joy to another's heart to be tasted, as the bee delivers its mouthful of honey to the lips of another bee. At length two children came puffing along, one of whom was tackled as pulling beast of burden to a wheelbarrow, and the other harnessed on in front as pushing driver. The barrow was freighted with six porous bags full of pine-cones which the poor span were hauling to feed a consumptive fire. The two frequently exchanged places, so as to hold out; and the driver always wanted presently to be the horse again. "My good children! can't your father push, then?" —"The tree has broken both his legs short off." —"Then certainly your big brother could go to the wood?" —"He has to plough over yonder." —Victor stood on the fallow-field beside a waistcoat with full as many colors as holes, and near a dirty bread-sack, both which belonged to the brother, who at a distance was ploughing on the stage of this scene with half a post-team of lean cows. The emptying of a full hand into the lap of misery lightened Victor's heavy soul, as did the outgushing, which followed, of the full eye; his conscience, not his selfishness, was his objector to the *greatness* of his gift—he gave it, however, but in coins of small denominations—the children left their merchandise, and while one of them ran across the field to the plough, the other ran down to the village to his mother. The ploughman in the distance pulled off his hat—would fain have uttered loud thanks, but could only blow his nose—went on ploughing without his hat; but when at length he called out his thanks after the youth, the latter had already escaped far beyond earshot....

Do not, dear reader, wish this or the succeeding interlude of human sorrow left out of the great scenes of happy nature; and may thy heart, like Victor, by giving deserve to receive!

In his good-hearted haste he soon overtook a journeyman blacksmith sick with fever, whose travelling-trunk or portmanteau was a filled handkerchief; he also carried on a stick a wretched, faded pair of boots, which he had to spare, because the other which he dragged along on other sticks, namely, on his legs, was still wretcheder and less without color than without soles. When he had tenderly greeted the feverish man and made him a present, he looked into his pale, livid face, and he could not deny him some smart-money.... Ah, the whole smart-money for this life is not paid out till we reach a higher! When he had civilly questioned him and informed himself about his hungry journeyings, about his correction-house fare, about his flights from one country to another, and about his thin viaticum which the mistress denied him when the master was out,—then was he ashamed, before the All-gracious One, of his flower-field of rapture, which he no more deserved "than that poor devil there," and he made him an additional present; and when he again waited for him to speak, and learned that he was fifty years old without any prospects, and when the distress overmastered him which he always felt at the sight of *old* but *undeveloped* men, gray apprentices, old clerks, old dispensers, old amanuenses, then was he somewhat excusable for running back again and silently giving the astonished old man the new signs of his overflowing, benignant soul; and when, at this renewed parting, he felt his heart, which was dissolved into love, and only floated, as it were, round his soul, thirst more and more for doing good, and felt an incomprehensible inclination for fresh giving, and a longing to pour out upon somebody to-day everything, everything, then for the first time did he perceive that he was now too tender and too happy and too giddy and too weak.

So soon as the people in the village had in hand the certain intelligence of this transit-toll of generosity, in the afternoon about fifteen children stationed themselves on different posts along the way, manned the narrow passes, and distributed sentries and *enfans perdus* to prevent evasion of the revenue-laws....

A man who, like Victor, construed three straight leagues into seven crooked ones, is often hungry, but certainly more so than he;—he took merely a Leibnitz's monad-meal out of his pocket, biscuit and wine, and appeased therewith the stomach which hung and drew upon his spirit, in order not to darken and foul, by throwing in any pieces of flesh, the clear lake of his inner being, with its reflected arch of heavenly blue and heavenly red. In fact, he hated gormandizers as men of too gross selfishness, as well as all living larders, where layers of fat crush in the spirit, as masses of snow do a house. The soul, he said, takes an odor from the contents of the body, just as wine does from the fruit which is near it in the cellar, and in the mephitic vapor in which the souls of the Flachsenfingenites bob up and down over the brew-kettles which seethe their potatoes and beer, the poor birds must surely fall down tipsy and stifled into this dead sea.

He broke his biscuit not in any house, but in the skeleton, i. e. framework of a house, which had just come from the hands and axes of the carpenters into the sight of the village. As he looked through all the divisions and subdivisions of this architectural skeleton, and saw at once through sitting-room, kitchen, stable, and loft, he thought to himself: "Another play-house for a poor, little human troupe, who are here to play out their benefit comedy, their Gay's Beggars'-opera, with no voice to cry from the stage-box, *Encore!* Ah! before these beams have blackened to ebony by the winter smoke, many an eye-socket will have grown red with grief; many a northwester of life will blow through the window upon trembling hearts, and into these nooks, which are yet to be darkly walled up, will many a back, sore with bruises from the warfare of common life, creep away to wipe off sweat or blood. But joy (he went on soliloquizing as he looked at the place for stove and table) will also set a gilliflower-tree or two before the window for your inmates, and drive up before your house-door, which is yet to be hung, and unload its freight of the three holy feasts, and the church fair, and the child's baptism.—Heavens! how foolish that I should prefer thinking all this in the mere ribs of a house to seeing it yonder in the walled-up houses of the village!"

During this table-talk and house-warming-oration, whereat, however, no drinking-glass was shivered, the white breast of a swallow swooped low across the road, and her bill took up a load of slacked lime for her little garret. The wasp shaved off from the joist-work paper-shavings for the layers of her bulbous sphere. The spider had already knit her spider's house into the larger one. All creatures played the carpenter and mason in building up for themselves their little islands in the infinite sea; but grovelling man looks not over his shoulder, and sees not that all is like him.

Sebastian quitted his wooden inn, his skeleton of a Frankfort Red House, more intoxicated with happiness than he could have gone from a fully-built one. In certain men a dark melancholy diffuses itself,—a shadow of the soul all the greater when the shadows around them are the smallest: I mean about one o'clock of a summer afternoon. When in the afternoon the lawns lie more intensely perfumed, and the woods with drooping leaves stand, more softly sighing and sleeping beneath the brooding sun, and the birds sit on the trees as dumb figurants or supernumeraries,—then in the Eden that lay sweltering under the cloud of blossoms an oppressive yearning seized upon his heart,—then was he wafted by his fancies under the eternally blue sky of the East, and under the wine-palms of Hindustan,—then did he rest himself in those still lands, where, without stinging necessities or scorching passions, he sank dissolved into the dreamy tranquillity of the Brahmin, and where the soul in its elevation holds itself steady and no longer trembles with the trembling earth, like the fixed stars whose gleam trembles not, seen on mountains,—then was he too happy for a German colonist, too poetic for a European, too luxurious for a neighbor of the North Pole.... Every summer morning he feared that in the summer afternoon he should fantasy too effeminately.

Fasting, wine, heaven, and earth had to-day so lavishly filled the chambers of his heart with the sleep-potion of rapture, that they must needs, when anything more was poured in, overflow through the eyes. These now gushed forth; and behind his dimmed eyes, in the overshadowed inner chamber, lined with the green of nature, and darkened, as it were, with curtains of evening redness, a colored night came on, wherein all the little shapes of his childhood rose cloudily before him,—the earliest playthings of life were laid out,—his first May months played like little angels on an evening cloud, and they could not in their wing-clothes fly round the great cloud, and the sun did not scorch them.

Ah! what he had long forgotten,—long lost,—long loved,—songs without sense and tones without words, nameless plays,—buried nurses,— dead servants,—all these came to life again; but before all, and greatest of all, moved the form of his first, his dearest teacher, Dahore, in England, who said to his melted soul, "We were once side by side." —O this eternally loved spirit, who even then saw in our Victor the wings that lift themselves toward the next world,—who even then was more the friend than the master of his so tender, tempestuous, loving, aspiring heart,—this never-to-be-forgotten spirit would not leave him; his form pushed aside the shroud, began to shine and to say, "Horion, my Horion, did I not hold thee by the hand, wast thou not in my heart? But it is long since we loved each other, and my voice is no longer recognizable to thee, scarcely my face; ah, the seasons of life roll not back, but onward, downward, forever." He leaned against a tree and kept drying his eye, which could no longer find the road, and his sight was fixed calmly on the woods which stretch toward St. Luna, and on the hazy hills that separate him from Maienthal and from his second teacher....

Kussewitz burst upon him. But too soon; his soul in its emotion was not ready to go among strangers. He was glad to come upon an overturned trough, out of which sheep were licking salt, and a hedge-pen, which folded them at night, and the hut on two wheels wherein their keeper slept. He had a peculiar curiosity and predilection for little copies of houses; he always walked into or up to every collier's hut, every hunter's and fowler's house, for the sake of saddening and comforting himself with his own confinement, and with the parodies of our little life and with the ground-floor of poverty. He never went blindly by anything small, over which the world's man and business man stalk so scornfully; just as, on the other hand, he never stopped before any pomp of citizenly life. He opened, therefore, a little door to the travelling bed of the shepherd: it looked so poverty-stricken in there, and the straw, which took the place of eider-down and silk pillow-cases, was so lowly and rumpled, that he felt an indescribable longing to enter; he needed now a diving-bell that should separate him from the rushing, crushing, sublime sea around him. I wish one could conceal the fact from the European cabinets, the Imperial Diet, and the Chief Commissary, that he actually laid himself down therein. But now the excitement of his senses, into which the door of his bedchamber admitted only a small section of the blue sky, soon passed over into the exhaustion of slumber, and over the hot eye the lid closed.

10
DOG-POST-DAY

Since the last Post-day our hero has been sleeping. The German *Reviewers* should do me the favor to start him up.

But they are knaves, these headsmen and partners of the censors; they wake up neither readers nor princes, but only Homeric sleepers. The sun already hangs low, and peers horizontally into his Dr. Graham's-bed, and he still lies there glowing in the face of it....

The sheep had to do it with their bleating and bells. When the belfry-bell of Great Kussewitz, with the accompaniment of sheep-bells, wafted into his opening ears an evening prayer set to music,—when into his opening eyes the red outline of the departed sun which had illuminated his to-day's paradises entered, and the evening glow, whose gold leaves the evening wind breathed upon the clouds,—when the air, bedewed like his nosegay, refreshed his bosom,—then was to-day's sultry afternoon rolled back a whole week; Victor had dropped upon a new island of the blest; new-born and rejoicing, he crept back out of his piece of travelling property. "O mad me!" he said; "but I do not rejoice extraordinarily in the fact that half an ounce of grains of sleep can eat away clean out of man a whole glowing world, and that the turning over of the body is the sinking of his paradise and his hell."

On the high road two sedan-bearers went jogging off at a short gallop between the supporting poles of their leather die.[112] He made after them,—their load, he thought, must be far lighter to them than a whole country and its sceptre, both which, however, a regent knows how to balance, as a juggler does a sword, dancing, on the nose, on the teeth, everywhere. They bore, however, the heaviest thing in the world, beneath which cities, thrones, and continents have often broken down.

"What are you moving round with at such a rate?" he asked. "With our most gracious Lord!" It was January,—it is, however, quite in accordance with the æsthetic and artistic tricks wherewith an author so extraordinarily excites the expectation of his readers, that I do not divulge what it was of January that sat in the bounding litter, until I utter the next word.

It was his image. The bust always travelled ahead before the bride, in order to arrive in season at her bedchamber, and hang itself up by a nail to the wall. On the whole *sentimental journey* the *cubic contents* of the bride had slept only in chambers, on which the *superficial area* of the bridegroom hung down like a garden-spider all night long....

As I do not mean in any manner to cut myself of, by the barrier-treaty which I have concluded with my cousin the reader, from the right of making, beside the Intercalary Days, extra-leaves, extra-leaflets, and pseudo-extra-leaves, inasmuch as I have, the rather, by certain secret and separate articles, which I have made merely in my own head, as the Pope does certain cardinals, reserved to myself the privilege, I will now exercise the right which my self-made By-Recess offers me on the spot.

EXTRA LEAFLET UPON THE ABOVE BUST-PIECES

"I maintain," said I, in the billiard-room at Scheerau, at a moment when I was not striking, "that dukes, margraves, and other graves, and many of high nobility, would be stupid, if in our day,—or, in fact, in future days,—when the crown grows bald before the chin gets a beard,—when many a face wants no requisite for spectacles except the bridge,—when particularly the man of rank is glad to be, instead of a *cast*, at least an *outline*, of a man,—they would not be wise, I recapitulate, if they celebrated no better marriage than a true one,—that is, no pictured—one; if their busts were stamped on nothing better—that is, on no breast—than on the pewter covers of beer-pitchers, so that they could *intoxicate* people in no other way than this latter; and if they, who uniformly act by plenipotentiaries, on imperial benches, in session-chairs, in bridal beds (marrying by ambassadors), should conceive that in the last-mentioned case there were any truer and more innocent chief commissary than their own picture on an ell of canvas." ... As we just then played in mass, and I happened to be king, and in my fiery state went on to say, "What the Devil! we kings understand how to substitute skilfully enough, for the *plastic* arts in virtue and in marriage, the *delineative* arts; and *not merely* in billiards does a king stand quite idle with his sceptre-cue!" — then the fire of my speech might well seem far from strange.

End of the Extra Leaflet on the above Bust-pieces.

At the house of the Count of O— (so was called also a famous officer in the Seven Years' War, and by Shakespeare the world, and the whole territory of an old lady; and, according to Bruce, with the Hebrews this vowel was a particular favorite; but this is, after all, unprofitable learning here) the Princess and the painted bridegroom alighted. Victor would not, with his to-day's dress and his to-day's heart, mingle in the tumult of the world; and yet he would gladly have seen all.

As he approached Kussewitz, a little red and white house peered forth to meet him,—red as a squirrel-cage, and smiling as a summer-house. He stepped up to it and to its gleaming windows, but immediately stepped back again; he would not hinder an old human couple, for whom the bell had been the organ, from finishing their prayer. When he entered, with his face exalted by the reflection of to-day's transfiguration, an old man turned a silver head, which stood like a mild moon over the evening of his life, and a face of smiling wrinkles, toward the guest. Only a hypocrite—that stockjobber of virtue—is not, after praying, more gentle and complacent. The old woman was the first to lay aside the look of devotion. Victor, with his victorious simplicity, asked a night's lodging. To grant it to him was what only such contented people as these could do; to request it was what none could do, except one who, like him, shunned landlords, because their cold, selfish sympathy and love, coming and going with every guest, was too repulsive to his warm soul. Secondly, he was attracted by the cleanliness which even the slut loves in *strangers'* houses, and which, in them, is a proof of contentment and of—childlessness. Thirdly, he wanted to remain to-day incognito, and out of the thronged streets, with his soul so consecrated by Nature.

He soon felt himself at home; even before the supper was washed and picked and ready, he found out, or, rather, took it in, that the gentle old man, named *Lind*, was a bee-keeper. The latter I believe; for otherwise he would not have been so mild, as, in fact, in most cases, animal society is less corrupting than human. Hence Plato assigns the Lange's colloquies of man with the animals as the best thing left of Saturn's golden reign. It is not all one whether one is a dog-keeper, a lion-keeper, or a bee-keeper; for our menagerie in the lower viscera, according to the Platonic allegory, barks and bleats in unison with the external one.—When Victor actually went with the old man round the house and among the bee-hives, then he came back into the supper-room with the face of a man who claimed already a seat in the Kussewitz Church and a page in the church-book. Did he not already know that the bee-father had followed three parsons and five squires in Kussewitz to the grave; that he had celebrated his first marriage with his "mother" (so he called his wife) at the age in which the silver wedding usually falls; that his head had still memory and hair; that he expected to carry black eyebrows under the coffin-lid; that he, Lind, had not the least need, like old *Gobel* and even the beadle *Stenz*, for the sake of his eyes, to take his place near the church-window, but could read his verse anywhere; and that he once every year went to Maienthal to church, and thrust a sovereign[113] into the church billiard-pocket,[114] because the churchyard there covered all his relations on the father's side?

O, this contentment with the evening-clouds of life refreshes the hypochondriacal hearer and spectator, whose melancholy strings in an old man's presence begin so easily to tremble like a death-watch; and an ardent old man seems to us an immortal being, hardened against the scythe of death, and a finger-post pointing to the next world! Victor especially saw, with heavy thoughts, in an old man, an organized past, a bent incarnation of years, the plaster cast of his own mummy standing before him. Every childish, forgetful, petrified old man reminded him of the masters of forges, who in their old age, like the human soul, have to undergo a crab-like promotion, and on account of their usual loss of sight become casters again,—then head smiths,—then foundery apprentices. The good Newton,[115] Linnæus, Swift, went back to be foundery-apprentices of learning. But so singularly timid is man, that, while he regards his soul, in its greatest *advantageous* dependence upon his organs, still as a *vowel,*—and justly,—nevertheless, in the case of an *injurious* dependence upon the same, fears it may be merely a *consonant* of the body,—and *that* unjustly.

As a walk about a strange place gives a traveller the best naturalization act, and as Victor was incapable of being anywhere a stranger, he went—out a little way. There are many nights when it is not night. He saw outside, not far from the garden-fence of the senior (not the seignior of nobility, but the senior parson), a very beautiful girl sitting, buried in a Latin Whitsuntide programme, and praying from it with folded hands. A case of beauty and craziness united he never could resist; he greeted her, and would not let her roll up and put up her Latin prayer-book. The good soul, having lost her prayer-book and paternoster, had easily despatched her devotions out of the Whitsuntide programme *De Chalifis literarum studiosis,* as she neither understood Latin nor how to read, and looked upon the folding of the hands as a Masonic finger-speech, which would be readily understood in the *higher places.* She unrolled from a paper a sixth finger which had been cut off, and said the cloister of Mary in Flachsenfingen, on whose mother of God her father had wished to hang it as a thank-offering, would not accept it, because it was not made of silver. As Buffon ascribes to man's fingers the clearness of his ideas, so that the thoughts may be dissected at the same time with the hand, it follows that one who has a *sext* [116] of fingers, must think 1/6 or 1/11 the more clearly; and such a one, with such a supernumerary writing-finger, could do more in the sciences than we with the whole hand.

She related that her father would not marry her till after two years, and that his son could get her sister, if she were not only just six years old,—and they two had been adopted as children by the six-finger,—and that he had his bijouterie shop wherewith he wandered from one ducal palace to another; just now in that of the Count of O—, together with board and lodging, and that he was an Italian, named *Tostato*. Heavens! Victor knew him full well. Without further question—for he loved besides to go a Sabbath-day's journey or two with any girl or any Pomeranian dog, and used to say he never would make the least distinction between a new face and a pretty one, even if he were obliged to—he marched off with her straight toward the Count's to see her father. He peeled off more and more of the hull of his little maid of honor: she was not only uncommonly beautiful, but equally— stupid.

But now she ran away from him; the Flachsenfingen Court came travelling along, and she must needs see the ladies alight. He kept close to the tail of the whole corps, which was still trailing along the street, while half the rump was already in the palace. The draggling tail was somewhat short and thin, consisting of the Court-apothecary Zeusel, who from vanity was on hand with his fifty-four years and his youthful clothes and his bumping coach to take part in the affair. The smallest man in the world, in the biggest carriage in the world, could so little be looked upon as an *entity*, that I count his coach as an empty ceremonial coach, in which the coachman shook him about like a dry kernel in a walnut.

I will describe more copiously how the coachman winnowed and bolted him, and will make it up by being shorter in matters of less consequence.

Of course, if I should lay such an imputation upon the coachman as to say that he knew how by speed and stones to give the coach-body that hard pulsation, which made Zeusel sit more on the air than on the coach-cushion,—then would Kästner in Göttingen reply to me, and prove that the apothecary himself, by the counteraction which he produced upon the cushion by his posteriors, was to blame for the repulsion of the homologous pole; but we have, I trust, less to do here with the truth than with the apothecary. Victor, as Court-doctor, took a *distant* interest in the apothecary; nay, he would gladly have begged the favor of being allowed to get in and sit by his side, that he might see more distinctly how the skilful Vetturino sent the ball, Zeusel, into the air. But to the weak nerves of Victor comic scenes, by the physical suffering which they in reality brought with them, were too hard and sharp,—and he contented himself with following behind the bouncing box, and merely conceiving how the thing inside rose like a barometer to indicate the pleasant weather of the drunken coachman,—he merely pictured it out to himself (therefore I need not) how the good little courtier at a climax, to which the fellow brought him (who ended every lift with a higher one), would thrust his left hand, not into his waistcoat pocket, but merely into the coach-strap, while in his right he would be obliged to warm and squeeze for an hour a pinch of snuff, which for want of a quiet moment he could not raise to his empty nose till the rascal of a coachman cried, Brrr!

Come along! said the stupid girl to Victor, and drew him to her father's. The Italian made his windmill gesture, and placed himself against Victor's ear and whispered into it, *Dio vi salvi!* [117] and the latter thanked him in a still lower voice in Italian, *Gran mercè!* [118] Thereupon Tostato breathed three or four uncommonly soft-voiced curses into Victor's ear-cell. He had not lost his wits, but only his voice, and that only by a cold. He cursed and condoled about it, that to-morrow, of all days, he should have to be dumb as a haddock, precisely when so much was to be cut. Victor congratulated him sincerely on that very account, and begged him to accept him till to-morrow, not only as Doctor, but also as partner and spokesman; he would talk for him in the shop to-morrow, in order the better and incognito to see all that went on. "If you will tell me to-day," replied Tostato, "one more funny story." And now when he actually produced the adventure of Zeusel with an Italian systole and diastole of the hands, and when Tostato grew foolish with laughing at the joke,—(the Italian and Frenchman laugh with the whole body, the Englishman only in the brain,)—then was it no wonder that he took him into partnership at once. His doctorship he began by pulling off the patient's stocking and binding it round the untuned throat, for a warm stocking is worn with equal medicinal benefit on foot and neck; with a garter it would be different.

Now the beauty and stupidity of the programme-pray-er appeared greater than ever in his eyes; he would gladly have kissed her, but it was impracticable: the Bijoutier followed him about everywhere, eager for his witty overflowings, and held both ears under to catch the drops.

He took this occasion, as he thought of the German indifference to wit and the fine arts, to lay down the fundamentally false proposition,— The Englishman, the Frenchman, and the Italian are *men*; the Germans are *citizens*. The latter *earn* life; the former *enjoy* it. And the Dutch are a cheaper edition of the Germans on mere printing paper and without engravings.

He was on the point of going back to bee-keeper Lind's: when at this late hour of the night—so late that the Court-courier had set down the appearance of this comet a whole hour too soon in his astronomical tables— the Princess with her attendant atmosphere arrived. As he had talked of her so long, he needed nothing more to make him love her, than to hear the rolling of her chariot and the silk-rustle of her walk. "A princely bride," he said, "can be much better endured than another; show me any other difference between a Crown-princess, a crowned bride, and a crowned wife, than that which the state-almanac assigns." Whoever shall further consider, that he knew her personal disinclination towards the Prince, who at his first marriage had postponed her for her sister,—and whoever reads now what I here mention that Tostato told him she had a handkerchief in her hand on alighting from her carriage,—such a one will already be wise enough not to be angry at his saying: "I would that these crown-beasts, who are suffered to snap off the fair white hands of such a beautiful child, as swine eat off the tender ones of children—I would... but my wares, of course, will be near enough to her to-morrow to admit my seeing the handkerchief, Mr. Partner."

At the Bee-father's, to whom he went home again, there was a more tranquil world, and his house stood in the green, silent as a cloister of sleep around a holy place of dreams. Victor pushed his little bed on the attic floor towards an opening through which the moon streamed in, and thus, overhung with hushed swallows' and wasps' nests, he saw peace in the form of Luna float down to his own nest; but she smiled upon him so potently that at length he sank away dissolved into guileless dreams. Good man! thou deservest the bright flower-pieces of dreams, and a fresh nosegay of head and breast on waking; thou hast never yet tormented any man, never yet supplanted any one, overcome no female honor, nor ever bartered away thy own; and thou art merely a little too volatile, too effeminate, too gay, too human.

11
DOG-POST-DAY

Voltaire, who never could write a good comedy, would not have been competent to create this Eleventh Dog-post-day.

In regard to the Eleventh Dog-post-day I remark, to be sure, that Nature has created plants with all variety of numbers of stamens, only none with eleven, and seldom also men with eleven fingers.

Meanwhile life, like shell-fish, tastes best in the months without R.

In reply to this, some say that the pen of an author goes, like a watch, the faster, the longer it has been going; but I reverse it, and say rather, men who write much make fast writers.

And yet people cannot well bear men who are the fifth wheel of a coach; but every baggage-wagon has a fifth wheel strapped on behind it, and in case of accident this is a true *wheel of fortune*. Reinhold read Kant's Critique through *five times* before he understood it. I pledge myself to be more intelligible to him, and require to be read only half as often.

To speak out freely, I cherish some contempt for a head full of elastic ideas, which jump with their spring-feet from one cerebral chamber to another; for I find no difference between them and the elastic worms in the intestines, which Götze saw, before a light, leap to the height of three inches.

Of course the following thought does not rightly hang together with the foregoing chain of conclusions and flowers; namely, that I am afraid of finding imitators, and so much the more as I am, here, myself, one of a certain class of witty authors. In Germany no great author can light a new torch, and hold it out into the world till he is tired and throws away the fag-end of it, without the little ones immediately pouncing upon it, and running round and shining round for half-years longer with the little end of a light. Thus have I (and others) in Ratisbon been run after a thousand times by the boys, who held in their hands remnants of wax-torches which the ambassadorial retinue had thrown away, and offered to light me to my landlord's for a few kreutzers ... *Stultis sat!* [119]

In the morning Victor hastened to the palace. He got a tradesman's dress and the shop. At ten o'clock came on the "transfer" of the Princess. The three apartments in which it was to take place stood, with their folding doors, opposite to his shop. He had never yet seen the Princess—except all night in his dreams, and he can hardly wait for it all....

Nor the reader either: does he not even now snuff his candle and his nose,—fill up pipe and glass,—change his position, if he rides upon a so-called *reading-ass*,[120]—press the book smoothly open, and say with uncommon delight, "I am somewhat sharp-set for that description!"—I verily, am not at all; I feel as if I were to be shot with arquebuses. Positively! an infantry-soldier who in midwinter storms a hostile wall of the thickest paper, in the opera, has his heaven on earth, compared with a mining-superintendent of my stamp.

For one who drinks coffee and sets out to make a description of any school-act of the Court,—e. g. of a Court-day, of a marriage, (in fact, of the preliminaries thereof,) of a Transfer,—such a drinker pledges himself to reproduce scenes, whose dignity is so extremely fine and fugitive that the smallest false by-stroke and half-shadow makes them perfectly ridiculous,—hence even spectators, on account of such accidental touches, laugh at them *in naturâ*;[121]—he pledges himself, I say, so to reproduce such scenes, bordering on the comic, that the reader shall remark the dignity, and be as little able to laugh at them as if he himself were one of the performers. It is true I may presume to count upon myself somewhat, or rather upon the fact, that I myself have been at Courts and acted the part of master of the Harpsichord (whether this was a mask of higher honors or not, I leave here undecided); from a privilege, then, which has fallen to me alone of almost the whole scribbling Hansa, and to which I actually and gladly own my indebtedness for that preponderance which has (by some) been detected in me over the so inferior crew of authors in the *Scientiâ media* [122] of courts,—therefrom, I say, one should promise one's self almost extraordinary things. I fear, however, we shall come off slimly; for I was not even able to rehearse to my pupil Gustav the crown-suit in Frankfort seriously enough to make him leave off laughing. So, too, Yorick never could scold in such a way as to drive his people off, but they always took it as a joke.

It would have been my misfortune if I had depicted the transfer of the Princess (I thought at first, to be sure, there would then be more dignity in it) under the figure of the transfer of a house to creditors sealed with a chip of the door, or as a transfer of a fief by *investitura per zonam*, or *per annulum*, or *per baculum secularem*.[123] But I have luckily hit upon the thought of portraying the transfer, under the poetic garb of a historical benefit-comedy, with that dignity which theatres give. I have, for that purpose, as much and more unity of place—(three chambers)—of time—(a forenoon)—and of interest—(the whole joke)—in my hands, as I need. And if an author reads through beforehand, into the bargain, as I do, the saddest serious works, Young's Night Thoughts, the uncatholic *gravamina* of the Lutherans, the third volume of Siegwart, and his own love-letters; if, further, he has never yet trusted himself, without first laying before him and running through Home's and Beattie's excellent observations on the source of the comic, in order to know at once what comic sources he was to avoid;—such an author can safely, without fear of vainglory, make and fulfil the promise to his readers, that, thus comically guarding himself against the comic, he may perhaps be able, not wholly without touches of sublimity, to deliver and depict the following

HISTORICAL BENEFIT-COMEDY OF THE TRANSFER OF THE PRINCESS

IN FIVE ACTS

The half-word Benefit signifies merely the profit which I myself gain from it.

Act First.—Of three chambers, the middle one is the scene of the play, the trading-mart where they exhibit, the hall of *correlation* (Ratisbonically speaking) where all matters of importance are referred and matured. On the other hand, in the first adjoining chamber is stowed the Italian, and in the second the Flachsenfingen court, each calmly awaiting the beginning of a part for which Nature has formed it. These two apartments I regard only as the sacristies of the central one.

The middle chamber, i. e. its curtain, which consists of two folding-doors, at last rises and shows to partner Sebastian, who is peeping out from his shop beside the catarrhal half of the firm, a great deal. There appears at the door of coulisse No. 1 a red-velvet chair; again, at the door of coulisse No. 2, another, a brother and relative of the first; these duplicates are the seats whereon the Princess sits in the course of the action, not because weariness, but because her rank, expressly desires it. One discovers now (caught in the Act it may be said to be) a long fringed table, dividing the middle chamber (which is itself a hyphen to the two coulisses) into two halves. One would not expect that this session-table, in its turn, would be again halved by something which a stupid person hardly sees. But let a man step into Victor's shop; then will he have a view of a strip of silk-cord, which, beginning under the pier-table, streaming across the agate floor and under the partition-table, ends in front on the threshold; and thus a mere silk-band easily divides the dividing-table and thereby the dividing-chamber, and finally the divided company of performers, into two of the most equal halves,—whence let us learn that at court everything is cut up, and even the prorector, in his time and turn, is stretched out on the dissecting-table. Of this silk-lace, wherewith the grand seignior divides his favorites from above downwards, but into fractions, we cannot and must not say any more in the First Act, because—it is over....

I found it uncommonly easy to draw up this scene in a serious manner; for as, according to Plattner, the ridiculous attaches only to man, the sublime, which in my performance assumes the place of the comic, was easy to be had in an act where nothing living played, not even cattle.

Act Second.—The stage grows now more alive, and upon it enters now the Princess, handed in by the Italian Minister from coulisse No. 1; both act at first, like nature, silently on this parade-ground, which on paper is already two pages long....

Just one look from the stage into the stage-box! Victor is playing also on his own account, in the fact that he picks out from the lorgnettes which he has to sell the most concave, and gets therewith a view of the heroine of my benefit-comedy.... He saw the confession- and praying-stool on which she had to-day already knelt. "I wish," he said to Tostato, "I had been her father confessor to-day; I would have pardoned her her sins, but not her virtues." She had, in fact, that regular statuesque and Madonna's-face, which covers quite as often hollow as well-filled female heads; her courtly *début* concealed, it is true, every wave and every gleam of wit and expression under the icy crust of decorum; but a soft, childlike eye, which makes us eager for her voice, a patience, which remembers rather her sex than her rank, a weary soul which yearned for a twofold repose, perhaps for her maternal fields, even an unnoticeable line around the eyes, drawn by pain in those organs, or perhaps by still deeper ones,—all these charms, which grew into sparks, cast into the dry tinder of the partner behind the eye-glass, made him in his box regularly half-crazy at the fate of such charms. And how could it do otherwise than make one's head hot, especially when the heart is already so, to think that these innocent victims, like the Moravian women, must see alps and oceans rise between their cradle and bridal-bed, and that cabinets export them like silkworm-seed in the cornucopia of despatches?... We turn again to our Second Act, wherein one proposes nothing more than to—arrive.

Coulisses Nos. 1 and 2 are still choke-full of actors and actresses, who must now come out. This is the day on which two courts, like two armies, are halted over against each other in two rooms, composedly preparing themselves for the minute when they are to march out and stand face to face, until at last it actually comes to that point, to which after such preparations and in such nearness to each other it very naturally must come, that of going away. The cubic contents of No. 1 stream after the Princess, consisting of Italians;—at the same moment, also, the court-retinue from coulisse No. 2 takes up its line of march towards head-quarters; it consists of Flachsenfingenites. At this moment two countries—properly only their abstracted and evaporated spirits—stand quite near each other, and now all depends upon the silken strings beginning to operate which I stretched across the room in the first Act; for the boundary shiftings and population-mixings of two so contiguous lands as Germany and Italy would be in one room almost as inevitable as in a *Papal brain-chamber*, had we not the string; but *that* we have, and this keeps two populations, threatening to run into each other, so effectually apart, that it is only a pity and a shame—honesty feels the greatest—that the German Cabinets have not drawn some such cordon between themselves and the Italian; and did it not, then, depend upon them, where they would apply the cord,—to the floor, or to Italian hands or to Italian necks?

When the English General History of the world and its German abridgment shall once have so nearly come up with the times as to take in hand and relate the year of this transfer, and among other things are able to remark that the Princess, after her entrance, seated herself in the velvet chair,—then should the Universal History quote the author from whom it borrows, namely, myself.... That was the second Act, and it was a very good one, and not so much comic as sublime.

Third Act.—In this there is nothing but talking. A court is the parlor or talking-room of the country; the ministers and envoys are *listening-brethren.* [124] The Flachsenfingen Secretary read at a distance an Instrument, or the emption-bill of her marriage. Thereupon speeches were whispered,—two by the Italian minister,—two, also, by the Flachsenfingen minister (Schleunes),—none by the bride, which was a shorter way of saying nothing than that of the ministers was.

Since, now, this sublime Act were verily ended, if *I* should say nothing: it will, I trust, be allowed me for once, after many weeks, to obtain by begging and to append a little *extra-leaf*, and therein to say something.

AN EXTRA-LEAF (BY GRACIOUS PERMISSION) UPON THE GREATER FREEDOM ENJOYED IN DESPOTISMS

Not only in Gymnasia and republics, but even (as may be seen on the former page) in monarchies, speeches enough are made,—not to the people, but still to their *curatores absentes.*[125] Even so is there in monarchies freedom enough, although in despotisms there may be still more of it than in them or in republics. A true despotic state has, like a frozen cask of wine, not lost its *spirit* (of freedom), but only compressed it from the watery circumference into a fiery point; in such a happy state freedom is distributed merely among the few who are *ripe* for it, the Sultan and his Bashaws, and that goddess (who is pictured still oftener than the bird Phœnix) holds herself indemnified, and more and better than that, for the reduced *number* of her worshippers, by their *worth* and *ardor*, since her few *epopts* [126] or *initiates*— the Bashaws—enjoy her influence in a measure of which a whole people is never capable. Freedom, like an inheritance, is lessened by the multitude of heirs; and I am convinced that he would be most free who should be free alone. A democracy and an oil-painting are to be put only on a canvas without *knots* (inequalities), but a despotism is a piece of *relieved* work,—or something still more rare: despotic freedom lives, like canary-birds, only in *high* cages; republican liberty, like yellow-hammers, only in *long* ones.

A despot is the *practical reason* of a whole country; the subjects are just so many impulses contending therewith, which must be overcome. The legislative power, therefore, belongs to him alone (the executive to his favorites);—even mere talented men (like Solon and Lycurgus) held the law-giving power in themselves alone, and were the *magnetic needle* which *guided* the ship of state; a despot consists, as their throne-successor, of almost nothing but laws, his own and others at once, and is the magnetic mountain, which draws the ship of state to itself. "To be one's own slave is the hardest slavery," said an old man, at least an ancient and a Latin; but the despot demands of others only the easier kind, and takes upon himself the harder. Another says *Parere scire, par imperio gloria est;*[127] a negro slave, therefore, wins glory and honor as much as a negro king. *Servi pro nullis habentur;*[128] hence it is that political nullities feel so little the pressure of the court atmosphere; whereas despotic realities earn their freedom by the very fact that they know so well how to feel and prize its worth. A republican in the nobler sense, e. g. the Emperor of Persia, whose liberty-cap is a turban and his liberty-tree a throne, fights for freedom behind his military Propaganda and behind his Sans-culottes with an ardor such as the ancient authors demand and depict in the Gymnasia. Nay, we are never justified in denying such enthroned republicans a Brutus's greatness of soul, before we have put them to the proof; and if in history good were delineated more than evil, one would have even now the means of showing, among so many Shahs, Khans, Rajahs, and Califs, many a Harmodius, Aristogeiton, Brutus, &c. who was able to pay for *his* freedom (slaves contend for another's) even with the death of otherwise *good* men and friends.

End of the graciously allowed Extra-leaf upon the
greater Freedom enjoyed in Despotisms.

The extra-leaf and the Third Act are ended, but the latter was shorter and more serious than the former has been.

Fourth Act.—By the act of dropping the curtain and raising it again, I have carried the world over from the shortest Act into the longest. To the Princess who now, as the German Imperial History announces, is sitting—came her compatriots in a body, who neither looked very honest nor very stupid, the chief-governess, the Court-confessor, the Court-Æsculapius, ladies and servants and all. This court-train does not say its farewell,—that has already been said privately,—but merely recapitulates it by a silent bow. The next step of the united Italians was from the middle chamber to—Italy.

The Italians passed along before Sebastian's warehouse, and wiped off from their faces, whose hard parts were *en haut-relief,*—the German were *en bas-relief,* a nobler glimmer than that which courts communicate: Victor saw among so many accentuated eye-sockets the multiplied signs of the melancholy with which he himself was oppressed as he thought of the willing stranger-heart which remained behind alone under the frosty canopy of the German throne and clouds, torn away from her loved ways and scenes, brought before microscopic eyes, whose focal point scorches into tender feelings, and bound to a breast of ice....

When he thought of all this, and saw the compatriots, how they pocketed their feelings and packed themselves off, because they were not permitted to exchange another word with the Princess; and when he looked upon the mute, submissive form within there, who was not allowed to show any other *pearls* than Oriental ones, (although the dream and the possession of the latter signifies Western ones, or of the evening land,—tears, I mean,) then did he wish, "Ah, that I could only, thou good creature, draw a treble veil over thy eye long enough for it to shed a tear!—might I only kiss that hand, so rudely set up at auction, as thy court-ladies are now doing, so as to inscribe with my tears upon the sold hand the nearness of a sympathizing heart." ...

Be tender and expand not your hatred of princes into hatred of princesses! Shall a bowed-down female head not touch our hearts with pity, because it leans on a mahogany table? and shall great tears not move us, because they fall upon silk? "It is too hard," Victor said, when in Hanover, "that poets and *magistri legentes,* when they pass by a chateau, make, with an envious, malicious pleasure, the remark, In there as much bread of sorrow is baked, perhaps, as in fishermen's huts. O yes, doubtless greater and harder loaves! But is the eye, out of which in the badger's kennel of a Scotchman nothing extorts a tear but the smoke of the room, worthy of a greater compassion than the tender one which, like that of an Albino, smarts at the very rays of joy, and which the spirit fills with spiritual tears? Ah, down in the valleys only the skin is punctured, but up on the high places of rank, the heart; and the index-hand of the village clock moves merely around the hours of hunger and sweat, but the second-hand, set with brilliants, flies round dreary, despairing, bloody minutes."

But fortunately never is rehearsed to us the passion-history of those womanly victims, whose hearts are tossed to the mint, and, like other jewels, cast among the throne-insignia,—who, as flowers with souls, hung upon an ermine-clad dead man's heart, fall to pieces, unenjoyed, on the bed of state, mourned by no one, save by a distant, tender soul, which finds no place in the Court-almanac....

This Act consists of nothing but *goings*: in fact, this whole comedy resembles the life of a child. In the first Act, there was *providing of household furniture* for the coming existence; in the second, the *arrival*; in the third, *talking*; in the fourth, *learning to walk*, &c.

When Germany had delivered discourses enough to Italy, and Italy to Germany, then Germany, or rather Flachsenfingen, or properly a piece of it, the Minister Schleunes, took the Princess by the hand and led her out of the torrid zone into the frigid; I mean, not from the bridal bed to the wedded bed, but—from the Italian territory of the apartment into the Flachsenfingenite, away over the silken Rubicon. The Flachsenfingen court stands over yonder as right wing, and has not yet gone into the fight. So soon as she had passed the silken line, then it was well that the first thing she did in her new land should be something memorable; and in fact she did, before the eyes of her new court, take 4½ paces and—sit down in the Flachsenfingen chair, which I set out vacant for that purpose in the very first Act. Now, at last, the right wing marched into fire, for the kissing of hands and sleeves. Each one in the right wing—the left not at all—felt the dignity of what he entered upon, and this feeling which melted into one with personal pride came— as according to Plattner pride is akin to the sublime—quite *apropos* to my Benefit-farce, in which I cannot succeed in being sublime enough. Great and silent, embarked in silken bow-nets, buried in a gulf of robes, the court-dames sail up with their lips to the still hand which is fastened with conjugal manacles to a stranger's. Less stately, but still stately, is urged on, also, the Adamitish portion of the *Dramatis Personæ*, among whom, unfortunately, I see the apothecary Zeusel.

We know no one among them but the minister, his son Mat, who does not observe anything whatever of our hero, the Physician in ordinary to the

Princess, Culpepper, who, transformed by fat and his doctor's beaver into a heavy Lot's-pillar-of-salt, pushes himself like a turtle into the presence of the Regent and Patient.

No mortal knows how Zeusel torments me. Contrary to all order of precedence, I prefer to present, sooner than I do him, the fat livery-servants, swollen into knavish stupidity, whose coats consist less of threads than of laces, and who bend themselves like yellow ribbon-preparations before weary eyes, wont to look on fairer forms. Victor regarded, through his English opera-glass, the Italian glazed court-faces as at least picturesquely beautiful; on the contrary, he found the German parade-masks so worn out and yet so starched, so languid and yet so on the stretch, their looks so evaporated and yet so brimstone-smoked!... I still keep Zeusel back by means of some Easter-lambs or *agnus Dei's* of pages' faces, soft and white as mites; a nurse would like to lay them with their nipple-glass-mouths to her breast.

Zeusel was no longer to be restrained; he has broken through and has the Princess by the wing—the whole joke of this play, I mean the whole serious meaning of it, is now once for all spoiled. This gray fool has in his old days—his nights are still older—buttoned himself into a complete historical copper-plate, that is to say, into a zoölogical fashionable waistcoat, wherein, with his four variegated rings, too, he looks for all the world like a green game-wagon, on which the animal pieces of the whole chase are painted, and four rings for the ringing of the swine's snouts are there *in naturâ*.[129] I must now see and suffer it,—as he does everything in the past,—while he, fuddled with vanity and hardly able to distinguish watch-chains from gala-coats, runs up and catches at some silken stuff to kiss it. It was easy to foresee that the man would spoil my whole altar-piece with his historical figure; I would absolutely have suppressed the ninny and covered him up behind the frame of the picture, had he not with his flappers and skippers stood out too prominently and made too much of a chattering; and then, too, my correspondent has expressly introduced and designated him among the benefit-confederates. It hardly pays for the trouble to write—

Act Fifth; since all is now thrown into pickle and the reading world is in a grin. In the Fifth Act, which I make without any gusto, there still continued to be nothing done,—whereas Tragedy-makers and Christians turn over the conversion and all important matter into the last Act, as, according to Bacon, a courtier thrust his petitions into the Postscript,—nothing, I say, except that the Princess let her new maids of honor do their first example in arithmetic and subtraction; namely, the problem of disrobing.... And as undressing concludes the fifth Acts of Tragedies, where Death does it,—

and of Comedies, where Love does it,—so, too, would this Benefit-Comedy, which, like our life, wavers between Comedy and Tragedy, wearily end with an undressing.

End of the Benefit-Comedy.

I was too much excited yesterday. To be sure the Apothecary is the Dog and Cat, in my picture, biting each other under the table of the Holy Supper; but, upon the whole, the very farce is sublime. Let one just consider that all is carried on in a monarchical form of government, which, according to Beattie, more than the republican form, helps out the comic,—that, according to Addison and Sulzer, precisely the most waggish men are the gravest, and that, consequently, the same thing must hold in regard to the stuff they work;—one must then see at once, from the comic element which my Acts contain, that they are serious....

My hero delivered in the shop a vehement Father Merz's controversial sermon *against* something which imperial cities and towns preach in favor of: "That men can act so without brains, the white or the gray, and without a particle of taste, as not to be ashamed sinfully and like dogs to fritter away the two or three years in which Pain has them not yet in his game-ticket, nor Death on his night-list,—not in doing absolutely nothing, or in the half bar-rests of chancery-holidays or the whole bar-rests of comitial holidays, or with the whimsicalities of joy,—what were more laudable?—but with the whimsicalities of torture, with twelve Herculean labors to do nothing, in the correction-houses of antechambers, on the *tratto di corda* of tight-strung ceremonials.... My dear seneschal, my fairest chief-governess, I approve all; but life is so *short* that it does not repay the trouble to make one's self a *long* queue[130] therein.—Could we not shake out our hair, and leap over all entrance-halls (or -hells), over all ushers and dancing-masters, away into the very midst of the May-flowers of our days, and into their flower-cups?... I will not express myself abstractly and scholastically; if I did, I should have to say, Like dogs, ceremonies grow mad with age; like dancing-gloves, each serves only for once, and must then be thrown away; but man is such a curséd ceremonious creature, that one must swear he knows no greater or longer day than the diet[131] of Ratisbon."

While Victor was at his meal, Tostato was not present, but in the shop. Now he had already, the evening before, been unable to get out of his head a design of kissing the pretty dunce. "If I can kiss a saint who is stupid as a cow but *once*, then I have peace for the rest of my life." But, unluckily, the so-called *smallest* (the sister), whose understanding and nose were too great, had to float round the dunce, as bob to the angle; and the bob would instantly have twitched, had he so much as put a lip to the bait. However, he was cunning, at least: he took our *smallest* on his knee, and danced her up as Zeusel's coachman did him, and called this *clever* one sweet names over her head, all of which he dedicated with his eyes to the *stupid* one (at court he will dedicate with reversed dissimulation). He covered up twice in joke the spying eyes of the *smallest*, merely in order to do it a third time in earnest, when he drew the dunce to himself, and with his right hand brought her into a position, where he could,—especially as she allowed it, because girls do not like to refuse a trick, often from the mere pleasure of guessing it,— amidst his court-services to the blind one, offer the other the hasty kiss, for which he had already contrived so many *avant-propos* and lines of march. Now was he satisfied and well; if he had been compelled to lie in wait two evenings longer for the kiss, he would have fallen deeply in love.

He was again sitting at his masthead when the Princess dined. It took place with open doors. She stirred up his wild-fire of love with the gold spoon as often as she pressed it to her small lips; she scattered the fire apart again with the two toothpicks (sweet and sour) as often as she resorted to them. Tostato & Co. disposed to-day of the most costly articles. No man knew the *& Co.*,—only Zeusel looked more sharply into Victor's face, and thought, "I must have seen you before." Towards half past two in the afternoon, good luck would have it that the Princess herself came to the shop, to look up Italian flowers for a little girl with whom she had fallen in love. In all masquerades, as every one knows, one takes masquerade liberties, and in every journey the freedom of a fair. Victor, who in disguises and on journeys was almost too bold, undertook to speak in the mother-tongue of the Princess, and, in fact, with wit. "The Devil," thought he, "cannot surely catch me for that." He remarked, therefore, with the tenderest complacency toward this fair child in Moloch's arms, simply this in regard to the silk-flowers: "The flowers of joy, too, are unhappily, for the most part, made of velvet and iron wire, and with the *shaping-iron*." It was only a miracle that he was polite enough to leave out the circumstance that it was just the Italian nobility who elaborated the Italian Flora. She looked, however, at his goods, and bought, instead of flowers, a *montre à régulateur*,[132] which she requested to have brought over to her.

He delivered the watch to her with his own hand; but, unfortunately, no less with his own hand—the reader will be frightened, but at first he himself was frightened, and yet thought over the conceit till at last he approved it—had he previously stuck on, above the *Imperator* of the watch, a delicate strip of paper, wherein, with his own hand, he had written, in pearl type: "*Rome cacha le nom de son dieu et elle eut tort; moi je cache celui de ma déesse et j'ai raison.*"[133]

"I know this people well enough," thought he; "they never open or wind up a watch in their life!" Ha, Sebastian! what will my reader or *thy* lady reader think?

She started this very evening for the country she had obtained by marriage, the future string-floor of her sceptre. Our Victor felt almost as if he had transferred another heart than the metal one with the billet, and thought with pleasure of the Flachsenfingen court. Before her ran her copied bridegroom or his litter, from which he alighted on the wall of the bedchamber. As he was her god, I can compare him or his image with the images of the ancient gods, who were carried round on a peculiar *vis-à-vis*, called a *thensa*,[134]—or in a portrait-box, called [Greek: ναος, naos],[135]— or in a cage, called [Greek: kadiskon].[136]

Thereupon Victor went with his commercial consul round behind the coulisses of the benefit theatre. He untied the silken demarcation-line and barring-chain,—drew it up like a disgusting hair,—felt of it,—held it first far from his eye, then near to it,—and pulled it apart, before he said: "The power may lie where it will,—a silk ribbon may insulate bodies politic as well as electrical, or it may be with princes as with cocks, who never can get a step farther, if one takes chalk and draws therewith a straight line from their bill to the ground,—nevertheless this much you see, partner,—if an Alexander should displace the boundary-stones, such a string would be, in opposition thereto, the best epitome of the natural law and a *barrière-alliance* of the same nature." He went into her bedroom, to the empty sepulchre,—that is, to the bed of the risen bride,—into which the *sponsus* could look down as he lay at anchor on the wall. Whole divisions of conceits marched mutely through his head, which, thus full, he pressed sidewise with his cheek against a silken pillow, as large as a lap-dog's, or the side-cushion of a carriage. Thus reclining and kneeling, he said, speaking half into the feathers:[137] "Would that on the other pillow also there lay a face looking into mine! Dear Heaven! two human faces opposite each other,—each drawing the other into its eyes,—listening to each other's sighs,—breathing away from each other the soft, transparent words,—that were what you and I absolutely could not stand, partner!"—He sprang up, gently patted down his hare's form smooth again, and said, "Lay thyself softly around the heavy head which sinks upon thee; smother not its dreams; betray not its tears." Had even the Count of O—, with his fine, ironical look, come in at this moment, he would not have minded this. It is unfortunate for us Germans that we alone—while to the Englishman even a world's-man sets down his hare's leaps, caprioles, and gambols as so many elegant *pas, forward capers* and *backward capers* and *side-capers*—cannot possibly march along with sufficient gravity and composure.

At evening he ran in again to the harbor of his beekeeper; and his tossing heart threw out its anchor into the tranquil, blooming nature around him. The old man had meanwhile mustered up all his old papers, baptismal and marriage-certificates, and private documents of reference for the Nuremberg Bee-father's case, and said, "Let the gentleman read them!" He wanted himself to hear it all over again. He showed also his "Trinity-ring" from Nuremberg, in which was inscribed:

"Here, by this ring, you see,
Father, Son, Spirit, three,
Make one sole Deity."

The Bee-father went on to make no secret of it, that he formerly, before he procured this ring in Nuremberg on a court-day, had not been able to believe in the Trinity; "but now one must be a beast, if he could not comprehend it." —The morning before his departure, Victor was in a double embarrassment, —he was very desirous of having a present; secondly, of making one. What he wanted to have was a plump hour-watch,[138] won at a raffle where the ticket was twenty kreutzers. This piece of work, whose thick hand had measured off the thread of the old man's life on the dirty dial-plate in nothing but gay, joyous bee-hours, he wanted as a Laurence's-box,[139] an amulet, an Ignatius's-plate,[140] against hours of Saul. "A manual laborer," said he, "needs really only a little sun, to go warmly and contentedly through life; but we, with our fantasy, are often as badly off on the sunny side as on the stormy side, —man stands more firmly in mud than on ether and morning-redness." He wanted to press upon the acceptance of the happy veteran of life, as purchase-money for the hour-watch and prize-medal for his lodgings, his own watch that told the seconds. Lind had not the heart for it, but grew red. At last Victor represented to him that the second-watch was a good fire-ball[141] for the Trinity-ring, a thesis-image of that article of faith, for the *threefold* hands made, after all, only *one* hour. — Lind *swapped*.

Victor could neither be the mocker nor the Bunclish[142] reformer of such an erring soul, and his sympathetic whimsicality is nothing but a doubting sigh over the human brain, which has its seventy *normal years*, and over life, which is an interim of faith, and over the theological doctors'-rings, which are just such Trinity-rings, and over the theological lecture-rooms and recitation-rooms, wherein just such second-telling watches indicate and strike.

—At last he leaves Kussewitz at six o'clock in the morning. A very beautiful daughter of the Count of O— did not come back until seven o'clock; that is fortunate for us all, for otherwise he would be still sitting there.

The Dog-post-day is run out. I know not whether I should make an extra-leaf or not. The Intercalary Day is at the door; I will therefore let it be, and only insert a Pseudo-extra-leaf, which, as is well known, differs from a canonical merely in this,—that in the apocryphal I do not give notice by any superscription, but only slip off from the history in an underhand way to mere irrelevant things.

I take up my historical thread again, and ask the reader what he thinks of Sebastian's flirtations. And how does he explain them to himself?— He replies, and philosophically indeed: "Through Clotilda; she, by her magnetizing, has put him *en rapport* with the whole female world; she has knocked at this swarm of bees, and now there is no more peace.—A man may sit for twenty-six years cold and sighless in his book-dust; but when he has once breathed the ether of love, then is the oval hole of the heart forever shut, and he must go forth into the air of heaven and be continually gasping at it, as I see by the coming dog-post-days plainly enough." The reader has accustomed himself to a quaint philosophical style, but what he says is true; hence a maiden never sues so eagerly for a second lover for her stage as after the decease of the first, and after her vows to throw away her recruiting-license.

But how could the reader fail to hit upon still weightier reasons,[143]—1. General love, and 2. Victor's maternal marks?

1. General love is too little understood. There is as yet no description of it extant but mine,—namely, in our days, reading-cabinets, dancing-halls, concert-halls, vineyards, coffee-tables, and tea-tables are the forcing-houses of our hearts and the wire-mills of our nerves; the former are too big, the latter too fine. Now when, in these marriage-seeking and marriageless times, a young man, who still watches like a Jew for his female Messiah, and still is without the highest object of the heart, accidentally reads with a dancing-partner, with a lady member of his club, or an *associée*, or sister in office, or other collaboratress, a hundred pages in the "Elective Affinities" or in the Dog-post-days,—or exchanges from three to four letters with her upon the culture of silk or clover, or on Kant's *Prolegomena*,—or scrapes the powder from her forehead some five times with the powder-knife,—or with her, and by her side, ties up the intensely fragrant kidney-beans,—or actually at the ghostly hour (which becomes full as often the sentimental hour) quarrels with her on the first principle of morals;—then is this much certain,—that the aforesaid youth (provided *refinement, feeling*, and *reflection* hold a mutual balance within him) must needs behave a little madly, and feel towards

the aforesaid collaboratress (that is, if she does not by some higglings of head or heart offend against his feelers) something which is too warm for friendship and too *unripe* for love,—which borders on the former, because it includes several objects, and on the latter, because of this it dies. And this is, in fact, neither more nor less than my general love, which I have otherwise called simultaneous and Tutti-[144]love. Examples are odious; else I would adduce mine. This universal love is a glove without fingers (or mitten), into which, because no partitions separate the four fingers, any hand easily slips; into the partial love, or the glove proper, only a single and particular hand can squeeze itself. As I was the first to discover this fact and island, I can give it the name wherewith others will have to name and call it. It shall be christened henceforward collective or simultaneous love, though I might also, if I and Kolbe chose, let it be named preluding love,—confederate-tenderness,—general warmth,—the fidelity of adopted childhood.

To please the theologians and humor their fiddle-faddle about final causes, I throw in here the following fixed principle: I should like to see the man who, without this general love, could in our times, when paired love is, by the demands of a greater *metallic* and *moral* capital, made more rare, hold out three years.

2. The second cause of Victor's so easily falling in love with women was his maternal mark,—i. e. a resemblance to his own and every mother. Besides, he asserted that his ideas had exactly the pace—that is, the leap—of woman's, and that he had, in fact, a great deal of woman in him; at least, women resemble him in this,—that their love springs up through talking and intercourse. Their love, it may safely be said, has not much oftener begun than ended in hatred and coldness. An imposed and hated bridegroom makes often a loved husband. "I will," he used to say in Hanover, "get into her heart's ears, if not into her heart. Could Nature, then, have built into the female bosom two such spacious heart-chambers—one can turn round therein—and two such neat heart's-alcoves—the heart's treasure-bag I have not yet touched upon—merely for this purpose, that a man's soul should hire these four apartments all alone without a mother's son beside, as a female soul inhabits the four cerebral chambers of the head's female suite? Quite impossible! and in fact they do no such thing: but (but whoever is afraid of immoderate wit, let him now step out of my track) in the two wings of this rotunda and in the side-buildings everything takes up its quarters that goes in, i. e. more than comes out—as in a toll-house or pigeon-house there is a constant coming and going—one cannot count, if one is there to see—it is a beautiful *temple* in which there is *right of thoroughfare.*—Such regard not the few who so shut themselves up as to give the chief box of the heart to only a single lover, and merely the two side boxes to a thousand friends."

Nevertheless Jean Paul never could succeed—though there might be ever so much surplus room—even so far as to get into the heart's ears, which, to be sure, is the very least thing. Because his face looks too meagre, his complexion too sallow, his head is much fuller than his pocket, and his income that of a titular-mining-superintendency: so they quarter the good rogue merely in the *coldest* place away up under the eaves of the *head* not far from the hair-pins,[145]—and there he is still sitting now and laughing out (in writing) his Eleventh Chapter....

12
DOG-POST-DAY

We are living now in the dark middle-ages of this Biography, and reading on toward the enlightened eighteenth century or Dog's-day. Still, even in this twelfth, as in the night before a fair day, great sparks fly. "Spitz," said I, "eat me out of what thou wilt, only enlighten the world."

Sebastian hastened on Saturday with joyful soul under an overclouded heaven to the island of Union. He could arrive there, if he did not delay, before the cloudiness was absorbed. Under a blue heaven, like Schickaneder[146] he brought out the Tragedies, but under an ashen-gray one the comedies, of his inner man. When it rained, he absolutely laughed out. Rousseau built up in his brain an *emotional* stage, because he cared neither to go out of the coulisse nor into a box of actual life; but Victor had in his pay between the bony walls of his head a *comic* theatre of the Germans, merely for the sake of not ridiculing *actual* men; his humor was as ideal as the virtue and sensibility of other people. In this mood he delivered (like a ventriloquist) purely internal discourses to all Potentates;—he posted himself on the bench of Knights with church-visitation-discourses,—on the bench of the cities with funeral-discourses,—in the Papal chair he held forth in straw-wreath[147]- discourses to the *virgin* Europe and the Ecclesiastical *bride*. The potentates had all, to answer him again, but one may imagine *how*—when he, like a minister from his prompter's hole put everything into their mouths;—and then, to be sure, he went his way and made fun of every one of them.

Mandeville says in his Travels, that at the North Pole in the winter-half of the year every word freezes, but in the summer-half thaws out again and is audible. This intelligence Victor pictured out to himself on the way to the island; we will lay our ears to his head and listen to the inner buzzing.

"Mandeville and I are not at all obliged to explain why at the North Pole words, as well as spittle, turn to ice as they fall, just as quicksilver does there; but we are obliged to reason from the phenomenon. If a laughing heir wishes there long years to his testator: the good man does not hear the wish sooner than the following spring, which may already have laid him dead. The best Christmas sermons do not edify good souls before haying-time. Vainly does the Polar court lay its New-Year's wishes before *Serenissimo*; he hears them not, till warm weather, and by that time half of them have already miscarried. They ought, however, to place a *circular stove* as speaking-trumpet in the antechamber, so that one might hear in the *warmth* the court speaker. An oratorical brother, without a stove-heater, would there be a defeated man. The faro-player, to be sure, vents his curses on St. Thomas's day; but not until St. John's day, when he has already won again, do they begin to travel;[148] and one might make summer-concerts out of the winter ones without any instruments: all one has to do is to seat one's self in the hall. From what other cause can it arise that the Polar wars are often carried on half-years before the declaration of war, except from this, that the declaration issued in winter does not make itself heard till *good weather*? —And so, too, one cannot hear anything of the winter-campaigns of the Polar armies till during the summer-campaigns. I, for my part, should prefer to travel to the Pole so as to be there only in winter, merely for the sake of uttering real insults to the people's, particularly the court-retinue's, face; by the time they came at last to hear them, the defamer would be snugly ensconced again at Flachsenfingen. —Their winter-amusements are not to blame for it, if the Northern administration fails to propose and decide a multitude of the weightiest things: but only during the canicular holidays is the voting to be heard; and then, too, can the decisions of the chamber upon matters of grace and *forest-law* take shape in speech. But, O ye saints, if I at the Pole—while the sun was in Capricorn and my heart in the sign of the Crab—should fall down before the fairest woman, and in the longest night make to her declarations of love all night long, which, however, in a third of a third[149] assumed the form of ice and reached her in a frozen state,—i. e. did not reach her ears at all,—what should I do in summer, when I had already grown cold and already possessed her, if at the very hour in which I was hoping to have a good quarrel with her, now, in the midst of the scolding, my Capricorn-love-declarations should begin to thaw out and to utter themselves? I could do nothing with any composure, but to make the rule, Let any one be tender at the Pole, but only in Aries or Cancer. And if, finally, the transfer of a Princess should take place at the Pole, and, in fact, at that point where the earth does not move, which is best suited to the twofold inactivity of a Princess and a lady, and if the transfer should actually occur in a hall, where every one, particularly Zeusel, had in the long winter evenings slandered her; then, when the air in the hall began to repeat the slanders, and Zeusel in his distress sought to escape,—then would I pat his shoulder in a friendly manner and say, Whither away, my friend?" —

"To Grosskussewitz, I help in the catching department," replied the veritable beadle of St. Luna, who behind some masonry had with one hand unclasped a book and with the other buttoned up a wallet. Victor felt a happy pressure upon his heart at an antique from St. Luna. He asked him about everything with an eagerness that seemed as if he had been away for an eternity *a parte ante*.[150] The reader who buttoned up his wallet became an author, and drew up at sight for the gentleman the year-books, i. e. hour-books of what had since occurred in the village. Into twenty questions Victor involved the one he had to put about Clotilda, and learned that she had been hitherto every day at the Parson's. This vexed him. "As if," thought he, "I had not strength of soul enough to look upon a friend's love,—and then too, as if—." In fact, he thought, at such a distance, he was the more at liberty to think of her.

The reading constable was a reader under my jurisdiction: the book which he carried about on his poaching-expeditions after thieves was the *Invisible Lodge*.[151] Victor requested the First Part to be handed to him: the Beadle was in the Second, just at the Pyramid, at the moment of the first kiss. Our hero made more and more rapid strides in reading and in walking, and ended book and walk together.

The island stood before him!—Here, on this island, my reader, open both eyes and ears!... Not that any memorable things presented themselves,—for these would of themselves make their way into half-open ears and pupils,—but for the very reason that only everyday matters are to be recorded.

His Lordship stood alone on the shore of the sea which flowed round the island, and awaited and received him with a seriousness which veiled his friendliness, and with an emotion which still wrestled with his wonted coldness. He was going now to cross over to the island, and yet Victor saw no means of transportation. There was no boat there; nor would it have been practicable to get one off, because iron spikes stood under the water in such numbers and direction that no boat could move. The guard that had hitherto been stationed on the shore to protect the island against the destructive curiosity of the populace was to-day removed. The father went with his son slowly around the shore, and dislodged out of their beds, one after another, twenty-seven stones which lay at equal distances from each other. The island had been constructed *before* his Lordship's blindness, and *then* was not yet prohibited to strangers; but during that affliction he had caused its interior to be completed and concealed by unknown nocturnal workmen. During the tour round the island Victor saw its fruit-espaliers of high tree-stems, which seemed to direct their shadows and voices toward the interior of the island, and whose foliage-work the tossing waves sprinkled with their broken suns and stars; bean-trefoils clasped the pine-trees, and round the cones ringlets of purple blossoms played their antics; the silver-poplar bowed down under the enthroned oak; fiery bushes of Arabian beans blazed from farther in out of leafy curtains; trees, grafted by approach, on double stems latticed up the avenues from the eye; and by the side of a fir, which overtopped all the summits, was a taller one, which had been bent down by storms half over the water, and which rocked itself above its grave. White columns lifted up in the middle of the island a Grecian temple, immovable above all the wavering treetops.—Sometimes a stray tone seemed to run through the green Holy of Holies. A tall, black gate reached to the tops of the pines, and, painted with a white sun-disk, looked toward the east, and seemed to say to man, Pass through me; not only thy Creator, but thy brother, has worked, here!—

Opposite to this gate lay the twenty-seventh stone. Victor's father displaced it, took out a magnet, bent down, and held its *south* pole to the gap. Suddenly machines began to gnar, and the waves to whirl, and an iron bridge rose out of the water. Victor's soul was overfilled with dreams and expectations. Shuddering, he followed his father, and set foot upon the magic island. Here his father touched a thin stone with the *north* end of the magnet, and the iron bridge sank down again. Before they stepped up to the elevated gate a key turned itself from within, and unlocked, and the gate flew open. His Lordship was silent. On his face a higher soul had risen like a sun: one no longer knew him; he seemed to be transformed into the genius of this magic island.

What a scene! So soon as the gate was opened there ran to and fro through all twigs an harmonious murmur; breezes flew in through the gate, and absorbed the sounds into themselves, and floated on with them, trembling, and reposed only on bended blossoms.—Every step opened farther a great, sombre stage.—Round about the scene lay marble fragments, on which the blacksmiths' coals had drawn forms of Raphael's, sunken Sphinxes, map-stones, whereon dim Nature had etched little ruins and effaced cities, and deep openings in the earth, which were not so much graves as moulds for bells that had been cast therein. Thirty poisonous trees stood twined round with roses, as if they were signs of the thirty years of man's passionate madness. Three-and-twenty weeping birches had bent themselves down to form a low bush-work, and were crowded into each other; into this bush ran all the paths of the island. Behind the bushes ninefold crape-veils, in waves that mutually swallowed each other, obscured the sight of the high temple; through the veils five lightning-rods rose into the heavens, and a rainbow, formed of two shoots of water that leaped up and arched over into each other, hovered glittering over the twigs, and evermore the two streams arched themselves aloft, and evermore they shivered each other to pieces overhead by their contact.

As Horion led his son, whose heart was grasped, affrighted, oppressed, kindled, chilled, by invisible hands, into the low birch thicket, the stammering dead-man's-tongue of an organ-trill began to speak, through the lone silence, to the sigh of man, and the tremulous tone sank too deeply into a soft heart. — There stood the two on a grave darkly built over with bush-work; on the grave lay a black marble, on which were chiselled a bloodless white heart, with a veil over it, and the pale words, "*It is at rest.*" "Here," said his Lordship, "my second eye became blind; *Mary's* [152] coffin lies in this grave; when that arrived at the island from England, the diseased eye was too severely inflamed, and never saw again." — Never did Victor shudder so; never did he see on a face such a chaotic, shifting world of flying, coming, conflicting, vanishing emotions; never did such an ice of brow and eyes congeal upon convulsive lips; — and so a father looked, and a son felt every sensation repeated in himself.

"I am unhappy," said his father, slowly; a more bitter, biting tear burned on the pupil of his eye; he hesitated a little, and placed his five open fingers upon his heart, as if he would grasp and pluck it out, and looked upon the pale stone one as if he would say, Why is not mine resting too? The good, dying Victor, crushed with the anguish of affection, melting into pity, longed to—fall upon the dear, desolated bosom, and to say more than the sigh, "O God, my good father!" But his Lordship gently repelled him, and the tear of gall, unshed, was stifled by the eyelids. His Lordship resumed, but more coldly: "Think not that I am specially affected; think not that I desire a joy or deprecate a sorrow: I live now without hope, and without hope I die."

His voice came cutting over ice-fields; his glance was made sharp by frost.

He continued: "When I have, perhaps, made *seven* human beings happy, then must it be inscribed on *my* black marble, *It rests....* Why dost thou wonder so? Art thou even *now* at peace?" — The father stared at the white heart, and then stared more fixedly straight before him, as if a shape had risen out of the grave, — the freezing eye laid and turned itself about on a rising tear, as if to smother it. Suddenly he drew back a veil from a mirror, and said, "Look in, but embrace me immediately after!" ... Victor gazed into the mirror, and saw, with a shudder, an eternally loved face appear therein, — the face of his teacher *Dahore*; his knees smote together, but still he did not look over, his shoulder, and embraced that father who was without hope.

"Thou tremblest far too violently," said his Lordship; "but ask me not, my dear boy, why all is so. At a certain stage of years one opens no more the old breast, full as it may be."

Ah, I pity thee! For *those* wounds which can be disclosed are not deep; *that* grief which a humane eye can discover, a soft hand alleviate, is but small; but the woe which a friend must not see, because he cannot take it away, — that woe which sometimes rises into the eye in the midst of blessedness in the form of a sudden trickle which the averted face smothers, — *this* hangs in secret more and more heavily on the heart, and at last breaks it, and goes down with it under the healing sod. So are iron balls tied to man when he dies on the sea, and they sink with him more quickly into his vast grave. —

He continued: "I am going to tell thee something; but swear, here upon these precious ashes, never to divulge it. It concerns thy Flamin, and from him thou must conceal it."

Victor, so hurled from one wave to another, started at this. He remembered that Flamin had wrung from him on the watch-tower the promise, that, if ever they should have offended each other too sorely, they would die together. He hesitated to take the oath; at last he said, "But shortly before my death may I tell it to him?"

"Canst thou know when that will be?" said his father.

"But in case — ?"

"Then!" said his father, coldly and curtly. —

Victor swore, and trembled at the future import of the oath.

He also had to promise not to visit this dark island before his Lordship's return.

They passed out of the leafy mausoleum, and sat down on an overturned stalactite. At times, during the conversation, a strange harmonica-tone fell from leaf to leaf, and, at a great distance, the four rivers of Paradise seemed to go sounding away under a zephyr that trembled with it.

The father began: "Flamin is Clotilda's brother, and the Prince's son." —

Only such a lightning-flash of thought could now have penetrated into Victor's already dazzled soul; a new world now started up within him, and snatched him away from the great one before his senses. —

"Furthermore," continued Horion, "January's three other children still live in England,—only the fourth, on the Seven Islands, is invisible." Victor comprehended nothing; his Lordship rent away all veils from the past, and introduced him to a new outlook into the life immediately before him, and into that which had flown away. I shall, in the sequel, communicate all his Lordship's disclosures and secrets to the reader; at present I will first relate the leave-taking of father and son.

While his Lordship accompanied his son into the dusky, subterranean passages of former times, and told him all that he concealed from the world, tears started from Victor's eyes at many a trifle which could not deserve any; but the stream of these soft eyes,—it was not the narrative, but the returning contemplation of his unhappy father and the neighborhood of the buried and mouldering fair form and of the funereal marble, that wrung it out of the incessantly weeping heart.—At last all tones on the island ceased,—the black gate seemed to shut to,—all was still,—his Lordship came to an end with his revelations, and said, "Fulfil thy purpose of going to-day to Maienthal, and be cautious and happy!"—But although he took his leave with that refined reserve which in his rank guides and governs the hands and arms of even parents and children, still Victor pressed his childish bosom, so big with sighs and emotions, to his father's, with such an intensity as if he would fain crush in two his impoverished heart for the sake of the tears which he was compelled to let rise to sight ever hotter and larger. Ah, the forsaken one! When the bridge which clove asunder the father's and the son's days had risen up, Victor went over it alone, staggering and speechless; and when it had sunk into the water again, and the father had disappeared into the island, pity weighed him down to the ground; and when he had drawn all his tears, like arrows, out of his suffering heart, slowly and dreamily he quitted the still region of riddles and sorrows, and the dark funeral garden of a dead mother and a gloomy father, and his whole agitated soul cried incessantly, "Ah, good father! hope at least, and come back again, and forsake me not!" —

And now all that in the foregoing part of the story has created obscurities, all that his Lordship exposed to his son, we will explain to ourselves also. It will still be remembered that, at the time when he set out for France to fetch away the Prince's children,—the so-called Welshman, Brazilian, and Asturian, and the *Monsieur*,—the dark intelligence of their abduction came to hand. This abduction, however, he had (as he now confessed) himself arranged,—only the disappearance of the *Monsieur* on the Seven Islands had occurred without his knowledge, and he could therefore with his untruth mix some truth, as mouth-glue. These three children he caused secretly to be taken to England, and educated at Eton for scholars, and in London for civilians,[153] in order to give them back to their father as blood-related assistants of his tottering administration. Hence he had helped the so-called Infante (Flamin) become an administrative councillor. So soon as he once gets the whole infant colony together, he means to surprise and bless the father with the delightful apparition. The (at present) invisible son of the Chaplain, who before the embarkation took the small-pox and blindness, he therefore keeps in the dark, because otherwise it would be too easily guessed to whom Flamin properly belonged.

Victor asked him how he would convince the Prince of a relationship to four or five strangers. "By my word," was Horion's first reply; then he subjoined the remaining evidences,—in Flamin's case, the testimony of his mother (the niece), who would come with him; in the case of the others; their resemblance to their pictures, which he still possessed, and finally the maternal mark of a Stettin apple.

Victor had already often heard from the Parson's wife that all January's sons had a certain mother's or father's mark on the left shoulder-blade, which looked like nothing, except in autumn, when the Stettins ripen; then it also grew red, and resembled the original. The reader himself must remember, in the annals of the curious and learned societies, whole fruit-basketfuls of cherries, whose red pencilling was only faint on children, and heightened in redness not until the ripening of the prototypes on the twigs. If I could believe a fellow-bather of mine, I myself should have such a Stettin fruit-piece hanging on my shoulder; the thing is not probable nor important; meanwhile next autumn,—for I have proposed it to myself several autumns, but now Knef, through his dog, reminds me of it,—so soon as the Stettins mature, I might, to be sure, take a looking-glass and examine myself behind.—And on the same ground this Stettin festoon puts off the return of his Lordship, at least the transfer and recognition of the children, till the autumnal season of its reddening.—

I make no scruple of communicating here a satirical note from my correspondent. "Make believe," he writes, "in regard to this intelligence, as if you did it at my behest, and, when you have once related his Lordship's *exposé* and revelation, very quietly relate it over to your reader a second time; so that he may not forget, or get it confused. One cannot cheat readers enough, and a clever author will be fond of leading them into marten-traps, wolf-pits, and deer-nets." I confess, for such tricks I always had a poor talent; and, in fact, will it not be more creditable, both to me and to the reader, if he fixes it at once in his mind, at first hearing, that Flamin is January's natural and Le Baut's assumed son,—that the Parson's is blind, and not yet apparent,—that three or four other children of January's, from the Gallic seaboard towns, are still to follow;—more creditable, I say, than if I should now have to chew it over for him a second time, (in fact, it would be a third time,) that Flamin is January's natural and Le Baut's assumed son,—that the Parson's is blind, and not yet apparent,—and that three or four other children of January's, from the Gallic seaboard towns, are still to follow?

The reason why his Lordship required of his son the oath of silence towards Flamin was, that the latter, by his native honesty, kept all secrets, but in a heat of passion betrayed all; because in such a case he would make his birth tell, merely for the sake of backing himself in a quarrel with an adversary; because he might the very next day, on account of this revelation, become, instead of a fencing-master with the sword of Themis, a fencing-scholar with the war-blade; and because, in fact, a secret, like love, fares still better between two partners than among three. His Lordship thought, too, that out of a man to whom you gave money in order that he might become something, more would be made than out of one who should be something because he had money, and who looked upon the coins as his hereditary arms, and not as the prize-medals laid out for his future redemption of them.

After all these developments, his Lordship made to our Victor still one more, and a weighty one, upon which he was always to look back on the icy career of his future court-life as to a warning-tablet.

When his Lordship was struck blind before the house that held the ashes of his beloved, his whole correspondence with England, with the niece and with the tutors of the princely children, was embarrassed, or at least changed. He was obliged to have the letters received by him read to him by a friend whom he could trust: but he could trust no one. Only one female friend he found out who deserved the distinguished preference of his confidence, and that was none else than Clotilda. He who did not, like a youth, squander his secrets, could nevertheless venture to put Clotilda in possession of his greatest, and to make her book-keeper and reader to him of the letters of her mother, the so-called niece. In fact, he held women's power of keeping a secret to be greater than ours,—at least in weighty matters and in the concerns of men whom they love.—But just hear what the Devil did last winter: to me it is memorable.

His Lordship received a letter from Flamin's mother, in which she renewed her old entreaties for a speedier promotion of the beloved child, and her inquiries after his fortunes at the Parsonage. Luckily just then Clotilda was making a visit at St. Luna, and saved him the journey to Maienthal. He visited the Chamberlain, to hear the letter from the mouth of his reader. He had great difficulty in securing in Clotilda's chamber an hour free from eavesdroppers. When he at last got it, and Clotilda began to read to him the letter, the latter was called away from the reading by her step-mother. He hears her immediately come back again, read the letter over in a sort of darkly murmuring tone, and say softly that she was going away again, but would come back in a moment. After some minutes Clotilda appears, and when his Lordship asks why she went out the second time, she denies a second leaving,—his Lordship insists,—she likewise persists,—finally Clotilda falls upon the bitter conjecture whether Matthieu may not have been there, and with his theatrical art and throat, which contained all human voices, himself have mocked and travestied her, in order under her credentials to read the important letter. Ah, there was too much in favor of the conjecture and too little against it! To be sure Matthieu could not now undertake upon Flamin, whose academic career had just expired, the October-test of the shoulder-device; but he stuck (so it afterward seemed to Clotilda and his Lordship) with his green-frog-feet to that good soul, and, under the cloak of love for Agatha and for his friend, hung out his threads, let the wind swing and stretch them across between the princely palace and the Parsonage-house,—kept on spinning one after another, until at last his father, the minister Schleunes, should have woven the right web for the entangling of the prey.... I confess, this conjecture throws light for me on a thousand things.—

Victor was even more astounded than we are, and proposed to his Lordship whether he might not, without injury to his oath, reveal to Clotilda his induction into these mysteries, as he had two reasons for it: first, her delicacy would be spared embarrassment at the appearance which her sisterly love must otherwise, in her opinion, have in his eyes;[154] secondly, one keeps a secret better, if only *one* more person helps him hold his tongue about it, as is well known from the case of Midas's barber and the reeds; the third reason was, that he had several reasons. His Lordship naturally did not refuse.

For the rest, he introduced his Victor with no pedantic rules of march to the ice-course and tilt-yard of the court. He merely advised him neither intentionally to seek nor to shun any one, particularly the house of Schleunes,—to unbridle his friend Flamin, who was in Matthieu's leading-strings, and to guide him, instead of by the bit, rather with a friendly hand,—and himself to covet the rank of a doctor, and nothing more. He said, rules before experience were like geometry before the operation for the cataract. Even after the harvest of experience Gratian's *homme de cour* and Rochefoucauld's Maxims were not so good as the memoirs and history of courts, i. e. the experiences of others. Finally he appealed to his own example, and said, it was only within a few years that he had understood the following rules of *his* father's.

The greatest hatred, like the greatest virtue and the worst dogs, is quiet.—Women have more *flow*, and fewer *overflows*, of emotion than we.— There is nothing one hates so much in another as a *new* fault, which he does not show till after some years.—One commits the most follies among people who are of no account.—It is the most common and pernicious delusion, that one always takes one's self to be the only one who remarks certain things.— Women and soft-hearted people are timid only in their own dangers, and courageous in those of others, where they have to save them.—Trust no one (and though it were a saint) who in the smallest trifle leaves his honor in the lurch; and a woman of that kind still less.—Most persons confound their vanity with their sense of honor, and allege wounds inflicted on the one as wounds inflicted on the other, and the reverse.—What we undertake from humanity, we should always accomplish, if we mixed in no selfishness with our motive.—The warmth of a man is by nothing more easily misunderstood than by the warmth of a young man.

The last observation, which perhaps had a nearer reference, he had made while he was already on the shore of the island in the attitude of leave-taking, which he did with that considerate courtesy which in his rank guides the hands and arms of even parents and children.[155]

THIRD INTERCALARY DAY

Meteorological Observations upon Man

When, in the former chapter, I wrote down his Lordship's pithy sayings, I found that some came into my own head, which might be serviceable for the Intercalary Day. I have never made one observation alone, but always twenty, thirty, in succession, and this very first one is a proof of it!

When any one remains modest, not after praise, but after censure, then he is really so.

The talk of the people, and still more the letters of maidens, have a peculiar euphony, arising from a constant interchange of long and short syllables (Trochees or Iambuses).

The two things which a maiden most easily forgets are, first, how she looks (hence mirrors were invented); and, secondly, wherein the pronoun *that* differs from the conjunction *that*. I fear, however, that they will from to-day forward observe the distinction, merely for the sake of upsetting my assertion. And *then* one of my two touchstones is lost[156] with which I have hitherto tested learned ladies; the second, which I retain, is the left thumb-nail, which the penknife has sometimes notched full of red marks, but seldom, however, because they drive the quill more easily than they make the pen.

One who has received many benefits ceases to *count*, and begins to *weigh* them, as if they were votes.

The transporting one's self into good characters does more harm to a poet or player, who retains his own, than entering into bad ones. A clergyman who, besides, is free to take only the first of these steps, is more exposed to moral *atony* [157] than the maker of verses and parts, who is able to make up again for a holy part by an unholy one.

Passion makes the best observations and the wretchedest conclusions. It is a telescope whose field is so much the brighter, as it is narrower.

Men require of a new Prince, Bishop, Domestic Tutor, Nursery Tutor, Capon-Stuffer, Town-Musician, or Town-Recorder *only in the first week* very special merits which were wanting in his predecessor; for in the second they have forgotten what they required and what they missed.

Such sentences please women most and stay by them longest.

Therefore, by way of reward, I will manufacture more than one upon themselves.—They regard others only as younger, not as fairer, than themselves.

They are even ten times more artful and false towards each other than towards us; but we are almost more honest to each other than to them.

They look to it only that one *does* justify himself with them, no matter *how*.

They forgive a loved man more stains than we do a loved woman. Hence the romance-writers let the heroes of their quill guzzle, storm, duel, and stay overnight anywhere and everywhere, without the least prejudice to the hero.—The heroine, on the contrary, must sit at home by her mother and be a little angel.

On the whole, they are so delicate, so mild, so sympathetic, so refined, so loving and love-thirsty, that I cannot get it into my head why it is that they cannot really like each other, unless it is for some such reason as this, that they are too courteous to each other to be formally reconciled or formally at variance with each other. You dear ones! you sometimes love a man because he has a friend and is one. O how beautifully would a friend of your own sex *fit* [158] you!

One learns taciturnity best among people who have none, and loquacity among the taciturn.

If self-knowledge is the road to virtue, so is virtue still more the road to self-knowledge. An amended and purified soul is darkened by the least moral poison, as certain precious stones are by every other, and now after the amendment one observes for the first time how many impurities still lurk in all corners.

I will close with some rules for improvement. Never, when the bosom has to fear that thorn in the side, anger, eloquently represent to any one his faults; for in the very act of convincing him of his guilt thou persuadest thyself of it, and so becomest exasperated. Picture to thyself every morning the possible situations and passions into which during the day thou mayst fall; then thou wilt deport thyself better, for one seldom behaves badly, in a repeated case, the second time.—Is thy friend angry with thee, then provide him an opportunity of showing thee a great favor. Over that his heart must needs melt, and he will love thee again.—No resolves are great save those which one has more than once to execute. Hence *forbearing* is harder than *undertaking*; for the former has to be kept up longer, and the latter is also linked with the sense of a double expression of power, a psychological and a moral.—Only despair not at a single failing; and let thy whole repentance be—a nobler action.—Only make thyself (by stoicism, or in ally way thou canst) *tranquil*, then wilt thou have little trouble in making thyself *virtuous* also.—Begin the culture of thy heart, not with the rearing of noble motives, but with the extirpation of bad ones. When the weeds are once withered or uprooted, then will the nobler flowerage spontaneously and vigorously spring up.—The virtuous heart, like the body, grows sound and strong more by *work* than by good *food*.

Therefore I can stop.

13
DOG-POST-DAY

In regard to his Lordship I have three words to say, that is, three opinions to state.

The first is wholly improbable; it is, that, like all men of the world and of business, he regards mankind as an apparatus for experiments, as so much hunting-gear, war-material, knitting-work: such men look upon heaven only as the key-board to earth, and the soul as orderly-sergeant of the body; they carry on wars, not for the sake of winning crowns of oak-leaves, but to secure the oak soil and acorns; they prefer the successful man to the deserving one; they break oaths and hearts to serve the state; they respect poetry, philosophy, and religion, but as means; they respect riches, statistics of national prosperity, and health, as objects; all they honor about pure Mathesis[159] and pure female virtue is the transmutation of each into impure for manufactures and armies; in the higher astronomy all they care for is the transformation of suns into odometers[160] and way-marks for pepper-fleets, and in the most exalted *magister legens* [161] they seek only an alluring tavern-sign for poor universities.

The second opinion is at least the opposite of the first, and an improvement upon it: it is, that to his Lordship, as to other great men, the race-course is the goal and the steps taken the garlands.—Fortune and misfortune differ, with him, not in *worth*, but in *manner*; both are, in his view, two converging race-tracks toward the eternity's ring of inner promotion; all accidents of this life are to him mere arithmetical examples in *unknown* terms, which he solves, not however as a merchant, but as an indifferentialist[162] and algebraist, to whom products and multiplicands are of equal interest, and to whom it is all one whether he reckons by letters or by hundredweights.

Verily, a man has almost as much to reproach himself with, if he is discontented, as if he had committed a crime; and inasmuch as it depends upon his ocean of thoughts, whether he will raise out of it as an island an Otaheite-Arcadia or the lowest hell, he deserves all that he creates....

Nevertheless, the third opinion is the true one, and at the same time it is mine: his Lordship, how much soever he may seem to be an indeclinable man, who has no object, but is a verb in *mi*, has nevertheless the following paradigm (and so inversely we find in the most ordinary man a short plan for the most singular one): he is one of the unhappy great ones who have too much genius, too much wealth, and too little repose and knowledge, to be habitually happy; they hunt pleasure instead of virtue, and miss both, and cry out at last over every bitter drop which is given them in a sugar-loaf; like silver-plate, precisely at the point of melting in the fire of pleasure are they the most inclined to overspread themselves with a dark skin; their ambition; which otherwise hides with plans the emptiness of high life, is not strong enough for their heart, which in this emptiness withers; they do good from pride, but without the love of doing it; they play with the empty shell of life as with a ringlet, and deem it not even worth the while to shorten it; and yet they do deem it worth the while, when they, who stand through this night-frost of the soul, outwardly smiling and cold, inwardly all in a fever, without hope, fear, or faith, renouncing all, making light of everything, and shut up in themselves,—when they feel a stroke of death, a great sorrow clutch at their unhappy hearts.—Ah the poor lord! can thy heart then find no rest till it finds it under the lid of black marble?

"Ah the poor lord!" his son incessantly repeated, as with oppressed soul he went toward Maienthal. The outward heaven around him was still; a great cloud completely overspread it, but rested on a blue rim along the whole circle of the horizon. In Victor's breast, on the contrary, streams of air rushed against each other and whirled together into a hurricane, drinking up brooks and tearing up trees. His father's image hung pale in this tempest. Victor's future days were hurled to and fro.—His future life was compressed into a narrow, veiled image, and it distressed him just as much to think that he *must* live it as *how* he must.

What saddened him most was the mere external and trifling circumstance that his father had remained alone and concealed in the depths of the island. Once the conjecture came over him, whether the greater part of what he had witnessed had not been mere dramatic machinery which his father (who in his youth had been a tragic poet) had employed to give more firmness to his vow of silence; but he was immediately disgusted at his own heart. Why are the purest souls tormented with a multitude of disgusting, poisonous thoughts, which like spiders crawl up on the shining walls, and which they only have the trouble of crushing to death? Ah, our *victories* are not wholly distinguishable from our *defeats*!

It is singular that the *perspective* thought of Clotilda's blood-relationship to Flamin was the one which he followed out least of all.

When man can obtain from reason no balsamic relief, he begs it at the hands of Hope and Illusion; and they two then willingly share his sorrow. Just as the blue sky of to-day by little and little peered through light seams in the clouds, and the sea of mist collected into hanging lakes, so also did the dark thoughts break asunder in Victor's soul.—And when the swollen masses of cloud in the broad blue passed into fleece, till at last the blue sea swallowed up all banks of vapor, and bore nothing on its infinite expanse but the blazing sun, then did Victor's soul also cleanse itself from vapors, and the sun-image of Emanuel, whom he was to-day to reach, shone soft and warm and cloudless into all his wounds.... The form of his loved Dahore, the form of his loved father, the form of his hidden mother, and all beloved images, reposed like moons in a mournful group over his head; and this sadness, and the sacred oath to keep himself virtuous and obey all his father's wishes, breathed upon his inflamed bosom some solace in regard to his father's fate.

He could even to-day see the sun go down behind the church-tower of Maienthal.

The broad cleared-up sky made him more tender, the thought of falling to-day upon the heart of a noble man, whose soul dwelt above this blue atmosphere, made him more exalted, the hope of being consoled by this man for his whole life made him more tranquil.—

He hastened, and, his haste drew out the saddest lute-stop of his soul. For he seemed not to be going over the summer fields, but they seemed rather to be hurrying along before him; landscape after landscape, theatres of woods, theatres of grain-fields, flew by; new hills rose with other lights, and lifted up their woods, and others with theirs dropped down; long, shadowy steppes ran backward before the flood of yellow sunlight; now valleys full of flowers billowed around him, now bare, hot hill-shores carried him upward; the stream murmured close to his ear, and suddenly its windings glistened from far away across poppy-fields; white roads and green paths met him, and fled from him, and led round the broad earth; full villages, with gleaming windows, swept by, and gardens with undressed children; the declining sun was now lifted up, now lost again, and now withdrawn to the summits of the hills.—

This fleeting of Nature's dissolving views bedimmed his moistened eye, and brightened the inner world; but the steady abiding of an incessant music, the constant choir of larks above him, whose contending cries melted to one in his soul, this distant hum from air and woods and bushes, this harmonica of Nature, moved him to say to himself: "Why do I in this solitude hold back every drop that would fall? No; besides, I am too sensitive to-day, and I will exhaust myself before I see the beloved man."

At last he ascended the broad mountain that stations itself with its scattered columns of trees and gray cubes of rock before Maienthal, which lies in greenness at its foot.... Then the earth, tuned by the Creator, rang with a thousand strings; the same harmony stirred the stream, divided into gold and gloom, the humming flower-cup, the peopled air, and the waving bush; the reddened east and the reddened west stood stretched out like the two rose-taffeta wings of a harpsichord, and a tremulous sea gushed from the open heavens and the open earth....

He burst into a mingling flood of tears at once of joy and sorrow, and the past and the future simultaneously stirred his heart. The sun with ever-increasing swiftness dropped down the heavens, and the more swiftly did he climb the mountain, the quicker to follow its flight with his eye. And there he looked down into the village of Maienthal, that glimmered among moist shadows....

At his feet, and on this mountain, lay, stretched like a crowned giant, like a transplanted spring-island, an English park. This mountain toward the south and one toward the north met and formed a cradle in which the peaceful village rested, and over which the morning and the evening sun spun and spread out their golden veil. In five gleaming ponds trembled five duskier evening heavens, and every wave that leaped up painted itself to a ruby in the hovering fire of the sun. Two brooks waded, in shifting distances, darkened by roses and willows, over the long meadow-land, and a watering fire-wheel,[163] like a pulsating heart, forced the sunset-reddened water through all the green flower-vases. Everywhere nodded flowers, those butterflies of the vegetable world, on every moss-grown brook-stone, from every tender stalk, round every window, a flower rocked in its fragrance, and scarlet lupines traced their blue and red veins over a garden without a hedge. A transparent wood of gold-green birches climbed, in the high grass over there, the sides of the northern mountain, on whose summit five tall fir-trees, as ruins of a prostrated forest, held their eyrie.

Emanuel's small house stood at the end of the village, in a tangled growth of honeysuckle, and in the embrace of a linden-tree which grew through it.—His heart gushed up within him: "Blessings on thee, quiet haven! hallowed by a soul which here looks up to heaven, and waits to launch into the sea of eternity!"—Suddenly the windows of the abbey where Clotilda had been educated flung upon him the flames of the evening-redness,—and the sun went, softly as a Penn, toward America,—and the thin night spread itself over nature,—and the green hermitage of Emanuel wrapped itself in obscurity.... Then he knelt there alone on the mountain, on that throne-step, and looked into the glowing west, and over the whole still earth, and into the heavens, and expanded his spirit to think on God.... As he knelt, all was so sublime and so mild, — worlds and suns came up from the east, and the little insect, with his play of colors, nestled down into his mealy flower-cup, — the evening-wind flapped its immeasurable wing, and the little naked lark rested warmly under the soft-feathered breast of the mother, — a man stood on the mountain-ridge, and a golden-chafer on the stamens; ... and the Eternal loved his whole world.

His spirit was now made up to take in a great man, and he yearned for the voice of a brother.

He staggered, without following any path, down into the village, with the pewit in its great circles, and the may-chafer in its little ones, sweeping around him. At the foot of the mountain the hybrid day grew darker, — in the starry heaven the curtain rose, — the vapor of evening, which had gone up hot, fell cold, as men do, back to the earth: one more loud lark went circling upward, as the last echo of day, over the mountain.

At last he neared Emanuel's linden. He would rather have embraced him under the great heavens than under the close ceiling of a room. Through the window he saw an uncommonly beautiful youth standing and playing on a flute. The player drew out of its heavenly gates a fugitive and floating elysium. Victor listened to him for a long time, in order to still his beating heart; at last, with tearful eyes, he went round the house, and would fain have fallen speechlessly and blindly on the necks of the youth and of Emanuel. As he passed along before the window, the youth did not return his greeting; as he opened the house-door, a soft chime of bells began to make music. Then the youth came out immediately, and asked him, in a friendly tone, who was there; for he was blind. Victor stepped into a Holy of Holies when he entered the apartment lined with linden-leaves, which was the nest of the winged man, who at this moment was out of it, under the great night of God. Emanuel was to return toward midnight. The room was open and clean; some leaves of fruits which had been eaten lay on the table; flowers glowed around all the windows; a telescope leaned against the wall; remains of an Oriental wardrobe bespoke the East Indian....

The voice of the beautiful youth had in his ear something inexpressibly touching, because it seemed like one he knew; it went deep into his heart, like the melody of a song that sounds up from childhood. He could rest freely with the steady gaze of love upon that face, that looked out into an eternal night; he wanted to kiss those childish lips full of melodies, and still he hesitated. But as he went out of the house again in quest of Emanuel, and when the bells began to chime again, — for they sounded whenever the door opened, to announce to the blind one every arrival, — then he could no longer restrain himself amidst the lovely music, but he touched the mouth of the blind one, as he leaned at the open window, with a kiss as soft as a breath. "Ah, angel! art thou, then, come down again from heaven?" said the blind one, confounding him with some well-known being or other.

How good was it to be out of doors! The evening-bell of the village sounded its call over the slumbering fields, and a distant soul was inclining its ear, perhaps, to catch the dying echoes of its broken tones. The evening wind, rustling through twigs full of green fruits, joined in. The evening star—the moon of our twilight—rested kindly on the road of the sun and of the moon, and sent its solace in the interval during the absence of both.— "Where mayst thou be at this moment, my Emanuel? Art thou resting, perhaps, in the sight of the evening-red,—or gazing into the starry sea?—art thou in the ecstasy we call a prayer,—or ..."

At this moment, all at once the thought flashed up in him, that, as to-night St. John's day began, his Emanuel might have expired in the enjoyment of the evening.... The more eagerly did he seek after him with his eyes under every tree, in every deeper shadow; he looked up to the hills, as if he might see him there, and to the stars, as if even there he might venture to seek him.—He went round the village, whose circular wall was a festoon of cherry-trees which silvered the green circumference with a milky-way of blossoms long since fallen, and hurried over the ruins of the houses which the children had built during the day, towards the fading windows of the abbey, which rose on the southern mountain down whose slope he had entered the village; for the blind one had told him that this mountain was Emanuel's observatory, and that he went thither every night. The green stairway, which made its successive landings of terraces and moss-banks, and on which a balustrade of bush-work ran upward, led him to a mountain which terminated sublimely in the ether with a tall weeping-birch. With every grass-plot, as from a bath, new limbs of dark Nature lifted themselves; he went on, as if from one planet to another. Across the ascending, darkling fields streamed the night-wind, and lonesomely swept on from wood to wood, and its ruffling fingers played with the plumage of the sleeping bird and the down of the whirring night-butterfly. Victor looked over toward the evening-red which Night had taken as a rose to wear on the bosom whereon suns repose. The sea of eternity lay in the form of night on the silver-sand of worlds and suns, and from the bottom of that sea the grains of sand glistened far up through the deep.

Around the weeping-birch swelled an unaccountable melodious murmur, which he had this very day heard on the island. At length he stood up there under the birch, and the music, like that of an harmonica which has just stolen over paradises and through hedges of flowers, was loud around him; but he saw nothing further, save a high grassy altar (the birthplace of Emanuel's letter) and a low grassy bench. From what invisible hand, he thought with awe, can these tones issue, which seem to glide off from angels, as they fly over the next world, from mingling souls, when a too great bliss breathes itself out into a sigh, and the sigh dissipates itself into distant dying sound? It must be forgiven him, if on such a day, which threw his soul into growing agitations, in this awful hour of night, under this melodious mourning-tree, on this Holy of Holies of the invisible Emanuel, he at last came to believe that *he* had this evening taken his flight from life, and that his soul, full of love, was still floating around him in these echoes and yearnings for the first and last embrace. He lost himself more and more in the tones and in the silence round about them,—his soul grew to a dream within him, and the whole nocturnal landscape grew to a cloud made of the sleep in which this light dream hung,—the fountain of endless life, flung up by the Eternal, flew far above the earth in the immeasurable arch with the spraying silver-sparks of suns over immensity; gleaming it encircled the whole vault of night, and the reflection of the Infinite overspread the dark eternity.

O Eternal One, if we saw not thy starry heaven, how much would our heart, sunk into the mire of earth, know of thee and of immortality?—

Suddenly in the east the night grew lighter, because the floating glimmer of the moon darted up on the Alpine ridges that hid the orb, and all at once the unaccountable tones and the leaves and the night-wind grew louder. Then Victor awoke as out of a dream and out of life, and clasped the harmonious, fleeting airs to his languishing bosom, and, amidst the gushing tears which, like a rain-cloud, veiled from him the whole landscape, he cried out, beside himself: "Ah, Emanuel, come!—Ah, I thirst for thee—Float no more in sound, thou blessed one; take thy deposed human face, and appear to me, and slay me by a shudder, and keep me in thy arms!" ...

Lo! while the dim tear-drop still stood in his eye, and the moon still lingered behind the Alps, there came up the mountain a white form with closed eyes,—smiling, transfigured, blissful,—turning toward Sirius....

"Emanuel, dost thou appear to me?" cried Horion, trembling, and melted into a new flood of tears. The form opened its eyes,—it spread out its arms. Victor saw not,—heard not; he glowed and trembled. The form flew to meet him, and he gave himself up, saying, "Take me!" They touched each other,—they embraced each other,—the night-wind swept through them,— the strange music sounded nearer,—a star shot down,—the moon flew up over the Alps....

And when with its Eden-light it suffused the cheeks of the unknown apparition, Victor recognized that it was his dear teacher, *Dahore*, who had to-day cast his image into the mirror on the island. And Dahore said: "Beloved son, dost thou still know thy teacher? I am Emanuel and Dahore." Then the embrace grew closer. Horion would fain have compressed his gratitude for a whole childhood into one kiss, and lay dissolved in the arms of the teacher and in the arms of loving ecstasy.

Twine around each other tightly, ye blessed ones; press your full hearts to each other even till you press tears out of them; forget heaven and earth, and prolong the sublime embrace!—Ah! so soon as it is dissolved, then has this frail life henceforward nothing firmer wherewith to knit you together than the beginning of the—second....

At last Emanuel drew himself out of the attitude of love, and, bending aside, gazed like a sun, with large and open look, into Horion's face, and confronted with rapture the ennobled spirit and countenance of his blooming favorite. The latter sank before the look of love involuntarily on his knee, and said, with uplifted face: "O my teacher, my father! O thou angel! dost thou, then, still love me so exceedingly?"—But he wept too much for utterance, and his words were unintelligible, and died in his heart....

Without answering, Emanuel laid his hand on the head of the kneeling pupil, and turned his glorified eye toward the glittering heavens, and said, with solemn voice: "This head, thou Eternal One, dedicates itself now to thee in this great night. Let only thy second world fill this head and this heart, and may the little, dark earth never satisfy them!—O my Horion! here on this mountain, on which, after a year, I go up from the earth, I conjure thee, by the great second world above us, by all the great thoughts wherewith the Eternal at this moment appears in thee,—I conjure thee to be still good, even when I shall have long been dead."

Emanuel knelt down to him, held up the exhausted youth, and bent towards his paling face, and said, in a low and prayerful tone, "My beloved! my beloved! when we both are dead, in the second world may God never part us,—never part me and thee!"—He wept not, and yet could say no more; their two hearts, knit together, rested on each other, and night veiled silently their mute love and their great thoughts.

14
DOG-POST-DAY

I have only two things to explain before going further,—the mysterious music and the shutting of the eyes. The former proceeded from an Æolian harp laid on the weeping-birch. As often as Emanuel came hither by night he let these breathed-out tones intermingle like blossoms with the whispering leaves, in order to exalt himself when he looked alone upon the exalted night. His eyes he often closed before the sun and the moon, whenever his inner man, winged like a cherub, had leave to bury itself in soft fantasies; into the streaming, many-colored waves of light which crowd through the eyelids he would then plunge, as into a zephyr, for a delicious swim, and in this light-bath the higher light-magnet within him drew heavenly light out of earthly light. As there are but few souls that know how far the harmony of outward nature with our own reaches, and in how very great a degree the whole creation is but an Æolian harp, with longer and shorter strings, with slower and swifter vibrations, passive before a divine breath,[164]—I demand not that every one should forgive this Emanuel.—

After this finding of each other again, which threw a far gleam over a whole life, the two came home to the blind youth; and his flute carried the heart softly over in dream from the tossings of fevered blood into the tranquil ether of heaven.

As I love so to be about Emanuel, the reader will not begrudge me the pleasure of turning over the leaves of all the hours which we are permitted to spend in his house, and to go along regularly, step by step.

The morning for the first time disclosed to the pupil of Emanuel, as it does to children, what a Christmas present the night had provided for his heart. What a form came before him in the morning-radiance, when the still, childlike, composed face of the teacher, over which storms had once passed, as on the soft, white moon volcanoes have flamed, smiled upon him in such wise that his inner being melted into mute bliss! Especially when beheld in *profile* did this lofty form appear to stand on the brink of earth, and to look down into the *second* hemisphere of the heavens, which is hid from us by the gravestone and the rich pasture-ground of this life. His countenance was transfigured when he lifted it to heaven, when he named God or Eternity, when he spoke of the longest day; in its light the leaf-gold of the present paled to the dead-gold of the past, and his spirit hung hovering over the body, as genii bloom out of flowers in arabesques. Never did Victor so easily attune himself, when coming out of a dream, to the new day, as he did this morning with Emanuel's voice, which was, so to speak, the music of the spheres to the blue heaven of his eyes, from which, as from that of Egypt, never a drop fell; from incapacity of the tear-glands, he could never weep; nor did this life any longer agitate his soul.

The pure morning-apartment seemed to make the soul pure and still. He was the greatest bodily Purist; he washed his body quite as often as his clothes; and the uncleanness of medical language, even to the very words, — as, e. g. toothpicks, &c., — was avoided by his stainless tongue. Even so did his heart remain unsoiled by so much as the images of great sins, and this unconscious innocence, as well as an unacquaintedness with our artful manners, made him, in the eyes of three different classes, either a child — or a maiden — or an angel.

The breakfast of fruits and water, which, in fact, made up his whole bill of fare, called up reprovingly before our Victor the wine and coffee-grounds wherewith he had sometimes had to manure, like earthly ones, the flowers of his spirit. Flower-pots were Dahore's snuff-boxes, and glowed under the linden-green, which, with two tame, and yet free, ground-sparrows skipping through it, was the live, growing ceiling-piece of the apartment. His soul seemed also, like a Brahmin, to live on poetical flowers, and his speech was often, like his manners, Indian, — i. e. poetic. So was there throughout, as with divers magnates of men, a striking pre-established harmony between outward nature and his heart; he readily found in the corporeal the physiognomy of the spiritual, and *vice versâ*; he said matter, considered as thought, was just as noble and spiritual as any other thought, and that we represented to ourselves in it, after all, only the Divine conceptions of it. For example, during breakfast he lost himself in the glimmering dew-drop on a stock-gillyflower, and, by moving his eye to and fro, played through the gamut of its harpsichord of colors. "There must," said he, "be some harmony or other of accordant sounds between this minute particle of water and my spirit, as between virtue and me, because otherwise neither could so ravish me. And is, then, this accord which man makes with the whole creation (only in different octaves) a mere play of the Eternal, and no resonance of a nearer, greater harmony?" In the same way he would often gaze at a glimmering coal, till in his eyes it had expanded to a flaming meadow, on which, illumined by tender fancies, he roamed up and down....

Have patience, reader, with this flowery soul; we will both think that men can more easily have one religion than one philosophy, and that every system presupposes its peculiar weaving in the heart, and that the heart is the bud of the head.

The only circumstance that pained the blessed Victor this morning was, that he could not embrace the fair blind youth, and ask, "Have we not already once lived together, and is not my voice as familiar to thee as thine is to me?" For he looked upon him (as I do too), for several reasons, as the concealed son of Pastor Eymann. But as Dahore kept silent on the subject,—into whose clear, bright heaven one could otherwise look down even to the least nebulous star,—he feared before these holy ears he should be speaking too near to the verge of his oath of silence, though he should only disclose his inquiring conjectures about the blind one. This Julius seemed to have only two root-fibres in his nature, of which the one went to his flute, and the other to his teacher. On his white face, whereon the rapture of the musical genius and the abstractedness of the blind dreamer were blended with an almost womanly beauty, lay the reflection of his teacher, and its fibres had, like lute-strings, stirred only to harmonious movements. The poor blind one, who looked upon his Dahore as his father, was turned about, like down, by his lightest breath. Victor often drew the head of the dear blind one close to his face, in order to inspect the disordered eyes, and judge whether they might be restored. But though he saw with pain that the unhappy one must remain incurable on the full, radiant earth, nevertheless he kept on repeating his minute investigation, merely for the sake of having the dear, enchanting form nearer to his eye and his soul.

In the morning Emanuel, as cicerone of Nature, led his guest through the ruins and antiques of the earth: for every tree is an eternal antique. How different is a walk with a religious[165] man from one with a vulgar, worldly soul! The earth appeared to him holy, just fallen from the hands of the Creator; it was to him as if he were walking in a planet hanging over us and clothed with flowers. Emanuel showed him God and love everywhere mirrored, but everywhere transformed,—in the light, in—colors, in the scale of living creatures, in the blossom and in human beauty, in the pleasures of animals, in the thoughts of men and in the circles of worlds; for either everything or nothing is his shadow. So the sun paints its image on all creatures,—great in the ocean, many-colored in the dew-drop, small on the human retina, as mock-sun on the cloud, red on the apple, silvery on the stream, seven-colored in the falling rain, and gleaming over the whole moon and over all its other worlds.

Victor felt to-day, for the first time, the enlargement and transfiguration of his conscious being before a spirit which, *like* his, but *excelling* his, like a spherical concave mirror reflected all the features of his nobler part in colossal size. The whole vulgar portion of his nature crept away when the higher, painted by Dahore on a large scale, erected itself above the low impulses. A man whom the perihelion of a great man does not set on fire and beside himself is nothing worth. He was hardly willing to speak, so that he might only hear *him* all the time, although he had it in mind to stay here a good many days. As before a higher being and before the woman of his love, in whose presence one will neither show his head nor his tongue, so had he, renouncing self, sunk into pure truth and love. All the varnish of the little relations of place and citizenly respectability had cracked so clean off, and they all stood before him there so moss-grown, that he would not so much as name the names of Göttingen, of Flachsenfingen, or empty incidents of life, or strange personalities. In fact, Victor had a slight contempt for men who care more for the directions to the bookbinder than for the book, and more for the review of an author than for his system, and to whom the earth is no deciphering chancery of the book of nature, but a parlor (a talking-room), a news-office of wretched personalities, which they care neither to profit by, nor to retain, nor to estimate, but merely to tell; and he was disgusted with the German societies, in which there is so little philosophizing.—Oh, how blest he was, for once to think a whole day in company with another, and, what is still finer, to be permitted to poetize with him!

His doubts upon the greatest matters which can weigh down our minds and lift up our hearts grew to-day to questions; the questions, to hopes; the hopes, to presentiments. There are truths of which one hopes that great men will be more strongly convinced than one can be one's self; and one will therefore by their conviction confirm and complete his own. Dahore held the two great truths (God and immortality) which, like two pillars, bear up the universe, firmly to his heart; but, like the rarer men to whom the truth is not merely the *shew-bread* of vanity and the dessert of the head, but a *holy supper* and *love-feast* full of the *spirit of life* for their weary heart, he cared little, if he could make no proselytes. Victor felt that *he* understood handling the artillery-train and the electric pistols and batteries of the art of disputation better than Emanuel; he would have abhorred his own tongue if he had directed its readiness against this fair soul. He was silent for two reasons. "Undertake," said he, "to give a molten image, an altar-piece, of a great, shining truth that embraces thy whole being,—to do this on the flying second-hand whereon one stands in transient conversation, with the few dry paints wherewith human ideas are to be colored, and with the clumsy human tongue wherewith you must daub on these grains of color,—I tell you, a *silhouette*, a transparent asterism, will be all you can produce." The light heaven of certain simple-hearted men of deep feeling veils, like the outer one, all its suns, except the warmest, under the sheen of a void blue; but the unclean heaven of others full of wit and logic is bedizened with *mock-suns*, bows, northern lights, clouds, and redness.

The second, better reason why he scorned the honor of opposition was his heart, which contained in itself more than the head could throw light upon. Certain views cannot be detached so easily as wall-pictures in Italy, and transferred from one head into another. The *light* which another can give thee *shows*, but *constructs* not, the house-furniture of thy interior, and what the light really *creates* with some is meteorological appearance, optical illusion, but no substance.[166]—Hence all turns not upon the showing and seeing of a truth, i. e. of an object, but upon the effects which it works through thy whole inner being. For how is it that there are men who, as Socrates did Aristides, make us better merely by our being with them?—How do great authors bring it about, that their invisible spirit in their works seizes and holds us fast, without our being able to quote the words and passages whereby they do it, as a thickly leaved forest always murmurs, though not a single branch stirs?—Why did Emanuel overmaster his beloved Horion—more than by broad thesis-formulas, *rationes decidendi* and *sententiæ magistrales*—merely by the transfiguration in his countenance, by the low echo-tone of his voice, by the radiance of his look, and by the devotion in his breast, when he spoke solemnly truths which were old to speech and new to the heart, like the following?—

Man goes, like the earth, from *west* to *east*; but it seems to him as if he went, with it, from east to west, from life to the grave.

What is highest and noblest in man conceals itself, and is without use for the practical world, (as the highest mountains bear no herbage,) and out of the chain of fine *thoughts* only some members can be detached as actions. [167]

Our aimless activity, our clutchings at the air, must appear to higher beings like the clutching of dying men at the bed-clothes.

The spirit awakes and will awake when the light of the senses goes out, just as sleepers awake when the night-light is extinguished.

Why did these thoughts linger like things of awe in the soul?—Because Horion felt something higher than language, which is invented only for every-day sensations, can ever represent; because, even in his childhood, he hated systems which thrust out of sight all that is inexplicable; and because the human spirit feels itself as much oppressed in the explicable and finite as it is in a mine, or in the thought of the heavenly space overhead being somewhere or other boarded up.

How should he have had the heart or the occasion on such a day to ask Emanuel about his dying-day, or about Clotilda? Victor had that poetry of fellow-feeling which easily puts itself into the place of the most unlike persons, of women and philosophers. In the evening Dahore went to the abbey to teach astronomy, his most beloved science. During the astronomical school-hour the open face of Julius became an open heaven; he told his Victor everything, as if he were a second father. Now he related to him frankly that the year before an angel had again and again come to him, who grasped his hand, gave him flowers, spoke to him kindly, and at last vanished from him into heaven, but had left him a letter, which he was permitted to have read to him a year after, at Whitsuntide, by Clotilda,— yes, and that this good angel had yesterday flown by him with a kiss. Victor smiled with delight, but concealed his conjecture that *he* looked upon the angel to be a shy, loving maiden from the boarding-school.—"But yesterday," said Victor, "I only was the angel that kissed thee *thus!*" and repeated it. Julius knew no fairer gift to make to those he loved than the picture of his father,—the portraiture of his exalted love, which forgot no human being, because it was based, not upon the superiorities, but upon the necessities, of men,—further, of his indulgence, of his disinterestedness, since a long virtue spared him the battle against his heart, and now he did nothing but what he wished to, and since the next world, hanging low down before him, preached a peculiar independence upon necessities. Five hundred thousand fixed stars of the first magnitude, according to Lambert, hardly give a light equal to that of the nearer full moon,—and so the present always outshines our inner world; but soar nearer to the fixed star of the next world, then does it grow to a sun, which transforms the moon of time and of the present into a petty nebula.—As to this Emanuel, all Maienthalers loved him (even the Parson, although he was a non-Catholic, non-Lutheran, and non-Calvinist); and he loved to be dependent on something, on others' love.[168]—During this description Victor yearned for him again with as much emotion as if they had been separated a year; accordingly, in the flush of evening he laid himself down under the birch-leaves opposite the school, in order immediately, with ardent arms, to take him prisoner.

And as Victor lifted his soul on the tall, white columns of the park planned by his Lordship, on the sublime sculpture which wrote out a great thought that looked like a tempest, and just as he had carried a bee that had dropped down, his wings being glued up with honey, to the beehive sill,—just then Dahore, with a friendly manner, came up. The latter entered, himself,—for Victor would have held the covert starting of a subject as a sin,—on that of Clotilda, and said this used to be her favorite spot, and the resting-bench of her quiet soul. The place was not grand, but, what is more, it was opposite to something grand (even physical greatness, e. g. a mountain, needs distance as a pedestal); it lay in the deepest part of the dell, encircled with Emanuel's flower-chains, which he often laid out without enclosure, because all Maienthalers respected his little joys,—breathed upon by great clover-fields,—overspread by the moon, which in spring, only after reaching the mountain-top, beamed down this deep valley with a mournful medley of birch-shadows, water-glistenings, and bright spots,—and, finally, adorned with a grassy bench, which I should not have mentioned had it not been planted at both ends with great, drooping flowers, which, with a tender feeling, no one crushed who sat down between them. How was Victor surprised or enraptured when Emanuel asked about this Clotilda! Like jewels of dew, like tears of joy, all the words of his teacher fell into his languishing heart, because they were eulogies upon her tender soul, which leads its own tears only into those of *others*, and hides them before dry hearts; upon her fine ambition, which men's criticism misconstrues into *coldness* and women's into *pride*; and on her warmth of love, which one would not have looked for in a heart like hers, fast closed as a bud, which now confounds inanimate with animated nature, in order by the former to learn to love the latter. It touched Victor even to tears when Emanuel so warmly praised his pupil, now withdrawn from this Eden; and when he actually went on to beg, in all simplicity, that he would be the friend of *his* friend, and now especially because he was going to die, and because she would never come back again,—for she had been here the last time merely for the purpose—on Whitsuntide, where her parents could not smile at it—of publicly taking the sacrament with the boarding-school girls,—that he would now take *his* place towards this starward-soaring eye, this heart aspiring to eternity,—then could he have fallen at the feet of his friend and *his* maiden friend for emotion and love.... From such lips praise bestowed upon its object always gives to love an extraordinary growth, because that sentiment always seems a pretext,[169] and ripens at once, so soon as it has found it.

If thy heart, my friend, does not beat quickly and intensely enough for another's,—although, in my opinion, it already pulsates at the fever-point, namely, a hundred and eleven times in a minute,—then just go, in order to transform thy cold fever into a warm one, thy quartan ague into a quotidian, to other particularly respected people, and let them praise her, the good soul, or only name her often before thee,—mortally sick, and provided with thy good hundred and forty pulsations to the minute, thou wilt go thy way, and have the desired fever.

The innocent Emanuel, who did not guess Victor's warmth, thought he must do still more by way of giving him the sevenfold consecration as priest of friendship for Clotilda, and gave him a—letter from her. *Thou* couldst do it, East Indian, since thou art here a child that has been made into an angel in the *limbus infantum* (the children's heaven), since thou hast no mysteries, excepting the mystery of the three children (hence his Lordship did not make thee the reader of his letters), and since thou dost not at all dream that the giving away of another's letter is anything wrong. Still thy scholar should not have read it.

But he did read it. He cannot defend himself by anything except by my reader, who here holds in his hand this very same letter of another who never wrote it for him, and nevertheless reads it through word for word in his chair. I, for my part, read nothing, but only copy off what the dog brings me.—It is a beautiful coincidence that this letter should have been written by her on that very same raining, melodious night of the garden-feast when he wrote his first to Emanuel.

"St. Luna, May 4, 179*.

"You will not, perhaps, expect any excuse from me, revered teacher, that, when I have hardly left Maienthal, I come back in the form of a letter. In fact, I meant to write it even while on the road, then the second day, and finally yesterday. This Maienthal will spoil for me many other valleys; all music will sound to me like an Alpine horn, making me sad, and bringing to my heart the remembrance of the Alpine life under the weeping-birch tree.

"In this mood I should not have been able to deny my heart the pleasure of opening itself and pouring itself out before yours in the warmest thanks for the most beautiful and instructive days of my life, had I not formed the resolve after some days to be in Maienthal again; after my second return home, my heart must have its will, and way.

"In our house I found nothing changed,[170] nor anything in our neighbor's; and I found in all souls the same old love with which we had parted from each other,—only my Agatha, to be sure, is merry, but yet less so than she used to be. The only change in Herr Eymann's house is a guest whom every one calls by a different name,—Victor, Horion, Sebastian, young Lord, Doctor. This last name he fully deserves by his first action and first joy in St. Luna, which was the healing of the blind Lord Horion. What a piece of happiness for the saved and for his saviour!—May this youth one day only pass through your Eden, and meet with your good Julius, so as to repeat upon him the beautiful art—Oh! as often as I think upon it, that the male sex is blest with the means of the greatest, godlike benefactions,—that they, like a god, can distribute eyes, life, justice, science,—whereas my sex must confine its heart, so yearning to do good, to lesser services,—to the drying away of a tear for another, to the concealing of its own, to the exercise of a secret patience with happy and unhappy;—then the wish rises, O that that sex which has the highest benefits in its hands would vouchsafe to us the greatest,—that of imitating itself, and getting into our hands good things which should bless us by our distribution of them!—-At present, a woman can have nothing in her soul to make her great, except only wishes.

"I have just come in out of the open air from a little garden-feast at my Agatha's; and never is any fair bit of deep-blue sky exactly right to me, if it does not stand over your weeping-birch, where your eye counts up all its treasures and suns, and shows my heart all the tokens of Infinite Power and Love. To-day, in the garden, I thought with almost too sad a longing on your Maienthal; Herr Sebastian reminded me of it still oftener, because he seems to have had a teacher who resembled mine.[171] He talked very well to-day, and seemed to be made up of two halves,—a British and a French. Some of his fine observations have not gone from me,—e. g., 'Sorrows are like thunder-clouds: in the distance they look black, over our heads hardly gray.—As sad dreams betoken a glad future, so may it be with the so-often-tormenting dream of life when it is over.—All our strong feelings, like ghosts, hold sway only up to a certain hour; and if a man would always say to himself, This passion, this grief, this rapture, will in three days certainly be gone from this soul,—then would he become more and more tranquil and composed.' I report all this to you so exactly, in order, as it were, to punish myself for a too hasty judgment which I passed some days since (though within myself) on his propensity to satire.—Satire, also, seems to be merely for the stronger sex; I have never yet found one of my own who had found in the works of Swift or Cervantes or Tristram anything to her taste.—

"*Two days later.*—I and my letter are still here; but to-day it starts four days in advance of me. I cannot help thinking, This last time every flower in Maienthal, and every word my best teacher says to me, will give me still greater and deeper joy than ever, because I journey thither right from the turmoil of visiting, and with such a melancholy heart. The morning after that lovely night of the church-going festival I sat alone in an arbor near the great pond, and made myself sadder with all that I saw and thought; for during that whole morning, by reason of a dream I had had, my faded friend[172] stood before my soul,—her grave lay transparent above her, and I looked down through it, and saw that lily of heaven lying within there pale and still,—I reflected, indeed, as the gardener buried flowers with their pots in the earth, that the body in which we are planted must, in like manner, go down into the earth for future blooming, but, nevertheless, I could no longer control my tears.—In vain did I look upon the sparkling spring, which draws every day new colors, new insects, new flowers out of the earth,—I only grew sadder, since it rejuvenates everything, but not man. [173]—And when I saw Herr von Schleunes with a frog-bow approaching the pond, I was obliged, as he could see my eyes at a great distance as he passed by, to make believe asleep, in order not to betray them.... But before my dearest teacher I would have opened them as now, because he forgives me my weaknesses.

"Clotilda v. L. B."

Victor had kept his left hand, with which he held the letter, too near to his heart, and his arm and letter began to tremble with the thumping heart, and he could hardly read and comprehend it for emotion. "Such a teacher! such a pupil!"—beyond that his looks could say nothing more.

There was a struggle within him whether he should tell his friend his love for Clotilda. In *favor* of the confession was Emanuel's request to seek her society,—that eye of his beholding, as if out of fixed stars, all trifles of earth,—Victor's grateful desire to repay one secret with another, and, most of all, oh! this love for his teacher, this love of his teacher for him.... And this, too, conquered, however much there was otherwise to be said *per contra*. For if Victor's whole nature glowed in the fire of friendship, so did his heart mount higher and higher, and burn to lay itself open,—he still wrestled with it, and still it was silent,—it loved boundlessly,—it lifted itself up as if by an invisible power,—at last it burst asunder,—his bosom opened wide as before God,—and now, beloved, look in, but forgive him all!

He was still in this inward conflict, when the moon, which had gone up behind their backs, projected their two shadowy knee-pieces before them.— He was reminded, by Emanuel's outstretched shadow, of a passage in his letter,[174] and of his sickly life and early passing away.... This clove open his inner being; he gently turned his Emanuel round toward the moon, now pouring down its radiance, and told him and showed him everything,— not merely his love, however, but his whole history, his whole soul, all his faults, all his follies,—everything; he was, at this moment, as eloquent as an angel, and full as great; his heart undulated in the melting glow of love; and the more he said, the more he wanted to have to say.

No sublimer and more blessed hour strikes on this earth than that in which a man erects himself, exalted by virtue, softened by love, and despises all dangers, and shows a friend how it is with his heart. This trembling, this dissolving, this exaltation, is more precious than the itching of vanity to disguise itself in idle refinings. But perfect sincerity comports only with virtue. Let the man in whom suspicion and darkness dwell by all means apply to his bosom night-screws and night-bolts, —let the bad man spare us his opening of coffins, —and whoso has no heaven's door about him to open, let him keep the hell-gate shut!

Emanuel felt the divine or motherly joy which a friend experiences at the virtue and improvement of a friend, and forgot in his joy the different occasions of it.

Reluctantly do I tear myself away for a night from this virtuous pair. May I get many more days of Maienthal to paint, and may Victor spend there many days more!

15
DOG-POST-DAY

Ah, he goes this very day! The emotions and conversations which we have described had shattered too severely the tender casing which enclosed, as a tulip does the bee, Emanuel's fair spirit; he rose pale and languid; and the blind one was the happiest, who saw neither this paleness nor the white handkerchief which he, during the night, instead of staining with tears, had stained with blood. He himself had still the pale evening red of yesterday's joy on his face; but this very indifference to the gradual extinguishing of his days, this growing feebleness and faintness of tone in his conversation, caused Victor to turn away his eyes from him whenever they had for some time rested upon him. Emanuel looked down calm as an eternal sun on the autumn of his bodily life; nay, the more the sand fell from his life's hourglass, so much the more clearly did he look through the empty glass. And yet the earth was to him a beloved place, a fair meadow for our earliest plays of childhood; and he still hung upon this mother of our first life with the love wherewith the bride spends the evening full of childish remembrances on the bosom of her beloved mother, before on the morrow she goes to meet the bridegroom of her heart.

Victor reproached himself with every drop of blood shed by Emanuel, and resolved to go to-day, because this Psyche, with her great wings, could no longer stir herself in her web without tearing it. In Emanuel's eyes there shone an inexpressible love for his sympathizing scholar. He began of himself to speak of his dying-day, in order to comfort him, and represented to him that he could not go hence till after a year. He based his enthusiastic prediction on two grounds;—first, that most of his male relatives had died on the selfsame day and in the selfsame climacteric[175] of life; secondly, that several consumptive patients before him had read in their diseased breast, as in a magic mirror, their last day. Victor disputed him; he showed that the foretelling of one's last appearance, as if the hectic man could easily feel beforehand, from the regular and gradual failing of the vital energy, the last step or freezing-point, was false, because feelings of the future in the present were contradictions (*in adjecto*), and because in the midst of life we could as little have a presentiment of the arrival of death as in our waking hours we can (notwithstanding a parallel gradation of steps in this case also) that of sleep. Victor represented all this to him; and yet he did not fairly believe it himself; he was overmastered by the lofty man who could announce his entrance into the shadow of death as calmly and confidently as an entrance of the moon into the shadow of the earth.... We will forgive the sick man, and not hold ourselves wiser than he is, because he is more enthusiastic than we. — Victor was most consoled by Emanuel's notion that his deceased father would appear to him for the first time just before his death.

Victor lingered, and tried not to linger; forbade, as physician, Emanuel's talking, in order to make the excuse to himself of a harmless postponement, and became more and more troubled, for the very reason that he cared little to speak himself. — How canst thou, good Victor, this very day hurry away from him, from this angel, who will perhaps disappear over the next grave? — It must be a sore thing for thee, since it is already so hard to quit a Maienthal full of blossoms, a blind one full of soft tones; painful is here the last pressure of hands, Victor, and sweet every delay!

He resolved to take leave at night, because a parting in the morning begets too long a sadness, and the place in the heart from which the beloved object was torn away continues bleeding all day long. Emanuel would of course, at evening, have betaken himself to the seminary, as he did yesterday; then would Victor, before the blind one, whom he would beg for the saddest melody in the world, be able to let his full eyelids, with which he always had to go out in order to relieve the anguish, stream down to his heart's content.

When at evening he had eaten his last meal, and the evening-bell began, his heart felt as if the breast had been lifted away from it, and needle-points of ice were blown upon it.[176] Full of love, he clasped the blind youth, whom he was not permitted to recognize as the playmate of his childhood, and who with his tones had given more raptures than he had in this night of his blindness received in return; and he let tears have their way, whose twofold, perhaps threefold, source Emanuel did not guess; for the sight of these eyes, which were nevermore to be opened, awoke in him now, since Clotilda's wish for their healing, much more sorrow. Emanuel he still begged, with a voice that hurried away over the incidental meaning, to accompany him a short distance, till Maienthal should be out of sight.

Out in the darkling and still country, all his sorrows lingered in his breast beside their sighs. "When the moon glimmers in upon this valley of blossoms," thought he, "I shall have left it for a long time." Only the altar-lights, the stars, burned in the great temple. He proposed to himself to part with his teacher on the mountain where their union had taken place; but he went up by circuitous ways,—Emanuel gladly following whithersoever he led,—in order during the circuit to overmaster his taciturnity and his tears.

But they arrived at the foot of the weeping-birch, and grief still held possession of his eye and his voice. "Ah!" thought he, "how great and glad was the first night here, and how painful is this!" They reclined on the earth beside each other on the grassy bank, solitary, silent, sad, before the darkly glimmering universe. Victor could hear the labored breathing of the diseased breast, and the future grave on this mountain seemed to open at his side. Oh! if it is bitter to stand by the bed wherein a loved and fading countenance lies with the hues of death, far more bitter is it, in the midst of the scenes of health, behind the erect form of the dear one, to hear the grave-digger Death softly at his work, and to think, as often as the loved face looks joyful, "Ah, be still more joyful! in a short time he will have gnawed round the roots of thy life, and thou wilt have passed away with thy joys and with mine!"—But ah! there is indeed no friend, man or woman, with whom we should not be obliged to think the same!—

He knew not why Dahore was so long silent.—He foresaw not that the moon would illumine the mountain sooner than the valley. The moon, that Pharos on the coast of the second world, now encircled men with pale fields, taken from dreams, with wan, gleaming meadows born of a super-terrestrial perspective, and the Alps and woods it resolved into immovable mists; *above* the hemisphere of earth stood deep the Lethe-flood of slumber, *below* the green crust stood the dead sea, and two loving men lived between the wide domains of sleep and death.... At this moment Victor thought to himself, indeed, still more keenly, "Here, beside this birch-tree, under this cold sod, will *his* crumbling breast be forever hidden, and his heart will bleed no more; but ah! it will beat no more." He thought, indeed, upon gloomy resemblances, as the *immovable* stars appeared to go *up* and *down*, merely because the playing *earth* turned itself about them, now *showing* and now *hiding* them; he turned, indeed, his melancholy glance away from the *ignes fatui*, that, gliding over valleys, danced only on the solemn darkness and on the graves, and which described round a solitary powder-house their deceptive circles.—

But still he was silent, and thought, "Ah, well! we have each other yet."

But then it was too much for his bleeding heart when the flute-wails of the blind one stole out from the solitary house into the night, and passed over the mountain and over the future grave.—Then were voices given to the sighs and death-bells to the future, and his sadness grew too oppressive, as he thought, amidst the flute-murmurs, how this unique, this irreplaceable man, who cherished so much love for him in his great heart, was going hence never to reappear.—Ah! and when, besides, just at this moment, Emanuel, who had been lying beside him silently lost in gazing on the heavens and like a departed one, changed his position on account of his painful and oppressed breathing, but with a countenance whose serenity was undisturbed by the pains in his breast, then a cold hand glided into Victor's swollen heart and turned itself about therein, and his blood curdled on it, and he said, without the power of looking upon him, in faint, supplicating, broken accents, "Do not die in a year, my dear Emanuel,—do not wish to die!"

The genius of night had stood till now, invisibly, before Emanuel, and poured high raptures into his bosom, but no passions; and he said: "We are not alone,—my soul feels the passing by of its kindred, and lifts itself up,— *under* the earth is sleep, *above* the earth is dream, but between sleep and dream I see luminous eyes move along like stars,—a cool breath comes from the sea of eternity over the glowing earth,—my heart mounts up, and will break away from life,—all around me is as great as if God passed through the night.—Spirits! grasp my spirit,—it climbs to your embrace,—and bear it up yonder...."

Victor turned round and looked imploringly into the beautiful, joyous, tearless countenance: "Thou *wilt* die?"

Emanuel's ecstasy soared above life: "The dark streak in the next world is only a meadow of flowers,[177]—suns shine to light us onward,—flying heavens come to meet us with spring-breezes. With only empty graves the earth flies round the sun; for her dead stand remote on brighter suns."—

"Emanuel?" said Victor, in a questioning tone, weeping aloud, and with a voice of the most fervent yearning,—and the flute-notes sank sorrowfully into the broad night,—"Emanuel?"

Emanuel, returning to himself, looked on him, and said, calmly: "Yes, my beloved!—I can no more accustom myself to the earth; the water-drop of life has become flat and shallow,—I can no longer move round therein,— and my heart yearns to be among the great men who have left this drop behind them.—O beloved, listen, I pray,"—and here he pressed to soreness the heart of his Victor,—"and hear this heavy breath going. See, I pray, this shattered body, this thick casing,—how it wraps round my spirit, and obstructs its passage.—

"See, here my spirit and thine cleave frozen to the ice-cake, and yonder the night opens all her heavens, reposing one behind the other; yonder in the blue, glimmering abyss dwells all the greatness which has disrobed itself on the earth, all the truth that we guess, all the goodness that we love.—

"See, how still is all up there in immensity,—how softly the worlds move, how silently the suns glow! The great Eternal reposes as a fountain, with his overflowing, infinite love, in the midst of them, refreshing and tranquillizing all; and around God lies no grave."

Here Emanuel, as if raised by an infinite blessedness, stood up and looked lovingly toward Arcturus, who still hung under the zenith of heaven, and said, directing his words toward the broad deep of brilliancy: "Ah, how inexpressibly do I yearn to come up to you! Ah, break in pieces, old heart, and hold me not so long in these bonds!"

"Die, then, great soul," said Victor, "and take thy way up yonder; but break with thy death my little heart also, and keep by thee the poor one who cannot forsake thee nor do without thee."

The flute had ceased; the two friends had sunk into each other's arms to end their farewell. "Dear, beloved, never-to-be-forgotten one," said Emanuel, "thou movest me too deeply; but when, a year hence, I go up from this mountain, then shalt thou stand by me, and see how man is released from his bonds. Thy tears will be my last earthly pangs; but I shall say, what I say now, We part by night, but we meet again by day." And so he went.

Victor had gently disengaged himself from the childlike lips,—he sought not to follow him on his night-track,—slowly he went along by one vast sleep.—Often he turned round and followed with eyes full of falling tears the falling stars over Maienthal; and at four of the morning he arrived with a heavenly soul at St. Luna, and entered the garden full of old scenes, and laid down in the familiar arbor his glowing head and his subdued heart in the dew of the morning for a cooling repose.

O rest thou, rest thou!—ah! sleep only, either on the earth or under the earth, can still the ever-agitated bosom of man....[178]

16
DOG-POST-DAY

One would certainly want to sleep in one's clothes, like old Fritz, so soon as ever one came to understand that in his shirt he is beset and attacked, as Victor and I sometimes are, by the vampires of midnight melancholy. They stay away when one sits up and has all his clothes on; especially do boots and hat retain for us the feeling of day in the greatest degree. —

A warm hand lifted up Victor's bedewed head from the sleeping-board,[179] and directed it towards the whole surging flood of morning-light. His eyes opened (as always) with indescribable mildness, and without night-clouds, before Agatha, and beamed on her with full radiance. But she hurried him away with his radiance out of the leafy bedchamber; for he must look himself up a dressing-comb and a morning-blessing, and, secondly, the table-couch was to be a tea-table for Clotilda, who liked to take *warm* drinks in *cool* places.

—And so he stands out there between parsonage and palace in mid-morning. All seemed to him to have been just built and painted during his journey; for all that dwelt therein seemed to have changed and made him melancholy. "The parents in there," he said to himself, "have no son, my friend has no sweetheart, and I—no tranquil heart." And now, when at last he entered the house, and became once more a bright triumphal arch of the loving family-circle,—when he was compelled to contemplate with sympathetic and yet enlightened eyes the tender illusions of the parents, the groundless hopes of his friend, and the coming up of stormy days,—then stood one fixed tear for the future in his eye; and it grew not less when his adoptive mother would justify it by tender glances.... Partly, however, this veil was wafted over his soul merely from the preceding night, whose glimmering scenes were separated from him only by a short interval of sleep; for a night spent in the watches of emotion always ends with a melancholy forenoon.

The Chaplain was just making butter-vignettes; I mean, he was cutting, with no other etching-tool than a penknife, and into no other copperplate except potatoes, printers' tail-pieces and quadrats, which were to be stamped on the July butter by way of ornament. One might have supposed that Victor would have helped himself out greatly by having wit enough to remark that the *old printed things* were, to be sure, quite worthy of long books upon them, and long universal German literary reviews of the books, but of no human thought, and were ten times more unenjoyable than these *newest* butter-*incunabula*;[180] for, if there could be anything wretcheder than the world's history (i. e. the history of rulers), whose contents consisted of wars, as the theatre-journal of *other* puppets does of cudgellings, it could only be the history of *littérateurs* and printers.[181] This, too, must have stood him in stead,—that he was, finally, philosophical, and demanded that man should be called neither a *laughing* nor a *reasoning*, but a *prinking* animal; to which remark the Chaplain's lady added nothing, except the application of it to her daughters.

But in men of his sort, sadness, satire, and philosophy have place beside each other. To the potato-medal-coiner and the Chaplainess, who reckoned all women on earth among her daughters, and pronounced similar castigatory sermons against them all, he described his journey with as many satires and rasures as were needful for both parties; but when he heard the wishes of the family expressed that his Lordship might have a happy journey back with the beloved son of the Prince, and the intelligence that the Regency-Counsellor had already everything packed up to start for the city any hour that he might choose, then had Victor nothing to do but to take the secretive tear-ducts in his eye-sockets out of the way.

But whither? Into the garden! That was not well-considered. Flamin followed, and they arrived together at the embowered closet in the presence of the tea-drinkers. Never did its branches overshadow a more embarrassed face, softer eyes, fuller looks, and livelier or lovelier dreams than Victor carried with him beneath them. He thought of Clotilda as now a wholly new being, and thought, therefore,—as he knew not whether she loved him,— very stupidly. Man, when he has climbed over the mountain, always regards the coming hill as nothing; Flamin had been his mountain, and Clotilda was his hill.—In all the shallows of conversation, where one is already half stranding or sinking, there is no grander ship's-pump than a story which one has to tell. Give me embarrassment, and the largest circle, and only *one* disaster,—that is, the anecdote of it, which no one knows but myself,—and I will soon save myself. Victor therefore brought out his, life-preserver,—that is, his log-book,—from which he made for the bower a practical extract. I confess, a newspaper-writer might have falsified more, might have been guilty of more sins of *commission*, but hardly of more sins of *omission*.

He gave himself, I fancy, a lift again with the Chaplainess, and injured himself unquestionably with Clotilda,—however much, out of good-will towards his hearers, and too strong a hatred of the court, he offended against Clotilda's satire-embargo in her letter,—when, without reflecting, too, that maidens love only the jest, not the jesters, he represented the benefit-drama of the Princess, not on the sublime side, as I did, but on the comic side. Clotilda smiled, and Agatha laughed.

But when he named the name of Emanuel, and his house, and his mountain, then did friendship and memory diffuse over the fairest eye above which an eyebrow-arch, drawn by a line of beauty, ever yet flowed, a soft glimmer which wanted, every moment, to grow to a tear of joy. But it had to become one of another nature, when, in answer to the question about his health which Clotilda hopefully put to him as an adept in science, Victor was compelled to give the (faintly paraphrased) history of his nocturnal bleeding. He could not conceal the pang of sympathy, nor could Clotilda conquer it. O ye two good souls! what sore wounds will your hearts yet receive from your great friend!

Whither could she now turn her loving and sorrowing eye, but to her good brother Flamin, towards whom her demeanor, in consequence of the double constraint which her silence and his interpretations imposed upon her, had been hitherto so indescribably mild?—As, now, Victor saw all this with such wholly different eyes,—as he stood before his poor friend, who with his present happiness was perhaps accumulating the poisonous nourishment of his future jealousy, and gazed openly and fixedly into the firm countenance which some time bitter days might rend with agony,— and as, generally, *past* or *future* sorrows of another took a stronger hold of him than *present* ones, because fancy had him more in its power than the senses,—in this state of things, he could not for a moment assert the mastery over his eyes, but they bent their look, encircled with compassionate tears, tenderly on his friend. Clotilda was embarrassed about the resting-place of his look; so was he too, because man is less ashamed of the most vehement signs of hatred than of the smallest signs of love. Clotilda understood not the coquettish double art of throwing others into embarrassment or drawing them out of it; and the good Agatha always confounded the latter with the former.... "Ask him what ails him, brother!" said Agatha to Flamin....

The latter led him out with like good intention behind the nearest gooseberry-bushes, and asked him in his firm way, which always held an assertion as a question,—

"Something has happened to thee?"

"Just come this way!" said Victor, and pulled him along behind some higher Spanish walls[182] of foliage.

"Nothing has happened to me," he began, at last, with brimming eye-sockets and smiling features, — "nothing more than that I have been a fool for some twenty-six years" (that was his age). "I know thou art unfortunately a jurist, and perhaps a worse oculist than I myself am, and hast, perhaps, read very little in Herr Janin.[183]—Am I right?"

Flamin's shaking of his head meant something more than No.

"Very naturally; but if thou hadst, thou couldst have it from himself, or from the translation by Selle, very finely shown, that not merely the lachrymal gland secretes our tear-drops, but also the crystalline body,[184] the Meibomian[185] glands, the lachrymal caruncle,[186] and—our afflicted heart, I add to the rest.—Nevertheless, of these aqueous globules, which are made for the sorrows of poor, poor mortals, not more than (if things go rightly) four ounces are filtered in twenty-four hours.... But, my dear one, the fact is just this,—that things do not go rightly, especially with me; and it vexes me to-day, not that thou hast never peeped into Herr Janin, but that thou dost not observe my confounded, cursed, stupid way."

"What one?"

"Yes, indeed,—what one? but I mean this of to-day,—namely, that my eyes—thou mayst boldly ascribe it merely to a too feeble *tear-siphon*, under which head Petit comprehends all absorbing tear-ducts—run over, when, e. g., any one does me an injustice, or when I merely desire anything too strongly, or imagine to myself an approaching pleasure, or only, in fact, a strong sensation, or human life, or the mere weeping itself." ...

His good-natured eye stood full of water as he said it, and justified all.

"Dear Flamin, I wish I had been a lady, or a Moravian, or a player;—truly, if I wanted to make the spectators believe I was going about it (namely, weeping), it would be actually a fact, too, on the spot." —

And here he fell softly and fondly, with tears which had an excuse for flowing, upon the beloved breast.... But for the viper-cure and iron-cure of his manliness he needed nothing but a "Hm!" and a shrug of the whole body; thereupon the youths went back as men to the arbor.

There was nothing left there: the girls had stolen away to the meadows, where nothing was to be avoided, except high grass and bedewed shadows. The empty arbor was the best absorbing tear-siphon for his eyes; nay, I gather from reports of the epistolary Spitz that he was vexed. As the sister came back by-and-by alone, his companion was vexed too. In fact, if somehow or other my hero—which would be a misfortune for me and him—should in time fall in love with Clotilda, then will the heroine make us both warm enough,—him in acting, me in copying,—for the very reason that she herself will *not* be warm, because she has neither superfluous warmth nor superfluous coldness, but always the alternating temperature which changes with the subject of conversation, but not with the speaker; because she takes away from a tenderly disposed fellow-man all pleasure in praising her, as she pays out no tithe thereof, or at least in offending her, as she issues no letters of indulgence; and because one really, in his agony, assumes at last that one can commit no other sins against her except such as are sins against the Holy Ghost. Jean Paul, who has been in such cases, and has often stood for whole years in one spot before such mountain-fortresses with his storming-ladders and labarums and trumpeters, and, instead of the garrisons, taken *himself* off by an honorable retreat,—this Paul, I say, can form a conception of what an amount of parchment, time, and printer's ink may have to be used up in the case of Sebastian *contra* Clotilda, before we get things even to a *war-footing*. In fact, with a perfectly *rational* woman a man never feels himself quite well; and only with a merely fine, fanciful, ardent, capricious one is he truly at home. One like Clotilda can make the best man, from mere distress and respect, frosty, stupid, and enraptured; and in most cases there comes in the additional misfortune, that the poor, worn-out, fond fool, by whom such an earthly angel absolutely will not let herself be worshipped, as the Apocalyptic one would not by the disciple John, can still seldom muster courage to say to the angel,—somewhat as one might to an angel of an opposite nature with the kingdoms of the world, demanding to be worshipped,—"Take thyself out of my sight!" Paul always in such cases takes himself away.—

Victor did not do this; he absolutely now could not get away from the house, i. e. from the village. The summer days seemed to him to rest in St. Luna, softly breathing, fragrant, blissful; and he was going to be cast out of this softly straying gondola into the slave-ship of the Court,—out of the milk-house of the Parsonage into the princely arsenic-house,—out of the *kindergarten* of household love into the ice-field of court love. That was a sore thing to him here in the arbor,—and so sweet a thing in Tostato's shop!—When man's wishes and situations exchange places, he accuses the situations, not the wishes. He could laugh at himself for it, he said, but he had a hundred reasons for lingering in St. Luna from one day to another: he was so much disgusted now with his intention of pleasing a man (the Prince) from any other motive than love; it was still more improbable that he should himself please than that he should be pleased; he would rather humor his own whims than those of crownéd heads, and he knew for certain that in the first month he should tell the Minister von Schleunes satirical things to his very face, and in the second even the Prince; and, in fact, now in midsummer he should just be fit to act the complete court-knave, whereas in winter, &c.

Beside these hundred reasons, he had still weaker ones which he did not at all mention,—for instance, some such as these: He would gladly be about Clotilda, because he must necessarily, as it were, to justify his conduct,—but which, then, my dear, thy past or thy future?—disclose to her his knowledge about her consanguinity to his friend. To this disclosure there was wanting, what in Paris is dearest, *place*,—and then, too, the exordium. Clotilda was nowhere to be met alone. Connoisseurs say that every secret one tells to one of the fair sex is a sticking-plaster which attaches him to her, and often begets a second secret: was it for some such reason that Victor was so eager to contrive a way of showing to Clotilda his acquaintance with her sisterly relation?—

He stayed day after day, as, besides, the butter-week[187] of the marriage must go by first. He had already marriage-medals in his pocket. But he never could see Clotilda except a second at a time; and, according to Bonnet, one needs half a second for a clear idea,—according to Hooke, a whole one, in fact. Therefore, before he could form a complete conception of this still goddess, she was always gone.

At last more serious arrangements were made, not for departure, but for forming the purpose of it.... The sweetest minutes of a visit are those which once more postpone its close; the sweetest of all, those in which one already has cane or fan in hand, and yet does not go. Such minutes now encircled our Fabius of love; softer eyes said to him, "Hurry not!" warmer hands drew him back, and the mother's tear asked him, "Wilt thou rob me of my Flamin so soon as to-morrow?"

"By no means," he answered, and kept his seat. Did not, I ask, the Chaplainess thrust for his sake her lingual executioner's sword into its sheath, because there was nothing he so hated as loud or silent defamations of a sex which, more unhappy than ours, sees itself maltreated by two sexes at once? For he often took maidens by the hand, and said: "Woman's faults, particularly *evil* reports, moodiness, and sensitiveness, are *knot-holes*, which in the *green* tree please us even into the honeymoon[188] as fine marble-veined *circles*, but which, in the *dry*, in the marriage-furniture, when the plug has shrunk and fallen out, gape open as ugly holes." Agatha now screwed her sewing-cushion to his writing-table and kissed him, whether he chose to look pleasant or sullen; Even the Chaplain sought to sweeten for him, if not the last days, which he dreamed away at his house, yet at least the last *nights*, for which purpose he needed nothing but a drum and a foot. The most fiery nocturnal witch-dances of the mice the Chaplain interdicted with his heel, that they might not wake up his guest; that is to say, he kept up against the foot-board of the bed from time to time a moderate cannonading, which knelled into the ear-trumpets of the dancers the more in proportion as it startled the ears of humanity. Against the Euler's knight's-moves of the rats he took the field with only a mallet, wherewith, breaking in like a day of judgment on their pleasure-parties and hunting-parties, he merely thumped once or twice on a drum, extemporized out of the bed-quilt.

Matthieu was invisible, and, as courtiers mimic princes in everything, was parodying the nuptial days of his prince at least by little nuptial *hours* of his own. The powder which issued out of cannons and the cornucopias of the firework-makers, the *vivat* which was prayed from pulpits and shouted from taverns, and the expenses one incurred for all this, were, I think, so considerable, that the greatest prince need not have been ashamed to illustrate therewith his marriage and his—ennui. Coldness has forever a *speaking-trumpet*, and sensitiveness an *ear-trumpet*. The arrival of an unloved princely corpse or bride is heard of at the polar circles; on the contrary, when we inferiors fill our graves or our arms with loved beings, there fall only a few, unheard tears, disconsolate or blissful.

Flamin pined for the session-table, whose labors were now soon to begin, and he could not comprehend this delay.... At last, for once, and with all seriousness, the day of departure was fixed, the 10th of August; and I am sure Victor would not have been on the 14th still in St. Luna, had not the Devil on the 8th brought along a Tyrolese.

It is the same fellow who day before yesterday made his entry among us at Scheerau, with a wax retinue which he had got together, half from the imperial states and half from among the literati, and with the wax hands of these twin brothers of man took money from our purse. It is stupid, that Spitz did not bring me the present dog's-day the day before yesterday; I could myself have asked the churl, who embossed, in St. Luna, Victor and the Chaplain in wax, what was the real name of Victor, and of Eymann, and of St. Luna itself. The result is, that I am still, with an allowable and biographical curiosity about this carpenter of men, who surrounds us with awful reflections of our little being, following on his heels.

Victor must, therefore, again tarry; for he had himself and the Chaplain baked in wax, in order to give, in the first place, to the latter, who had a childish fondness for all casts, dolls, and puppets, and, secondly, to the family, who longed to quarter the waxen mock-Victor in his vacated chamber, a greater pleasure than to himself. For he had a horror of these flesh-colored shadows of himself. Even in childhood, among all ghost-stories, those of people who had seen themselves crept with the coldest hand over his heart. Often at evening, before going to bed, he surveyed his trembling body so long, that at last he detached it from himself, and saw it standing thus alone beside his self and gesticulating as a strange form; then he would lay himself down, quaking, with this strange form, in the grave of sleep, and the darkling soul felt itself like a Hamadryad, grown over by the pliant fleshy bark. Hence he felt deeply the difference and the long interval between his self and its bark, when he looked for some time on another's body, and still more deeply when he contemplated his own.

He sat opposite the embossing-stool and the embossing-tools, but fixed his eyes on a book again, so as not to see the corporeal form, in which he carried himself round, distant and duplicated. The reason why he nevertheless could endure the reduplication of his face in the glass can only be, that he regarded the supernumerary in the glass either merely as a superficial portrait without cubic contents, or as the only archetype with which we compare other duplicates of our person.... Upon these points I can never speak, myself, without a certain tremor....

The wax-copy of Victor, to express his majority, was arrayed in a *toga virilis*, an overcoat which the original had cast off; likewise the chamber which the living one vacated was cleared out. The Chaplain proposed to himself to place this cheap edition of Horion in the window when the better one was gone, in such a manner that all the school youth, who learned from the chorister manners and *mores*, should doff their hats to it when they came tearing out of the school-house.

Now at last!—For Mat came. The wrung-out cheeks of the latter, and his whole body, which had been under the lemon-squeezers of night-feasts, gave evidence that he did not lie when he said the princely bridegroom looked even eight times wretcheder, and was prostrate with the gout. He added in his bitter way, which Victor little liked, that these pale great people had in fact no blood except the little they cupped from their subjects or what stuck to their hands, as insects carry no red blood about with them, save what they have sucked from other creatures. This reminded Victor of his medical duties to this prince. Either Mat's wasted form,—for immoral night-life makes features and complexion still more repulsive than the longest confinement to the sick-bed,—or the recollection of his Lordship's warnings, or both, made him quite as odious to our court-physician as the latter through his court-doctorship had become to him: this secret poison of Matthieu's, however, manifested itself, not by an abated, but by an increased, almost ironical courteousness. On the contrary, Mat and Flamin seemed to be more familiar with one another than ever.

In the forenoon, after shaving, Victor jumped up without washing himself again, and immediately packed up his boot-jack, and burst the suspenders of his pantaloons, and bespoke additional hands to discharge his life-ballast, (on account of his miserable packing,) and then stow it again. For he always gave over the whole trusteeship of the lumber of our petty life's furniture to strange hands, and that with such a contempt for the trumpery and such a recklessness of expenditure,—I never mean, indeed, to calumniate my hero, but, notwithstanding, it is proved by Spitz that he never collated the current money of a gold-piece when he changed it into silver, nor ever beat down in trade a Jew, Roman, or Moravian,—to such a degree, I say, did he carry this, that the whole female Hanse in St. Luna cried, "What a fool!" and that the Chaplainess always in the market-square slipped herself into his place. But he was incorrigible, because he made the journey of life, and therefore the luggage of the journey, look so diminutive through his philosophic eyes, and because nothing made him blush like the least appearance of self-interest: he ran off from all arrangements, outriders, and stage-rehearsals, when they appeared on his account; he was ashamed of every pleasure which was not to be divided, at least into two bites, one for a fellow-eater; he said, the forehead of a Hospodar[189] must have assumed the hardness of his crown, for otherwise such a man could not possibly endure what often, merely on his behalf, was done by a whole county,— the music, the triumphal arches, the odes, the cries of joy in prose, and the frightful cannonades.

He had now nothing more to discharge in St. Luna than a mere flat civility; for thus much may I well assert without vanity, that a hero whom I have chosen for mine will have, I trust, sufficient good-breeding to go to the Chamberlain Le Baut and say, "*Au revoir!*" Besides, to such state visits he must now accustom himself.

Mat, too, was over there, that image of a Cupid with bristly, plucked, drooping wings, tossed to the Chamberlain's lady: the latter joked with him about those vacant looks, which betrayed the intermittent pulse of his love. Le Baut was playing chess with Mat,—Clotilda sat at her little work-table full of silk-flowers, in the midst of this noble trio.... Ye poor daughters! what people have you not often to welcome and hear through! To Clotilda, however, this family friend was nothing but a stuffed-out mummy, and she knew not whether he came or went.

Sebastian, as adoptive son of Fortune, as heir of the paternal post of favorite, was to-day received at the Chamberlain's with uncommon civility.

Verily, if the courtier shuns unfortunates because sympathy for their sufferings comes over him too heavily, so does he gladly seek the society of the fortunate, because he loves to participate in their joy. The Chamberlain, who even continued to bow before one who, in his fall from a throne, hung midway in the air, naturally bent himself still lower before one who was in the act of making the opposite passage.

Victor joined the women, but with an eye that strayed away to the chess-board, in order, if he should be embarrassed, immediately to have at hand a pretext for changing his attention or taking his leave. It was ingenious: for every word which he or the women said was a move at chess; he was obliged to conceal his coldness toward the Le Baut, that is, toward the stepmother,—how much did she know that nothing graces a mother more than a perfect daughter?—and his *warmth* toward the stepdaughter. The reader must not ask: "What warmth, then, could the old stepmother desire?" For in the higher ranks claims are not altered by blood-relationship or age; merely in the lower is this the case; hence I always fear that what I address to the daughter may weary the mother, and I always cast about, and rightly, when she comes, for a better thread of discourse. Victor easily concealed his *coldness* by virtue of humanity, which, with him, so often degenerated into a good-natured flattery of immoral hopes; and when a woman wanted to have him fall in love with her, he would say: "I cannot really tell the good little lamb, 'I would rather not.'" His *warmth* toward Clotilda he concealed—badly, not because it was too strong, but precisely because it was not yet enough so. It is natural: a young man of education can, if he will, conceal and bury in silence his *reciprocated* love, without making a pulpit announcement, but an *unreturned* love, one which he himself calls nothing more than mere regard, he lets blaze out from him without cover. For the rest, I beg the world to sit down and consider, that my hero has not the Devil in his skin or sixteen years over his head, but that he cannot possibly feel a love for a person who hangs a Moses' veil over her sentiments and over her charms. Love begins and rises, throughout, only on reciprocal love, and with the lovers' mutual finding-out of each other. He has merely regard, but a very great, a growing and anxious regard; in short, his regard is that cold pulsating point in the yolk of the heart—the metaphor is drawn from an egg—to which the least outward warmth, often after years, imparts growing life and Cupid's wings.

He now at the work-table investigated Clotilda's warmth with the pyrometer; but I cannot go beside myself for joy, that he found, on a scale subdivided into the minutest parts, her warmth to have risen 1/111 of a line. For he is off the track: I would sooner rely on Lavater's forehead-measurer than on the heart- and warmth-measurer of a love-seeking man, who confounds his interpretations with his observations, and accidents with intentions. His pyrometer may, however, be right; for towards good men one is, when bad ones are by, (consider only Mat,) warmer than usual.

Let no one blame Herr Le Baut and Frau Le Baut for congratulating my hero on the good fortune of going to such a court, to see such a prince, — the greatest in Germany, said *he*, — to such a princess, — the loveliest in Germany, said *she*. Mat smiled between Yes and No. The old man went on with his chess, the old woman with her praise. Victor saw with contempt how little possible it would be, in the case of two such souls, who held the steps of the throne for a scale of being, and the glacier of the throne for an Olympus and an Empyræum, and knew not where, except on this eminence, to find their happiness, — to give them better ideas of happiness, and worse ones of the eminence. Nevertheless, he was obliged to confess to Clotilda, who had on her face more than a No to the *eulogy*, that he negatived the whole of it as nobly as she. He therefore kneaded praise and blame together, according to an Horatian mixture, in order to make neither satirical nor flattering allusions to two dismissed court-people.

"It is painful to me," said he, "that there are only pleasures there, and no occupations, — mere baskets of confectionery, and not a single work-bag, not to say no work-table like this one."

"Do you think," asked Clotilda, with striking earnestness, "that all court-feasts pay for a single court-service?"

"No," said he, "for one ought to be paid for the feasts themselves. I maintain there is nothing but drudgery there, and no enjoyment: all their amusements are only the illumination, the interlude, and the decorations, which please the player, who is thinking of his part, less than the spectator."

"It is, at all events, good *to have been there*," said the old woman.

"Certainly," said he; "for it is good not always to stay there."

"But there are persons," said Clotilda, "who cannot make themselves happy there, simply because they do not love to be there."

That was very fine and forbearing, but intelligible only to Victor's heart.

"I would advise a fine enthusiast" (said he, and made no account, as usual, of the apparent contradiction between Victor's *life* and Victor's *opinions*) "or a fiery poet to stay at home, — the *flights* of either, instead of *pas*, would be in court-life what an hexameter is in prose, which the critics cannot bear, — and to the soul with the softest sensibilities I would say, Be off with them! the *heart* is there treated as a superfluous member, as in the six-fingered family in Anjou the sixth *finger* is." ...

The old woman shook her head quickly to the left.

"And yet," he continued, "I would take all three for a month to court and make them unhappy, in order to make them wise."

The Chamberlain's family could not accommodate themselves to Victor's style so well as my reader, who to my exceeding delight so cleverly distinguishes humor and the talent of looking at all sides of a thing from flattery and skepticism. Clotilda had slowly shaken her head at the last proposition. In fact, all battled to-day *for* and *against* him, in that partial tone which women and relatives always assume towards a stranger, when an hour before they had carried on the same suit, but with a practical application, with their own kin.

Victor, who had long been fearing: that he should become disconcerted, went off at last to where he had been so often looking,—to the chess-table, where they were playing with the greatest desire to—lose. The Chamberlain,—we all know how it was with him; he wrote nothing but commendatory letters for the whole world, and the sacramental cup would have been more to his taste, could he have drunk from it a *toast* to some important man's health,—that personage only promoted as well as he could with the dry chess-statues another's success at the expense of his own; he was glad to lose, provided only Matthieu won. And then, too, he resembled those shamefaced souls who love to bestow their benefits secretly, and he could not find it in his heart to tell his adversary that he was securing him the victory; he took almost greater pains to conceal himself as a courtier than to *conquer himself* as a Christian. Such a love ought, it would seem, to have been more warmly requited than by open malice; but Mat had the same object in view, and declined the victory which the other threw into his hands, like a real sharper. In vain did Le Baut devise the best moves for checkmating one's self. Mat matched him with still better ones, and threatened every minute to be checkmated too. And every one pities the poor Chamberlain, hunted about on the chess-board, and fearing, like a coquette, that he shall *not* be conquered. It became at length, for a soft-souled eye, which certainly forgives the weak one sooner than the wicked one, no longer endurable; Victor, with a thousand excuses to the weak one and full of malice toward the malicious one, entered into the steeple-chase, and obliged the Page to accept his advice and his charitable subsidies, and to lay hold of military operations which he proposed of such worth, that the man with the office of Chamberlain's key, at last, in spite of his fears and in spite of the worst prospects,—lost the game. All present saw through all present, as princes do through each other in their public—playbills.

He got at last his farewell audience, but very small solace. The fair form, beneath which all his ideals of beauty stood only as heraldic bearers and caryatides, was even colder than at the reception, and persisted in being only the echo of the parental courtesy. The only thing which still kept him up was a—thistle: namely, an optical one which had been sowed on the mosaic floor. That is to say, he took notice that Clotilda during the farewell avoided with her foot this flower-piece (which she certainly must have known) as if it were the original. In the evening he drew his chains of inferences, as they are taught in the universities; he engrafted upon this mock-thistle all the roses of his destiny. "She was certainly *distrait*, and why? I ask," he said, speaking into his pillow; "for, besides, they have not yet detected my feelings over yonder," he asserted, as he laid himself on the second pillow. "O thou sweet eye that went down on the thistle, rise again in my sleep, and be the moon of my dreams!" said he, when he was already half-way into both. It was merely out of modesty that he thought he was not discovered, because he did not look on himself as remarkable enough to be observed.

The 20th of August, 179-, was the great day when he took up his march to Flachsenfingen. Flamin had already trotted off at four o'clock in the afternoon, in order to avoid a leave-taking which he hated. But our Victor loved to bid farewell, and loved to tremble in the last silences of parting. "O ye poor, egoistic mortals!" he said,—"besides; this polar life is but so bald and cold; besides, we stand weeks and years near each other without stirring with the heart anything better than our blood,—only two or three glowing moments hiss and go out on the glaciers of life,—why do you still avoid everything that draws you out of your commonplace, and that reminds you how man loves? No! and if I went to the bottom, and if I could thenceforward no longer console myself, I would still, with bare heart and with all my wounds bleeding, dissolved and sinking, I would still press to my bosom the beloved being who must leave me, and would still say, It does me good!" Cold, self-seeking, comfortable persons avoid leave-taking, just as unpoetic ones of too intense sensibilities do; women, on the contrary, who alleviate all their sorrows by talking, and people of poetic temperament, who relieve all theirs by fantasying, court it.

At six o'clock in the evening,—for it was only a skip to Flachsenfingen,—when the cattle came home, he sallied forth, accompanied by the whole family. On his more fortunate arm—mine has to bestir itself only for the good of science—hung the Britoness, and on his left Agatha; to the sister the poor house-poodle (Apollonia) had buckled herself, who thought, nevertheless, she might touch and enjoy, despite the sisterly interpolation and mediating spirit, the dear Doctor. So do the sparks of love, like the electric and magnetic element, dart through a medium of twenty interposed bodies. A philosopher, who sits down and considers that our fingers come not, in fact, a thumb nearer to the beloved soul, whether only the globe of the brain or that of the earth lie between them and it, will of course say, "All very natural!" Hence this sedentary philosopher explains why maidens half-love at the same time the male acquaintances of their beloved,—why the cane-chair of Shakspeare, the clothes-drawer of Frederick II., the bob-wig of Rousseau, content our yearning hearts.—

But no one, except the queen-bee of this streaming swarm, wanted to go back again. "Only just as far as the six trees," said Agatha. When they had arrived at these frontier posts and boundary-trees of to-day's pleasure, there were seven of them, and there was a general agreement that *they* were not meant, and they must go farther. The one who is escorted grows generally more and more nervous, and the escort more and more delighted, the longer it lasts. "Do let us go as far as that ploughman!" said the sharp-sighted Britoness. But at last our hero observed, that this Pillar of Hercules of their journey was itself a moving column, and that the ploughman was only a wayfarer. "The best thing is," said he, and turned about, "for me to go back, and not start till to-morrow." The Chaplain said: "As far as the old palace" (i. e. there was still *one* wall of it remaining); "besides, I usually go there evenings!" But beyond this frontier fort of the loveliest of evenings the chattering column deceptively extended its march, and the eyes were forgotten for the ears. As, consequently, in these boundary disputes, one main article after another was broken by separate articles, there was really nothing further to be done, except to make the following attempt. "Only so far did I mean to have you go," said Victor;—"now you must keep on with me and spend the night at the apothecary's." "In fact," said the Chaplain's wife, coolly, "we'll go along together till sundown; we surely are not going to turn our backs upon this lovely sun." And certainly the evening had kindled nothing but *feux-de-joie* in the sun, in the clouds, on the earth, and on the water.

On the hill they saw already the spires of the city; the sun, that chosen turnstile of the escort, poured out of his deep hiding-place his gold-trailing purple streams over the beds of shadow. There, on the hill, as the sun vanished, Victor folded his arms round the married couple, and said, "O, make yourselves as happy as you do me, and return to your home in gladness!"—and then he took the sisters to his enraptured heart, and said, "Good, good night! I love you!"—and then he saw them all going back with their hidden sighs and tears; and then he called out, "Truly, I shall soon come back; it is really only a jump from one place to the other"; and then he cried after them, "I shall be a poor devil, if we are separated!"—and then his heavy eye followed them through all branches and hollows, and only when the loving company had sunk into the last valley, as into a grave, did he close his eyes and think on the ceaseless separations of man....

At last he opened his eyes toward the outspread, obscured city, and thought: "Amidst that raised-work, in which men nestle with their little life, thy little days, too, are shut in,—this is the veiled birthplace of thy future tears, thy future raptures;—ah! with what eyes shall I look down again, years hence, over this misty environment,—and ... I am a fool! are, then, 2,300 houses standing only on my account?"

Postscript. This sixteenth post-day the Mining-Superintendent has concluded in regular order at the end of June.

FOURTH INTERCALARY DAY,

AND

PREFACE TO THE SECOND PART

I am going to weld Intercalary Day and Preface together. Therefore, unless there is to be mere trifling with the matter of the Preface, the Second Part must be here, in some measure at least, touched upon. It deserves to be noticed by critics, that an author who in the beginning has before him for his domain eight pages of white paper—just as, according to Strabo, the territory of Rome was eight leagues broad—gets on by degrees so far, and peoples the scribbled paper with so many Greek colonists,—for such our German characters are,[190]—that at last he has often marched through and settled a whole alphabet. This puts him into a condition to begin the Second Part. My second is, as I know for certain, much better than the first, although it is, to be sure, ten times worse than the third. I shall be amply rewarded, if my work is the occasion of one review more being made in the world; nor can I conceive of anything, unless it be this very thought, that books must be written, so that the learned notices of them may go on, which could keep an author up to the unspeakable labor of standing all day at the inkstand, and dyeing whole pounds of paper-rags *Berlin-blue....* And now let this cool, serious, *hocus-pocus* of a Preface—an expression which Tillotson maintains to be an abridgment of the Catholic formula, *hoc est corpus*—suffice for good reviewers and universities.

I return to that which I properly meant by this whole episode. I have conceived the idea, namely, of not only announcing my intention to give the extra leaflets and side-shoots wherewith the Intercalary Days are to be filled up, in alphabetical order,—for disorder is the death of me,—but also to make a beginning here on the spot, and continue as far as the letter I.

INTERCALARY—AND SIDE-SHOOTS, ALPHABETICALLY ARRANGED

A

Age of Women.—Lombardus (L. 4. Sent. dist. 4) and Saint Augustin (l. 22. de Civit. c. 15) prove that we all rise from the dead at that age at which Christ rose, namely, in the thirty-second year and third month. Accordingly, as in the whole of heaven there is no quadragenarian to be found, a child will be as old there as Nestor, namely, thirty-two years and three months. Knowing this, any one will highly esteem the fine modesty of women, who after the thirtieth year give themselves out (like relics) to be older than they are; for it would be enough, if a quadragenarian, or one of eight-and-forty years, should make herself out as old as good Rhine wine, or, at most, as old as Methuselah; but she thinks it is being more modest, if she ascribes to herself at once, however much her face contradicts it, the extreme old age which she can have only when her face has lain some thousands of years in the earth, namely, thirty-two years and three months. The merest dunce can see that she means only her future resurrection-age, and not any earthly age,—because she does not deviate from that standing year, which in eternity, indeed, when no human being can grow an hour older, is a matter of course. This unity of time they introduce into the *Intrigue drama* of their life already in the thirtieth year, for the reason that after that time in Paris no woman can any longer dance in public, and (according to Helvetius) no genius can any longer write in a masterly style. This last fact they perhaps took into account in old times in Jerusalem, where any one after his thirtieth year, but no sooner, could get an office as teacher.

B

Basedow's School System.—Basedow proposes in his *Philalethia* to hedge up thirty uneducated children in a garden, to leave them to their own development, and to assign them only mute attendants, who should not even wear human clothing, and then to publish in a protocol the results of the experiment. Philosophers are so preoccupied with possibility that they do not see reality; otherwise Basedow must have observed that our country-schools are just such gardens, in which Philosophy would try the experiment of what will at last come of human creatures, if they are absolutely deprived of all culture. I confess, however, that all these attempts must continue uncertain and imperfect so long as the schoolmasters cannot refrain from imparting to these little probationers some instruction, though it were the least possible; and the thing would work better with wholly dumb teachers, as there are deaf and dumb pupils.

C (*vide* K)

D

Divine Poet.—The Poet, although he paints the passions, nevertheless will hit them best at that period of life when his own, have slackened,—just as convex mirrors, precisely in those summers when the sun burned the faintest, have acted the most intensely, and in the hot ones the least so. The flowers of poesy are like other flowers, which (according to Ingenhouse) thrive best in a dim, hazy sunlight.

E

Emotion (Sentimental).—Sentimentality often imparts to the inner man, as apoplexy to the outer, greater sensibility and yet paralysis.

F (*see* Ph)

G

Goddess.-As the Romans would rather recognize their monarchs as gods than as masters, so do men like to call the directress of their heart *goddess* rather than mistress,—because it is easier to adore than to obey.

H

H.—I have often seen people who had the wherewithal of living and knew how to live,—which are not two different things,—first, flutter about the best and most superior women and suck from the honey-cup of their hearts; and, secondly, I have seen them on the same day fold their wings and light on a miserable ninny, that the ninny might inherit their—heirs. But never have I compared these butterflies to anything but butterflies, which all day long visit and rifle flowers, and yet spawn their eggs on a dirty cabbage-stump.

H

Holbein's Leg.—I prefer repeating the H in the place of I, because under the Rubric of the I would come the *Invalides*, of whom I had meant to assert, that, as people who have had limbs taken off become full-blooded, so they have the less bread handed to them the more limbs they have had shot or cut off, and that this is called the Physiology and Dietetics of the military chest.—But I have pitied these (half) poor devils too much to do it.

The famous legs of Holbein afford a better joke than legs that have been taken off. That is to say, this painter used his brush in Basle only upon Basle itself; and the self-same circumstance that drove his genius to this architectural dyeing-business compelled it often to hold recess-hours therein,—namely, he guzzled terribly. A house owner, whose name is wanting in history, often came to the house-door, and swore up at the scaffolding, when the house-stainer's legs—for that was all of the painter that could be seen—were standing or staggering in the neighboring wine-cellar. Then when Holbein by-and-by came stalking along with them across the street, a quarrel came to meet him and went with him up the scaffold. This irritated the painter, who made a study even of his cups, and he proposed to himself to reform the owner. That is to say, as he owed his misfortune wholly to his legs, whose festoons the man wanted to see under the scaffolding, he resolved to make a second edition of his legs, and paint them on the house in a hanging posture, so that the man, when he looked up from the house-door below, should get the idea that the two legs and their boots were painting away up there busily. And the owner took this idea, too; but, as he observed at last that the counterfeit foot-works hung all day in one spot and never moved along, he wanted to see what kept the master so long improving and retouching at one part, and so up he went. Up there in the vacuum he easily saw that the painter ceased where the knee-pieces began, at the knee, and that the trunk, which was wanting, was again guzzling in an *alibi*.

I do not blame the owner for not at once on the scaffolding drawing a moral from the leg-works; he was too furious.

I meant to have appended a further history of the princely portraits which hang there behind the President in the Session-Chambers instead of the originals, by way of casting-votes,—but I should disturb the connection; here, too, was formerly the end of the First Part.

17
DOG-POST-DAY

When I was in Breslau, I said, "I wish I were the Fetzpopel!"[191] just as I was devouring the portrait of that personage. The Fetzpopel is a silly woman whose face is stamped on the Breslau ginger-cookies. I say what follows not merely on my own account, for the sake of getting my own head on to such gingerbread paste, but also for the sake of other literati, whom Germany honors with monuments as little as it does me,—for instance, Lessing and Leibnitz. As one must always feel so disagreeably in the German circles, until half a rod of stones, at least, are got together for the monument of a Lessing or other magnate, (the most that we have as yet is what few stones good reviewers throw at a literary man, as the ancients did upon graves,)—accordingly, I expressed myself freely in the Breslau market-place before I had bitten into the Fetzpopel: "Either the temple of fame and the bed of honor for German authors are on this gingerbread here, or else there is no fame at all. When will it be the time, if it is not now, to expect of the Germans that they shall take the faces of their greatest men and emboss them upon eatables? because, certainly, the stomach is the most important German member. If the Greek lived only among statues of great men, and thereby became great himself, then surely would the Viennese, if he had the greatest heads always before his eyes and on his plate, fall into enthusiasm and an emulous desire to promote himself and his face also on to gingerbread, and other cakes, pies, and cracknels. Meusel's learned Germany might be copied in baker's-work,—one might emboss great heroes upon army-biscuit, in order to set on fire the common soldiery and make them hunger for glory,—great poets I would sketch on bridal-cakes in inlaid sculpture, and heraldic geniuses on oatmeal bread,—of authors for women sweet box-pictures might be designed for sugar-work. If this were done, then would heads like Hamann or Liskov meet more generally the German *taste* in such dress; and many a scholar who had not a loaf of bread to eat would at least ornament one; and we should have, beside the paper nobility, a baked one also." As regards myself, who up to this time never saw my face anywhere except in the shaving-glass, they shall mould me (for I am least known in Westphalia) on Westphalia rye-bread.

Now to the story again. A tall, curly-haired man stands in the night before the many-colored house of the apothecary Zeusel, peeps up at the lighted third story, which he is about to occupy, and at last opens, instead of the wooden door, the glass one of the apothecary's shop. O my good Sebastian! a blessing on thy entry! May a good angel give thee his hand, to lift thee over boggy roads and man-traps; and when thou hast fallen into a snare and been wounded, then may he fan the wound with his wing, and a kind man cover it with his heart!

In the apothecary's shop, which blazed like a ballroom, one of the fattest court-lackeys was begging of one of the leanest dispensers a maniple more and a little pugillus[192] of moxa[193] for his Highness. But the lean man took behind his scales a half-open handful of moxa, and four finger-tipfuls more (for in fact a little pugillus amounts to only three finger-tips), and sent it all to the feet of the Prince. "When we have burnt all this," said he, pointing to the moxa, "his Highness will soon have a podagra as good as can be found in the country."

The reason why the dispenser gave more than the recipe said was that he also wished to have his pew in the Temple of Fame; therefore he would first think over a recipe that was handed to him until he approved it, and then he always weighed out 1/11 or 1/17 of a scruple too much or too little, in order to take off from the doctor's head the civic crown of the recovery and put it on his own. "Only with such gifts can I work my cures," said he. Victor did not begrudge him the illusion. "A dispenser," said he, "who leads the whole column of convalescents, and turns over to the doctor merely the rearguard of corpses, has already laurels enough for this short life *under* his brain-pan."

The apothecary Zeusel has good breeding enough not to bore his tenant by forcing upon him a reception-dinner, and merely gave him *this* newspaper article from his oral *Morning Chronicle* of the city, that the Prince had not so much got the gout as that he was trying to get it and settle it. He also gave him the Italian servant whom his Lordship had hired for him, and his chamber.

—And therein Sebastian is now sitting alone on the window-seat, and seriously considering, without glancing at the beauties of the room or the prospect, what he properly shall have to do here to-morrow, and day after to-morrow, and longer. "To-morrow, I blaze away at once," said he, and twirled the tassel of the curtain-cord; "I and the gout must settle ourselves down with the Prince. It is hard when a man has to use the gouty matter of a Regent for water to turn his mill: a polypus in the *heart* or dropsy on the *brain* would annoy me less as a courtier; either would be respectable *means of grace* and fins for swimming upward. No, I will stand straight and firm, entirely upright; from the very first I will not yield an inch, so that they shall always find me the same. Not so much as quartering and anchoring in antechambers is to be thought of." (Indeed, his Lordship had already stipulated to the soliloquist an exemption from the annoyance of court etiquette.) "Ah, ye fair spring-years! Ye are now flown away over my head, and with you peace and mirth and studies and sincerity, and none but good, genial hearts!" (He suddenly twirled the curtain-tassel up shorter.) "But, thou good father, thou hast not even had such good years, — thou roamest over the earth and givest up thy days to the welfare of men! No, thy son shall not spoil nor embitter for thee thy sacrifices, — he shall conduct himself here discreetly enough, — and then, when thou comest back again and findest here at court an obedient, favored, and yet uncorrupted son..." When the son actually thought to himself, that, if he should thus culminate in a right ascension at court, he might win the heart of the Chaplaincy, the heart of Le Baut, that of his father, those of his whole kindred, and (provided he thought of *that*) even the heart of Clotilda, — by that time he had twisted off the curtain-tassel and held it like a tuberose in his hand, ... and so he thought best to lay himself quietly down in his bed.

—Get up, my hero! The morning sun already reddens thy balcony, — jump up amidst the ringing of the bells for the week-day sermon, and amidst the din of this market-day, and look round on thy bright chamber! Thy father, of whom thou hast been dreaming all night, has furnished it full of musical and artistic instruments and apparatus, and thou wilt think of him the whole morning; and yet the balcony offers thee still more, — the sight of a green strip of fields, and, toward the west, of the heights of Maienthal, the whole market-place, the private residence of the senior parson of the city opposite, into all the rooms of which, that he lets to thy Flamin, thou canst look!

Flamin, however, is not in there just now: for it was he who had already laid hold of my hero, and accosted him in those words of mine, "Get up!" A new situation is a spring-cure for our hearts, and takes away from them the oppressive feeling of our transitoriness; and beneath such a cheerful sky of life my Victor to-day dances with everything and everybody, — with the forenoon hours, — with the Regency-Counsellor, — with the apothecary, — out through the apothecary's shop right before the dispenser, on his way up to the palace to make a few passages with the gouty Januarius.

—He has hardly been at the Prince's half an hour, when Zeusel sees him running back again into his medicinal warehouse.... "Heigh! heigh!" thinks the apothecary.

But it was quite different from what he thought. Through an abatis of uniforms—for the entrances to princes' apartments are almost like lanes of tents, and rulers cause themselves to be guarded as anxiously as if they feared they might be the *first* or the *last*—Victor made his way into the sick-chamber. Before a patient who lies in a horizontal position one can keep a perpendicular one more easily. Great folk often confound the effect of their apartment and furniture with their own: if the *savant* could come upon them on a common, in a wood, in a cabbage-field, he would know how to deport himself. Victor, however, had himself been brought up in apartments that were embroidered, and furnished with gold corner-clips. So when he found his father's friend in pain and with his legs packed up, he exchanged his English composure for the professional, and, instead of awaiting haughty princely questions, began to propose medical ones. When the doctor's medical confessional session was at an end, he laid his hand, instead of on the head of the penitent, on the Bible which lay by it, and was going to swear, but gave that up because a better idea had occurred to him, and he opened—this was what had come into his head—the gospel of the paralytic: "For the podagra in this case is not to be thought of," said he. He showed him that his whole complaint was—wind (figuratively and literally speaking),—that it lodged itself in the relaxed vessels of the system, and insinuated itself, like the Jesuits, under every different form, through all the members,—even his pain in the calf was nothing more than that displaced human or intestinal ether. The physician in ordinary, Culpepper, is to be excused for his error in regard to the Prince; for every physician must make his selection of some universal malady, into which he resolves all others, which he treats *con amore*, in which, as the theologue does in Adam's sin, or the philosopher in his first principle, he detects all the rest. It rested, therefore, with the free will of Culpepper, whether to pick out for himself as the radical malady, to be the nest-egg and mother-bulb of his pathology, the podagra in the case of men, with women the flux, or not. When he has once made his choice, then he is obliged to endeavor to fix it upon his Highness, like pastel or quicksilver. January had never, even from his chapel, heard anything more agreeable than Victor's assertion, which set him free from the prostration, dosing, and starving which he had had to go through. Victor, in his joy at the lightness of the malady, hurried away to give his recipe for it, after he had asserted, by way of consolation, that "an *ethereal* body was still to be taken along with him, and would serve the soul, not indeed for a heavenly Graham's-bed,[194] but still for an air-bed, which made itself up. Only poor women's-souls—if one rightly regarded their bodies—might be said to lie on thorny straw sacks, smooth hussars'-

saddles, and sharp sausage-sledges[195]; whereas shaven and tattooed spirits (monks and savages) wrapped themselves up with such fine bodies stuffed with whalebone shavings."[196]

Away he flew; and I have already reported that the apothecary presently thought to himself: "Heigh! heigh!" In the apothecary's shop Victor said to the dispenser, at whom he flew like saltpetre: "Sir colleague, what think you about it, if we should have nothing to cure in the case of his Highness but wind? You must advise me. For my part, I should prescribe:—

> *Pulv. Rhei Orient.*
> *Sem. Anisi Stellati*
> *—Fœniculi*
> *Cort. Aurant. immat.*
> *Sal. Tart. āā dr. I.*
> *Fol. Senn. Alexandr. sine Stipit. dr. II.*
> *Sacchar. alb. unc. sem.—*

"If you agree with me, I have nothing more to say, except, *C. C. M. f. p. Subt. D. ad Scatulam, S.* Colic-powders, one teaspoonful as often as occasion requires."[197]

As the dispenser looked at him seriously, he looked at him still more seriously; and the medicine was prepared without a change in the dose. When he had gone, the dispenser said to his two startled pages: "You couple of stupid epiglottises, don't you suppose he has sense enough to ask?"

The biographer has no need whatever to justify the circumstance—since the powder and the hero justify it—that January got upon his legs the very same day.

As princes feel no pressure of the atmosphere, except that of the air which is in their bodies, January's gratitude for his deliverance from this pressure, was so unbounded that for the whole day he would not let the Doctor go from his side. He must dine,—sup,—ride,—play with him. In the palace it was tolerable; it was not like Nero's, a city within a city, a Flachsenfingen in Flachsenfingen, but merely barracks and a kitchen full of soldiers and cooks. For before every mouldy archive, before every room where lay genuine diamonds, before every door-lock, and before every stairway a bayonet was planted, with the protector and patron who was attached to it. The numerous crew of kitchen-servants lived and fired up in the palace, because his Highness was continually eating. By this continual eating he would make his fasting easier for him; for at the three ritual mealtimes of men he touched—because Culpepper would so have it—desperately little, and could not wholly contradict the courtiers who praised his strict diet. A watchmaker from London had done the most to help him out in this moderation by contriving for him a servant's bell, and a spring-work whose index stood upon a great dial-plate in the servants' apartment; the margin of the dial-plate was encircled, instead of the hours and the days of the month, with the names of viands and wines. January had only to ring the bell and press the spring, and the household immediately knew whether the tongue and the victual-index pointed to pastry or to Burgundy. In this way, by tinkling like a mill when his inner man had nothing more to grind, he was most easily enabled to observe a stricter diet than physicians and moralists could well demand, and he shamed more than one grandee, whom, after eviscerating in death, they were obliged to lay out upon the bed of state with the hungry stomach under one arm and the thirsty liver under the other, as they give to capons also their two viscera as a body-guard between their two wings.

Victor was as much at home in the palace as in the parsonage; for the court proper, the proper courtly worms'-nest and frog-spawn, was resident merely in the palace of the actual minister, Von Schleunes, because he had to do the *honneurs* of the throne, to invite ambassadors, strangers, &c. The Princess resided in the large old palace, which was called the Paullinum. Thus, then, did January spend his days without pomp, but with comfort and convenience, in the true solitude of a philosopher, and passed them away in eating, drinking, and sleeping; hence could the Flachsenfingen Prorector compare him, without flattery, to the greatest of the old Romans, in whom we admire a similar hatred of show and state. January had, in fact, no court, but went himself to the court of his actual minister; with extreme reluctance, however: he could not love anything there,—neither the Princess, who was always there, nor Schleunes's unmarried daughters, which would have been against his London vow.

About twelve o'clock at night Zeusel would have been glad to find out how all was going on, and brought to the physician in ordinary his niece *Marie*, whom he offered to him as a female lackey. The physician, who could not play the fool with any fool in the world, especially under four eyes, thrust before the slender pike a crateful of the food of truth, which the latter greedily devoured as if it were pine-apple. Marie was a relative and a Catholic, impoverished by a lawsuit, and disappointed in love, who, in the cold, hollow family of the apothecary, received and expected nothing but thrust-wounds of words and shot-wounds of looks; her broken and crushed soul resembled the marsh-willow, of which one can strip down backward all the twigs with the mere hand. She felt no longer pained at any humiliation; she seemed before others to crawl, but in truth she lay continually prostrate on the ground. When the gentle Victor saw this meek, averted form, over which so many tears had flowed, and this once beautiful face, on which, not the sorrows of fancy had laid their charming painter's-touches, but physical pangs had emptied their poison-bags, then did the fate of mortals bring sadness to his heart, and, with the softest of courtesy towards Marie's station, sex, and sorrow, he declined her services. The apothecary would have despised himself if he had taken this politeness for anything else than fine raillery and good breeding. But Victor threw her off once more; and the poor girl withdrew in silence, and, like a maidservant, without spirit enough for courtesy.

Nevertheless, in the morning the rejected one brought him his breakfast with downcast eyes and painfully smiling lips; he had heard in his bed how the apothecary and his hard sprouts of daughters had twitted Marie with her "doleful whining air," and therefrom inferred a "*refusal* from the jesting gentleman" overhead. His soul bled within him, and at last he accepted Marie;—he made his eye and his voice so soft and sympathetic that he could have lent either to the most tender maiden; but Marie took nothing of it to herself.

January could hardly wait for him to come again.

The third day also it was just so.

And so, too, the next week.

—But I could wish my readers had all ridden in a body, at this time, through the Flachsenfingen gate, and that this learned company had scattered itself through the city in order to institute inquiries about our hero. The reading scouts sent by me to the coffee-houses would learn that the new English doctor had already unseated the old one,—helped the parson's son at St. Luna to the post of Regency-Counsellor,—and that great changes in all departments were at hand. The division which I distributed among the butlers, butchers, fishery-masters, castellans, and valets of the court, would bring me word that the Prince had patted the Doctor, not on the fingers, but on the shoulder,—that he had day before yesterday showed him with his own hand his picture-cabinet, and sent him the best piece out of it,—that in the theatre he had looked out with him from the stage-box,—that he had presented to him a snuff-box rich with jewels (the usual civic crown of rulers, and their calumet, as if we were Greenlanders, who never love to receive any other present so much as snuff),—and that they would travel together. Two of the very finest and most dignified readers whom I had detached from these columns, and of whom I had despatched the one to the Paullinum to the Princess, the other to the actual Minister, would at least report to me the news that Prince and Doctor had called together upon both, and that both had looked upon my hero as a singular, shy, taciturn Englishman, who owed everything to his father.

But the last piece of news which the readers have related to me they cannot, I am sure, possibly know; and I will myself tell it to them.

—Before I deliver this, let me first simply explain in three words how it was that Victor rose so rapidly. There may be Evangelist-Matthieus among my readers who take this sudden rise, like that of the barometer, as the sign of a speedy fall,—who will say that laurels and salad, which have been forced to ripen in twenty-four hours by spirit on a cloth, wither again just as soon,—nay, who will even joke about the matter, and give out that the Prince's intestines, with their ether, are a fish's swimming-bladder to my hero, who only by its inflation mounts upward. Mining-superintendents laugh at such readers, and inform them that men, particularly the occupants of thrones, look upon a new physician as a new specific,—that they are always most ready to obey a new one,—that Sebastian always deported himself towards every one the first time in the finest manner, whereas with old acquaintances he never said unnecessarily anything witty,— that January loved every one whom he could see through, and that he fortunately recognized in my hero merely a gay fellow fond of life, and did not remark around his head any of Bose's Beatifications,[198] which smell of phosphorus and emit painful sparks,—that Victor was not, like Le Baut, a *pot-plant* in a crown, but a hyacinth hanging in the open air high above it,— that he was cheery, and made every one else so,—and that another mining-superintendent would not have made so much ceremony with his readers as I: *he* would merely have told them the main circumstance, that in Victor, in his waggery and behavior generally, the Prince had found and fallen in love with an enchanting resemblance to his fifth son, the *Monsieur* (lost on the Seven Islands), and that he had made this observation even in London, although Victor was five years younger than the latter.

January chose, himself, to present his favorite to everybody, and so to the Princess too. The philosophers have it to explain why Sebastian never once remembered, until he sat beside the princely bridegroom on the coach-cushion, the mad, enamored little strip of paper which, in Kussewitz, he had pasted above the Imperator of the *montre-à-regulateur*, and thrown into the Princess's bargain. He started, and held it to be impossible that he should have been such a fool. But such a thing is easy for a man. His fancy flung back upon every scene, upon every idea, so many focus-lights from a thousand mirrors, and spread around the future, which stretched out beyond, so many colored shadows and so much blue mist, that he was really frightened when a foolish action came into his head; for he knew, that, when he should have rejected it ten times and then thought it over thirty times more, then, after all, he should go and do it.—When the two appeared before the Princess, Victor was in that agreeable frame, which is nothing new to tutors and young scholars, which stiffens the limbs to bone, and sends the heart up into the mouth, and petrifies the tongue;—it was not the certainty that *Agnola* (that was the name of the Princess) had read the aforesaid advertisement on the watch, which so disconcerted him, but the uncertainty whether she had or not. In his agony he never thought of *this*,—that she, of course, did not even know his handwriting or the authorship of the little slip; and even if one does think of that in his agony, still it does not leave him.

—But all was, at once, above, below, and contrary to his expectation. The Princess had laid aside the face of sensibility with her travelling-dress, and had put on instead a fine, firm gala-face. The crowned bridegroom January was received by her with as much warm decorum as if he were his own ambassador of the first rank. For January, the disk of whose heart charged itself full of sparks on the electrizing-cushion of a fair cheek or a bosom-handkerchief, had for that very reason towards Agnola, with whom merely from policy he had concluded the concordats of marriage, all the warmth of the month after which he was named. Towards Victor, the son of her hereditary foe, the successor to the house-thief of princely favor, she cherished, as is easy to guess, true tenderness. Our poor hero, surprised at January's coldness, which seemed to promise on the part of the wife no special warmth toward himself, demeaned himself as gravely as the elder and younger Cato at once. He thanked God (and so do I) that he came away.

But all the way back he kept thinking: "If I could only have got my missive out of the watch-case! Ah, then I would have done everything, poor Agnola, to reconcile thee to thy fate and thy husband!—Ah, St. Luna," he added, as they passed along before the city parson's house, "thou peaceful spot, full of flowers and of love! The masters of the hunt send thy Bastian from one baiting-house to another!"

For he must also, for politeness' sake, go at least to the actual Minister's, and January took him along with him. Thither he went with gusto, as if into a sea-fight, or into a quarantine hospital, or into the Russian ice-palace.

Furniture and persons in the house of Schleunes were in the finest taste. Victor found there, from the wabble-headed figures[199] and court-people, even to the basaltic busts of old philosophers, and to the dolls in the shape of Schleunes's daughters, from the polished floor to the polished faces, from the powdering cabinet to the reading cabinet,—both of which painted the head in the mere passage through them,—in short, everywhere he found all that the sumptuary laws have ever forbidden. His first embarrassment with the Princess gave him the pitch for a second. It was no longer the old Victor at all. I see beforehand that the worthy schoolmasters at the Marianum in Scheerau will be hard upon him for it,—especially the rector,—that he should have so little knowledge of the world as to be, while in this company, witty without vivacity, constrainedly free without complaisance, too constantly in motion with his eyes, too immovable in his other members. But one must suggest to these courtly and scholarly people, that he could not help it. The rector himself would have been embarrassed as well as Victor before the *bel-esprit* of a minister's lady, whom, though, to be sure, Meusel has not introduced her into his, the court has into *its* Learned Germany,—before her quizzing daughters, especially the handsomest, who was named Joachime,— before a number of strangers,—before so many people who hated him on his father's account, and who watched him in order to explain and verify his relations with the Prince,—before the Princess herself, whom the Devil had also brought hither,—before Matthieu, who here was in his element, and in his leading character and bravura air,—and before the Minister,— especially before this last. Victor found in him a man full of dignity, from whom business did not take away politeness, nor thinking wit; and whom a little irony and coldness only the more exalted, but who seemed to despise feeling, scholars, and mankind. Victor generally imagined to himself a minister—e. g. Pitt—as a Swiss glacier, on which the clouds and dew that nourish it freeze overhead, which oppresses the low places, and, in its alternation between melting and congealing, sends out great torrents down below, and out of whose clefts corpses are drifted.

January himself was not quite comfortable among them: what availed him the finest dishes, if they were embittered by the finest conceits? The card-table was, therefore, especially upon the peaceful arrival of his spouse, his quiet place of anchorage; and his Victor was for this once also glad to anchor beside him. My correspondent thinks that the tuning-key to this over-fine, demi-semi-*tone* was turned by the Minister's lady merely, who had all sciences in her head, and to be sure at-her tongue's end, and for that reason held a weekly *bureau-d'esprit*. In this ridiculous position, Sebastian played away his evening and gobbled down his *souper*; he could tell a good story, but he had no story to tell,—in the few *contes* which stayed by him all was anonymous, and to the circle about him the names were precisely the things of the first importance; nor could he make use of his humor either, because a humor like his places the possessor himself in a mild comic light, and because, therefore, only among good friends whose respect one cannot lose, but not among bad friends whose respect one must hold by defiance, can it venture out in its sock and harlequin's-collar,—he did not even enjoy the happiness of inwardly laughing at them all, because he had no time for it, and because he never found people ridiculous till their backs were turned.

He was confoundedly badly off. "You'll not catch me here again very soon," he thought to himself; and when, through the two tall glass doors of the balcony, which looked out upon the garden, the moon stole in with its dreamy light, which out there fell upon stiller dwellings, fairer prospects, and calmer hearts,—then he stole out upon the balcony (as his partnership at the card-table was broken up by the Prince after supper), and the night that glistened on the earth and in the heavens exalted his bosom with greater scenes. With what love thought he then of his father, whose philosophic coldness was like the January snow, which covers the seed from the frost, whereas that of the court resembles the snow of March, which devours the buds! How sorely did he reproach himself for every discontented thought about his honest Flamin's slight want of refinement! O, how his inner man erected itself like a fallen and forgiven angel, when he imagined to himself Emanuel leading Clotilda by the hand, and rapturously asking him, "Where hast thou found to-day an image of this my friend?" At this moment he yearned inexpressibly to be back again in his St. Luna....

His quickening heart-beats were all at once checked by *Joachime*, who came out with a burst of laughter directed toward the parlor. As it was a burden to her to sit for a single hour, (I wonder how she could lie in bed a whole night,) she extricated herself as often as she could from the curb-bit of the card-table. The Princess released her this time, who suspended this *night-work* of great people on account of the weakness of her eyes. Joachime was no Clotilda, but still she had two eyes polished like two rose-diamonds, two lips like painted ones, two hands like casts, and, in fact, all the duplicate members were very pretty.... And with these a court-physician can keep house well enough, though the single ones (heart, head, nose, forehead) are not those of a Clotilda. As now under the open heaven he recovered his spirits, and on the balcony, which for him was always a parlor, the use of his tongue,—as Joachime's tone attuned him again to his own,—as she assailed the taciturnity of the English, and he defended the exceptions,—as he could now run, like a spider, up and down along the thread of the conversation, and was no more to be disturbed by the Princess, who had followed after to cool off in the night-air her inflamed eyes,—and as one complains of feeling ennui only when one himself inflicts it,—and as I transcribe all this, I do enough (I think) for a reviewer, who stands up behind the coach-body of the Prince, and reflects and wonders what he shall have to hold on to (except the footmen's straps), in case Victor, sitting before him in the carriage, does not during the ride home wish the Minister's house at the Devil, but thinks more contentedly,—Well, it's tolerable enough![200]

Victor's society agreed so well with the Prince, that he fancied he could as little do without him as a canoness out of the house can think of taking the badge of her order off her person. He always plunged into the sacred cup and welcome of the warm spring of a new friendship as immoderately as a guest at Carlsbad does into his. When he felt ennui, the Medicus was besought to come and drive it away; when he experienced an inward jubilee, that person was again entreated to appear, that he might participate in the jubilation. Only those times at which January felt neither ennui nor the contrary were left to his friend to spend entirely at his own pleasure. Victor had sworn beforehand to make an easy matter of refusing, and had broken out upon people of easy consent; now, however, he said, "The Devil may say, No! Just let a man find *himself* in the same situation first!" ... And so must our poor Victor describe nothing but empty, dizzying gyres in the court-circle of the throne, among people for whose tone he could more easily have an *ear* than a *tongue*, and whom he could read, but could not win.

A youth in whose breast hang the night-pieces of Maienthal and St. Luna,—or one who has just arrived from a watering-village,—or one who has it in mind to fall in love,—or one who, in great cities or in their great circles, must be an *idle* spectator,—every such one is also, for that very reason, a *dissatisfied* spectator therein, and blows into his critical pipe against the trifling company, till he himself is drawn in. But when all these causes actually meet in one and the same man, then can he find no relief against his gall-bladder nor any biliary duct, except to take some fine paper and send off to the Eymanns in St. Luna a confounded satirical letter upon what he has seen.

My hero despatched the following to the Parson:—

My dear Sir and adopted Father:"—

"I have not had hitherto spare time enough to lift my eyes up and see what moon we have. Verily, a court wants time for virtue. The Prince carries me about with him everywhere, like a smelling-bottle, and shows up his foolish Doctor. Erelong they will not be able to endure me: not because I am good for anything,—on the contrary, I am convinced they could bear the most virtuous man in the world quite as well as the worst, and that merely because he would be an Anglicism, an *homme de fantaisie*,[201] a *lusus naturæ*,—but because I do not talk enough. Business-people never trouble themselves about any conversational or epistolary style; but with court-people the tongue is the artery of their withered life, the spiral-spring and flag-feather of their souls; they are all born critics, who look at nothing but fine turns, expression, fire, and speech. This comes of their having nothing to do; their good works are *bon mots*,[202] their exchange business consists in visiting-cards, their housekeeping is a card-party, and their agriculture a hunting-party, and the *minor service* a physiognomy. Hence they must have other people's faults all day long in their ears as an antidote to tedious leisure, as the physicians inoculate with the itch to counteract stupidity; a court-establishment is the regular penny post-office of the smallest items of news, even about you commoners, when you happen to have done anything really ridiculous. It were to be wished that we had festivals, or card-parties, or plays, or assemblies, or *soupers*, or something good to eat, or some amusement or other; but that is not to be thought of. We have, to be sure, all these things, but only their names; the President of the Exchequer would shrug his shoulders, if we should undertake to be, four times in a year, so brilliantly happy as you are four times a month. As our week consists of seven Sundays, it follows that our amusements are only signs in the calendar, epochs of time, to which no one pays heed; and a festival is nothing but a play-room for the plans which every one has in his head, the boards on which he is to act his leading part, and the season for continuing the intrigue against victims of love and of ambition. Here there is, every minute, a stinging mosquito, and the thistle-seed of beautifully painted trouble flies round far and wide.

"There are many women here who are good, and disciples of Linnæus, and their eyes classify men botanically, according to his fine and simple *sexual*-system; they make a great distinction between virtuous and vicious love,—namely, that of *degree*, or at least of time; and the *best* often speaks on the subject like the *worst*, and the worst like the best. Meanwhile we have here female virtue and manly fidelity, in their way,—but no idea of them can be communicated to a parson; for these two jellies are so soft and delicate, that, if I should undertake to carry them down over all the steps of the throne to the parsonage, they would arrive there in such a spoiled and ruined state, that one would give them down below there the two opposite names,—for which, however, we ourselves have up here our special and corresponding objects. Your commoners would find our elderly men ridiculous in matters of love, as *they* would your daughters. But what often embitters for me this happy court-life is the universal want of dissimulation. For no one believes here what he hears, and no one thinks how he looks; all must, according to the regular laws of the game, like cards, have the upper side uniform, and put on an external stillness of face as a cover to the internal fire, as the lightning destroys only the sword and not the scabbard. Consequently, as a universal dissimulation is none at all, and as every one gives every other credit for poison, no one can *deceive* another, but only *outwit* him; only the understanding, not the heart, is taken in. Meanwhile, to speak the truth, that is not truth; for every one has two masks,—the general and the individual. For the rest, the colors which are used upon the scientific, refined, and philanthropic painting of the outer man are necessarily scraped off from the inner man, but advantageously, since there is not much on the inner man, and the study of appearance lessens reality: so have I often seen hares lying in the woods that had not an ounce of flesh or a drop of fat on their bodies, because all had been absorbed by the monstrous fur which had continued to grow after their death.

"If one compares the substantial value of the throne and that of the low ground of the commonalty, the physical and moral exaltation of men appears to bear an inverse relation to that of their soil, just as the inhabitants of marshy lands are larger than mountaineers. But, nevertheless, those elevated people bear the state easily on butterfly-wings, survey its wheel-work with the hundred-eyed papilio's eye, and with a walking-cane defend the people from lions, or chase therewith the lions among the people, as in Africa the children of the herdsmen scare away with a whip the real lions of Natural History from the grazing cattle.... Dear Mr. Court-Chaplain, this satire began to pain me already on the former page; but here one is malicious, just as he is vain, without knowing when: the former, because one is obliged to take too much notice of others; the latter, because he is compelled to think too much of himself. No! Your garden, your sitting-room, are pleasanter; there, is no stony breast on which one *crucifies* the arms and veins of friendship like a tree trained on an espalier; there, one is not obliged, as I am, to be twice a day under the barber's hands, and three times a day under the hair-dresser's; there, one has leave at least to put on his polished boot. Write soon to your adopted son, for I still deny myself the festival of a visit to you. Are there many baptisms and burials? What is *Fox* [203] doing, and the deaf bellows-blower? At this very moment I hear the mortar, instead of your rat-drum, pounding down below. Farewell.

"And now at last I greet you, beloved mother! My hand is warm, and in my heart a pair of souls are beating; for now your face, full of motherly warmth, shines on all my satirical ice-peaks, and melts them into warm blood, which will throb for you and for you flow. How good it feels to love again! Your second son, Flamin, is well, but too busy, and at present in St. Luna.[204] Greet my sisters and all that love you.

"Sebastian."

++++[326=361

He reserved the letter in order to despatch the Regency-Counsellor, who wanted to take his person along with him, with a freight at least.

Meanwhile his and January's joint visits, with their stage entanglements, grew to quite other ones, even a ganglion of friendship between January and himself,—and at the same time gave this friendship increased notoriety. In St. Luna, in Le Baut's house, three times as much was made out of it as there was in it,—in the parsonage, nine times. To this was added a trifle, namely, a scuffle,—properly, two. I have the incident from Spitz,—Victor got it from Flamin,—he from Matthieu,—in whose noble historical style it can here be handed over to posterity. The Evangelist was never ashamed of a commoner, provided he could make a fool of him. Therefore he visited the court-apothecary without scruple. To the latter, who cordially hated the barrack-physician, Culpepper, on account of his coarse arrogance, and on account of the reason given in the note[205] below, Matthieu had long since promised to upset the Doctor. As the latter and the podagra had actually been banished by Victor from January's feet, the Evangelist gave the apothecary to understand that he himself would, without *his* hint and wishes, have contributed far less to the fall of Culpepper than he had done. Zeusel, especially as he had the successor of the barrack-physician in his house, came after some days to the billiard-table with the certain conviction that he, from his apothecary's-shop, had thrust under Culpepper's posteriors the invisible leg, and hurled him down from the steps of the throne. There were present, unfortunately, the barrack-physician himself, and the noble Mat. Zeusel came upon this stage with the festoons of three watch-chains, with a pair of breeches on whose knees some Arabesques were printed, with a double waistcoat and double neck-tie, and with double signs of exclamation in his face at the barrack-physician;—his money-purse lay exactly under the *os sacrum*, because he, like some Englishmen, had caused his breeches-pocket to be concealed in the region of the breeches buckle. He had with him as his chamber-moor his long, lean dispenser, who in the adjoining drinking-room encountered the very short dispenser of the second apothecary's-shop, or shop of the *canaille*. The short dispenser, out of malice, followed the tall one about everywhere, merely to vex him; but this time he had just come back from the country with some hens'-eggs which he had collected as fees from convalescent patients.

Matthieu, after an exegetic hint to Zeusel, took the liberty of being of Culpepper's opinion in regard to the Prince's gout. Culpepper, who would fain be an old German,—such old Germans can never dissemble when they are angry, though they can very well do so from self-interest,—fired away and said the English doctor was a complete ignoramus. Zeusel displayed with a broad smile, as with a printer's vignette, his contempt for the coarse man. The Medicus looked like the Equator, the apothecary like Spitzbergen. Now the tourney went on merely upon the subject of the gout. The second and umpire, Matthieu, gave it to be understood, that "Zeusel, to be sure, loved his prince and lord, but still he could wish that this love had had the best means and the wholesomest influences. "In bawdy-houses," said Culpepper, "*that fellow there may* have influence." When the apothecary, at these words, proudly and contemptuously straightened himself up, the Doctor slowly jammed him down on the chair and on his money-purse, and, bringing down his fist upon his shoulder, nailed the little coxcomb with his purse to the seat.

This pinning-down vexed the tailor-bird most of all, and he replied, trying to get up, that "he would this very day, if he were consulted, advise his Highness to adhere to his present better choice." The barrack-physician might perhaps have too hurriedly withdrawn his hand from the shoulder which it covered; for he grazed with it, as with a cannon, the nose of his adversary, whereupon the latter, like Saint Januarius, discharged some blood. The Evangelist was personally grieved "that two such sensible men could not fall out and fight with each other without personal hatred and heat, since they *might*, like princes who go to war, attack each other without either,—but the bleeding too well attested Zeusel's ebullition." ... Zeusel cried out to the Doctor, "You lout!" The latter, in his fury, actually took Matthieu's opinion, that the former bled only from fury, and compared him to those corpses which in old times bled, indeed, at the approach of the murderer, but from none other than quite natural causes. The Medicus, therefore, looked for his cane, which like a prince was gold-headed, and took his leave with the crowned stick, drawing it a few times, as with magnetic passes, across Zeusel's fingers; but I would call the staff, if I were in the place of other people, neither an ear-trumpet for Zeusel, which the physician applied to him, as they often do to persons hard of hearing, that the latter might hear better, nor yet a door-knocker, which he stretched out before the truth, that it might the more easily get admission into the apothecary. What he wanted was merely to oblige him to let his handkerchief drop, in order that he might look him in the face as he bade farewell, which he clothed in the following forbearing and neatly turned remark: "You tell your Doctor that he and you there are the two greatest blockheads in town."

Under these last words both dispensers kept themselves still enough in other respects, though not with their tongues, indeed; for the tall dispenser saluted, as second chorus, the short one with the same war-song, and was a genuine Anti-Podagrist. Whoso considers that the tall one loved my hero on account of his politeness, and could not bear the short one, because

Culpepper sent all his prescriptions to *his* shop,—such a one cannot expect anything less of the couple than a reflection of the scene in the billiard-room; but the tall dispenser was composed, and never, like Portugal, propagated edifying truths with blood, but—the moment the barrack-doctor called the court-physician a blockhead—he quietly took the hat of the short dispenser, who had deposited his income of eggs therein to guard them from being broken, and coolly, without the least resentment, placed the aforesaid hatful of eggs on the head of the professional brother; and by a slight squeeze fitted the Doctor's hat, which sat half an ell too high, upon the head of his friend,—with all the more propriety, as Castor and Pollux also had on egg-shells,[206]—and having effected this promotion, he went his way, without exactly caring to have much thanks for the felt-stuffing and the streaming face-poultice.

Fisticuffs spread abroad lesser truths, as wars do great truths. The Court-Chaplain Eymann sent a long letter of congratulation to Victor, and called him "January's kidney-keeper," and begged for his promised visit. A travelling[207]-advocate knocked at his door as at that of a superior court, and begged him for a princely injunction against the Regency-College. The apothecary, with his application about the *lavement*,[208] still holds back.

Victor still laid up for himself his first visit to St. Luna like a ripening fruit, and thereby vexed the Regency-Counsellor, who wanted to persuade him into it. But he said: "Those who are left behind in a place long indescribably for him who has gone from it, until he has made his first visit; and so, too, with him. After the first, both parties wait quite coolly and composedly for the second."—What he neither said nor thought, but felt and feared, was this: that his demigoddess, Clotilda, who inhabited the most holy place in his breast, and who by her invisibleness had become dearer, more indispensable, and for that very reason more sure to his soul, would, perhaps, at her appearance, take away at once all hopes out of his heart.

It was on the evening of the day when he received Eymann's letter, that he thus fantasied: "Ah, if January would only continue so well! He must have exercise, but of an unusual kind,—the rider must walk, the pedestrian must drive. We ought to travel together on foot through the country, in disguise. Ah, I might, perhaps, be of service to many a poor devil! We would steal homeward through St. Luna,—No, no, no!" ...

He started back himself, affrighted at a certain idea,—for he feared he should, when he had once had it, even execute it; hence he said to it three times, No. The idea was this,—to persuade the Prince to visit Clotilda's parents. But it was of no use; he remembered that his father had held too strict a court of cognizance over the Chamberlain and the Minister. "And yet, what harm can Le Baut do to me? If I should only draw three sun-glances from January upon the poor fool! The wisest thing for me is, not to think any more about it to-day."

The dog will bring us the answer; I, for my part, make a bet—a fine connoisseur of human nature on my island bets the contrary—that he does not carry out this joke.

18
DOG-POST-DAY

To be sure he did—carry out the joke; but still at bottom I do not lose my bet. For it happened in this way. From the day when Doctor Culpepper had made that pass with his coarse hand, as with an electrical discharger, before the full-blooded nose of Zeusel, the man with three watches pressed his company upon my hero, who carried only one, and that, too, the clumsy one of the Bee-father. Zeusel always thanked God, if only a court-courier got drunk at his house, or the court-dentist over-ate himself. He always brought with him, when he came, certain secret items of intelligence, which were to be published. He kept nothing to himself, not though one had threatened to hang him in the cellar of his shop. He told our hero that the Minister was making interest in behalf of his Joachime for the place of second maid-of-honor to the Princess, who could select only the female part of her service for herself,—but that he could not fairly do it, because he, or his son Matthieu, had promised the Chamberlain Le Baut to procure the same place for Clotilda; he therefore begged my hero, who, as he saw, he said, was Matthieu's friend, to spare him the embarrassment, and induce the Prince (which would cost only *one* word) himself to intercede with the Princess in behalf of Joachime; the Princess, who, besides, patronized the Minister, would, on more than one ground, do it with pleasure, and then the Minister could not help it, if the Chamberlain, the enemy of his Lordship, went away empty.

The simpleton, as one can see, had guessed out, merely from the two accounts, which he had got hold of, of the two office-seekers, the whole of the remaining case; and the very circumstance, which Matthieu disclosed to him, that the Minister was vacating a quarter of a wing of his palace, for a companion of his deceased daughter Giulia, had only strengthened his conviction. To such a degree does malice supply the place, not only of years, but also of information and insight!

My hero could say nothing to him except that—he did not believe a word of it. But after three minutes of private reflection he believed it all: for that was the reason, he saw, why the dear Clotilda had to come back from the seminary just at the arrival of the Princess,—that was the reason why Le

Baut built around the Minister's son so many altars of incense and thank-offerings,—that was the reason why the old lady (in the Sixteenth Dog-Post-Day) serenaded, and so loudly, court-life,—in fact, as he further saw, two such outlawed, captive Court-Jews in Babylon must have the live Devil in them, until they are reinstated in the old holy city, and if they happen to have a handsome daughter, they will use her as the relay of their journey, and the Montgolfier of their balloon-ascension....

"O, only come, Clotilda!" he cried, glowingly;—"the court-pool will then be to me an Italian cellar, a flowery parterre. If thou art only once settled at the Minister's, then I shall have spirits enough and sparkle properly. What will my father say, when he sees us stand with two leading-strings, with one of which thou holdest the Princess, and I, with the other, the husband?" ... At this moment, Clotilda's recent objections to court-life fell like ice-flakes into his boiling blood; but he thought to himself: "Women, however, are a little mite more pleased with the court-residence of splendor than they themselves suspect or say, and far more than men are. Cannot he, too, bear, then, with a like soul-edifying position? She, as step-daughter of the Prince, is only half-miserable, compared with him,—and does she know, then, whether she may not some time be recalled from her *field-état* to the court-garrison by an accident?" By this *accident* he meant a marriage with Sebastian. Finally, he tranquillized himself with something which I also believe,—namely, that she had at that time, merely out of politeness, made a show of a certain coldness towards her new separation from her parents, and therefore towards the new place also; and then, too, pleasure at such a prospect might have been taken for warmth toward *somebody* or other at court, e. g. toward her—*brother*, he thought to himself.

And now yesterday's idea, upon which I have lost my wager, came forth again, having shot up astonishingly in *one* night,—namely, that, if he could persuade the Prince to make the journey and the visit to the Chamberlain, and while they were still on the road, could plead with him for a good word to the Princess in behalf of Clotilda,—then was it, in the first place, impossible for the stepfather to refuse a prayer for the most beautiful stepdaughter,—and, secondly, impossible for the Princess, when her spouse should exercise the privilege of the first petition, not to draw all possible advantage from the first opportunity of laying him under obligations to her.

—Eight days after, just at dusk,—in the autumn days night comes sooner,—the Court—Chaplain Eymann was standing on the observatory and peering at the sun, not for its own sake, but in reference to the evening-redness and the weather, because he wanted to sow the next morning,—when suddenly and with alarm he sprang down from the watch-tower into his house, and delivered the Job's tidings, that the Consistorial Messenger would be there in a moment, together with a French emigrant, and for the one there was not a farthing, and for the other not a bed in the house....

No soul came.

I can easily comprehend it; for the Consistorial Messenger reconnoitred around the parsonage, and so soon as he saw the court-physician, Victor, in wax, sitting up at the window, he marched instanter out of the village, straight back to Flachsenfingen. The emigrant had turned in at his professional cousin's, Le Baut's.

The two travellers were named January and Victor, and were returning this very day from their facetious flying tour.

That is to say, seven days ago, the Prince, who loved mask-dances and incognito-journeys and the ways of the commonalty, and who wished only the Minister's mental masks and incognito *further*, had started off on foot, with Victor, behind a fellow who had sallied forth in advance on horseback with the masquerade dresses and masquerade refreshments. January carried a sword in his hand, which was contained, not in any sheath, but in a walking-cane,—an emblem of court-weapons! He gave himself out in the market-town for the new Regency-Counsellor, Flamin. My hero, who at the outset had passed himself through the mint, and come out stamped as a travelling dentist, recoined himself in the third village into a Consistorial Messenger, simply because the couple met the true Messenger. This financial collector of the Consistory was made to hand over to the physician for this week—it cost the Prince only a princely resolution and an indulgence—his receipt-book and his ecclesiastical robe of office, together with the tin-plate sewed thereto. These plates are attached to Messengers, and the silver stars to coats of distinction, as the leaden ones are to bales of cloth, that one may know what the trumpery is worth.

For Büsching such a Rekahn's journey would be a windfall,—to me it is a true torment; for my manuscript is, besides, so large already, that my sister sits on it when she plays the piano-forte, because the seat is not high enough without the addition of the Dog-Post-Days.

What did January see, and what Victor? The Regency-Counsellor, January, saw among the public servants nothing but crooked backs, crooked ways, crooked fingers, crooked souls. "But a bow is crooked, and the bow is a sector of the circle, that emblem of all perfection," said the Consistorial Messenger, Victor. But what vexed January most was, that the officials respected him so exceedingly, when after all he gave himself out only for a regency-counsellor, and not for a regent. Victor replied: "Man knows only two neighbors: the neighbor at his head is his master, the one at his feet is his slave; what lies out beyond either of these two is to him God or beast."

What did January see still further? Untaxed knaves he saw, who enriched themselves at the expense of taxed poor men,—honest advocates he heard, who did not, like his courtiers or the English highwaymen, steal under the mask of virtue, but without any mask, and to whom a certain remoteness from enlightenment and philosophy and taste will not after death be prejudicial, because they can then in their own defence set up against God the exception of their ignorance, and represent to Him, "that no other laws but those of their own sovereign and of Rome can bind them, and that neither is God Justinian, nor is Kant Tribonian."[209] He saw hanging from the heads of his country-justices bread-baskets, and from those of their subjects muzzle-baskets; he saw, that, if (according to Howard) it takes two men to support one prisoner, here there must be given twenty incarcerated ones, that one city-magistrate may live.

He saw cursed stuff. But, on the other hand, as an offset, he saw on pleasant nights the cattle in fair groups feeding in the fields,—I mean the republican ones, namely, stags and wild boars. The Consistorial Messenger, Victor, said to him, that he had to thank the masters of the chase for this romantic spectacle, whose tender hearts had been as little able to execute the princely order of shooting wild game as were the Egyptian midwives to execute that of slaughtering the Jewish male children. Nay, the Financial Messenger at an alehouse had some yellow ink and black paper brought to him, and there,—while the slater drummed away on the roof to get some more slates brought to him, and the guests knocked on the pitchers to get them replenished, and the tavern-boy *tooted* in at the window through a beer-siphon,—amidst this Babylonian din the Consistorial Tithingman drew up one of the best petitions that the noble gentlemen of the chase ever yet despatched to the Prince.

A PLAIN RELATION, FROM THE PETITION OF
THE CHIEF MASTERS OF THE CHASE

"That, as the wild game could neither read nor write, it was the bounden duty of the masters of the chase, who could, to write for them, and on conscience report that all the wild game of Flachsenfingen was pining under the tyranny of the peasant, as well the red game as the black.[210] That it made a chief-forester's heart bleed, to stand out of doors at night and see how the country-folk, out of an incredible ill-will to the deer, all night long, in the coldest weather, kept up on the borders of the fields a noise and fire, whistling, singing, shooting, so that the poor game might not be able to eat. To such hard hearts it was not given to reflect, that, if one should station around their potato-tables, as they do around their potato-fields, just such shooters and pipers, who should shoot away every potatoe from their mouths, that then they would necessarily grow lean. From just this cause the game was so haggard, because it could but slowly accustom itself to such treatment, as cavalry-horses learn to eat their oats from a beaten drum. The deer had often to go miles away, like one who, in Paris, picks up his breakfast at the inns,—in order, at last, to dash into a cabbage-field, which was beset by no such coast-guards and adversaries of the wild game, and there get a good bellyful. The dog-boys, therefore, said justly, that they trampled down in *one* stag-hunt more grain than the game got to eat the whole week. These, and none other, were the reasons which had moved the chief masters of the chase to appear before his Highness with the humble prayer—

"That your Highness would be pleased to enjoin it upon the country-people to stay at night in their warm beds, as thousands of good Christians do, and as the game itself does by day.

"Thereby—the majors of the chase were emboldened to promise—a lift would be given at once to the country-folk and the stags, the latter could then graze the fields in peace, like the day-cattle, and would certainly leave the countryman the gleanings, while they contented themselves with the first-fruits. The country-folk would be happily freed from the ailments which come of night-vigils, from chills and exhaustions. But the greatest advantage would be this,—that, whereas hitherto peasants had grumbled at the hunting-socages (and not wholly without justice), because they delayed the time of the harvest, that then the deer in their place would undertake the harvest in the night, as the young men in Switzerland took upon themselves to cut the grain over night in the place of their sweethearts, so that the latter, when they came to their work in the morning, should find none there,—and thus would the hunting-socages no longer disturb any one in the matter of the harvest, except at most—the game," &c.

But what have we to tell of the Consistorial Fee-Messenger, Victor? That ecclesiastical collecting-servant astonished all parsons by his drollery, and all parsons' wives by his readiness, and nothing but his tin and his papers could adequately certify the genuineness of such a specimen of a Messenger. He collected all that the Consistorial Secretary had liquidated, and excused himself by the plea that it became neither him nor the Secretary in this case to be conscientious. In his brief administration, he bagged without shame all back-standing marriage-pledges of the smallest value, ("We in the College," said he, "are greedy for a half-bats,"[211])—moneys, when parties were divorced,—moneys, when marriages were concluded by councils, whether by indulgences for mourning-time, for blood-relationship, or for want of parental consent,—moneys, when the moneys were only once (*or twice*) paid, but not yet for the second (or third) time, although the Consistory always required this after-ring or resonance of the money in the single case where people had lost the receipt,—moneys which the parsons had to pay down merely for decrees wherein they were *exempted* from payment.—

Thereupon he emptied his bag before the Prince, and flattened down the billow of money, and began:—

"Your Highness!

"The Devil is in the Consistory: it might be a Lutheran *Penitentiaria* for all the Commandments, and is so only for the sixth. What an honest Consistorial administration has been able to scrape together lies there on the table. The pile might be as broad again, if the Consistory had sense enough to say, 'Who buys? fresh, new letters of indulgence for everything!'—It has shown, that, beyond certain degrees of relationship, it can grant bulls of dispensation as well as the Pope: why will it not, then, apply its indulgence to any nearer degrees? It would be able to dispense from great as well as from small, if it really set about it, and just as well from fast-day penances as from mourning, and thrice publishing, that erotic fast-time. By Heaven! if a single man, like the Pope, can be the spiritual washing-machine of whole continents, and can clean souls in bundles in the year of jubilee, then surely we all in the College may serve for the washing-machine of a single country. If that is not done, then we take—for we mean to live—sin-money and perquisites for the few things which we have graciously to wink at; and if in Sparta the *judges* worshipped the goddess of Fear, so with us the *parties* revere this fair *ens*.[212]—Had we only, at least, power to absolve from five or six great sins,—only, e. g., from a murder,—then could we allow divorces and expeditings of marriages, (these wholly opposite operations we perform successfully, just as the Karlsbad water at the same time dissolves the stone in the bladder and petrifies what is dipped into the well,) and do it for half the money."

Then, after a long pause,—"Your Excellency, it is, after all, impracticable, because the Devil has the secular counsellors mixed in among the ghostly; a half-*profane session-table* cannot by any cabinet-making process be made over into a *holy chair*; there is, therefore, nothing to be wished—except a good digestion[213]—but a spirit of concord, that clerical and secular counsellors may properly feed upon the parties around which they sit, saving a couple of bones, that shall fall to us scribes and messengers. So have I often seen on the carcass of a dead horse starlings and ravens at once, in a motley row, sitting amicably together, and pecking away and devouring."—

My correspondent assures me that by these addresses the Court-Physician effected more with January than the Court-Chaplain by his. Many parties got their money, and some judges a most gracious letter, from the Prince's own hand.

Before I arrive with our disguised span in the suburbs of St. Luna, one or two things are still to be mentioned. To January's soul more knee-pedals were attached than to a pianoforte, which the favorite's knee, while it seemed to bend itself, moved at its pleasure. He was always the son of the present moment, and the reflection of his company. If he read in Sully, then he did not neglect for a week at a time the Regency-College, and sent for the President of Finance. If he read in Frederick II., then he was for furnishing the imperial contingent and himself commanding it, and went forenoons to the parade. He contemplated with pleasure the ideal of a good government, whether in print or in a speech, and often attempted approximations to it, reformations, investigations, and compensations, for whole weeks,—with the exception of *retrenchments*, which, after all, are the only merit a prince can earn without the help of others. During the whole crusade he was a true Philosopher Antoninus, and stood ready everywhere to reward and to punish and to enact; he felt, too, that he could make it practicable, if one only did not absolutely require him to *labor* and to *abstain*; under *that* the other part also went to the Devil.

In the beginning, he was pleased with the sentimental journey; when it was over, he was so again; but in the midst of it, all that was pressed out after the first runnings grew more and more bitter, and he wished for himself, instead of the country bill-of-fare, his dietetic dial-plate. Then, too, he had accustomed himself so much to valor, that, for want of it,—i. e. of his body-guard,—he was, so to speak, timid; hence, on one occasion, in the dark, at the tavern, he was while in bed, about to run through a young weaver with his cane-sword, because the weaver had confounded at night the princely bed with one of more peaceful contents. For the rest, all the rays of his favor now converged to a focus upon the single man of rank, the only courageous and confidential friend whom he had,—his Victor.

But my hero had everywhere something to enjoy,—at least, the thought of St. Luna; everywhere something to eat,—at least, when they came to a fruit-tree; everywhere something to read,—and though it were only charms against fires on the house-doors, old calendars on the walls, exhortations to charity on the alms-boxes; everywhere something to think of,—of the travelling pair, of the four acts of Nature's seasons, which are annually given over again, of the thousand acts in man, which never return; and everywhere something to love and to dream of,—for this was the very road which Clotilda had so often gone over on her journeys between Maienthal and St. Luna, and the friend of her rich heart found on this classic avenue nothing but great remembrances, magic passages, and a long, quiet, homelike bliss....

"St. Luna!" cried January, delighted at the mere thought of seeing once more a man of the world,—Le Baut. The mask of an emigrant was a thought he had himself hit upon, the better to draw out the Chamberlain, with whom he meant finally to give himself out as an hereditary foe of the Prince. Had there been in Le Baut's soul a higher nobility than the heraldic, or had Victor but known that the Chamberlain would recognize the Prince at the first glance, and that he would be able to do so for the very reason that the genuine suspended Consistorial Messenger had probably before this whispered the whole secret in the ear of the city of Flachsenfingen, he would have dissuaded him from the *noble masque*.

Sebastian, as we have mentioned, stayed back and in the open air, probably out of shame at his part, and evidently from a longing to look upon Clotilda's sunny face, which for so long a time had not risen upon him, in a scene more convenient and congenial to his heart. "And the parents will be glad to see me again," he thought beside, "when they have something to thank me for,"—namely, Clotilda's place at court. More than once did he start, as he stood watching there behind the blanket of the dark, to hear his name called out of the Parsonage, and, in fact, with such love and such longings for his answer that he could almost have given one. But it was only the people of the Parsonage talking with his little godson, and saying to him, "Dearest good Sebastian! Just see here: what have I got for you?" How the veiled paradise of to-day's spring lay in old relics around him! How he envied the shadowy heads in the palace, which he saw moving about the lights, and the old Parson's pug-dog, who would fain wag him in to the Parsonage-inmates, and who continued in there to perform his part on the stage of so sweet a past! But when some thistles round the palace reminded him of the mosaic ones on the floor within-doors, then was the envier to be envied, and, with the fairest dreams that were ever traced over the ground of his dark life, he went back to the Apothecary's.

The next day January followed, delighted with the parents, enraptured with the daughter, because they were so fine and she so fair. It cost my hero nothing but a word to move the step-father to the intercession for the appointment of the step-daughter, which our hero and the father had so often longed to see; and it cost the step-father, too, only a word with the Princess to get his and their petition granted.... Clotilda became maid-of-honor.

Immediately upon that, the Minister von Schleunes, in a congratulatory letter, pressed upon Clotilda's parents the quarter-wing of his house, and was happy, in the epistle, "that a higher petition had *repeated* his own with such effect." I set up this nobleman as a model to all people of the world; although, at present, all writes itself *noble* in the *moral*, as the Viennese do in the *heraldic* sense.

Victor, who with his soul's eyes was peeping all day long into the Chamberlain's window, could hardly wait to see Clotilda, first in St. Luna, and next at court. He put off the visit from day to day, and night after night made it in dream. Not even his visiting-card—his letter to the Parson—had he sent off; he wanted, not only to carry it, but actually to supersede it, himself. But this, last thought—of suppressing the letter, for fear Clotilda might possibly get hold of this malicious conduct-list of courts, and therefrom contract a repugnance to the new office—he hurled forthwith out of his soul, as Paul did the viper from his hand. Woe to the heart that is not sincere towards a sincere one, is not great towards a great one, and warm towards a warm one, when it should be all this even towards one that is nothing of it all!

For the rest, he needed such a visit, and such a reciprocal visit, every day more and more; for he was not happy; and for this there were, besides himself, to blame, first, the Prince, secondly, Flamin, thirdly, nine thousand and thirty-seven persons. The Prince could not well help it; he poured out the whole cornucopia of his love on the Doctor, and took away from him all the freedom which the latter had been minded in the beginning so sacredly to maintain. Victor shook his head as often as he wrote in his journal, or log-book of his voyage of life, (at his father's behest,) and saw by his chart that he had passed over quite other seas and degrees of latitude and longitude than he or his father had desired. "However, I shall land right, at least," said he.—

But his Flamin brought still more sadness to his soul, which everywhere at once sought and bestowed love. He wanted to impart to the Counsellor, with the news of Clotilda's appointment, a joy like his own; but his friend received it as coldly as he did its bearer. The dust of law-papers lay thick on the organ-pipes of his spirits.—Chained to the session- and writing-tables, he was now, like chained dogs, wilder than he had been before when unfettered.—The efforts of his colleagues to dislocate the body politic into an anagram did not get from him the approbation which they deserved.—Then, too, there lodged itself in his soul the leaven of the jealousy of friendship, which could not feel it right that his Victor should see him seldomer and others oftener.[214]—But most was he affronted by Victor's refusal, when he besought his company to St. Luna.... In a word, he was vexed.

The nine thousand and thirty-seven men who were to my hero nine thousand and thirty-seven tormenting spirits are the gentlemen of Flachsenfingen jointly and severally, by means of their absurd character, which deserves not to be sketched here, but in an extra flyleaf.

EXTRA FLY-LEAF,

Wherein is sketched the Ridiculous Character of the People of Flachsenfingen, — or Perspective Plan of the City of Little Vienna.

Little Vienna is the name many give to my Flachsenfingen, just as we have a Little Leipsic, Little Paris,[215] &c. There can hardly, however, be two cities wider apart in manners than Flachsenfingen, where one gluts and drowns his life and his soul, and Vienna, where one, perhaps, does not sufficiently shun the opposite fault of a Spartan asceticism. The Little-Viennese, or Flachsenfingeners, open their hearts to the enjoyment of Nature far less than the orifice of the stomach.—Pastures are the kitchen-pieces of their cattle, and gardens those of the owners thereof; the Milky Way does not chain and satisfy their spirits half so much (though it is longer) as the Königsberg sausage of 1583 would have done, which was five hundred and ninety-six ells long, and four times as heavy as the learned man himself who has portrayed it to posterity,—Herr Wagenseil.[216]—Are these the traits upon which carriers ground the name of Little Vienna? I have often been in Great Vienna, and am personally acquainted with the grand crosses, little crosses, and commanders of the Order of Temperance, which is there so common. I can certainly, therefore, represent a valid witness, and must be believed, when I say, that, while in Little Vienna they guzzle extraordinarily, of Great Vienna, and emphatically of its cloister-people, I can and must maintain something very different: they have not only all the time the greatest thirst,—which certainly must needs be gone, if they quenched it,—but they also make use, against drunkenness, of a fine method of Plato's. That ancient advises us, in case of drunkenness, to look into a glass, in order, by the distorted figure therein which reminds us of our desecration, to be forever warned away from the vice. Hence whole chapters, the dean, the sub-senior, the junior canons, &c., often set vessels full of wine or beer before them, and lift them to their eyes, and in this *metamorphotic* or caricaturing glass, which, by shaking, distorts still more the distorted features, contemplate themselves, according to the philosopher's advice, a good long while. I ask whether people who peer so deeply into the glass can love drinking?—

It does not, however, follow from this, that I deny the Great-Viennese a resemblance to the Flachsenfingeners, in such traits as do honor. Thus, for example, I must gladly allow a similarity of the former to the latter in this respect, that they, neither of them, are ever down with the disease of poetry or enthusiasm or sentimentalism,—which are all one. Victor would make this eulogy sound in his language somewhat thus: "The Viennese authors (even the best of them, only Denis and hardly three others excepted) give the reader no wings to bear him up over the whole world of the actual by that nobility of soul, by that contempt of the earth, by that reverence for old virtue and freedom and the higher love, wherein other German geniuses shine as in holy rays."[217] And he would refer for proof to the "Vienna Sketches," to "Faustin,"[218] to Blumauer,[219] and to the "Vienna Almanac of the Muses." This reproach even a Viennese would accept and turn to his credit, by asking us whether we have to show (like him) a "Musen-Almanach," with a sediment of filth, whereupon one might write, "With approbation of the brothel."—This feeling of literary difference compelled even a Nicolai,—otherwise no special *amoroso* of the Vienna authors,—in his "Universal German Library," to build up for them a separate side-box, although he throws writers of all other German circles together into *one parterre*, or pit. In like manner have I seen in Bavaria, on the gallows, beside the usual post for the three Christian fellow-confessors, a special schismatic cross-beam attached, to which only the Jew tribe were strung up.

The Flachsenfingener knows that there is nothing in poets; and in books, where rills of verse run through the prose, he skips clean over the rills, just as certain people come late to church in order to escape the singing. He is a true servant of the state, who knows of what use the poetic golden vein is in the revision-, commission-, relation-, and enrolling-systems,—none at all; meanwhile, although he cannot appreciate a Klopstock or a Goethe, nevertheless he will not, in his leisure hours, despise a doggerel verse or crambo-rhyme. A soul of such a fortunate, robust nature, wherein one aims less to exalt his spirit than his income, makes it, to be sure, comprehensible how there may be a kine-pox, by means of which the Flachsenfingener has been able, like Socrates, to wander round alone in the plague of sentimentalism without being infected. The full moon produced with them full crabs, but no full hearts; and what they planted under it, that it might favor the growth, was not love, but—turnips. The genuine Little-Viennese shoots at much nearer targets than that white one over yonder. They marry there with true gusto, without having first shot themselves or sighed themselves to death,—they know no obstacles to love but ecclesiastical,—female virtue is a belt-buckle, which must hold as long as the surname of the daughter,—the hearts of daughters are there like letter-envelopes, which, when they have once been superscribed to one lord, can easily be turned so as to be addressed to another man,—the girls love there, not from coquetry, but from simplicity, any devil, except poor devils....

In short, my correspondent, from whom I have all this, is almost prepossessed in favor of Little Vienna, and therefore contradicts vehemently the author of the "Travelling Frenchman," who is said to have said somewhere—if I had him in the house, I should know how Little Vienna is properly named—that the Flachsenfingener has not energy enough to be at least a highwayman. Knef says, however, he will not give up the hope that they have been thieves, and backs himself by the cases of those that have been hung.

End of the Extra Fly-Leaf, wherein was sketched the Ridiculous Character of the People of Flachsenfingen,—or of the Perspective Plan of the City of Little Vienna.

But among such people my hero, with all his toleration, could not take any comfort whatever,—he who so hated all selfishness, especially in the sensual form, and who would gladly have attended Dr. Graham's lectures, wherein he taught men to live without eating,—he who so gladly opened his heart to the seed of truth winged by poesy,—who bore an Emanuel in his heart, and held the want of poetic feeling even as a sign that the *moral* man had not yet laid aside all caterpillar-skins,—he who looked upon this whole life and the whole body politic as the hull in which the kernel of the next life ripens,—O, whoever thinks this is too lonely among them that think otherwise!—

So it stood with the world around him, when he got a line from the good wife of the Parson:—

"The general talk here is that you are dead. But I express my mind against people, that, as you let so little be heard from you, and have forgotten all the world, you must, for that very reason, be still alive. Do confirm my proposition! We all have a fond and foolish longing for you, and I should like to beg you to come on the twenty-first (if the wedding at the senior Parson's hinders you no more than it does my Flamin). We have nothing to offer you here, but the birthday of our Clotilda. O good my Lord, and my beloved Lordship, how has it been possible for you hitherto to remain so long mute and invisible? A true friend, who has nothing at all of the ladies of your court about her, not even their fickleness, wishes heartily to have you before her eyes and beside her ears,—and that lady is myself,—and when I see you come, I shall certainly weep for joy, let me laugh or pout the while as I will.

"E."

When did he receive this letter, so full of soul? And what answer did his make to it?—

It was on the loveliest evening, which announced the coming of the loveliest Sunday morning and of the magic after-summer,—he looked at the evening red under which lay Maienthal's mountains, and his heart beat heavily within him,—he looked toward the dawning red of the full moon which kindled over St. Luna, and his yearning thitherward became inexpressible,—he thought of Clotilda, whose birthday fell upon to-morrow,—and so, very naturally, as to-day closed, he went—to bed.

19
DOG—POST-DAY

The October Sunday with which I fill up this Dog-Post-Day was, even at nine and a half o'clock in the morning, such a glad, glistening day in St. Luna, that the whole Parsonage thought of the Court-Physician.—"Ah, he ought to come to the concert this evening!" The *virtuoso* Stamitz was to give one in Le Baut's garden.—"O, better earlier, even to dinner!"—"And to my forenoon sermon, if he will not come to the children's catechizing." Eymann, as he said this, had, more than anything else, his newly dressed peruke in his head, which Herr Meuseler had to-day placed *on* it. This clever peruke-maker visited those of his diocesans (the parsons) who wore no hair of their own, often and with greater benefit to their heads than the Superintendent himself, that *Commander of the Faithful*, to whom most chaplains said, Your Excellency! If he could only have weaned himself from singing, lying, and drinking too much,—the *friseur*,—most of the clergy would have ordered their toupees—those artistic cock's-combs—of him; but as it was, they did not.

As the Chaplain loved to make the *confitures* of Fate, among which false hair is to be reckoned, bitter in some way, and to give them, as it were, an infusion of hops, he naturally sought to embitter to-day's peruke (for whose false curls he gave, in place of payment, genuine hair cut off from his people's heads) by the misgivings which he conjured up about the long staying away of Victor. He bethought himself: "We must have affronted him in some way,—he does not even write,—he has, perhaps, fallen out with my son,—something has occurred,—and then, too; the old Lord no longer gives us a side-glance,—our rats, also, had a hand (or a foot) in helping drive him away."

By such elegies he threw at first himself, and at last even his hearers, into agony. He was not to be refuted in any way, except by one's bringing out some new subject of distress. The breaking-away spot in his cloud, or his *little book for help in distress*, was this time a literal book, the "Anecdotes for Preachers," by Teller, of Zeitz, which he to-day received through the peruke-maker from the clerical reading-circle. Clergymen, especially country clergymen, carry everything out with a minute, punctilious solicitude, into which they are partly scared by their reigning bugbear and dragon of a Consistory. Now in this book-club there was a law current—commentators and editors keep it—that every member who should find a grease-spot or ink-stain or rent in the book he was reading should enter it on the fly-leaf in an index and inventory of spots, together with the number of the page "where." Very naturally, every one who was even half-way an honest Lutheran would deny the *immaculate re-*(or *con-*)*ception* of it, and the freckles were therefore all regularly registered, but nobody fined. Only the conscientious Court-Chaplain took upon himself, as scapegoat, the punishment of other people's sins; for he never could sleep a wink the whole night, when he found in a book more blots than in the sin-register, because he clearly saw that he should be made adoptive father of the anonymous smutch and buyer of the book.—Now Teller's Anecdotes for Black-Coats was a complete pile of linen for the wash, black with dirt. Was there not one dog's-ear upon another,—compound dog's-ears,—blot upon blot? were not the leaves regular *proof-sheets,*—and, in fact, speaking *without metaphor?* Eymann began, "And if money should come flying in to me through the window"....

Just then Victor's letter flew in at the window, and its—author through the door.

But, of course, the case was this:—Victor, before pleasant weather, had pleasant dreams; before bad weather, Satan and his kin appeared to him. The beautiful weather of Saturday, and the thought of Clotilda's birthday and of the after-summer, gave him a morning dream, which, in turn, gave him a stage on which only her sweet image played. A person whom he had seen behind the veil of dream stood before him all the next day in a magic reflection. With him dreams,—those night-moths of the spirit,—like the real moths, strayed out beyond the bounds of night and sleep; at least for the forenoon, he went on loving, awake, every person whom he had begun to love in dream. This time, by an exactly reverse process, waking love flowed on into dreaming love, and the actual Clotilda coincided with the ideal to form one saintly image, so radiant that any one who knows his dream will easily enter into the rest. Therefore must the dream be given to the readers, the poetic ones especially: for others I should be glad to prepare an expurgated edition of the Dog-Post-Days, in which it should be left out; for unpoetic souls that have no dreams themselves should not read any.

But to you, ye good, seldom requited female souls,—ye who have a second conscience of your own, beside the first, for pure manners,—whose single virtue, when one looks at it nearly, is seen to bloom up into one wreath made of all the virtues, as nebulous stars, seen through glasses, fall into millions,—ye who, so changeable in all purposes, so unchangeable in the noblest one, go from the earth with unrecognized wishes, with forgotten worth, with eyes full of tears and love, with hearts full of virtue and grief,—to you, dear ones, I gladly tell the little dream and my long story!...

"A hand which Horion did not see laid hold of him; lips which he saw not spake to him, 'Let thy heart now be clean and holy, for the genius of female virtue resides in this region.'—Lo! there stood Horion on a field clothed with forget-me-nots, over which the sky like a blue shadow fell; for all the stars had been withdrawn from it, only the *evening star* stood gleaming alone up in the place of the sun. White ice-pyramids, streaked with down-trickling lines of evening redness, closed in, as with a wall of gold and silver ore, the whole dark horizon.—Therein Clotilda passed by, sublime as one dead, serene as a human being in the next world, conducted now by winged children, now by a veiled nun, now by an earnest angel, but she passed forever by before Horion; she smiled upon him in blissful lovingness while thus passing, but she passed by.—Flowery hillocks, almost like graves, rose and sank, for every one was stirred by the breathing of a bosom slumbering beneath it; a white rose stood over the heart that lay veiled below; two red ones grew over the cheeks, where tender blushes hid themselves in the earth; and overhead in the night-blue of heaven the white and red reflections of the hill-flowers glided fitfully into each other as often as the roses of the heart and the cheeks swayed with the hillock.—Dying echoes, awakened, however, by unheard voices, gave answer to each other behind the mountains; each echo lifted the little hills of slumber still higher, as if a deep sigh or a bosom full of rapture heaved them; and Clotilda smiled more blissfully, sinking at every resonance more deeply into the flowery earth.—The tones were too full of ecstasy, and the dissolved heart of man was fain to die therein. Clotilda sank now into the graves up to her heart; only her silent head still smiled above the meadow; the forget-me-nots at last reached up to the sunken eyes that were full of blissful tears, and bloomed over them.—Then suddenly a hill of slumber crept over the saint, and from beneath the flowers her words came up, 'Rest thou, too, Horion!'—But the sounds, growing more distant, transformed themselves during the burial into dim harmonica-tones.... And lo! as they sank into silence, there came up a great shadow like Emanuel, and stood before him like a short night, and covered the unknown moment as with a hand from a higher world. But when the moment and the shadow had passed away, then had all the hills sunk.—Then the reflections of the flowers, flowing together, gilded over the undulating heavens.—Then were seen *white* butterflies, *white* doves, *white* swans, climbing up to the purple peaks of the ice-mountains with outstretched wings as with arms, and behind the mountains, as if by an uncontainable transport, blossoms were flung up, and stars and garlands.—

And there on the highest ice-mountain, as it rose tranquil in clear radiance and purple blaze, stood Clotilda, glorified, consecrated, radiant with supernatural rapture, and on her heart fluttered a nebulous globe, which consisted of little vaporized tears, and on which Horion's pallid form was delineated, and Clotilda spread wide her arms." —

But to embrace? or to soar away? or to pray?... Ah! he awoke too soon, and his eyes streamed down in greater tears than the nebulous ones, and a sinking voice cried incessantly all around him, "Rest thou, too!"

O thou soul of woman, — thou that goest, weary and unrewarded, wounded and bleeding, but great and unspotted, up from the smoking battle-field of life, — thou angel, whom the heart of man, reared by storms, soiled by the world's dealings, can respect and love, but cannot reward or reach, — how does my soul at this moment bow down before thee! how do I wish thee now the soothing balm of Heaven, the requiting goodness of the Eternal! And thou, Philippina, precious soul, glide away into a secret cell, and, amidst the tears which thou hast already so often shed, lay thy hand upon thy soft, rich heart, and swear, "Forever shalt thou continue consecrated to God and virtue, even if not to repose!" To thyself swear it, — not to me, for I believe it without an oath. —

What a parade-night, full of stars and dreams, was that! and what a gala-day of Nature followed upon it! In Victor's brain stood nothing but St. Luna, veiled in blue, bespangled with silver dew-drops, and graced by the loveliest angel, who to-day raised moist, glad eyes to the friendly heaven, and thought, "How beautiful art thou to-day, just upon my birthday festival!" — Even the Senior Pastor and his daughter, who both made a wedding, — the former an anniversary second wedding with his Senioress, the latter a first one with the preacher of the Orphan Asylum, — slipped themselves into the procession of his joyous thoughts as two new couples.

He did not mean to go to St. Luna, but he said; "I will dress myself up just for a little walk." —

"It is all one where I go to-day," he said, when he was out of doors; and so he took the St. Luna road. —

"I can turn round at any time," he said, when he had gone half-way. —

"But it would be something still more ridiculously funny, if I should be at once correspondent and postman, and deliver my own letter," said he, and drew it out. —

"And answer my good mother's orally by the same opportunity," he continued, half in dream, and full of greater love towards her who had sent him the sweet nocturnal one by the intelligence of the birthday. —

—But when he heard the first bells of St. Luna ringing for church, then he sprang up, and said, "Now I will no longer embitter the way by further scruples, but will march boldly and decidedly into the village."

And so, taking the hand of Fortune, with all Nature smiling after him, with dreams in his heart, with innocent hope in his freshly blooming countenance, he entered into the Eden of his soul.

Flamin he had not asked to go with him, in order not to rob the Senior Pastor of his wedding-guest, and because he did not know, himself, that he should reach St. Luna, and perhaps, too, because he did not want to have his fantasying attention to the sparkling morning disturbed by any news about juristic cases. In fact, he would rather take a walk with a woman than with a man. Men are almost ashamed, beside one another, of any except silent emotions; but womanly souls love to unfold to each other their bashful sensibilities; for they cover up the naked heart with maternal warmth, that it may not become chilled during the unveiling.

As Victor passed round the Parsonage below, he saw himself up at the window, in his *second edition for a few good friends*; but the wax Victor had forthwith to be banished behind a false partition, that it might not frighten the fleshly one. The reception of the latter, and the feast of jubilee thereupon, need not be described by me in a more lively manner than by my saying that the pug-dog was almost crushed underfoot, the bulfinch hopped round in vain for his breakfast, nor did the Parson's wife offer any to the guest, in her joy at staring at him, and church did not begin till after the double usance of half an hour; so that this time more parishioners went to church drunk than usual.

Victor, too, went thither intoxicated, but with joy. There is nothing more agreeable than to be a parson's wife, and to say to one's husband, while putting on his clerical bands, "Make the service a little longer to-day, else the mutton will not be quite roasted through."—Domestic trifles gratified my hero full as much as courtly ones provoked him.

He went with the Parson and with the Parson's wife, who abridged all the processes of kitchen and toilet in a summary and manlike way. His toleration for the faults of the clerical order had nothing in common with that of the distinguished people who are fit for high dignities and dinners, which arises from supreme contempt, and which can endure a Christian priest as easily as an Egyptian; but it grew out of his opinion that the churches are still the only Sunday-Schools and Spartan school-gates for the poor commoners, who cannot hear their *cours de morale* from the *state*. Besides, he loved, as a youth, the favorites of his childhood.

Many preachers try to combine the rule of Quintilian, who requires that *bad* arguments should be put forward in the earlier part of the discourse, with that of Cicero, who is for keeping them back till the latter part, by posting them in *both* places; but Eymann held good feelings to be better than bad reasons, and wound around the peasants chains, not of reasoning, but of flowers.

The *friseur* above-mentioned, at first, would not go to church, because it was beneath his dignity, but afterward he could not do otherwise; for, on account of the court stranger present to-day, church-music was to be made.

It is the only fault of the peruke-maker Meuseler, that he loves to sing too well, and is too fond of intruding his natural pipes into all church-music that is made in his perukial diocese, especially on Holy Whitsuntide. The St. Luna chorister could never bear this; but how to cheat him and feast a thousand ears? Simply thus: He frizzled out to-day what was still to be frizzled, (not to-day alone, but it was always so,) and merely glided up the choir-steps. Here he leaned and watched, till the chorister, seated on the musical sausage-sledge, struck with his finger the first note of the church-music. Then, like a sunbeam, he darted up into the choir, and filched away from the young counter-tenor his part, and sang it into the ears of the congregation, but with much whining and puffing, as if he were chanting his manuscript to the reviewers. For one must now, once for all, make it known to the world, that the enraged musician at the clavichord had, with a sharp-cornered triangle of elbows, furiously thrust back at the frizzling counter-tenor, in order to push the strange singing-bird out of the bird-house of the choir. But as the singer made his right arm the firm note-desk of his text, and the other a war-club,—like the Jews, who built up Jerusalem with one hand full of building-tools and the other full of weapons,—one sees that the peruke-maker, even amidst this continuance of fighting and fa-sol-la-ing, could do his very best, and execute somewhat during the musical truce of God. But so soon as the music had drawn its last breath, then the harmonious bird-of-passage and stormy-petrel skipped nimbly out across the choir, accompanied by the memory of a thousand ears and a single elbow. The chorister could not catch him, nor get scent of him.

If, on the contrary, he had the good fortune to be passing with his bandboxes through a village just as parson and schoolmaster and pedagogic frog-spawn were quacking and croaking[220] round a deaf corpse,—all which many name, more concisely, a dirge,—then could the *virtuoso*, without the counter-prop of elbows, spring gayly with both feet into the motet,[221] work out the funeral serenade given to the dead man by his heirs, throw in gratis some final cadences to the funeral procession, and yet have time to offer in the village to the bailiff an entirely new bag-wig.—

To our hero the music in country churches gave the greatest satirical pleasure. But little should we get by it, had I not the forethought to beg leave just for one poor little extra-syllable—one shall hardly see it—upon church-music.

POOR LITTLE EXTRA-SYLLABLE ON CHURCH-MUSIC

It always gives me pleasure to see the people keep their seats during church-music, because it is a proof that no one is bitten by the tarantula; for, if they should run out, one would see that they could not endure any discords, and so had been bitten. I, as profane music-master, compose for few churches,—that is to say, only the consecration-noise for new ones, or old ones that have been repaired,—and therefore, in truth, I understand nothing of the matter whereupon, in passing, I purpose to express myself; but thus much let me still be allowed to assert, that the Lutheran church-music is good for something,—in the country, not in the capitals, where, perhaps, the fewest discords are correctly delivered. Verily, a miserable, sottish, blue chorister, who in bravura-airs sings himself brown and beats others brown,—there are, therefore, two kinds of *bravura*-airs,—is able, with a few mechanics who on Sundays work at the fiddle, with a trumpeter who might blow down without an instrument the walls of Jericho, with a smith who lays about him with the sticks of the kettle-drums, with a few spasmodic youngsters that do not yet even understand singing, and still resemble a female singer, who labors, not, like the fine arts, for *ear* and *eye* alone, but also (only in a worse acceptation than the youngsters) for a third sense, and with the little wind which he draws from the lungs of the organ and his own lungs,—such a thumper, I say, is able, with so extraordinarily little musical rubbish, nevertheless, to get up a much louder thundering and fiddle-rosin-lightning around the pulpit Sinai—I mean, to draw a far more vehement and discordant church-music out of his choir—than many much better sustained theatre-orchestras and chapels, with whose harmonies temples are so often desecrated. Hence such a noisy man is pained afterward, when people misunderstand and falsely judge his church scraping and squeaking and groaning. Shall, then, the soft, low Moravian music steal into all our provincial churches?—Fortunately, however, there are still city choristers who are working against this, and who know wherein pure choral tone and discord are to be distinguished from court-tone.

I expect, not readers, but organists, to know why mere dissonances—for consonances are to be endured only among the voices of the instruments—belong to the choir. Dissonances—according to Euler and Sulzer—are relations of tones which are expressed in high numbers; they displease us, therefore, not on account of their incongruity, but on account of our inability to reduce them rapidly to an equation. Higher minds would find the near relations of our harmonies too easy and monotonous,—the larger ones of our discords, on the contrary, charming and not above their comprehension. Now, as divine service is held more in honor of higher beings than for the profit of men, the church style must insist upon this, that a music shall be made, suitable for higher beings,—namely, of discords,—and that precisely that which is the most abominable to our ears shall be chosen as most appropriate for the temple.

If we once open the church-doors to the instrumental music of the Moravians, then we shall at last be infected with their singing, and by degrees all that vocal bleating and bellowing will be lost which makes our churches so lively, and which to castrated ears is such a disagreeable hammer of the law, but for us so good a proof that we resemble the swine, which the Abbé de Baigne, at the command of Louis XI., arranged according to the scale, goaded with jacks, and set to squealing.—These are my thoughts on church-music, or modern German battle-song.

End of the Extra-Syllable on Church-Music.

I should not have let the hair-dresser sing and strut so long, if my hero had been available for anything else, all this Sunday, than a supernumerary; but he did nothing of consequence the whole day, except, that, out of a sort of humanity, by unpacking, himself; her chests-of-drawers and bandboxes, he compelled old Appel, who would rather dress hams than her person, to prepare the usual Sabbath edition of the latter, printed with typographic splendor, as early as three o'clock in the afternoon; otherwise she would not have delivered the same till after supper. The Jews believe that they get, on the Sabbath, a new Schabbes-[222] or Sabbath-Soul: into maidens there enters one at least; into the Appels, two or three.

But why do I expect my hero to make any more active demonstration to-day,—him who, to-day, buried in that dream-night and in the coming evening, his emotions stirred by every kindly eye, and by the *rudera* [223] and urns of a spring which he had dreamed away,—softly dissolved by the calm, bland summer, which still lay smiling and dying on the incense-altars of the mountains, on the crape-clad fields, and amidst the mute funeral escort of birds, and at the rising of the first cloud would pass away from the boughs,—Victor, I say, who to-day, greeted with a melancholy smile by nothing but tender remembrances, felt that he had hitherto been too mirthful? He could only look upon the good souls around him with glistening eyes of love, then turn them away, more intensely glistening, and go out. Over his heart and all its notes stood written, *Tremolando*. No one is more profoundly sad than he who laughs too much; for when this laughter ceases, everything has power over the exhausted soul, and a meaningless lullaby, a flute-concert,—whose D sharp and F sharp keys and mouthpieces are merely the two lips wherewith a young shepherd whistles,—opens the flood-gates of the old tears, as a whisper loosens the poised and trembling avalanche. He felt as if his dream of this morning absolutely did not allow him to address Clotilda; she seemed to him too holy, and still escorted by winged children, and placed upon icy thrones. As, upon the whole, he had to-day neither a tongue nor an ear for Le Baut's conversations in the realm of the morally dead, he preferred to listen unseen in the great leafy garden to this Stamitz concert, and at the farthest let himself be introduced to the company by accident. His second reason was, that his heart was made for a sounding-board of music, and gladly drank in the fleeting tones without disturbance, and loved to conceal their effects upon him from ordinary men, of the world, who can truly quite as little do without Goethe's, Raphael's, and Sacchini's things (and for not a whit inferior reasons) as without Löschenkohl's own. Emotion, it is true, raises one above being ashamed to show emotion; but while his emotions lasted, he hated and shunned all attention to another's attention, because the Devil smuggles in vanity among the best feelings, often one knows not how. In the night, in a shady nook, tears fall more gracefully, and by-and-by evaporate.

In all this he was strengthened by the Parson's wife; for she had secretly sent to town and invited her son, and artistically prepared in the garden a surprise.

The Parson's family repaired at last to the embowered concert-hall, and gave not a thought to the consideration how much they were despised by Le Baut's household, who held only noble metals and noble birth, never noble deeds, to be cards of admission, and who, highly valuing the people of the Parsonage as friends of his Lordship and of Matthieu, would, however, have valued them still higher as lap-dogs of either.

Victor kept back a little in the Parsonage garden, because it was still too light, and also because he pitied poor Apollonia, who was peering solitary and unseen, in full finery, from the window of the summer-house, out into the air, and dandling perpendicularly the little god-son, whom she hung now over her head, now under her stomach. After the manner of a cit, he did not put on his hat in the summer-house, in order to strengthen her spirit by courtesy. An infant is, as it were, prompter and bellows-blower to the nurse: the young Sebastian sent Appel timely and sufficient succor under the siege by the elder one, and she undertook at last to speak, and remark that the god-son was a dear, good, beautiful, little "Basty." "But," she added, "the young leddy (Clotilda) must not hear that: she will have it that we should call him Victor, when she hears father call him Basty." Now she began to magnify how Clotilda loved his godchild, how often she would snatch the little monkey and smile on him and hug and kiss him; and the eulogist repeated on a small scale everything that she praised. Nay, the grown-up Sebastian did it after her, but he sought on the little lips only the kisses of *others*; and perhaps, in Appel's case, again, *his* were among the things which are sought. Made happier himself, he left one whom he had made happier; for Love despatched now one gayly attired hope after another as messengers to his heart, and all said, "Truly, we do not deceive thee: trust us!"

At last Stamitz began to tune up, about whom the stiff family of the Lord Chamberlain would certainly not have concerned themselves, because to-day there were no strangers present, had not Clotilda begged for this garden-concert as the only festival of her birth-night. Stamitz and his orchestra filled a lighted bower, — the noble audience sat in the next brightest niche, and wished the thing were already over, — the commonalty sat farther off, and the Chaplain, for fear of the catarrhal, dewy floor, twisted one leg round the other above the thighs, — Clotilda and her Agatha reclined in the darkest leafy box. Victor did not steal in, till the overture announced to him the seats and the seating of the company: in the remotest arbor, in a true aphelion, this comet took its place. The overture consisted of that musical scrawling and flourishing, of that harmonious phraseology, that crackling of fire-works produced by the mutual contact of sounding passages, which I so extol, when it is nowhere but in the overture. There it is in place; it is the sprinkling rain which softens the heart for the great drops of the simpler tones. All emotions in the world need *exordia*; and music paves the way, or the tear-ways, (lachrymal ducts,) for music.

Stamitz — after a dramatic plan which not every conductor marks out for himself — gradually descended from the ears into the heart, and from allegros to adagios: this great composer sweeps in ever-narrowing circles around every bosom in which there is a heart, until at last he reaches it and folds it in a rapturous embrace.

Horion trembled alone, without seeing his loved ones, in a gloomy arbor, upon which a single withered twig let in the light of the moon and of its pursuing clouds. Nothing ever stirred him more during music than to look at the chase of the clouds. When he accompanied with his eyes and with the tones these nebulous streams in their everlasting flight around our shadowy globe, and when he imparted to them all his joys and his wishes, then he thought, as in all his joys and sorrows, on other clouds, of another flight, of other shadows, than those above him,—then did his whole soul pine and languish; but the strings stilled the panting bosom, as the cold leaden bullet in, the mouth allays thirst, and the tones discharged the heavy tears from the full soul.

Dear Victor! there is in man a mighty wish which was never fulfilled: it has no name, it seeks its object, though all that thou namest it and all joys are not its reality; but it recurs, when in a summer night thou lookest to the north or towards distant mountains, or when moonlight is on the earth, or the heavens are studded with stars, or when thou art very happy. This great, vast wish lifts our soul aloft, but with sorrow: ah! here below we are thrown upward in a prostrate position like epileptics. But this wish, to which nothing can give a name,—our strings and tones name it to the human spirit; the yearning soul then weeps more profusely and can no longer comprehend itself, and calls inward in rapture of lamentation between the tones: "Ay, all that ye name to me is what I want!" ...

Mortal man, the enigmatical creature, has also a nameless, monstrous dread, which has no object, which awakes at hearing of spiritual apparitions, and which one sometimes feels when one only speaks of it....

Horion yielded up his bruised heart, with quiet tears which no one saw flow, to the high adagios which laid themselves with warm wings of eider-down over all his wounds. All that he loved entered now into his shady arbor,—his oldest friend and his youngest; he hears the thunder-storm-bells of life toll, but the hands of friendship stretch forth to meet each other, and they clasp each other, and even in the second life they hold each other fast in withering grasp. All tones seemed the unearthly echoes of his dream, sent back by beings whom one neither saw nor heard....

He could not possibly stay longer in this dark inclosure with his burning fancies, at this too great distance from the Pianissimo. He went—almost too boldly and too closely—through a leafy avenue up to the tones, and pressed his face far through the leaves, in order at last to see Clotilda in the dim and distant green glimmer....

Ah, and he saw her! But in too angelic, too paradisiacal a form! He saw not the thinking eye, the cold mouth, the calm person, that forbade so much and desired so little; but he saw for the first time her mouth encircled by a sweet harmonious sorrow, with an inexpressibly touching smile,—for the first time her eye weighed down under a brimming tear, as a forget-me-not bows itself beneath a tear-drop of rain. O, this good soul surely concealed her fairest feelings most of all! But the first tear in a beloved eye is too mighty for a soft heart.... Victor knelt down, overpowered by reverence and rapture, before the noble soul, and lost himself in the darkling, weeping form, and in the weeping tones. And when he saw at length her features turned to paleness, because the green foliage overspread her lips and cheeks with a deathly hue from the reflection of the lamps,—and when his dream came back to him, with Clotilda sunk under the flowery hill,—and when his soul, dissolved into dreams, into sorrows, into joys, and into wishes for her who consecrated her birthday festival with devout tears,—oh, was there then any need, for the completion of his euthanasia, that the violin should die away, and that the second harmonica, the *viole d'amour*, should send its music-of-the-spheres to his naked, enkindled, palpitating heart? O, the pang of bliss quieted him, and he thanked the Creator of this melodious Eden, that He, with the *highest* tones of His harmonica, which with unknown forces shiver the heart of man to tears, as high tones shatter glasses, had at last exhausted his bosom, his sighs, and his tears: amidst these tones, after these tones, there were no more sounds; the full soul was wrapped up in foliage and night and tears; the speechless swelling heart drank the tones into itself, and took the outer ones for inner ones; and at last the tones played like zephyrs around the head that was drowsy with bliss, and only in the innermost part of the dying soul still stammered the too happy wish: "Ah, Clotilda, could I surrender to thee to-day this mute, glowing heart!—ah, that I might on this imperishable heavenly evening, with this trembling soul, sink dying at thy feet, and say the words, 'I love thee!'"

And as he thought of her festive anniversary, and of her letter to Maienthal, which had given him the greatest praise, that of being a scholar of Emanuel, and of little tokens of her regard for him, and of the sweet fraternization of his heart with hers,—ay, then did the heavenly hope of winning this ennobled heart for the first time draw near to him amidst the music, and that hope caused the sounds of the harmonica, like dying echoes, to float far and wide over the whole future of his life....

"Victor!' said some one, in a slowly lengthened tone. He sprang up and turned his exalted features toward the—brother of his Clotilda, and embraced him with joy. Flamin, into whom all music flung war-flames and more open sincerity, looked at him wonderingly, inquiringly, and with an imperceptible suspicion, and with that friendliness which resembled scorn, but which was never anything but the smarting of injuries received.

"Why didst thou not take me, too, with thee to-day?" said Flamin, in a friendly tone.

Victor pressed his hand, and was silent.

"No! speak!" said he.

"Let it be for to-day, my Flamin; I'll tell thee some time," replied Victor.

"I will tell it to thee myself," Flamin began, more quickly and warmly. "Thou thinkest, perhaps, I shall be jealous. And look thou, did I not know thee, I should be so: truly, another would be so, if he had thus lighted upon thee here, and put all things together,—thy late retreat from our summer-house out into the foliage, thy writing without a light, and thy singing of love"—

"To Emanuel," said Victor, softly.

"Thy sending off that leaf to her"—

"It was another from her album," said he.

"Still worse; *that* I did not even know. Thy lingering in St. Luna, and a thousand other signs, which do not immediately occur to me,—thy going off alone today"—

"O my Flamin, this is going too far! thou seest with other eyes than those of friendship."—

Here Flamin, who never could dissemble without immediately becoming what he assumed, and who could never recount an offence without falling into the old anger, grew warmer, and said, in a less friendly manner,—

"And others, too, see it,—even the Chamberlain, and the Chamberlain's wife."

This tore Victor's heart.

"Thou dear old friend of my youth! so, then, we are to be drawn and torn asunder, bleed we ever so much; so, then, this Matthieu is to succeed (for all comes from him, not from thee, thou good soul!) in getting thee to torment thyself, and me to torment thee. No, he shall not succeed; thou shalt not be taken from me. See, by Heaven!" (and here the feeling of his innocence stood in Victor erect and sublime,) "and though thou shouldst for years misunderstand me, still the time will come when thou shalt start back, and say to me, 'I have done thee wrong!'—But I shall gladly forgive thee."

This touched the jealous one, who to-day, indeed, (for a special reason,) was more composed.

"See," said he, "I believe thee always: say, dost thou never do anything against me?"

"Never, never, my dear fellow!" answered Victor.

"Now, then, forgive my heat," the other continued. "Thus have I already, with my cursed jealousy, once tormented Clotilda herself in Maienthal. But wrong not Matthieu; it is he, rather, who tranquillized me. He told me, to be sure, what Clotilda's parents thought they observed; nay, still more,—see,

I tell thee everything,—he said they had even, on account of thy presumed liking and thy present influence, which the Chamberlain would fain avail himself of for his reinstatement, spoken of a possible betrothal to their daughter, and had even spoken to her and sounded her on the subject; but (to thee, however, this is a matter of indifference) my beloved remained true to me, and said, No."

Now was the hitherto so happy heart of our friend broken: that hard No had never yet been uttered to him. With an inexpressible, crushing, but meek woe, he said, softly, to Flamin,—

"Be thou, too, always true to me, for I have very little; and never torment me more as thou hast to-day."

He could say no more; the stifled tears stormed surging up over his heart, and painfully collected themselves under the pupil; he must needs now have a still, dark place, where he could weep to his heart's content; and in his lacerated and smarting bosom there remained only one soft and balmy thought: "Now, in the night, I can weep as much as I will, and no one can see my shattered face, my shattered soul, my shattered fortune."

And when he thought, "Ah, Emanuel, if thou shouldst see me as I am to-day!" he could hardly any longer contain himself.

He fled, with suppressed tears, unconcerned who saw it or did not see it, out of the garden, over which a dark angel let float a great funereal banner and the music of a dirge. He bruised himself against a stone garden-roller which was used to crush the *sprinkled* grass-blades and *flowerets*,—he wept not yet, but on the observatory there would he satisfy himself and steep himself in abundant sorrow,—he kept repeating, "But she remained true, and said, No, no, no!"—the concert-tones glided after, like fire after the conjurer,—he waded through moist, slumbering lawns, which concealed their flowers, and, swifter than he, swept over the earth the shadowy outlines of the clouds overhead chased by the wind,—he stood at the foot of the observatory, still held back every tear, and hurried up,—he threw himself on the bench where he had seen Clotilda for the first time afar off, in a white dress,—"Rest thou, too, Horion!" she had called to him out of his dream from under the flowery hill, and he heard it again.—

Here he tore open joyfully all his wounds, and let them bleed out freely in tears; they overspread with mournful streams the face which once had often smiled, but always good-naturedly, and which from other eyes had never wrung any, but only wiped them away; every flood was a load taken off, but the heart grew heavy again upon it, and poured out a fresh one.—At last he could hear the tones again; most of them sank and were lost before they were wafted to the tower; little ones arrived dying, and expired in his darkling heart; every tone was a falling tear, and made him lighter, and expressed his anguish. The garden seemed to consist of softly resounding, dark-green waves of shadow, veiled under a broken twilight. Stung by memory, he tore his eye away from it: "What does it concern me any longer?" he thought. But at last from this shadowy Eden and from the *viole d'amour* came up the song, "Forget me not," to his weary heart, and gave him back the softer pang and the past love. "No," said he, "I never will forget thee, though thou hast not loved me! thy form will assuredly forever move me, and remind me of my dreams! ah, thou heavenly one, it is, indeed, now, the only thing that does not pain me, to think I forget thee not!"

All was silent and extinguished; he was alone in the presence of night. At length, after remaining a long time in silence, he went down and back to Flachsenfingen, exhausted with weeping, and a poor man. And as, on the way, he cast a hurried glance up at the dark-blue heaven, in which floating clouds lay flung around the moon like *scoriæ*, and a hurried glance again over the half-annihilated shadowy landscape, over the shadow-hills and shadow-villages, all appeared to him dead, empty, and vain, and it seemed to him as if, in some brighter world, there were a magic-lantern, and through the lantern glasses moved on which earth and springs and human groups were painted, and we called the descending, dancing images of these glasses *us* and an earth and a life; and *after all that was bright and many-colored, a great shadow followed on.*—

Ah, I stir up, perhaps, once more, in many a breast, long-forgotten troubles! But it is good for us—since sorrows occupy so large a place in our memory—that this bitter winter-fruit should grow mild by lying, and that there is but a small difference between a past sorrow and a present bliss.

Poor Victor arrived after midnight, with a pale face and burning eyes, at the house of the Apothecary. He asked for nothing, that he might not betray his broken voice. When he saw his every-day overcoat hanging in the moonbeams, and when he imagined himself a strange person to whom the coat belonged, and who took it off so joyfully in the morning and now would put it on again so sorrowfully, then did a certain compassion which he had for himself seize again with too strong an impression his exhausted heart. Marie came, and he turned not away from her even the signs of this compassion. She stood surprised; he said to her with the softest voice, woven of sighs, that he wanted nothing; and the good soul went slowly out without courage to console or to weep, but all night long she shed invisible tears for those of another, and for a woe which had not been whispered in her ear.

Why did Fate to-day, of all days, open all the veins of his heart? Why must the Senior Pastor's silver wedding and the first marriage of his daughter to the preacher of the Orphan-House fall just on this day? Why, if indeed the two nuptial feasts had to coincide on this day, must they last till after midnight, when they gave poor Victor occasion to gaze into all the mouldering scenes of his burnt-up hopes, when he could see from his dark chamber, in a brilliantly lighted room, the love which linked hand in hand, pressed lips to lips, and mingled eyes and souls? At another time he would have smiled at the Orphan-House preacher and at two catechists of the poor; but tonight he could only sigh over them,—and it is a soft line of beauty on his inner man, that he did not grudge, but felicitated, the poor people's possession of what he was deprived of himself. "Ah, you are happy!" said he. "O, love each other truly, press your throbbing, transitory hearts ardently to each other, ere the wing of Time shatters them, and glow on each other's bosoms during the short minute of life, and exchange your tears and kisses ere eyes and lips freeze in the grave! Ye are happier than I,—I, who can give my heart full of love to no one but the worms of the grave, and on whose coffin a joiner shall paint the inscription, which like myself shall be buried in the earth: 'Ye good children of men, you loved me not, and yet I loved you so well!'"

Every happy smile, every fleeting touch of the violin, every thought, became now, to his soft tear-bathed heart, a hard, sharp corner,—just as a hand which dips itself under the water feels everything hard to the touch.

His unbounded sincerity, his unbounded tenderness, he could now satisfy in no other way than by a letter to Emanuel, into which he let his whole soul overflow.

"O Dearly Loved Friend!

"Ought I to hide it from thee, when griefs or follies unman me? Ought I to show thee the faults I have repented of, and never my present ones? No, come hither, dear one, to my wounded breast! I will lay open to thee the heart therein, let it bleed and beat under the exposure as it will. Thou wilt, perhaps, still cover it up again with thy fatherly love, and say, 'I love thee still.'

"Thou, my Emanuel, reposest in thy lofty solitude, on the Ararat of the saved soul, on the Tabor of the shining One: there thou gazest, softly dazzled, into the sun of Deity, and seest calmly the cloud of death swim in over the sun; it veils the orb: thou growest blind under the cloud; it melts away, and again thou standest before God. Thou lovest men as children who cannot offend,—thou lovest earthly enjoyments as fruits, which one plucks for refreshment, but without hungering for them; the storms and earthquakes of life pass by thee unheard, because thou liest in a life-dream full of tones, full of songs, full of meadows,—and when death awakes thee, thou art still smiling over the bright dream.

"But, ah! more than one tempest thunders into the life's-dream of the rest of us, and makes it distressful. If a higher being could enter into the hurly-burly of ideas which encompasses our spirit, and from which it must draw its breath, as we breathe in an air composed of all kinds of gases poured together,—if he were to see what kinds of nutriment pass through our inner man, from which it has to extract its chyle: that medley of comic operas,—Bayle's Dictionaries,—concerts of Mozart,—Messiahs,—military operations,—Goethe's poems,—Kant's writings,—table-talks,—lunar observations,—vices and virtues,—men and sicknesses and sciences of all sorts:—if the Being should examine this *olla-podrida* of life, would he not be curious to know what heterogeneous and mutually repulsive juices thereby run together in the poor soul, and would he not wonder that anything settled and uniform is left as a residuum in man? Ah, Emanuel! if thy friend is now in a fine banquet-hall, now in a garden, now in an opera-box, now under the great night-heavens, now in the presence of a coquette, and now before thee,—surely, this ambiguous alternation of scenes must bring him sorrows, and perhaps leave stains....

"No, I will not deceive my Emanuel—O, are, then, the trifles and the pebbles of this life worth our choosing crooked paths to avoid them, as the sapping-caterpillar submits to winding courses through the twig-work of its leaf? No, all that I have said is true; but I should not have said it, had not other sorrows led me to speak of these also; and yet, thou innocently, simple-heartedly, sublimely trusting teacher, thou wouldst have believed me! Ah, thou hast too good an opinion of me!... O, it is a long and weary step from admiration to imitation! But now look into my open heart!

"Since I have, here in the charnel-house of my childish joys, in the beds where my childhood's years bloomed and faded, been conversing with perhaps too many dreams of the past,—and, still more, from the day when thou gavest my heart the provocative to the fever-stroke which has shaken my whole life,—since thou disclosedst to me the life wherein man exfoliates, and the thin, sharp moment whereon he so painfully stands,—since that farewell-night when my soul was great and my tears inexhaustible,—an eternal wound has been running within me, and the sigh of a longing which nothing can name but dreams and tears and love has lain like a stagnant vein, oppressive and consuming in my breast.—Ah! I still smile as ever, I still philosophize as ever, but my innermost heart only the beloved friend sees to whom I now lay it bare.

"O Fate, why dost thou strike in man the spark of a love which must be smothered in his own heart's blood? Have we not all, abiding within us, the sweet image of a beloved, of a friend, before whom we weep, after whom we seek, for whom we hope,—ah, and so vainly, so vainly? Does not man stand before a human bosom, as the turtle-dove before a mirror, and, like her, coo himself hoarse before a dead, flat image therein, which he takes for the sister of his complaining soul? Why is it, then, that every fair spring-evening, every melting lay, every overflowing rapture, asks us, 'Where dost thou find the beloved soul to which thou wilt tell and impart thy bliss?' Why does music give the tempest-stricken heart, instead of peace, only greater waves,—as the tolling of bells, instead of dispelling, draws down the thunder-storms? And why is it, that out of doors, on a fair, still, bright day, when thou lookest over the whole unrolled picture of a landscape, over the seas of flowers that tremble upon it, over the shadows flung down by the clouds which fly from one hill to another, and over the mountains which stretch like shores and walls round our flowery circle,—why does then a voice within thee cry incessantly, 'Ah! behind the smoking[224] mountains, beyond the clouds that repose upon them, there rests a fairer land, there dwells the soul thou seekest, there heaven lies nearer to the earth'? But behind the mountain and behind the cloud there sighs also an unappreciated heart, that looks over towards this thy horizon, and thinks, 'Ah, in that far region I should doubtless be happier!'

"Are we *not*, then, all happy?—Do not assert it, nor say to me, Emanuel, that, in the winter of this life, the few warm sunbeams that interrupt it burst and destroy the better man like a vegetable; say not that every year steals away something from our heart, and that, like ice, it grows less and less, the farther it drifts down the stream of Time; only say not that the wandering Psyche, though she hears her second self in her prison, yet can never get into its arms.—But thou hast already somewhere said: 'All loving souls on earth dwell apart from each other in two bodies, as on two hills; a waste lies between them, as between solar systems; they see each other, speak across by distant signs; at last they hear each other's voices from hill to hill; but they never touch each other, and each embraces only its thought. And yet this poor love crumbles like an old corpse, when it is exhibited; and its flame flickers like a burial-lamp, when it is uncovered.'

"Are we, then, all not happy?—Do not say so!—Ah, man, who, even from childhood up, has been calling after an unknown soul that grew up in *one* heart with his own,—that entered into all the dreams of his years, and therein gleamed from afar, and, after his waking, started his tears,—that in spring sent him nightingales, that he might think of her and long for her,— that in every tender hour visited his soul, with so much virtue, so much love, that he would so gladly have offered in his heart, as in a sacrificial chalice, all his blood to the beloved,—but who, alas! never, appeared, and only sent her image in every fair form, but forever kept back her heart;—oh, if at last, oh, if suddenly, oh, if blissfully, her heart beats against his heart, and the two souls embrace each other forever, he can no longer say it, but we can: 'This man, indeed, is happy, and is loved.' ...

"Good Emanuel, thou forgivest me the pain of the fear that I may never be the happy man,—no, never!—Oh, even for this earth, broken up into graves, I should be perhaps too happy, I should be permitted to enjoy, perhaps, too great an Eden for so young a life, and one justified by such slight merits, if my too soft soul, which even now gives way under three happy minutes, which loves every human being, and hangs with the arms of a child on the heart of the whole creation,—oh, which is already made too blissful by this mere dream of love, and is overpowered by this description!—no, it were too blessed, such a soul, long since dissolved by melancholy and humanity, if it should once, after such a long, deathly yearning, at last, at last—O Emanuel, I tremble again for joy, and yet it can never, never be!—if it should find all its wishes, its whole heaven, so much love, accumulated in one dear, dear soul; if in the presence of great Nature, and before the face of Virtue, and before God himself, who gave love to her and to me, I could dare to say, weeping, to this only, this sweet, this beloved—O God, how shall I name her? this fore-loved one, whom in my frenzy I would now name: 'At last my heart has thee, thou good soul! to-day God gives us to each other, and we remain together through all eternity!' No, I would not say it; I should for ecstasy be dumb and die!

"—Lo! it seemed to me just now as if a form passed across my chamber, and called, 'Victor!' I looked round, and beheld my empty room, and the Sunday clothes which I had taken off, and now, for the first time, I remembered that I was unhappy and not loved.

"But thou, irreplaceable friend, misunderstand me not. I swear to thee that I will give thee these sheets unaltered, though to-morrow, when the whirlpools of to-night flow stiller and smoother, I should find all sorts of alterations necessary. Thy foolish friend remains, nevertheless, thy friend forever.

"S. V. H."

20
DOG-POST-DAY

"Poor Sebastian!" said I, as I opened to-day's letter-bag, "before I get it open, I know already beforehand, that, after such a night, thou must have shut thyself up all day, to turn thy pale, exhausted face toward the garden of sorrow, that thou to-day lovest these poison-drops better than the vulnerary balsam, and that thou lookest into the glass to weep for this still, innocent form which it shows thee with its gashes, as if it were the form of a stranger.—Oh, when man has nothing more to love, he embraces the gravestone of his love, and sorrow becomes his loved one! Forgive one another the short delusion of mourning; for, among all the weaknesses of man, this is the most innocent, when, instead of soaring away like the bird of passage above winter, and flying to warmer zones, he sinks before it, and helplessly stiffens in his cold grief."

Victor coffined himself, so to speak, that day in his chamber, which he opened to no one but a next-door neighbor of sorrows,—Marie,—whose form affected him as softly as an evening sun. Every other female face on the street gave him stings; and the brother of the lost Clotilda, whom he saw at the window, and to-day would gladly have embraced, lent to the remembrance which tears had dimmed, new colors.... Reader!—my female reader will be, of herself, more reasonable,—laugh not at my good hero, who *is* none precisely where the strength of the soul becomes the strength of sorrow: at least, let me not hear it. Whoever has the sympathetic nerve of life—love—tied up or cut asunder, can well, if for no other reason, sigh and say, "Anything on earth can man lose more patiently than fellow-men."

And yet at evening an accident—namely, a letter—made all his sorrows pass once more through his weary heart. A short letter from Emanuel—not, however, an answer to the one just sent to him—arrived.

"My ever-loved one!

"I have learned the day of thy entrance upon a new scene of tumultuous life, and I have said, 'May my beloved still continue happy! may the tranquillity of virtue wall in his heart as with a breast against the frosts and storms of his new life! may neither his sorrows nor his raptures be loud!

may he mourn softly and silently as a princess in soft white! may he enjoy softly and silently, and in the temple of his heart may Pleasure play only as a noiseless fluttering butterfly in a church! and may Virtue float before him in the higher heaven above our sun, and warm and irradiate and gradually attract to herself his heart!'

"In thy affectionate anxiety for my parting life, thou wilt not have me write often: so little, dear one, dost thou believe my hope! Oh, the weights of my machine, as they run down, fall slowly and softly upon the grave; this earthly life arrays itself to my soul in ever fairer colors, and adorns itself for the farewell; this mock-summer around me, which stands beside the August summer like a mock-sun,—this and the coming spring take me beguilingly out of the arms of Nature.

"So does the All-Gracious overhang with foliage, overspread with flowers, the churchyard-wall of life, as we cover the wall of an English garden with ivy and evergreen, and gives the end of the garden the appearance of a new thicket.—

"So ascends the spirit even here in this *dark* life, as the barometer ascends even during thick weather, and feels the influence of the *brighter* life even under the clouds.

"But I obey thy love, and will write to thee no more, except once in winter, when I describe to thee the great night wherein I told my blind Julius, for the first time, that there is an Eternal One.—In that night, my beloved, rapture and devotion bore me too high, and came near to rending my thin life. I bled a long time. In winter, when the charms of heaven take the place of those of earth,[225] forbid me not to paint the summer picture.

"O my son!—I was compelled, indeed; to write to thee, because my friend Clotilda complains that the new year will draw her out of the green bower of solitude to the crowded market-place of the court; her soul is dark with sorrow, and stretches out its arms after the tranquil life which is being taken away from her. I know not what a court is; thou wilt know, and, I conjure thee, release my friend, and turn aside the hand that would draw her from St. Luna. If thou canst not do it, still forsake not at court the beloved soul; be her only, her most ardent friend; draw the bee-stings of earthly hours from her gentle heart. When cold words, like snow-flakes, fall upon this flower, then let the breath of love melt them to tears that shall flow before thy sight; when a tempest shall come up, over her life, then show her the angel who stands in the sun, and draws over our tempests the rainbow of hope. O thou whom *I* so love, my sister also will so love thee; and when my friend discovers to her his gentle heart, his tender eye, his virtue, his soul, the home of Nature and of the Eternal, then will he see my sister grow happy before him, and the exalted countenance which melts into tears and smiles and love before him will remain forever in his heart.

"Emanuel."

Lo! in this glowing moment the exalted form which he had seen yesterday appeared again before his heart, with the sadly smiling lips and the eyes full of tears; and as the form continued floating before him, and gleamed and smiled, his soul rose up before her as before one dead, and during the uplifting of himself all his wounds began to bleed again, and he cried, "Now, then, never do thou vanish from my heart, thou sublime shape, but rest forever on its wounds!" Disconsolateness, exhaustion, and sleep overwhelmed his spirit, as well as his latest thought,—to go back shortly to St. Luna, and persuade her parents not to force her to court...

The long sleep of death closes our *scars*, and the short sleep of life our *wounds*. Sleep is the half of time which heals us. On awaking, Victor, whose fever of love had yesterday been so aggravated by sleeplessness, saw today that his sorrow had been unmoderated because his hope had been immoderate. At first he had wished,—then observed,—then assumed,— then seen,—then interpreted,—then hoped,—then sworn to it. Every little circumstance, even his share in Clotilda's nomination as maid-of-honor, had poured mild oil of love into his flame. "Oh, fool that I am!" said he, with the three swearing-fingers placed upon his forehead; and, like all energetic men, he was so much the more spirited in proportion as he had been spiritless. Nay, he felt himself all at once too light; for a too sudden cure betokens, in the case of souls also, a relapse. A new consolation was his yesterday's resolve, that he would render Clotilda a service,—namely, save her from the court-service. He still reflected upon his determination to see her again.—Feelest thou, haply, Victor, that everything which Love does, in order to die, is only an expedient for rising again from the dead, and that its epilogues are only prologues to the Second Act?

But a basket of apples in the market confirmed him again in his resolution. That is to say, Flamin came in. He began immediately with questions about the disappearance on Sunday, and with reports of the general uneasiness about the dear runaway. Victor, heated again by the whole recollection, and almost a little enraged against the image-breaker and government-attorney of a vain love, gave him the true answer:—"Thou tookest away from me in part my pleasure; and why should I, at so late an hour, come upon the stage?" The more vividly Flamin painted the affectionate concern of the Parson's wife and Clotilda about his disappearing, so much the more painful grew the maze of contending feelings within him. But for his conscience calling him back, it would now have been easier for him to confess the love that was hopeless, than formerly the love that was hopeful.—Accidentally Flamin wondered at the ripeness of the apples down below in the market, and desired some. A lightning beam now darted before Victor's eye at the inherited fruit-pieces on Flamin's shoulders, which always appeared in the after-summer at the time of the apples' ripening, but which, in the previous whirl of his feelings, he had forgotten. Heaven knows whether it has not escaped the reader himself, that Flamin bears this winter-fruitage (his maternal mole) on his back, which may become a Sodom-apple and Eve's-apple for him. Might not Matthieu, who until now could not examine upon Flamin this seal of his princely relationship, suddenly become convinced of all that which, with his thievish glances at his Lordship's letter, he had only been able to guess? And might he not afterward go to the Prince, and there mix for all our friends the most poisonous broths?—As, however, the magic image generally faded in one week, Victor needed for only so long a time to keep its wearer out of sight; he therefore laid before his friend, thus tattooed by Nature, the request to take for once a social walk to St. Luna, as they had day before yesterday missed each other.

"I can't do it," said Flamin, who had the lesser delicacy not to avail himself of the request for company on account of the reproaches in Le Baut's garden, and forgot in that the greater delicacy of not imputing such a reference to his Victor.

The latter, in a passionate hurry to avert two such evils (Clotilda's court-office and Matthieu's inspection), seized upon the singular expedient of proposing to the page to share the journey with him.

"With pleasure!" said the Evangelist; "*this* week I have to do cabinet-service, but I can *next* week."

And it was precisely this week that Victor wanted it to be done.—So many sudden miscarriages confounded him to such a degree, that he, whose careless and innocent heart was always an open letter with flying seal, dissembled now towards his dear, good friend Flamin.—He wanted at least to investigate the maternal mole and its distinctness for himself. He therefore went to him, and found him bent over his writing, and with a glowing work-face. He conjured him to consider that recreation and holidays were indispensable to him, and urged it upon him that he should work, like a compositor, standing. Then he came gradually upon the subject of Flamin's full-blooded chest, and upon the question whether it could bear his exertions without stingings and oppressions. Then he arrived at the point, and proposed that Flamin should, at all events, have a Burgundy-pitch plaster applied as lung-conductor to his shoulder-blades; yes, he would himself do it for him now, and show him how all was to be prepared.

He hoped, besides, to draw thereby a curtain around the apple-piece. But he dissembled so wretchedly,—for he always succeeded in his innocent intrigues with maidens, and comic disguises for satirical purposes, while his serious ones always miscarried,—that even Flamin heard him out, and dryly replied, he had already had on such a plaster for two days, and—Matthieu had advised, and himself applied it.

There was a fix.—Sebastian had nothing further left him than, with a singular *sangfroid*, which, on the St. Luna road, was mixed only with a few stings from the old thorny latelings of his withered Paradise, to go unaccompanied to the Chamberlain Le Baut, to say what was to be said, hardly to peep into the Parsonage, and quietly to trudge off again without a single—hope.

Dear Fortune! better beheaded than scalped,—better *one* disaster than ten miscarriages; I mean, break man upon thy wheel rather from above than from below upward!—

Victor, to be sure, knew as yet not a word of the turn he should give to the subject, in order to put two such court-emigrants as the Le Bauts, who knew nothing holier than the *Latreia* towards a prince, the *Douleia* towards his minister, and the *Hyperdouleia* towards his w—, out of humor with Clotilda's promotion; but he thought, "I will do what I can."

Clotilda's parents received him with so much civility,—i. e. with so much courtesy of the body, with so much powdered sugar on every feature, with so much sirup of violets on every word,—in short, he found the report which Matthieu had rendered to Flamin of their amiable disposition towards him so well grounded,—that he could have selected no better opportunity than this to dissuade them from the transplanting of their daughter, had they not begun to thank him for having been himself the very transplanter. They had learned or guessed all, and thanked him for his intercession, to which they probably attached more self-interested views than the daughter did. It would have been ridiculous, in Clotilda's presence, to advise *her* against Flachsenfingen, and dissuade from that for which they thanked him; still, however, he attempted something. He told the Chamberlain "his daughter deserved rather to *have* a court than to adorn one; nay, that *he* deserved at most in the whole matter—an excuse, as Clotilda would certainly prefer the society of her parents to the constraint of court; in that case, he would promise to put the index back again with the Prince, and rectify everything without disadvantage." The father took this expression for a strong deprecation of gratitude; the step-mother, for some piece of knavery or other; the daughter, for—words. She said, a little curtly, "I think it was easy to choose between disobedience and absence." For, unbending as she was to her step-mother, she willingly followed the hints of her father, whom, with all his weaknesses, and as the only soul on the earth attached to him, she tenderly loved. Victor, at last, though reluctantly, was forced to give it up; but why does man find it harder to resign himself to the future than to the past?—The coldness of the daughter was naturally not less (but sincerer) than the warmth of the parents.... And this coldness was precisely what refreshed his glowing brain. This cold, indifferent form was wrapped as a veil about the sublime and loving one, as it ever floated before him with that melancholy look which he could not endure. Without the consciousness of anything wrong, satisfied with his obedience to Emanuel's request, he withdrew, with his feelings oppressed by decorum, returning coldness with greater coldness.—He would have been a poor lover, if he had known what he wanted; for otherwise he never could have desired of Clotilda, even in case of her love for him, any extraordinary warmth towards a medicus whom her parents forced upon her (which injures a man even more than ugliness), who so impolitely took himself out of the garden without a birthday *carmen*, and who pressed her into the seven gilded towers of court-service, despite her reluctance, despite every probability of her future *prison-fever*.—But for the *vacant freehold* of his heart this very vexation was wholesome....

If my good reader ever has to take an eternal farewell of a too dear friend, let him take it *twice*.—The *first* we all understand, as a matter of course, when he sinks in the intoxication of sorrow, in the hemorrhage of heart and eyes, and when the beloved object burns itself with flames into the tender soul; but *then* he will never be able to forget the being thus torn from his heart. Therefore he must take a *second* farewell, which is colder even for the reason that passionate emotions admit no *dal segno* [226] of repetition; nay, (if he will take the wisest course of all,) he must endeavor, after the first tragic leave-taking, to see her in a public place (e. g. at a coronation), where she must appear cold. Her frosty face will then snow over her glowing one in his brain; and my good reader has, undoubtedly, collected together again wits enough to know what he reads in the Dog-Post-Days....

—Upon my word, if Jean Paul does not write industriously, then no one does; it has already struck one, and he took it for a quarter to twelve; my sister will already be folding her hands before the tucked-up smoking pike, which, like the serpent of eternity, has his tail in his mouth, and saying, incessantly, "It is all growing cold!"—"It must be so, after such glowing chapters," say I, "if thou meanest the reader and the author."—Already, while I still sit over the twentieth chapter, the post-dog is frisking round in the chamber with the twenty-first; and yet I will starve myself, unless I can still utter before dinner, like the seven wise men, seven golden sayings:—

1. When one who is stung by a bee or by fate does not keep still, the sting tears out, and is left behind.

2. Miserable earth, which three or four great or bold men can reform and agitate! Thou art a true stage: in the foreground are some fighting players and a few canvas-tents; the background swims with painted tents and soldiers!

3. States and diamonds are in these days, when they have stains, cut up into little ones; and as

4. Men in great states and bees in great hives suffer a loss of courage and warmth; accordingly now-a-days they join to small countries other small countries, as they do to beehives colony-hives.

5. Man takes *his* suffering for that of *humanity*, as the bees take the dropping of their bee-stand, when the sun already shines out again, for rain, and stay in-doors.

6. But he commits daily a *lesser* error: he regards as an *eternity* (that Aristotelian Unity of Time to the drama—of Existence) at first his present *hour*,—then his *youth*,—then his *life*,—then his *century*,—then the duration of the *globe*,—then that of the *sun*,—then that of the *heavens*,—then (this is the least error) *time* itself....

7. There are in man, in the beginning and at the end, as in books, two blank bookbinder's leaves,—childhood and old age; and so, too, in the Dog-Post-Days: see the end of this day and the beginning of the next.

FIFTH INTERCALARY DAY

Continuation of the Register of Extra-Sheets.

K

Cold.[227]—In our age decrease of *stoicism* and increase of *egotism* are found side by side. The former covers its treasures and germs with ice; the latter is itself ice. So, in physics, *mountains* wear away, and *glaciers* increase.

L

Library (Circulating) for Reviewers and Young Ladies.—I still always adhere to my purpose of having it inserted in the Intelligence-leaf of the Literary Gazette, that I shall not destroy the purchase-money which I raise upon my *evening star* [Hesperus], nor, like Musæus, fritter it away in the purchase of summer-houses, but shall lay out the whole capital upon a complete collection of all German *prefaces* and *titles* that appear from fair to fair. I can carry out the plan, if I give out a preface a week, on the payment of a penny, to reviewers, who do not care to read the book itself when they review it.

That not even the surplus of the aforesaid mintage may lie as dead capital in my house, I shall employ it—if I do not change my mind—in getting the bookbinder to publish the *heavier* German masterpieces,—e. g. Frederick Jacobi's, Klinger's, Goethe's Tasso,—likewise the better satirical and philosophical ones, in a *lighter* ladies' edition, which shall consist wholly of so-called *puzzle-volumes*, which have no book slid into them. I shall thereby, methinks, be playing something pithy into the hands of my fair readers, which shall be as well bound and as well titled as the booksellers' edition, and in which—because the hard stone-fruit is already *shelled out*, and there is nothing inside—they can lay not only just as much of silk threads and silk snippings as in the printed edition, but six ounces more. *Allwill's* correspondence—a heavy, two-yolked ostrich's egg of the author's, which I have had *blown out* by the bookbinder in this manner, because most of the fair readers are too *cold* to hatch it—is now quite *light*. But of the German romances I shall never prepare such a work-box edition of empty state-carriages of the God of the Sun and the Muses, because I fear the trade would cry out about *piracy*.—A happy man were I, if the joint subscribers to my circulating-capsule-library had only been shown round as much as twice in some Italian and Portuguese bookeries:[228] they would there, where often only the titles of works—and of the stupidest, into the bargain—are daubed on the wall, be astonished to see what a miserable figure such useless libraries, beside my bookery of regular puzzle-books, which I select from so many departments and with some originality, cannot do otherwise than cut.

—Thus, of course, German capsule-readers among the ladies will never be overtaken by you Portuguese women! Much rather will the former follow in the footsteps even of the men, advocates and business people, who subscribe to similar capsule-journalistics, and jointly read and circulate the covers of the best German journals,—which latter are often annexed as *curiosa* even to the capsules, and fill them out.... Such is my plan and sketch; but even sheep would presume I were merely playing off a joke here, unless I really carried it through.

M

Maidens.—Young maidens are like young turkey-hens, that thrive poorly, if one touches them often; and mothers keep these soft creatures, made of floating pollen, like *pastel-pictures*, under window-glass—because everything is afraid of us princess-stealers and fruit-thieves—until they are fixed. Meanwhile the proper crown-guard around a female heart is neither solitude,—which leads only to an untried innocence,[229] that falls, to be sure, not before the debauchee, but yet before the hypocrite,—nor society, nor hard labor,—otherwise no country girl would ever fall,—nor good teachings,—for these are to be had in every mouth and in every circulating library; but these four first and last things do it all at once, and they are at once superseded, united, and replaced by a wise and virtuous mother.

N

Names of the Great.[230]—When I see, as I do, how they scatter their productions for the Fair, occasional writings and fugitive pieces (children born out of wedlock) as anonymously as if they were reviews, then I say: "Herein I recognize genuine modesty; for natural children are precisely their best and their own, and can, besides, be acknowledged by the Prince *as* genuine; whereas their supernatural [or extra-natural] ones born in wedlock have to do without the certification; and yet they will not let the world know the name of the benefactor, but quite as often (nay, oftener) get people *into it* as *out of it* secretly. What the child in other cases first learns to pronounce, such parents speak to him last,—their name. Methinks they follow herein Goethe's fine ear; for they hide themselves, while they fill the orchestra of the world with children's voices and with *vingt-quatre*,[231] and with alarm-works and repeating-works, (what a juxtaposition of unlike things!) just as Goethe demands of the playing musical artist that he shall work for the ears, but hide himself for the sake of sparing the eyes. Quite as beautifully do they do the thing when they finally adopt as children, and show to the world, their children by the thirtieth marriage (often after the five or twenty years' limitation), and thus imitate the greenfinches, which, it is said, make their nest and its inmates invisible by means of the so-called greenfinch-stone, till the latter are fledged."

O

Ostracism.—It was among the Greeks, as is well known, no punishment. Only people of great merits achieved it; and so soon as this banishment from the country was lavished upon bad men, it went entirely into disuse. An imperial citizen must lament that we, who have a similar public educational institution,—namely, banishment,—squander it often upon the very wretchedest rascals, and therefore—with the design of making one circle or country the spit-box and secreting-vessel of another—drive out of the country scoundrels who are hardly fit to stay in it. Thereby is this clearing of the country deprived for the most part of the honorable and distinguishing feature which it might have for the man of merit, and an honest man—e. g. a Bahrdt[232]—is almost ashamed to be invested with such an honor. There should, therefore, be an imperial police-regulation that only ministers, professors, and officers of decided worth, like important documents, should be dismissed and banished. To similar men I would also limit hanging. With the Romans, in truth, only great heads and lights were interred on the *way* [233] at the expense of a whole state; but what shall I think of the Germans, with whom seldom serviceable subjects, but mostly finished rogues, are buried at public expense, which they call hangman's fees, having been previously hanged on the gallows by the roadside?— Not even in his lifetime can a man, unless he has extraordinary, and often *eccentric* merits,—although eccentric men fall back into the truth, as *comets* do into the *sun*, as fuel,—make his calculations upon being, in some manner, as the ancients duplicated their noble men in statues and pictures, hung up in *effigy* in a thick stone frame.... Let me have an answer; I allow myself to be talked with.

P

Philosophy.—Some critical philosophers have now borrowed from the algebra a mathematical method, without which one cannot for a single minute—not so much think as—write philosophically. The algebraist, by the transposition of mere *letters*, catches truths which no chain of reasoning could ever draw out of the deep. In this the critical philosopher has imitated him, but with greater advantage. As he cleverly mixes together, not letters, but whole *technical words*, there rises from the alliteration of the same a cream of truths which he could hardly have dreamed of. Such philosophers are forbidden, and rightly, like the preachers of Gotha (Goth. Public Ordinances, P. III. p. 16), to use allegories, or any flower of speech, which, as other flowers do for the drawing-hounds, would spoil the scent.— Properly, however, the picturesque style is more definite than the technical word-style, which finally, as all *abstract words are pictures*, is also itself a picturesque style, only one full of pictures that have run out and faded. Jacobi is not obscure in consequence of his *images*, but in consequence of the new *ideas* which through them he would communicate to us.

I have lately been looking over the birth-lists of the learned and teaching republic, and counting up the young little Kants whom the old Kant— otherwise unmarried, like his cousin Newton—has for the last ten Fairs begotten. Demetrius Magnus, who wanted to make a book of authors of the same name, must have been very stupid, if he had undertaken to write in our times, and yet at the same time, though he nevertheless communicated that there had been sixteen Platos, twenty Socrateses, twenty-eight Pythagorases, thirty-two Aristotles, had very sinfully omitted to say that there are now as many philosophers and philosophists as those make when reckoned all together—namely, ninety-six—who could bear the name of Kant,—that is, if they chose to. Such mechanics—thus may I call the magisters, because formerly the mechanics, inversely, were called magisters, and the upper master arch-magister—one should take into account as the best propaganda which bulky books can have. They are, at best, competent to diffuse the system, because they know how to separate from it the incomprehensible, the spiritual, and to extract what is popular and palpable, i. e. the words for readers, who, otherwise simple, nevertheless would not die without a critical philosophy. The most miserable theological and æsthetic stone receives now a Kantian setting in words. Although every new system introduces a certain *one-sidedness* of view into all heads,—especially as every cold philosopher has so much the more *one-sidedness*, precisely as he has the more *insight*,— still that is no matter; for great bars of truth come forth through the joint digging of the whole thinking-works.[234] Whoever has seen Kant standing on his mountain among his learned fellow-laborers, is reminded with pleasure of a similar incident in Peru, which Buffon communicates. When Condamine and Bouger were measuring there the equatorial degrees of the earth (as Kant did of the intellectual world), whole troops of apes appeared as coadjutors, put on spectacles, looked at the stars and down at the clocks, and reduced one thing and another to writing, although without salary, which is their only distinction from the vicariate Kants.

Every man of genius is a philosopher, but not the reverse. A philosopher without fancy, without history, and without a *general knowledge* of the most important things, is more one-sided than a politician. Whoever has adopted, rather than discovered, a system; whoever has not had beforehand dark presentiments thereof; whoever has not at least pined for it beforehand; in short, whoever does not bring with him a soul like a full, warm, ground filled with germs, which waits only for its summer,—such a one may indeed be a teacher, but not a scholar of the philosophy which he degrades to a mercenary profession; and, briefly, it is all one what place one climbs as his philosophical observatory,—a throne, or a Pegasus, or an Alp, or a Cæsar's-couch, or a bier,—and they are almost all higher than the desk in a lecture-room and hall of disputation.

Q (see K)

R

Reviewers.—An editor of a review should have six tables. At the first should sit and eat the advertisers of the *existence* of a book; at the second, the wholesale appraisers of its *value*; at the third, the epitomists of it; at the fourth, the grammarians and philologists, who distribute to the public *catalogues raisonnés* of other men's grammatical blunders; at the fifth, the fighters, who refute a new book, not by a new book, but by a sheet; at the sixth should stand the critical, princely bench, on which might sit Herder, Goethe, Wieland, and perhaps yet another, who survey a book as a human life, who apprehend its *individuality*, indicate at once the spirit of the literary creation and creator, and separate that incarnation and embodiment of the divine beauty which takes the form of an individual *from* the beauty, and then disclose and pardon it.

These six critical benches, which might edit six different literary periodicals, are now thrown over each other, and form *one.*—Frankly, however, as I come out against this jumbling together of learned (1) advertisements, (2) reviews, (3) extracts, (4) verbal and (5) real criticisms, and (6) artistic judgments, still I am ready and glad to admit that the critical *Fauna* and *Flora* of the first *five* tables root out, perhaps, full as many shoots of weeds as they put forth themselves from their own germs; and I therefore appeal to a private letter of my own, which is beyond the suspicion of flattery, and wherein I associate it with a toadstool, which, although it produces, itself, upon an affusion (in this case, of ink), whole hosts of insects, nevertheless eradicates the flies.—But as among the reviewers there are also authors, like myself; as among the Portuguese inquisitors there are Jews; and, in fact, as I should want to talk whole intercalary years on the subject,—why talk a whole intercalary day?

S

Stripes.—"He that knoweth his Lord's will, and doeth it not, shall receive double stripes."—Who, then, gets the single ones? Not he, surely, who knows not the will and does it not?—It follows, therefore, that greater knowledge, not *aggravates*, but itself *creates*, moral guilt; for in so far as I absolutely do not discern a moral obligation, my offence against it is surely not less, but none at all.

I will be my own Academy of Sciences, and assign to myself the following prize-question, which I will myself answer in a prize essay: "Since only such actions are virtuous as proceed from love for goodness, it follows that only those can be sinful which proceed from mere love of evil, and reference to self-interest must lessen the degree of a sin, as well as that of a virtue. But, on the other hand, what could there be but self-interest in our nature, which should impel us to what is bad? And if evil were done from a pure propensity to evil, then there would be a second, although opposite, autonomy[235] of the will."

T

Trouble, Tribulation.—Now, as I write these distressful sounds, which announce to me that Nature makes only *thorn-hedges*, but men *crowns of thorns*, all pleasure in lashing about me with the thorns of satire dies away, and I would rather draw some thorns out of your hands or feet.

21
DOG-POST-DAY

The following remark comes not from the dog's knapsack, but from my own head: One needs not to be a panegyrist of our times, to see with pleasure that authors, princes, women, and others have now mostly laid aside the unnatural *false* masks of virtue (e. g. bigotry, pietism, ceremonial behavior), and have entirely assumed instead the *genuine* tasteful *show* of virtue. This improvement of our character-masks, whereby we hit more finely the exterior of virtue, is contemporaneous with a similar one on the stage, where they play their antics and their tragics no longer, as once, with *paper* clothes and badly imitated laces, but with the *true* ones.—

"The Princess wanted you yesterday," said the Prince to the Court-Physician, almost as soon as he had entered with his exhausted face. The inflammation of Agnola's eyes had, in consequence of the autumn weather, night-feasts, and Culpepper's bold practice and her own—for the red capital letters of beauty (namely, painted cheeks) she was always putting on afresh—very much increased. Properly, Victor was too proud to let himself be sent for as a mere physician; nay, he was too proud to let himself be in demand for anything else (and though it were philosophy or beauty) than his character; for his father, who had just as much delicate pride, had taught him that we must not serve any one who does not respect us, or whom we ourselves do not respect,—nay, that one must not accept a favor from any one to whom one can only return outward, but not inward thanks. But this tender sense of honor, which never came into an unequal conflict with his self-interest, though it might well with his humanity, could never bind the hands wherewith he might relieve an unhappy Princess—unhappy, like himself, from a famine of love—at least of the pains of her eyes; perhaps, also, of *younger* pangs; for his good-heartedness suggested to him nothing but reconciliations,—of the Prince with Le Baut, with the Princess, with the Minister. Nothing is more dangerous than to reconcile two persons,—unless, indeed, one is himself one of them; to set them at variance is much safer and easier.

He found Agnola, even in the afternoon, still in her chamber, because its green tapestries flattered (not the face, to be sure, but) the hot eye. A thick veil over the face was her screen from daylight. When she, like a sun, lifted her veil, he could not comprehend how in Tostato's shop he could make, out of this Italian fire and these quick court-eyes, the face, red with weeping, of a blonde. A part of this fire belonged, to be sure, to her sickness. Her first word was a decided disobedience to his first; meanwhile she flew in the face of the Messrs. *Pringle* and *Schmucker*, as well as himself; for the whole triune College advised leeches round the eyes; but those were disgusting to her. The medicus then suggested cupping-glasses at the back of the head; but her hair was more precious to her than her eyes.

"Must, then, everything be bought with blood?" said she, with Italian vivacity.

"Realms and religions ought not to be, but health should," said he, with English freedom of speech.

Once more he demanded her blood. She would not give it to him, however, until he changed the sacrificial knife, and proposed opening a vein in the eye. Persons of rank, like learned men, are often ignorant of the commonest things: she thought the Doctor would open the vein. And as she thought so, he did it, with a hand trained by the couching-needle.

Meanwhile, if (according to Pliny) a kiss on the eye is one on the soul, the opening of a vein in that organ is no joke; but one may, while he inflicts a wound, himself get one. The poor Court-Medicus must, with his swimming, friendly eye, from which only within a few days the tear of love has been dried away, boldly gaze into the sun pent up in an eye-socket, and, what is more, softly rest his finger on the warm face, and from the fountain of tears make bright blood spurt out.... One ought, before undertaking such an operation, to have a similar one performed on himself, for the sake of the cooling. But, in truth, fate had given him nothing this week but lancet-cuts into his heart's arteries. Let one, further, represent to himself how the whole female sex appeared to him like a magic, far-receded shape, which had once gleamed near to him in a dream, and as a paled moon by day, which he had worshipped in a bright night; and then will one have opened his good innocent heart to behold therein, beside a great ever-active sorrow, a thousand sympathetic wishes for the compassionated Princess. Despite her singular mixture of pride, liveliness, and refinement, he still thought he discovered a change in her, which he could explain partly by his to-day's assiduity and partly by his influence on the Prince, which had been thus far so favorable to her,—a change which would have given him greater courage, had he not insisted upon being threatened with special drafts upon his courage by the billet above the imperator of the compass-watch. At the former and first visit his courage was lamed, because he thought himself avoided, as the son of a father who seemed to fortify his influence by his care for natural children; for a man full of love beside one full of hatred is dumb and stupid.

What put him most in heart to-day, next to the quarrels in which he was defeated (as the one about leeches, &c.), was the last and following, in which he conquered (one grows more courageous and prosperous when one contradicts a proud woman than when one flatters her): He saw a mask lying there; now, as he knew that in Italy ladies wore them in bed, as ours do gloves, using them as a sort of glove to the face, he straightly forbade her the mask, as being tinder to the inflammation of her eyes. It was no flattery when he said to her that the mask might take from her more than it gave. In short, he insisted upon it. —

He was, perhaps, too tolerant towards the doubt which only a woman could make *endurable* and *enduring*, —the doubt which one she mistook for the other, the Court-Physician or the favorite; for at last—though not without a fear of saying too much, which, with people of his fiery temperament, is a sign that the thing has already happened—he told her, what he had in the beginning kept back, that the sympathy (*empressement*) of the Prince had sent him to her; and he extolled the latter at his own expense, and so much the more, as he had nothing further of an extraordinary nature to adduce with regard to him, but only that he had—sent him to her.

Then he went. With the Prince he bestowed on her as many *beatifications* and as many *canonizations* (two contrarieties on this earth) as decorum and his humor (two still greater contrarieties) would allow. Singular! she had, for all her fire, no humor. He knew January succumbed, not merely to the slanderer, but also to the flatterer. The crowned theatre-managers of the earth have determinations put into their hearts, and decrees into their mouths; they know what they mean and what they say two or three days later than their throne-prompter. A favorite is a Shakespeare and poet, who, from behind the persons he makes act and speak, never peeps or coughs out himself, but is a ventriloquist, and gives *his* voice the sound of another's.

When he visited his patient the next day, the eye-sockets were cooled down, though not the eyes. Agnola sat convalescent in a cabinet full of images of the saints. With the indisposition of her eyes had been taken away, at the same time, a source of conversation; and her pride blocked up the way at once to his sensibility and to his humor. Although he said to her a hundred times in his innermost heart, "Torment not thyself, proud soul; I am no favorite; I will not rob thee of anything, least of all of thy pride or another's love,—oh, I know what it is to win none,"—nevertheless he remained (in *his* opinion) cold before her, and retired with the annoying prospect that his successful cure had cut off his return; for the other court visits were, after all, no confidential visits to the sick. Of the plaguy compass-watch he stood daily less and less in terror, except just when he was happier than usual.

—Many people would sooner live without houses than without building-schemes; Victor, sooner without air to breathe than without castles in the air. He must always have on hand the lottery-chance and stocks of some plan or other for the future; and a woman was, in most cases, the partner in this grand-adventure trade. This time he was keenly bent upon the reconciliation of January and Agnola. He reasoned thus:—"It is easy on both sides. January will now always seek Agnola's society, though merely out of cunning, for the sake of getting with more decency into that of her future maid-of-honor, Clotilda, whom, in her condition of singleness, he can, according to his *vow*, still love with impunity. As he can neither withstand a long praise nor a long intercourse, this will imperceptibly accustom him to Agnola. She, who is now left alone on the side of the Minister Schleunes, will not reject the united regards of Victor and January," &c.... But whether only the beauty of the action, and not also the beauty of the Princess, incited him to this mediatorial office, that is what the Twenty-First Chapter cannot yet know; meanwhile, so far as I am concerned, let the following stand: his cold inner man, exhausted by bleeding, from which the harpsichord and the name of Clotilda and the awaking at morning still draw bloodless daggers, needs so much indeed the din of the world and everything that may benumb its wounds!

With the design of such preliminaries to a peace, he excused his future disobedience to his father, who had counselled him against frequenting the house of Schleunes; for as the Princess always went there, it was the fittest neutral place for the peace-congress. Oh for only half an—

EXTRA-LEAF ON HOUSES FULL OF DAUGHTERS!

The house of Schleunes was an open bookstore, whose works (the daughters) one could read there, but not carry home. Although the five other daughters stood in five private libraries as wives, and one, under the earth at Maienthal, was sleeping away the child's plays of life, there were, nevertheless, in this warehouse of daughters, three free copies left for sale to good friends. The Minister, at the drawings of the lottery of offices, loved to give his daughters as premiums for great winnings and prizes. To whom God gives an office, to him he gives, if not understanding, yet a wife. In a house rich in daughters, as in St. Peter's Church, there must be confession-pews for all nations, for all characters, for all faults, that the daughters may sit therein as mother-confessors, and absolve from everything, celibacy alone excepted. I have, as naturalist, often admired the wise arrangement of Nature for the propagation as well of daughters as of vegetables. Is it not a wise provision, I said to the natural historian Goetze, that Nature gives precisely to those maidens who need for their life a rich mineral fountain something *attaching,* by which they may fasten on to miserable nuptial finches, who shall carry them to fat places? Thus Linnæus[236] observes, as you know, that those kinds of seeds which only thrive in rich earth have little hooks on them, in order to hang the more easily on the cattle which carry them to the stable and manure-heap. Wonderfully does Nature scatter about by the wind—father and mother must make it—daughters and pine-seeds into the arable places of the forests. Who does not observe the final cause why many daughters receive from Nature certain charms in designated numbers, that some canon or other, a German Herr, a cardinal-deacon, an appanaged prince, or a mere country squire, may come along and take the aforesaid charmer, and, as groomsman or English bride's-father, hand her over, ready finished, to some blockhead or other, in a distant place, as a ready-made wife on sale? And do we find in the case of bilberries any less precaution on the part of Nature? Does not the same Linnæus observe, in the same treatise, that they are enveloped in a nutritious juice, that they may attract the fox to eat them, whereupon the knave—he cannot digest the berries—becomes, for all he knows, the sower of them?—

Oh, my innermost spirit is more serious than you think. I am vexed with those parents who are traders in souls; I pity the daughters who are negro slaves. Ah! is it any wonder, then, if the daughters who were obliged to dance, laugh, talk, and sing at the West Indian market, in order to be carried home by the master of a plantation, if they, I say, are treated just as much like slaves as if they were sold and bought? Ye poor lambs!—and yet ye are quite as hard as your sheep mothers and fathers. What shall one do with his enthusiasm for your sex, when one travels through German cities, where every richest or most distinguished man, and though he were a distant relation of the Devil himself, can point with his finger to thirty houses, and say: "I don't know,—shall I pick out and marry one from the pearl-colored, or from the nut-colored, or perhaps from the steel-green house? The shops are all open for purchasers."—What, ye maidens! is, then your heart so little worth that you can cut it down, like old clothes, to suit any fashion, any breast? and is it, then, like a Chinese ball, now great, now tiny, in order to fit into the ball-form and wedding-ring case of a man's heart?—"It must indeed be so, unless one will continue to sit alone, like the Holy Virgin over yonder," is the reply of those to whom I make no reply, because I turn away from them with contempt, in order to say to the so-called Holy Virgin: "Forlorn, but patient one! Unappreciated and withered one! remember not the times when thou still didst hope for better ones than the present, and never repent the noble pride of thy heart! It is not always a duty to marry, but it is always a duty not to forgive one's self anything, never to be happy at the expense of honor, and not to avoid celibacy by infamy. Unadmired, solitary heroine! In thy last hour, when the whole of life and the former goods and scaffoldings of life, crushed into ruins, sink beforehand,—at that hour thou wilt look out over thy emptied life; thou wilt see there, it is true, no children, no husband, no wet eyes; but in the vast, void twilight a great, saintly form; angelically smiling, radiant, godlike, and soaring to the divine ones, will hover, and beckon to thee to ascend with her. Oh, ascend with her; that form is thy *virtue*."

End of the Extra-Leaf.

Some days after the Princess gave the Prince an *eye en médaillon* with the fine conceit: she gave this *votive-tablet* to the saint (this was so much the more *apropos* as the Prince was named *Januarius*) who had sent her his wonder-worker, and who now received that which he had caused to be healed. January said to Victor, to whom he showed the eye, "She confounds St. Januarius with you, with St. Ottilia,"—who, as is well known, is the patroness of eyes.

Victor was glad that Matthieu came to him to go with him to St. Luna; for the latter begged him, because this was done without him, to go with him to his mother's, "because to-day at the Princess's there was a great *souper*, but at his mother's not a soul,"—that is, hardly more than nine persons. Victor therefore—it mattered not to-day that the distinguished and interesting eye-sufferer was absent—gladly followed into Schleunes's Nuremberg *Exchange Library* of daughters behind the tender Jonathan-Orestes-Mat, whom he, in fact, out of forbearance towards their mutual friend Flamin, treated now with more toleration. *Men*, like *ideas*, are associated together quite as often on the principle of *simultaneousness* as on that of *similarity*; and as little can be inferred from the choice of *acquaintances* as to the character of a youth, as in regard to that of a woman from her choice of a husband. Matthieu introduced him to his mother in the reading cabinet, just as she was hearing an English author read, with the words, "I bring you here a real live Englishman." Joachime was reading in a catalogue,—it was not a catalogue of books, but of stock-gillyflowers,—in order to select some gillyflowers for herself, not for the purpose of planting, but of imitating them—in silk. She hated flowers that grew. Her brother said, ironically, "She hated changeableness, even in a flower." For the truth was, she loved it even in lovers, and was quite different from April, which, like women, is in our climate far more steady than is pretended. In the cabinet there were also two fools, whom my correspondent does not so much as name to me, because he thinks they would be adequately designated and distinguished, if I should call the one the fragrant fool, and the other the fine one.

Both fools were buzzing round the beauty. In fact, whenever I have wanted to study fools at great parties, I have always looked round regularly for a great beauty; they gather round such a one like wasps around a fruit-woman. And if I had no other reason—I have, however—for marrying the handsomest woman, I would do it for this reason, if for no other, that I might always have the queen-bee sitting in the hollow of my hand, after whom the whole foolish bee-swarm would come buzzing. I and my wife would then be like the fellows in Lisbon, who, having in their hands a pole of parrots strung together, and at their feet a leash of *monkeys* skipping after them, trudge through the streets, and offer their crazy *personæ* for sale.

The fragrant fool, who was to-day on the *sunny side* of Joachime, was reading to the mother; the fine one, who was on the *weather-side*, stood near Joachime, and seemed not to trouble himself about her *cooling of the temperature*. Victor stood there as transition from the torrid zone to the frigid, and represented the temperate; Joachime played three parts with one face. The fragrant fool shot, with his left hand, the swivel-gun of a silver *joujou*. This hanging seal of a fool he kept in motion, either, as the Greenlander does a block with his feet, for the sake of keeping himself warm,—or he did it, as the grand sultan for similar reasons must always be whittling with a jackknife, in order not to be always having somebody killed out of love,—or in order, as the stork always holds a stone in his claws, to have all the time an Ixion's-wheel in his hands, as a rowel on his heels,—or for the sake of health, in order to counteract the *globulus hystericus* [237] by the motion of an external one,—or as rosary bead,—or because he didn't know why.

Each was satisfied with himself. When the mother begged our Englishman to read to her with his native accent, the *fine* fool said, "The English, like certain sentiments, is easier to understand than to pronounce." That is to say, this fine sheep had universally the habit of being metaphorical. If a maiden said to him, "I cannot keep myself from feeling cold to-day," he made out of it coldness of the heart. One could not say, "It is cloudy, warm, the needle has pricked me," &c., without his taking this as a ball-drawer, to extract his heart from the fire-arm of his breast, and exhibit it. It was impossible in his hearing not to be fine, and from your good-morning he twisted a *bon-mot*. Had he read the Old Testament, he would not have been able to admire sufficiently the fine turns that occur there. On the other hand, the *fragrant* fool limited his whole wit to a lively face. He unfolded before you this bill of invoice and insurance-policy of a thousand bright conceits, and held it up to you, but nothing came. You could have sworn by the advertising-poster of wit in his fiery eye, "Now he is going to blaze out,"—but not in the least! He used the weapon of satire, as the grenadiers do hand-grenades, which they no longer throw, but only wear imitated on their caps.

When the fine one had said his erotic *bon-mot*, Joachime looked at our hero, and said, with an ironical glance at the fine one, *"J'aime les sages à la folie."*

The pride of the fragrant one in his to-day's superiority, and the apparent indifference of the fine fool to his own neglect, proved that neither was often in to-day's ease, and that Joachime coquetted in a peculiar style. She always made fun of us stately male persons, when two were with her at once,—of one alone less so; her eyes left it to our self-love to ascribe the fire in them more to love than to wit; she seemed to blab out what came into her head, but many things seemed not to come into her head; she was full of contradictions and follies, but her *intentions* and her inclination nevertheless remained doubtful to every one; her answers were quick, but her questions still quicker. To-day, in the presence of the three gentlemen,—at other times she did it in the presence of the whole *bureau d'esprit*,—she stepped up to the looking-glass, took out her paint-box, and retouched the gay box-piece of her cheeks. One could not possibly think how she would look if she were embarrassed or ashamed.

The virtue of many a lady is a thunder-house, which the electric spark of love shatters to pieces, and which they put together again for new experiments; to our hero, spoiled by the highest female perfection, it appeared as if Joachime must be classed among those thunder-houses. Coquetry is always answered with coquetry. Either this latter it was, or too feeble a respect for Joachime, which led Victor to make the two adorers ridiculous in the eyes of the goddess. His victory was as easy as it was great; he encamped on the foe's position,—in other words, Joachime took an increased liking to him. For women cannot bear him who, before their eyes, succumbs to another sex than their own. They *love* everything that they *admire*; and one would not have made such satirical explanations of their predilection for physical courage, if one had considered that they feel this predilection for everything that is distinguished,—for men distinguished by wealth, renown, learning. The dry and wrinkled Voltaire had so much fame and wit, that few Parisian hearts would have rejected his satirical one. Add to this, that my hero expressed his regard for the whole sex with a warmth which the individual appropriated to herself; then, too, his favorite universal-love, furthermore his eye swimming in sorrow over a lost heart, and finally his infectious human tenderness, secured him an attention from Joachime which excited his to the degree, that he proposed to himself the next time to investigate what it might signify.—

The next time soon came. So soon as the advent of the Princess was predicted by the Apothecary,—for *he* was for the little future of the court his witch of Endor and of Cumæ, and his Delphic cave,—he went thither; for he did not drive. "So long as there is still a shoe-black and a pavement," said he, "I do not drive. But as to the more distinguished gentry, I wonder that they even travel on foot from one wing of the palace to the other. Could not one, just as they have a penny-post for a city, introduce a conveyance for the interior of the palace? Might not every chair be a sedan-chair, if a lady were less afraid of an Alpine tour from one apartment to another? And various circumnavigatresses of the world would even venture to make a pleasure-tour through a large garden in a close litter."—Victor's own journey lay straight through one,—namely, that of Schleunes. It was too bright and pleasant as yet to let him screw himself like a sewing-cushion to the card-table. He saw in the garden a gay little party strolling about, and Joachime among them. He joined them. Joachime expressed an artist's pleasure at the groupings of the clouds, and it was becoming to her beautiful eyes when she lifted them in that direction. As they had nothing clever to say, they sought to do something clever, so soon as they came to the *carrousel*.[238] They seated themselves in it, and caused it to be set agoing. Many of the ladies had absolutely not the courage to climb this potter's-wheel; some ventured into the seats; only Joachime, who was full as daring as she was timid, mounted the wooden tourney-steed, and took the lance in hand, to spear away the ring, with a grace which was worthy of finer rings. But in order not to expose herself to being thrown by the whirling Rosinante, Joachime had set my hero beside her as a banister, that she might hold on to him in time of need. The revolution of the axle grew more rapid, and her fear greater; she clung to him more and more firmly, and he clasped her more firmly in order to anticipate her effort. Victor, who understood very well the legerdemain and hocuspocus of women, easily saw through Joachime's Wiegleb's-natural-magic and "Trunkus Plempsum Schallalei";[239] besides, the reciprocal pressure had passed to and fro so rapidly, that one could not tell whether it had an originator or an originatress....

As they are now all within doors, and I stand alone in the garden by the horse-mill, I will reflect ingeniously on the subject, and remark that great people, like women and the French and the Greeks, are great—children. All great philosophers are the same, and, when they have almost destroyed themselves with thinking, revive themselves by child's fooleries, as, e. g., Malebranche did; even so do great people refresh themselves for their more serious, noble diversions by true childish ones; hence the hobby-horse chivalry, the swing, the card-houses (in Hamilton's *mémoires*), the cutting out of pictures, the *joujou*. With this passion for amusing themselves, they are in part infected by the custom of amusing their superiors, because the latter resemble the ancient gods, who, according to Moritz, were appeased, not by atonement, but by joyous festivals.

As he was acquainted with the whole theatre-company of the Minister, and, secondly, as he was no longer a lover,—for such a one has a thousand eyes for *one* person, and a thousand eyelids for the rest,—he was not embarrassed at the Minister's, but actually enjoyed himself. For he had, to be sure, his plan to carry through there; and a plot makes a life entertaining, whether one *reads* or *executes* it.

He was successful to-day in having a tolerably long talk with the Princess, and, to be sure, not about the Prince,—she avoided that subject,—but about her trouble of the eyes. That was all. He felt it was easier to play off an exaggerated regard than to express a real. The apprehension of appearing false *makes* one appear so. Hence a sincere man has the look, with a suspicious one, of being half false. Meanwhile, with Agnola, who, in spite of her temperament, was coy,—hence a peculiar, lowered tone reigned in her presence at Schleunes's,—every step sufficed which he did not take backward.

But toward the sprightly Joachime he took half a step forward. Not so much she, as the house, seemed to him to be coquettish; and the daughters therein—they constitute the house—he found to resemble the old Litones,[240] or people of the Saxons, who were one third free and two thirds serf, and who therefore could mortgage a third of their estate. Each had still a third, a ninth, a segment, of her heart left to her own free disposal. In fact, whoso has ever seen codfishing can learn the thing here from metaphor,— the three daughters hold long fishing-rods over the water (father and mother splash, and drive the codfish along), and have their hooks baited with state-uniforms or their own faces,—with hearts,—with whole men (as luring rivals),—with hearts which have already been once taken out of the stomach of another captured codfish;—from this, I say, one can see in some sort how they catch the other cod in the sea, precisely as they do the stock-fish on land,—namely, besides what has been mentioned (now let one read back again), with bits of red rag, with glass-pearls, with birds' hearts, with salted herrings and bleeding fishes, with little cods themselves, with fishes which one has taken out, half digested, from stock-fish formerly caught.— Victor thought to himself, "Joachime may be only lively or coquettish for all me; I can easily skip over marten-traps which I can see set right before my nose." Well, run, Victor; the *visible* steel shall lead thee precisely upon that which is *concealed*. One may observe in the same person coquetry towards every other, and yet overlook it toward himself, as the fair one believes the flatterer whom she sets down as a consummate flatterer of all others.—He observed that Joachime had somewhat oftenish looked up at the new ceiling this evening, and he could not rightly tell why it pleased her. At last he saw that she was only pleased with herself, and that raising her eyes was more becoming to them than looking down. He undertook presumptuously to investigate this, and said to her, "It is a pity the painter of the Vatican had not made it, that you might look up at it oftener." —"Oh," said she, in a tone of levity, "I never would look up with others; I do not love admiration." By and by she said, "Men dissemble, when they wish to, better than we; but I tell you just as few truths as I hear from you." She confessed outright that coquetry was the best remedy against love; and with the observation that his frankness pleased her, but hers must please him too, she ended the visit and the Post-Day.

22
DOG-POST-DAY

The reader will be vexed with this Dog-Post-Day; I, for my part, have already been vexed about it. My hero is evidently becoming entangled in the meshes of two female trains, and even in the bonds of the princely friendship... Nothing more is wanting than that Clotilda should actually be joined to the hurly-burly.—And something of this kind it becomes necessary for a mining-superintendent, an islander, to communicate confidentially to the people on the mainland.

Besides, it must be done chronologically. I will dissect this Dog-Post-Day, which reaches from November to December, into weeks. Thereby more order will be observed. For I understand the Germans. They want, like the metaphysician, to know everything from the beginning onward, very exactly, in royal octavo, without excessive brevity, and with some *citata*. They furnish an epigram with a preface, and a love-madrigal with a table of contents; they determine the zephyr by compass and the heart of a maiden by conic sections; they mark everything, like merchants, in black-letter, and prove everything, like jurists; their cerebral membranes are living parchments, their legs private surveyors'-poles and pedometers; they cut up the veil of the Nine Muses, and apply to the hearts of these damsels turners'-compasses, and insert gauging-rods in their heads; poor Clio (the muse of history) looks, for all the world, like the Consistorial Counsellor Büsching, who trudges along slowly, bent up under a land freight of surveyors'-chains, clocks to calculate *thirds*, and Harrison's longitude-watches, and interleaved writing-almanacs, so that I specially weep for the poor Büsching as often as I see him striding along, since all Germany, (from which I should have expected something different,)—every magistrate, every stupid justice of the peace, (only we of Scheerau have never saddled him,)—has loaded down the good topographical carrier and Christopher (cross-bearer), like a statue hung with pledges, from knee to nostril, (so that the good man is hardly to be seen, and I wonder how he stays on his feet,)—has palisaded, I say, and built him in with all sorts of cursed devil's whisks, with village inventories, with advertising sheets, with heraldic works, with books of ground-plats and perspective plans of pigsties.

They have even—that I may only *relate* an example out of my own history of the German statistic stupidity, although in the very doing of it I *give one*—infected Jean Paul. Is it not an old story that he has approximately assigned in degrees, by means of a Saussure's cyanometer,[241] the blueness of the fairest eyes into which an *amoroso* ever looked, and inspected the fairest drops that fell from them during the measurement, correctly enough, with a dew-measurer?—And has not his attempt to catch and prove female sighs by a Stegmann's measurer of the purity of the atmosphere found more than too many imitators among us?—

WEEK OF THE 22d POST-TRINITATIS, OR
FROM NOV. 3d to 11th (EXCLUSIVE)

Almost the whole of this week he sat out at the Minister's. Many people, when they have been only four times in a house, come again daily, like the quotidian fever,—in the beginning, like the spring sun, every day earlier; afterward, like the autumn sun, every day later. He saw, indeed, that he could not contribute anything at this court-and-ministerial party, either a mystery, or property, or a heart, because it would resemble honest courts of justice, which—just as the monks call their property a deposit, and say nothing belongs to them—inversely promote every deposit into a piece of property, and say all belongs to them. But he made no account of that. "I come indeed only for fun," thought he, "and no harm can be done to me."—

The Minister, whom he met only over the table, had all the civility towards him which can be united with a face full of persiflage, and with a class of society in whose eyes all the world is divided into spies and thieves; but Sebastian perceived, nevertheless, that he looked upon him as a smatterer in medicine and the serious sciences,—as if they were not all serious,—and as an adept merely in wit and in the liberal arts. He was, however, too proud to turn to him any other than the empty new-moon-side, and concealed from him all that might convert him. Consequently, Victor must needs, in the eyes of the stupidest government-officer who had seen it, have deprived himself of all respect by the fact that, when the Minister started an interesting conversation with his brother, the Regency-President, about imposts, alliances, or the exchequer, he either did not attend, or ran off, or looked up the women.—Then, too, he loved in the Prince only the man; the Minister loved only the Prince. Victor could himself, when with January, deliver discourses on the advantages of republics, and the latter would often, in his enthusiasm, (if the supreme courts and his stomach had allowed it,) gladly have raised Flachsenfingen to a free state, and himself to the President of Congress therein. But the Minister hated all this with a mortal hatred, and fastened on all political free-thinkers—on a Rousseau, on all Girondists, all Feuillants, all Republicans, and all philosophers—the name of *Jacobin*, as the Turks call all foreigners, Britons, Germans, Frenchmen, etc., *Franks*. Meanwhile this was a reason why Victor now took a greater liking to Mat, who thought better on this subject, and why he fled from the father to the daughter.

This week he got into Joachime's good graces. She gave to the fine and fragrant duo of fools, as we do to *virtue*, only the second prize, and to my hero, as we do to *inclination*, the prize-medal. But as he respected, at most, merely a certain sentimentalism in friendship and in love, he could, he thought, have ridden through the moon with this waggish girl, without sighing *for* her (though he might, indeed, *over* her). But these jolly ones, my Bastian, have seen the old Harry; for whenever they change to anything else, one changes with them to the same thing. She told him she wanted to give *pleasure*, like a Lutheran holy picture, but she would not be *adored*, like a Catholic one. She prepossessed him most by the gift peculiar to her sex, of understanding tender allusions,—women are so easy at guessing the meaning of others, because they always oblige others to guess their meaning, and *complete* and *conceal* each *half* with equal success. But among her attractions I reckon also her constraint before the Princess, and before those who listened with their—eyes. For the rest, his heart, which Clotilda had rejected, was now in the situation of children who have made a bet that they will receive blows upon their hands without crying, and who still continue to smile when the tears already flow.

WEEK OF THE 23d POST-TRINITATIS, OR 46th OF THE YEAR 179-

Now he is there even in the forenoon. It is worthy of notice, that on St. Martin's day he scraped her powdered forehead with the powder-knife, and that he applied to her for some court offices in connection with the toilet. "I can be your rouge-box bearer, as the Great Mogul has tobacco-pipe and betel-bearers, or else your *cravatier ordinaire*, or your *sommier* (i. e. prayer-cushion-bearer).—I would, if you did not kneel yourself on the cushion, myself do it before you.—I knew in Hanover a handsome Englishman who had his left knee stuffed and padded, because he did not know whom he should to-day have to adore, and how long."

It is something quite as important, that on St. Jonas's day he forced her to accept a pair of fine gloves, on which a very simple face was painted. "It was his own," he said; "she should have the face only by night, in bed, in, or on, her hand, that it might look as if he kissed her hand through the whole November night."

I go on with my pragmatic extracts from this siege-journal, and find recorded on Leopold's day that, as early as in the forenoon, Joachime said she would have her parrot, if she kept a master of languages for him, repeat nothing out of the whole dictionary except the word *perfide!* "Every lover," said she, "should keep a poll for himself, which should incessantly cry out to him, *perfide!*" —"The ladies," said my hero, "are alone to blame: they want to be loved too long; often whole weeks, whole months. The like of that is beyond our powers. Have not the Jesuits made even love to God periodical? Scotus limits it to Sunday, others to the festival days.—Coninch says, it is enough if one loves Him once every four years.—Henriquez adds a year more to it.—Suarez says, it is enough if it is only done before one's death.— To many ladies the intermediate times have hitherto fallen; but the hours of the day, the seasons of the year, the days of betrothal, of burial, form just as many different sects among the Jesuits of Love."—Joachime made a beginning of putting on an angry look. The court-physician loved nothing better with a fair one than a quarrel, and added: "*C'est à force de se faire haïr qu'elles se font aimer—c'est aimer que de bouder—ah, que je vous prie de vous fâcher!*" —His humor had carried him beyond the mark.—Joachime had reason enough to fulfil his prayer for her wrath.—He wanted to continue the quarrel in order to settle it, but as there are cases where the *aggravation* of an offence brings about forgiveness quite as little as the *taking of it back* step by step, he did wisely in coming away.

He wondered that he should think of her all day long. The feeling of having done her wrong brought her face with a suffering expression before his softened soul, and all her features were at once ennobled. Tacitus says, we hate another when we have offended him; but good men often love another merely on that account.

The day following, Ottomar's day,—*Ottomar!* great name, which makes the long funeral procession of a great past sweep by all at once before me in the dark,—he found her serious, neither seeking nor shunning him. The two fools remained in her eyes the two fools, and gained nothing in any way. As, therefore, he clearly perceived that out of a transient resentment there had grown true repentance for her previous openness,—of which he seemed to have made too free a use and too selfish an interpretation,—it was now his duty to do in earnest that which he had hitherto done in joke, namely, to seek her and get her to be reconciled.

But she stood all the time by the Princess, and nothing was done.

I have not said it myself, because I knew the reader would see it without me,—that my hero thinks Joachime regards him as the image-worshipper of her charms, and as the moon-man, or satellite attracted by her. My hero has, therefore, long since made up his mind to leave her in this error. As to removing such an error,—for *that* a man or a woman seldom has strength enough; but Victor had, besides, several reasons for indulging her with faith in his love (that is, himself, also, with faith in hers). In the first place, he wanted to conceal the reason of his coming; secondly, he knew that in the great world, and among the Joachimes, a lover is sought for only as third man in the game,—with them there is no dying of love, one does not even live on it; thirdly, he reserved for himself in all cases the sheet-anchor of making earnest out of jest; "when the knife is at my throat," thought he, "then I will set myself down and fall truly in love with her, and then all will be well"; fourthly, a coquette makes a *coquet*.[242] ... Here I began already, as is well known, to be vexed about the 22d Post-Day, although I know as well as anybody why all mankind, even the most sincere, even the male kind, incline to little intrigues towards their beloved; that is to say, not merely because they are little and *reciprocated*, but because one thinks by his intrigues to give more than he steals. Only the highest and noblest love is without real trickery.

WEEKS OF THE 24th AND 25th POST-TRINITATIS

On Sunday there was a ball. "Very naturally," said he, "she will not look on me. In ball-dress the fair sex are more implacable than in morning dress." Hardly had she seen him when she came to meet him, like an agitated heaven, with her fixed stars of brilliants and her pearl-planets, and in this splendor begged of him the forgiveness of her freak. She had at first made believe angry, she said, then had actually become so; and not until the next day had seen that she did wrong to appear so and had a right to be so. This prayer for forgiveness made our Medicus more humble than was necessary. She begged him sportively to beg her pardon, and made him acquainted with her percussion-gold of sudden resentment.

For a space of two days this Westphalian peace was kept.

But one quarrel with a maiden, like one fool, makes ten; and unfortunately one only likes the angry one so much the better (at least, better than the indifferent), just as people run most after *those* Methodist preachers who damn them the most roundly. Joachime grew daily more susceptible of anger,—which he ascribed to an increasing love,—but so did he, too. Let them have spent the whole visit in the finest imperial and domestic peace, at the leave-taking all was put upon a war-footing again, ambassadors and furloughed ones (if I may be allowed these poetical expressions) recalled. Then with the angry sediments in his heart he withdrew, and could hardly wait for the moment of the next interview,—i. e. of his or her justification. Thus did they spend their hours in the writing of peace-instruments and manifestoes. The matter of dispute was as singular as the quarrel itself: it concerned their demands of friendship; each party proved that the other was the faulty one, and demanded too much. What most enraged our Medicus was, that she allowed the fine and the fragrant fools to kiss her hand, which she forbade him to do, and in truth without any reasons for the decision. "If she would only lie to me, and say, such or such is the reason,—that at least would be something," said he; but she did him not the pleasure. To my sex, refusal without reasons, even conjecturable ones, is a pit of brimstone, a threefold death; upon Joachime, reasons and cabinet-sermons had equal influence.

EXTRA-LEAF ON THE ABOVE

I have a hundred times, with my legal burden of proof on my back, thought of women who are able, with a certain effort, to act as well as to believe without any reasons. For surely, in the end, everybody must (according to all philosophers) reconcile himself to actions and opinions for which reasons are entirely wanting; for, since every reason appeals to a new one, and this again rests upon one which refers us to one, which again must have its own reason, it follows that (unless we mean to be forever going and seeking) we must finally arrive at one which we accept without any reason whatever. Only the scholar fails in this, that precisely the most important truths—the highest principles of morals, of metaphysics, &c.— are the ones which he believes without reasons, and which, in his agony,— thinking to help himself out thereby,—he names necessary truths. Woman, on the contrary, makes lesser truths—e. g. there must be drives, invitations, washing to-morrow, &c.—the necessary truths, which must be accepted without the insurance and reinsurance of reasons;—and just this it is which gives her such an appearance of soundness. For them it is easy to distinguish themselves from the philosopher, who thinks, and into whose eyes the sun of truth flames so horizontally that he cannot see, for it, either road or landscape. The philosopher is obliged, in the weightiest actions,—the moral,—to be his own lawgiver and law-keeper, without having the reasons therefor given him by his conscience. With a woman, every inclination is a little conscience, and hates *Heteronomies*,[243] and beyond that pronounces no reasons, just as the great conscience does. And it is precisely this gift, of acting more from private sovereignty than from reasons, which makes women so very suitable for men; for the latter would rather give them ten commands than three reasons.

End of the Extra-Leaf on the above.

What was full as bad was, that Joachime at last, only for the sake of removing his documentary piles of complaints and imperial grievances, allowed him her fingers, without giving him the least reason for it. He could, therefore, show no title of possession, and, in case of need, would have had no one who could protect him therein.

There is, however, a well-grounded rule of right or Brocardicon[244] for men: that everything grows firmer with women, when one builds upon it, and that a little stolen favor legitimately belongs to us, so soon as we sue for a greater. This rule of right bases itself upon the fact that maidens always abate with us, as one does to Jews in trade, the half, and give only a couple of fingers when we want the hand. But if one has the fingers, then arises, out of the Institutions, a new title, which adjudicates to us the hand: the hand gives a right to the arm, and the arm to everything that is appended to it, as *accessorium*. Thus must these things be managed, if right is to remain right. There will, in fact, have to be a little manual written by me, or some other honest man, wherein one shall expound and elucidate to the female sex with the torch of legal learning the *modos* (or ways) *acquirendi* (of winning) them. Otherwise many modi may go out of use. Thus, e. g., according to civil law, I am rightful proprietor of a movable thing, if it was stolen thirty years ago (in fact, it should be further back, and I should not be made to suffer for it, that one began the stealing later); so, too, by prescription of thirty minutes (the time is relative) everything belonging to a fair one lawfully falls to me, which (of a movable nature—and everything about her is movable) I may have purloined from her, and therefore one cannot begin soon enough to steal, because before the theft the prescription cannot begin to take effect.

Specification is a good modus. Only one must be, like me, a Proculian,[245] and believe that a strange article belongs to him who has imparted to it a different form; e. g. to me, the hand which I have put into another shape by pressure.

The late Siegwart said: *Confusio* (mingling of tears) is my modus. But *commixtio* (mixture of dry articles, e. g. the fingers, the hair) is now with almost all of us the *modus acquirendi*.

I was going once to treat the whole thing according to the doctrine of the *Servitudes*,[246] where a woman has a thousand things to suffer (though all these servitudes are entirely extinguished by the consolidation[247] of marriage); but I do not myself any longer rightly retain the doctrine of the Servitudes, and would much rather examine any one in them than be examined myself.—

I return to the Medicus. Since, then, he knew that a kissed hand is a warrant to the cheeks,—but the cheeks the sacrificial tables of the lips,—these of the eyes,—the eyes of the neck;—accordingly he would have proceeded exactly according to his text-book. But with Joachime, as with all antipodes of coquettes, *no favor paved the way for another, not even the great one for the small one*; you passed from one antechamber to another,—and what said my hero to this? Nothing but "Thank God that for once there is one better than she seemed, who, under the appearance of being our plaything, plays with us, and makes her coquetry the veil of virtue!"

He felt now, as often as her name was mentioned, a soft warmth breathe through his bosom.

FROM THE END OF THE ECCLESIASTICAL YEAR (Dec . 1) TO THE END OF THE CIVIL (Dec. 31)

Flamin, whose patriotic flames found no air in the session-chamber, and stifled himself first, grew shyer and wilder every day. It was something new to him, that it took whole boards and commissions to do what one person might have done,—that the limbs of the state (as is also the case, indeed, with the limbs of the body) are moved by the *short arm* of the lever, so as to do less with greater power, and a board, particularly, resembles the body, which, according to Borellus,[248] spends 2,900 times as much strength on a leap as the load which it has to lift requires. He hated all great people, and never went to see any: the page Mat did not even get visits from him. My Sebastian made his visits to *him* seldomer, because his leisure and his calms of dissipation fell exactly upon Flamin's working hours. This separation, and the eternal sitting at Schleunes's,—which Flamin, from not being acquainted with Joachime's influence, was obliged at all events to ascribe to Clotilda's, for future visits to whom Victor must be creating a pretext by his present ones,—and even the Prince's favor towards the latter, which in Flamin's eyes could not be any result of his spirit of freedom and his sincerity;—all this drew the intertwined bonds of their friendship, which had made life to them hitherto a four-handed piece of music, further and further asunder; the faults and the moral dust which Victor could once brush off from his darling he hardly dared to blow off; they behaved towards each other more delicately and attentively. But my Victor, to whose heart Fate applied so many tongues of vampyres, and who was compelled to shut up in *one* breast the bitterness of lost love and the woe of failing friendship, was made by it all—really merry. O, there is a certain gayety of stagnation and grief, which is a sign of the soul's exhaustion, a smile like that on men who die of wounds in the diaphragm, or that on the shrivelled, drawn-back lips of mummies! Victor plunged into the stream of amusements, in order, under it, not to hear his own sighs. But often, to be sure, when he had all day long been sprinkling over ruined follies comic salt, which full as often bites the hand of the sower and makes it ache, and when he had not been able all day long to refresh himself with any eye, to which he would have dared to show a tear in his own,—when, thus weary of the present, indifferent to the future, wounded by the past, he had just passed by the last fool, the Apothecary, and when from his bow-window he looked out into the night hanging full of worlds, and into the tranquillizing moon, and upon the eastern clouds over St. Luna,—then were his swollen heart and his swollen eyeball sure to burst, and the tears which night concealed to stream down from his balcony on the hard pavement. "O, only *one* soul," cried his innermost being with all the tones of melancholy,—"give but *one* soul, thou eternal, loving, creative nature, to this poor, languishing heart, which seems so hard and is so soft, which seems so joyous and yet is so sad, seems so cold and yet is so warm!"

It was well that, on such an evening, no chamberlain, no man of the world, stood in the balcony, just as poor Marie—on whom her former life has been precipitated like a crushing avalanche—came to desire his breakfast-orders; for he would get up, without wiping away a drop, and advance kindly to meet her, and grasp her soft, but red and hard-worked hand, which from fear she did not draw back,—although from fear she did turn away her face, hardened into stone against hope,—and say, as he softly stroked her eyebrows horizontally, with a voice rising from a heart full of the deepest emotion, "Thou poor Marie, tell me—I am sure thou hast little comfort—is it not so? There seldom comes any longer into thy gentle eyes anything that they love to see, unless it is thy own tears? Dear girl, why hast thou no courage before me? why dost thou not tell me thy woe? Thou good, tortured heart,—I will speak for thee, act for thee: tell me what weighs on thee, and if ever of an evening thy heart is too heavy, and thou mayest not venture to weep down below, then come up to me ... look at me now frankly ... truly I will shed tears with thee, let them say what they will and be hanged." Although she held it to be uncourteous to weep before so distinguished a gentleman, nevertheless, it was impossible for her, by a forcible bending away of her face, to thrust aside all the tears which his voice, full of love, drew in rivers from her eyes.... Take it not ill of his over-boiling soul, that he then pressed his hot mouth to her cold, despised, and unresistingly trembling lips, and said to her: "Oh, why are we mortals so unhappy, when we are too soft-hearted?"—In his chamber she seemed to take all as jest,—but all night long she heard the echo of the humane man;—even as jest, so much love would have been a comfort to her; then her past flowers once more crystallized in the window-frost of her present wintry-time; then she felt as if she were to-day, for the first time, unhappy.—In the morning she said nothing to any one, and towards Sebastian she was merely more devoted, but not more courageous; only, at times, she would concur with the dispenser down below, when he praised him, and say, but without further explanation, "One should cut up one's own heart into little bits, and sacrifice it for the English gentleman."

Poor Marie! my own innermost heart repeats after the Doctor, and adds besides: Perhaps at this very moment, just such an unhappy woman, just such an unhappy man, is reading me. And I feel as if; now that I have struck the funeral bells of their past sad hours, I must also write them a word of consolation. But for one who has to be ever striding across new gaping ice-chasms of life, I know no resource but my own: the moment things grow bad, fling all *possible hopes* to the Devil, and with utter renunciation fall back upon thyself, and ask, How now, if even the worst should come, what then? Never reconcile thy fancy to the *next* misfortune, but to the greatest. Nothing relaxes one's spirits more than the alternation of warm hopes with cold anguish. If this method is too heroic for thee, then seek for thy tears an eye that shall imitate them, and a voice that shall ask thee why thou art thus. And reflect: the echo of the next life, the voice of our modest, fairer, holier soul, is audible only in a sorrow-darkened bosom, as the nightingales warble when one veils their cage.

Often did Sebastian worry himself about this, that he could here exert so little his noble powers in behalf of humanity; that his dreams of preventing evil and accomplishing good through the Prince remained fever-dreams, because, e. g., even the best men at the helm of the state filled offices entirely according to circumstances and recommendations merely, and held offices, whether those of others or their own, never as obligations, but as mining-curacies. He was troubled about his uselessness; but he consoled himself with its necessity: "in a year, when my father comes, I set myself free and rise to something better," and his conscience added, that his own personal uselessness was serviceable to the virtue of his father, and that it was better to be, in a wheel, with all one's fitness for a pendulum, a tooth, without which the machinery would stop, than to be the pendulum of a toothless wheel.

In such cases he always asked himself afresh: "Is Joachime, perhaps, like me, better, tenderer, less coquettish than she seems? and why wilt thou condemn her on the strength of an outward appearance, which is, to be sure, the same as thine own?" Her conduct seldom confirmed these favorable suppositions, nay, it often absolutely refuted them; nevertheless, he went on to expose himself to new refutations and to desire confirmation still. The necessity of loving drives one to greater follies than love itself; every week Victor let himself abate one perfection more from the female ideal, for which, as for the unknown god, he had already for years had the altar set up in his brain. During this haggling the whole of December would have slipped away, had it not been for the first day of Christmas.

On that day, when he saw through every window laughing faces and gardens of Hesperides, he too would fain be joyful, and flew amidst the church-chorals to Joachime's toilet-chamber, in order there to make himself a Christmas pleasure. He had brought her for a present, he said, a bottle-case of liqueurs, a whole cellar of Rataffia, because he knew how ladies drank. When, at last, he drew his gantry full of bottles out of his—pocket: it was a miserable little box full of cotton-wool, in which stood imbedded neat little bottles of sweet-smelling waters, almost as long as wrens'-eggs. What is neat always pleases girls—as well as what is splendid. He delivered a long discourse to Joachime upon the temperance of her sex, who ate as little as humming-birds and drank as little as eagles: with a few show-dishes and a smelling-bottle he would feast an army of the female sex five thousand men strong, and there should still be something left. The physicians observed that they who had borne hunger longest had been women,—even in the middle classes the whole bee-flora on which these saints lived consisted of a colored ribbon, which they wore as sash or scarf, by way of a nourishing poultice and portable soup, and to which they attached nothing further, except at most a lover. Joachime, during the eulogy, drew out a bottle, because she thought it wax. Victor, by way of refuting her—or for some other reason— pressed it tightly into her hand, and fortunately crushed it. A mining- superintendent of my disposition would hardly introduce the crushing of a bottle, not big enough to cover one of Eymann's cucumbers with, into his Dog-Post-Days,—because he loves to serve up things of importance,— did not the bottle itself acquire an importance from the fact that it cut the softest hand upon which the hardest jewel ever yet threw lustre, till it ran blood. The Doctor was startled,—the patient smiled,—he kissed the wound, and these three drops fell like Jason's blood, or like a blood rectified by an alchemist, as three sparks into his inflammable veins, and the blood-coal of love assumed three glowing points;—nay, a little more, and he would have obeyed her, when she playfully commanded him (in order to spare him a greater embarrassment than he had) to revive the antiquated fashion of the Parisians, of writing to ladies with rose-colored ink, and here on the spot to despatch three lines to her in her own blood. Thus much is, at least, certain, that he told her he wished he were the Devil. To the last-named personage, as is well known, the warranty-deed or rather partition-treaty of the soul is despatched with the blood of the proprietor as fist-[249]pledge and consideration. Blood is the seed of the Church, the Catholic Church says; and here we are speaking of nothing less than the *temple* of the fair.

So it was—and so it stood—when the Court of the Princess was announced for to-day. This was, in the first place, plaguily awkward for him, because this evening was spoiled; and, secondly, it was agreeable to him, because Joachime was obliged to-day to put away the hat which he and she so loved. Since, as is customary, ladies had the robes and frisures prescribed to them by the Princess, in which they must celebrate in her presence the court-day, i. e. the incendiary Sunday of their freedom: accordingly, she could not to-day keep on the crape-hat which she so loved, and Victor too, but not on her; for it was just the mate of that which Clotilda had worn when, during the concert, she covered her moist eyes with the black-lace veil, which from that time always hung down over his bereaved eyes.

I will describe the Court-day.

The main object of the Court in setting forth at six o'clock in the evening was, to drive home again at ten o'clock in a right sulky mood. I can, however, deliver this ten times as copiously:—

At six o'clock Victor, with the rest of the communion of brethren and sisters under orders, drove to the Paullinum. He envied, or rather blessed, the weaver, the boot-polisher, the wood-cutter, who had at evening his jug of beer, his prayers, his Johnny-[250]cakes and his trumpeting children; likewise their wives, who already had foretaste of the morrow, namely, of the marbled, speckled dresses which were to array them for the second holiday. In the May-colored atmosphere and zodiac stood the Princess as a sun, full as unhappy as her unhappy planets; *only dream* (thought he) *can make a king happy or a poor man unhappy.* When he saw how they all, after a scanty frog-rain of words; and after refreshments, i. e. beatings and exhaustions, were harnessed, one post-team after another, according to the Court almanac and directory, to the card-tables,—to every board came the same motley set of old faces,—he wondered first of all at the universal patience; on a negro of the gold coast of the court (he swore to himself) if one only considers what he has to *hear* and to *endure*, the *ears* and the *skin* are certainly, as in the case of roasted sucking-pigs, the best parts. Here the lion must beg *that* animal to let him have his skin for a domino, which has usually borrowed his of him. Here among these forms bent up by small souls (as leaves also crook up when leaf-lice live on them) no great, no bold thought can be carried: like wheat which is *beaten down*, they can yield only *empty* grains.

Before the sitting down at table, that part or segment of the—halo[251] encircling the Italian *sun*, which was not invited, drove home, disgusted at the tediousness of play, and still more disgusted that certain persons in particular were honored with the tediousness of a seat at the table.

Joachime, in whom the retiring Agnola found little satisfaction, went away with them, but not the Doctor, nor her brother Mat either, who had the honor of making, behind the chair of the Princess, in the column of march formed by herself, her chamberlain, a page, and a court lackey, exactly the central point; he stood, as every one knows, immediately behind the chamberlain, and was the only one who looked like a legible lampoon upon the *tout ensemble*. About the table, during[252] which there was little said, at most in a very low tone by two neighbors, here also there shall be nothing said.

After dinner the Prince came and disturbed the stiff ceremonial, which he hated from love of comfort, just as Victor despised it on philosophical grounds. "Verily, an archangel," Victor would often say, "who should remark the wisdom and virtue observed by mortals in all trifles at their session-tables, altars, receptions, must needs bet his heaven and his wings that we are worth a farthing—or at least something—in greater things; but we all know where the conclusion limps; and this very disgust at the stiff, pedantic, decent micrology and machinery of men is the humor of the satirist. Moral deterioration comes about, it is true, through trifles, but not improvement: Satan creeps into us through Venetian blinds and *sphincters* [253]; the good angel enters through the front door."—Agnola rewarded our hero to-day for his previous so well meant assiduity with a warmer attention, which was made more beautiful in his eyes by her ornaments— she wore those of the former princess, her own, and those of her mother before her—and by her whole state-attire; for he loved finery on women and hated it on men. His esteem borrowed a tender warmth from the painful fact that she confounded January's selfish intentions in his visits (with reference to the future Clotilda) with fairer ones, and that nevertheless one could not say so to her. How came it that Agnola reminded him then of Joachime; that the latter was the *conductor* of regard for the former; and that all loving emotions with which the Princess inspired him turned out wishes that Joachime might deserve and receive them?

With a soul full of such longing, he drove back this very day without ceremony to that Joachime on whose hand, as we know, he had left a slight wound. He said to her, "He must, as murderer and Medicus, look once more to-day after the wound"; but a charming new trouble on Joachime's face fell like sunshine with a warming influence into his soul. He was impatient to go out with her on the balcony, to talk about it. Out there, he in a few minutes made the gash and the December chill a pretext for taking the hand and the gash into his own to warm it. "Cold is bad for wounds," he said; but the fine fool would here have had his own comment on the subject. The vacant evening, the remembrances of the childish joys of Christmas, the starry heaven, looking down from overhead, which magically illuminates all dark wishes of man, like flowers in the night,—these and the silence surcharged and burdened his forlorn soul, and he pressed the only hand which human kind at this moment extended to him. He put the question to her directly about her trouble. Joachime answered more softly than usual, "I was going to ask you the same; but with me it is natural." For she had, she related, on her return found the luggage of Clotilda and the news of her arrival, and—which is the precise point—the clothes of her sister Giulia, which Clotilda had hitherto given a place among her own. This Giulia, it will be remembered, had expired on Clotilda's heart, a day before the latter removed from Maienthal to St. Luna.

A chaos shot through his heart; but out of the chaos only the faded Giulia took shape,—for Clotilda daily receded into a duskier sanctuary of his soul; her pale Luna-like image caressed with rays of another world his sore nerves, and he willingly suffered himself to believe that Joachime had her form. In his poetic exaltation, so seldom intelligible to women, the dead threw the halo which Clotilda diffused over her back again upon her sister. Joachime had to-day read over again the letter which Giulia had dictated to her in her last hour through Clotilda, and she still had it with her. Probably a heart full of unrequited love had borne the fair enthusiast down under the earth. Victor with gleaming eyes begged her for the letter; he opened it in the moonlight, and when he saw the beloved handwriting of his lost Clotilda, his whole heart wept.

"Good sister!—

"Forever farewell! Let me say that first, because I know not what moment may close my lips. The tempests of my life are going home.[254] I speak this farewell and my heartiest wish for thy welfare through my friend Clotilda's pen. Give the enclosed to my dear parents, and join thy prayer to mine, that they will leave me in my beautiful Maienthal, when I am gone. I see now through the window the rose-bush which stands by the sexton's little garden in the churchyard: there a place is given me, which like a scar shall testify that I once existed, and a black cross with the six white letters *Giulia*,—no more. Dear sister, do not, I beseech thee, allow them to confine my dust in a tomb!—O no! it shall flutter in the shape of Maienthal's roses, which I once so loved to sprinkle!—Let this heart, when it shall have dissolved into the pollen of a new eternal heart, play and hover in the beams of the moon, which has so often in my lifetime made my heart sad and soft. If thou ever drivest, dear sister, along by Maienthal, then will the cross peep out upon the road through the roses; and if it does not make thee too sad, then look over to me.

"It seemed to me just now, for some minutes, as if I drew breath in ether,—in little thin draughts. It will soon be over. But tell my playmates, if they ask for me, that I was glad to go, though I was young. Very glad. Our teacher says, the dying are flying clouds, the living stationary ones, beneath which the former glide away, but verily at evening both are gone. Ah, I thought I should have to yearn for death a long time yet, from one year of sorrow to another; ah! I feared these pale cheeks, these eyes sunk with weeping, would not prevail upon death, that he would let me grow superannuated, and not take away my withered heart until it had throbbed itself to exhaustion: but, lo! he comes sooner. In a few days, perhaps in a few hours, an angel will appear before me and smile, and I shall see that it is death, and I, too, shall smile and say most joyfully, Take my beating heart into thy hand, thou ambassador of eternity, and care for my soul.

"'But art thou not young?' the angel will say; 'hast thou not just stept upon this earth? Shall I recall thee so soon, even before it has its spring?'

"But I shall answer: Look on these sunken cheeks, and these exhausted eyes, and only shut them to. O, lay the snake-stone[255] on my bosom, that it may suck out all the wounds, and not fall off till they are healed. Ah! I have haply done no good in the world, but also no evil.

"Then will the angel say: 'If I touch thee, thou becomest stiff,—spring and mankind and the whole earth vanish, and I alone stand beside thee. Is, then, thy young soul already so weary and so sore? What sorrows, then, can there be thus early in thy breast?'

"Only touch me, good angel!—Now he says, 'If I touch thee, thou crumblest to dust, and all thy loved ones see nothing more of thee—'

"O, touch me!..."

Death touched the bleeding heart, and a human being had passed on....

While Victor read the sorrowful sheet, the sister of the dead one had several times wiped her eyes, because she imagined to herself what he was reading, and when he looked up at her, there glimmered therein the seed-pearls of a tender soul. But he wished now that his face could be invisible, or that he could be in the balcony of his chamber, so as to give way to all sighs and emotions unseen. Had he been in a citizen's house, he might now have gone without being derided to the unpacked clothes, and into the future apartments of Clotilda; and he might have seen again, as it were, the green lawns of Maienthal, if he had seen the romantic dresses, wherein Giulia had roamed through them, locked up amidst the last kisses of a sister. But in such a house it was an impossibility.

He could now, as he seldomer had the enjoyment of another's sensibility, easily pardon its even being carried to excess. That it shatters the body was to him the wretchedest objection, because, indeed, everything of a nobler sort, every effort, all thinking, wears it out; in fact, the body and life were only means, but not an end. "Giulia's heart in Giulia's body," said he, "is a pure dew-drop in a tender flower-cup, which everything crushes, chokes, dries up, and which yet has escaped the noonday sun; such souls, too pliable for a world full of storm, which have too many nerves and too few muscles, deserve for their sensibility's sake not the corroding salt of satire, which gnaws them like snails. Earth and we can give them few joys; why will we take from them the rest?"

But the lines of sorrow which sympathy now drew through Joachime's smiles imprinted themselves distinctly in Victor's heart, and that which she would here conceal made her more charming than all that she had ever sought to show.

Nothing is more dangerous than—as he had done some weeks before—to make believe he was in love: one becomes so forthwith in reality. Thus, the voluptuary *Baron*, when he had played one of Corneille's heroes, himself was one for some days. Thus Moliere died of a *malade imaginaire*, and Charles V. of a rehearsal-burial. Thus the paper crown which Cromwell had worn in a school-drama made him covet a harder one.—The second lesson which is to be learned from this (this, however, to be sure, presupposes Joachime's being a coquette) is, that a hero may scent coquetry, and yet run into the trap; a poet, like the nightingale (which he resembles in plumage, throat, and simplicity) sits up on the tree, and sees the snare set, and skips down and—into it.

After some days,—while the question about Joachime's worth and his own love was rising and falling like a wave in Victor's mind,—while he stood on bad terms with Flamin, good ones with the Princess, and better with the Prince, who kept asking every day when Clotilda was coming,—she came.

23
DOG-POST-DAY

"Ay, I must confess," said Victor, as on the day after Clotilda's arrival he ran round in his chamber, "I could look with more courage into a thunderstorm or a tempestuous sea than into that little face,—into a radiant heaven, three noses long." He got relief, however, by striking a detached fortissimo chord on the piano: then he could go to see Clotilda. Only on the way he said: "Nowhere is there so much jangling as within a man. What a devilish uproar in this five-foot Disputatorium about the smallest trumpery, till a bill grows into an act! A portable national convention *in nuce*,[256] that is what I am; I cannot take a step, without the *right* and *left* first haranguing on the subject, and the *enragés* and the *noirs*,[257] and the Duke of Orleans and Marat. The most detestable thing about this interior Ratisbon diet of man is, that Virtue sits therein with ten seats and one voice, but the Devil with one rump and seven votes." —

By these humorous soliloquies he sought to divert himself from the aspect of his confused, stubborn, cold-sore spirit, which was always lifting Joachime to the level of Clotilda. He was finally put in perfect tune again merely by the virtuous resolution not to conceal now his love for Joachime, — "not to be ashamed of her," he had almost thought to himself. "If I *feign* myself to be somewhat warmer toward Joachime and colder towards the other than I perhaps am, then the Devil must have his game in it, if I do not finally *become* so."

But the Devil had his game, and in fact a true game of Ombre[258] for *four* persons,[259] with a dummy:[260] this croupier[261] had made the original vault of playing out the face[262] of Clotilda with a wholly different *color* from what he had given her in Le Baut's palace. Victor found her, on meeting her again at Schleunes's, infinitely more beautiful than he had left her, — that is to say, more *pale*. As she was no nervous patient, never avoided the cold, even on December evenings walked out alone in the village, her cheeks were usually more like dark rosebuds than opened and whitened rose-leaves. But now the sun had become a moon: she had, in some sorrow or other, like the sapphire in the fire, lost nothing but color; instead of the blood, the soul, grown more still, lovely, and tender, seemed itself to look more nearly through the white crape curtain. All the blood which had receded from her cheeks flowed over into his, and rose like a magic potion into his head; meanwhile he tried to get into the latter the thought, "Probably it is more the quarrel with her parents, and less the affliction of being driven hither, that has made her sick."

When one has once proposed to himself to make believe cold, one becomes still more so when one finds reasons for *not* being so: Victor was made still colder by Clotilda's parents, who had come with her, and from whose faults the mantle seemed to him to be at once removed. Upon persons whom, for the sake of a third, one has esteemed too highly, one avenges himself, when the third no longer exerts the constraining influence, by a so much the greater depreciation of them. Then, too, he said to himself: "As she now seldom sees her brother Flamin, it would be a piece of simplicity to expose her to a minute's embarrassment by the announcement that I know the relationship." Poor Victor! Nevertheless, it was impossible for him even to charge his heart with so much electrical warmth—though he might rub it with cat-skins and beat it with fox-tails—as would be requisite in order that his pulse should beat full for Joachime, not to say feverishly; but *this very thing* decided him to conduct himself exactly as if heart and pulse were fuller. "It were ignoble," thought he, "if the good Joachime should be made to atone for it, that I once had other hopes and wishes than my hitherto newest ones." This sacrifice warmed him to a proper degree of regard; this regard gave him the manly pride, which defies with its love and its choice all the four quarters of the world; this pride, again, gave him freedom and joy,—and now he was in a condition to talk with Clotilda like a reasonable man.

All this inner history occupied, of course, twelve times as great a space of time as Mohammed's journey through all the heavens,—almost a good hour. But an accident threw itself into the midst of all his ideas. Namely, as the Minister's lady was a true female philosopher,—she knew that a couple of quartz crystals with some preparations and a drowned fœtus do not make a philosopher, but nothing short of a lecture-room full of natural curiosities, and a reading cabinet,—and as the Chamberlain Le Baut was a philosopher, for his cabinet was quite as large,—the collection was exhibited to the Chamberlain, which he had himself helped to enrich. One would suppose that they must have laughed at each other in their sleeves, and taken each other for fools; but they really held each other for philosophers; for with great folks the fruits of the tree of knowledge grow so into the window and into the mouth,—they have so much facility in gaining knowledge (and therefore a second in showing it),—they so seldom seek in the wells of truth anything else than their own knee-pieces made with water-colors, and to wade into the depths of this fountain would give them such a chill,—and yet, on the other hand, they converse with so many sorts of persons of information in all departments,—that they get a smattering of everything over the table, and by oral tradition, like the disciples of the ancients, become through the ears living cyclopædias. If, afterward, they actually know how to absolutely renounce that which they have never heard, what difference is there, then, between them and the poorest philosopher, except in consciousness?

In the cabinet of books and natural curiosities lay the whole New-Year's freight of buzzing chafers, with golden wing-sheaths minus wings,—I mean the gilt Musen-Almanachs. Matthieu, that mimic of the actual nightingales, was the sworn foe of the human ones, namely, the poets. He said,—what would have suited better for a Review,—"He was a great friend of verses, but only in winter,—for when he went roaming so through the flower-beds of an Annual, he became, like one who walks through a poppy-field, drowsy enough, and could go to sleep. And just as the nights grew longer, and one therefore needed a longer sleep, it was a fine thing that the Annuals should appear, exactly at the beginning of winter, and that these flowers should bloom at the same season of the year with the mosses; in this way one could at least be lulled to sleep beside the brook that murmured in the verses, when there was no more murmuring or sleeping on the frozen meadow."—

Our Victor was as satirical as the Evangelist; he had in Hanover laughed as well as this fellow here,—e. g. he had complained that most Annual-minstrels unfortunately labored more for *connoisseurs* than for dull readers, and were well contented if they only got the former to sleep,—that a man who could not write prose should try whether he might not make a popular bard, as only those birds can *sing* who do not learn to talk,—that he could get through a good Annual at the quickest and most agreeable rate, if he only ran over the rhymes,—and that flat heads, like flat diamonds, to which no facettes can be given, became *hearts*, and instead of thoughts gave us tears, in which there swam not so much as the infusorium of an idea....

But he saw still one side more than Matthieu, namely, the noble side. It was his custom to turn this side forward precisely when another had been showing the bad side, and *vice versâ*. His opinion was, that the poets were nothing but intoxicated philosophers,—but whoever could not learn philosophizing from them, would learn it quite as little from the systematicians. That philosophy made only the *silver-wedding* between ideas, but poetry the first marriage; empty *words* there might be, but no empty *sensations*. That the poet, in order to move us, has only to take for his lever all of noble that there is on the earth,—Nature, Freedom, Virtue, and God; and the very magic-words, the magic-rings, the magic-lamps wherewith he sways us, react at last upon himself.

He delivered this opinion—when Matthieu had given his and Joachime her own, namely, that there were three or four leaves, at least, in the Musen-Almanachs which pleased her, namely, the smooth parchment leaves—much more briefly than we have put it;—the Minister's lady was of his opinion (for she herself was a versifex);—the Chamberlain said, "Every city and every prince did indeed adore the poets in appropriate temples,—namely, in the play-houses." Clotilda ventured now to join herself to the victors:[263] "When one reads a poet in January, it is as lovely as when one goes to walk in June. I cannot read either philosophers or learned men; there would, therefore, be left to me" (she meant to say, to her sex) "quite too little, if one should take from me the dear poets." "You would at most," said the Minister at last, "find your disciples in them; poets, like the saints, concern themselves little about the world and its knowledge; they can sing of the state, but not instruct it." "O thou grinning mummy!" thought Victor, "a precious stone which thou canst not work into the wall of the state-building is less to thee than a block of sandstone. If thou couldst only install every flaming soul sent into the world as a completion of the republican antiques, in the office of under-clerk, custom-house collector, or warden of the treasury (as the people of Grand Cairo transform their ruins into stables and horse-troughs)!" The noble Mat merely subjoined: "There was a painter in Rome who never talked with any one but by singing; and I knew a great poet who not even in common life could speak prose; but he could not do much beside, and had little of the world, but a great many worlds in his head. When he comes out in print, he will hardly play off more deception on his readers than any one has already played off on him, who chose to."—Victor saw, by Clotilda's downcast eye, that she observed, as well as he, that the Devil meant her Dahore: but he was silent; his soul was sad and embittered: he had, however, long since been hardened by court life to endure those whom he must needs hate.

During this disputation the noble Mat had, unobserved, cut out the whole group in black paper. "Ah!" said Joachime, "this is not the first time that he has given *blackened* likenesses of companies." But as Victor could never see silhouette-groups, without thinking of us fleeting shadows of mortals, of this dwindling and drying-up dwarf-life, of the night-pieces drawn upon life, and of the shadowy companies called peoples,—and as he was reminded of this not only by his melancholy, and not only by a wax-skeleton, by Madame Biheron,[264] which stood there among the natural curiosities, but still more by the pale form of Clotilda,—and as, casting a glance of comparison at the skeleton and the profile, she said softly to Victor, "So many resemblances might at another time make me sad,"—then was his full heart transpierced with a sharp pang at the thought of his eternal poverty, and at the certainty, "This great, beautiful heart will never stir for thine, and when her friend Emanuel is dead, thou art left forever alone"; and he stepped to the window, threw it open violently, drank in the north-wind, pressed his fist against his two eyeballs, and went back with his former expression of countenance to the rest of the company.

But for to-day such agitations had torn deeply into his heart. And when Clotilda, at a solitary second, said to him that the Parson's wife and Agatha were angry at his staying away, then was he, to whom at these names the whole beclouded past opened like a heaven, in no condition to give an answer.

When he returned home, Clotilda's voice, which he could of all her attractions least forget, kept incessantly speaking, and like the echo of a funeral-song, in his soul.... Reader, when that which thou lovedst has long vanished from the earth or from thy fancy, then will nevertheless the beloved *voice* come back and bring with it all thy old tears, and the disconsolate heart which has shed them!... But not merely her voice,—everything came thronging back in the darkness upon his fancy: her modest eye, which did not in court-like style sparkle and bid defiance and express desire, as did those of the others,—that watchful delicacy, which since his entrance on court-life no longer appeared to him, either in her or in his father, too great,—to this add the image of Joachime and his chaos of inconsistencies, and the remark that a man whom the most certain proofs have satisfied that he is not loved, still suffers afresh at a *new* one,—and then one can understand the commotions which sleep, that lull on life's ocean, had in his case to appease.—

"That was the last fever-shake," said he the next morning, relying upon his present heart, whose eruptions, like those of volcanoes, daily burnt out its crater more and more. He enjoined upon himself, therefore, a weekly flight from the too dear soul, with the design that the new resonance of his love might cease its vibrations in his heart, and all become still again within him.

But after a week he saw her again: verily, there sat the Devil again at the card-table, and played another color against him,—the *red*. Clotilda looked, not pale, but, though only slightly, red. This redness made a great blot on his inner man, and adulterated his inner coloring, as black does every color of the painter. For when he found her well again; it was not so much *agreeable* to him,—for he saw how few claims he any longer had upon her tranquillity,—how she did not so much as distinguish him in this warehouse of human waste-paper, and how stupid he had been in letting himself dream so secretly, so very secretly, that her previous paleness proceeded actually from her vain longing after such a one as he;—at the same time it was not *disagreeable* to him,—for he would have poured out all his heart's blood, if he could thereby have brought a single artery in her to its old course;—I say it was not so much either agreeable or disagreeable to him, as it was both, as it was unexpected, as it was a hint to—give himself to the Devil. His heart, and the image which had been too long therein, were absolutely crushed in two. "Be it so!" said he, and bit the convulsive lip with which he said it. For some days he cared not even to see Joachime. "Has *she* then an eye for nature and a heart for eternity?" asked he, and he knew well the answer.

Now came on a time for him, which was the precise opposite of the Sabbatical weeks,[265]—one may call them the *race-weeks* or the *Tarantula-dancing-hours* of visiting. It is a cursed time; man knows not where he stands. With Victor it fell just upon the winter-months, when, besides, the honeymoons of city and court occur. I will now portray them regularly.

Victor sought, namely, to drown deeper his unhappy, discordant heart,—not with the drum-roll of amusements; under this it would only bleed the more, just as wounds flow more strongly under the sound of drumming; but with—people; these were the blood-stanching screws which he applied to his soul. His body was now, like the Catholic reliquiary body of an Apostle, in all places; he spent the whole day in running to and fro, now with the Prince and now without him.

At last there was not a lady left in Flachsenfingen whose hand he had not kissed,—nor a toilet-table where he would have been satisfied. He made in the *racing-weeks* double-knots, French *pas,*—dotted sketches of patterns,— little plays,—charades,—receipts for canary-birds,—verses for fans,—a thousand visits,—and still more, morning notes....

These last, which he received and sent, were written in French and folded French-wise,—namely, crushed into the shape of hair-rollers. "They are," said he, "the hair-rollers of the fibres of the female brain,— the cartridges full of Cupid's powder,—the cocoons of loving-butterflies": he spoke of the rise and fall of these female notes, and called them still further the proof-sheets of the female heart, and the outer-title-pages of the coquettish Edicts of Nantes. "I assert this," he added, "to distinguish myself from the page Matthieu, who denies it, because he actually contends, that at first one presses letters upon the fair sex, then things of more cubic contents, e. g. fans, jewels, hands, then finally one's self; just as the mails at first only took letters, then packages, finally passengers." —

He found those women daily more amusing who steal away from us people of understanding the heart out of the breast and the brain out of the head, and, to be sure, (as a certain nobleman did other stuff,) not from love for the stolen goods, but from love of robbery itself; the next morning, like the nobleman, they honestly send the goods back again to the owner. Their refinements,—his own,—his turns to escape theirs,—the attention which one had to bestow upon one's self,—the opportunity of bringing all emotions under the finest dissecting-knives, or solar and lunar microscopes,—the facility of taking away from the most sincere truths the sour taste and from the most agreeable the sickly-sweet,—all this made the toilet-tables of women, particularly of coquettes, to him *Lectisternia* [266] and tables of the gods. "By heaven," said the toilet-table-boarder or pensioner,[267] "a man is merely a Dutchman, at most a German, but a woman is a native Frenchwoman, or in fact a Parisian: man conceals his moral as he does his physical breast: thoughts and flowers, which do not fall through the racks of the four faculties, emotions which cannot be described in the acts or in a physician's report, one must really say only to a woman, and not to a man, especially one of Flachsenfingen"—or Scheerau.

By way of excusing himself for associating with coquettes on the footing of a general lover, he appealed to his motive,—that of merely wishing to become acquainted with their ways,—and to the excellent Forster, who in Antwerp *knelt down*, as well as any born Catholic, before Rubens's altar-piece of the Virgin Mary ascending to heaven, merely to examine her more nearly.

He had a still more dangerous excuse. "Man," said he, "should be everything, learn everything, try everything,—he should labor for the *union* of the two *churches* [268] in his soul,—he should, if only for a couple of months, have been a city-musician,[269] grave-digger, gallows-*pater*,[270] an engineer, tragedy-manager, upper-court-marshal, an imperial vicar, deputy sheriff, a reviewer, a lady, in short, everything a man should have been for some days, in order that the hues of the prism might at last melt together into the perfect white."

These principles are the more dangerous with one like him, who, strung with the tense strings of the most dissimilar powers, easily gave every one's note, not from dissimulation, but because his social poetic faculty could transport itself deeply into another's soul; hence he gained, tolerated, and copied the most unlike persons, notwithstanding his sincerity. But I pity him, that he has everywhere so much to suppress, his seeing through the Prince, his state of heart toward Clotilda, his conciliatory intrigues towards Agnola, his knowledge of Flamin's relations, &c. Ah, reserve and dissimulation easily run together; and must not a constant dropping, when one stands directly under it, at last wear scars in the most solid character?

Nothing chills the noblest parts of the inner man more than intercourse with persons in whom one cannot take any interest. This hotel-life at court, this daily seeing people who never even say "I," whose relations one ignores as indifferently as their talents, unless some necessity seeks them,—this snatching only at the next moment, this racing by of the finest and most intellectual strangers and ant-swarms of visitors, who in three days are forgotten,—all this, which makes palaces like Russian ice-palaces, where even the stove full of naphtha flames is a lump of ice, and to which I need not at all add the *comic* salt, which, besides, chills all warm blood, as that of *Glauber* does hot water,—all this made his heart desolate, his days bald and burdensome, his nights distressful, his conduct too cold towards the good, too tolerant towards the bad.

In addition to this, his Emanuel was silent, and, like nature, shut up his flowers within himself. He whom nature nourishes and builds up, is not in so good a mood in winter as in summer. The earth had on her powder-mantle of snow, and her night-gown on all day; the trees had wrapped up their buds in fleecy hair-papers, and the twigs looked like hair-pins. Victor's soul was like nature: O may Heaven soon warm in both the flowers of spring!

As the pathological history of my Victor reminds me too painfully of the latent poisons in the human body, it shall soon come to an end. It pleased him that he became, by this fluttering round, more and more gallant and cold towards all women: the cord of love cuts less deeply into the bosom, when, plucked out into threads and floss, it flutters about everybody. He who, like his namesake, Saint Sebastian, looked like one stuck all full with (Cupid's) arrows, shot off arrows of another kind against the whole sex, though never against individuals. In this last circumstance his bitterness differed from Matthieu's, who could say of his own cousin, for example, who had lost her beauty by a late attack of small-pox: "Her beauty held out right valiantly against the small-pox, and brought off from this victory the most glorious *scars*, and all of them indeed, like those of Pompey's knights;[271] in front and in the face."

As assafœtida is used for *haut gout*, so does one season the finest *savoir vivre* by sundry bold incivilities. Bastian in the Tarantula-season was not to be embarrassed by anything: he went and came like a Parisian, without ceremony; he sought often bold, but advantageous postures of his body; during the play he made tours through the boxes as the Prince did through the coulisses; five times he carried matters so far (though with difficulty, and always only by means of setting before himself the example of the courtiers), that he listened indifferently, or absolutely looked away, when another was, telling him a story: all which things, if not essential, are nevertheless incidental to true politeness.

Nor will I let it be unnoticed in his praise, that he took to himself the regular *exotic* and *satirical* liberties of the *Gallican* Church toward several women at once, for in the presence of a single one he had still the old veneration of a noble heart. I will give at least one example of that. Once he was among five slanderesses (the company consisted of six females and a male person); the ugliest blackened all maidens, even those in print, e. g. the deceased Clarissa, whom she charged with not having in her intercourse with Lovelace been quite able to *sauver les dehors de la vertu.*[272] One can anticipate how the Königsberg school will receive it in their reviews, that he let himself down on one knee before the calumniatress, and said with some seriousness: "*O Clarisse! voici votre Lovelace; retranchons quatre tomes, commençons comme les faiseurs d'Epopées par le reste.*"[273]

To be sure, he frequently during the Tarantula-season reproached himself for the Tarantula-season; and when the Gentile-fore-court of his heart grew so full of women, while in the Holy of Holies there was nothing but mute darkness, and when his brain became an entomological cabinet of court trifles, then, of course, he often sighed in his balcony: "O come soon, good father, that thy sinking son may soar out of this unclean March fog into a clearer life, before he has utterly stained himself, so as no longer even to frame this wish." And as often as he got sight, in Joachime's chamber, of the views of Maienthal,—which Giulia had had taken by the painter of Clotilda's portrait,—then in the midst of his jestings he turned his eye away from them with a sigh.—But he was not healed, until fate said, Now! Then all at once the theatre-key struck, which bids men come and act in the players' rehearsal of life;—the play itself is not given till the next life;—and then transpired something which I shall at once report in the following chapter, when I have done relating in this one how Victor stood with all the people about him.

With many, properly speaking, badly,—in the first place, with Clotilda. She resided, to be sure, at the Minister's; as maid of honor, she would have belonged in the Paullinum, only the Prince had so contrived it for the greater facility of seeing her; but she was always about the Princess, with whom she was soon linked in intimacy by a similarity of seriousness and a similarity of reserve. Her indifference to one who had with her a common friend and teacher inspired this Victor with a still greater, especially as he knew she must feel that, in this cold mountain- and court-air, only a single, though faded, carnation slip of her fair soul bloomed, namely, himself. Then, too, the obligation of decorum, to look upon her coldly, must become a habit. The worst thing for him was that she was indifferent towards him without ill-feeling, and cold towards him with respect. Others were quite furious about the "phlegmatic virtue of this Pygmalion's statue." The noble

Mat called her often the *Holy* Virgin, or the Demoiselle Mother of God. It is made out very clearly by the Dog-documents, which I have opened, that some gentlemen of the Court, after various abortive attempts to explain to themselves a virtue irreconcilable with so much beauty, now on the ground of temperament, now of concealed love, and now of a coquettish coyness, ending at last, like the water at St. Clermont, in petrifying and becoming *its own bridge over itself,*—that these cunning gentlemen most felicitously fell upon the conjecture that Clotilda wore this mask over her face as a copy of the face of the Princess, for the sake of continuing in favor. Hence Clotilda's discreet virtue was judged by most with greater indulgence, while one could excuse it, as an intentional imitation of a similar fault in the Princess, even by the example of like imitations, as courtiers often aped the greatest external natural faults, nay, even the virtues of a prince. So thought at least the more reasonable portion of the Court.

Agnola was assiduous in testifying an ever increasing gratitude to our hero for January's visits, although, as I think, she could detect the faithless intentions of the Prince in the presence of Clotilda full as well as she might sometimes see into Victor's soul in the presence of Joachime.... In fact, I should have begged the reader long since to be on the look-out; I deliver the facts with excusable stupidity, though with historic fidelity; if, now, there are therein fine, knavish, significant, intriguing traits and hints, it is without my knowledge, and therefore I cannot point them out to the reader with an index-hand, or announce them with a fire-drum,[274] but he himself—as he understands court histories—must know what I mean by my hints,—not *I*.

With Joachime Victor would have gone on very well,—as he set down all faults which he found in other women, and not in her, to her credit as virtues, and as he grew more intimate with her personally; for the faults of maidens, like chocolate and tobacco, appear at first the more odd to the palate the better they taste to it afterward: he would have got on very well, but for two sharp corner-stones; but they were there. The first was,—for I will not reckon his slight annoyance at the short duration of her Christmas sentimentality,—that she was always finding fault with Clotilda, particularly with her "affected" virtue. The second was, that Clotilda sought her society quite as little: Victor could love no one whom Clotilda did not love. And now the race-weeks and visiting-Tarantula-dance hours of one man are at an end; but, alas! all posterity must yet cross the same hot *line* of folly and of youth.

24
DOG-POST-DAY

On the 26th of February Victor found in the morning at Joachime's—the proud Clotilda. I know not whether it was by accident that she was here, or from politeness, or for the purpose of meeting more nearly a person whom Victor treated with some interest. But, O heavens! the cheeks of this Clotilda were pallid, her eyes were as if breathed over by an eternal tear, her voice emotional, as it were broken, and the pale marble body seemed only the image standing on the monument of the departed soul. Victor forgot the whole past, and his innermost soul wept for longing to succor her and wipe out from her life all dark winter landscapes. "I am as well as usual to-day," said she to his professional inquiry, and he knew not what to make of this unexpected paleness; he could not, in fact, to-day make anything, not so much as a joke or a piece of flattery; his soul, dissolved into sympathy, would not take any form; then, too, he was embarrassed. Clotilda soon took leave;—and it would not have been possible for him to-day, not for all Great Poland (that ice-floe beautifully ground down under the sledging of emigrating nations and crowns), after she was gone, to stay half an hour longer.

Besides, he would have been obliged to go; for the page Matthieu called him to the Princess. The time was unusual; he could not wait to see, nor could he guess what was the matter. The Evangelist smiled (that he did now somewhat often when the Princess was the subject), and said: "To Princes and Princesses weighty things were trivial and trivial things weighty, as Leibnitz[276] said of himself. When the crown and a hair-pin fall from their heads together, they look first of all for the hair-pin."[277]

By the way! It would be malice on my part toward the noble Matthieu, if I should longer suppress, the fact, that for some time he has been much more tender and ardent towards my hero,—which on any other man than he, I mean on a lurking villain, would be a Cain's-mark, and would have somewhat of the same meaning as the wagging of a cat's tail.

Victor was astonished at the request of the Princess,—that he would cure Clotilda: that is to say, not at the fact of her making a request,—for she often did him that honor,—but at the intelligence that Clotilda, on whose cheeks he had hitherto seen the apple-blossoms of health at his soul's expense in the *race-weeks*, had worn only dead blossoms,—namely, rouge, which the Princess had been obliged to enforce upon her for the sake of having a uniformity of bloom with the remaining red copper-flowers[278] of the court. Agnola, who, like her rank, was quick, besought him further, when he was appointed to the medical upper-examining-commission, to enter on his office as soon as might be, this very day forthwith, at the play, where he would find the candidate for examination.

And he found her. The play was a sparkling brilliant brought from Eldorado,—Goethe's *Iphigenia*. When he saw the patient again with the evening-red of the rouge, wherein she was to glow at another's behest even during her going down,—when he saw this still victim (marked red, as it were, for the altar), which he and others had driven away from its meadows, from its solitary flowers, to the midst of the sacrificial knives of the Court, mutely enduring, the extinction of its wishes, and when he compared with woman's dumb patience man's raging restlessness,—and when it seemed as if Clotilda had lent her sorrow to Iphigenia with the prayer, "Take my heart, take my voice and mourn with it,—mourn with it over thy separation from the fields of youth, over thy separation from a beloved brother,"—and when he saw how she tried to fasten her eyes more steadfastly on Iphigenia, when she pined for her lost brother, in order to control their overflow and their direction (towards her own brother in the Parterre, towards Flamin), O then did such great sorrows and their signs in his eyes and looks need a pretext like the omnipotence of genius, in order to be confounded with pangs growing out of poetic illusion!

Never did a physician question his patient with greater sympathy and forbearance than did he Clotilda in the next interlude: he excused his importunity with the commands of the Princess. I must first state that the fair patient—although he had been hitherto a falling Peter, whom many a cock-crow had brought rather to tears than to repentance—nevertheless remained the *second person*, whom he never denied, ... i. e. whom, he never addressed with the frivolous, whimsical, bold, entrapping turns of conversation now so common with him. The *first person*—whom he esteemed too highly to write to him in the present state of his heart—was his Emanuel.

Clotilda answered him, that "she was as well as ever; the only thing there was sickly about her," she said, smiling, "namely, her color, was already under the hands of a female surgeon, who, against her inclination, healed her only outwardly." This playful allusion to the rouging decreed by the Princess had the double design of excusing her painting and of diverting the Doctor from his tender-hearted seriousness. But the first was unnecessary,—since in the theatre even ladies who never wore rouge put it on as they entered the box and wiped it off on going out, in order not to hang there as the only quinces on a tree full of glowing Stettin-apples, and as, in fact, mineral cheeks were required of the whole female court-retinue as facial court livery. The second was vain; much more likely were the wounds of his heart to be aggravated by two causes: by that cold, almost fanatical resignation to fading away,—and by something inexpressibly mild and tender which, in the female face, often betokens the breaking heart, the failing life, as fruit by *soft* yielding to *pressure* announces its ripeness.

O ye good creatures, ye women, while joy already beautifies you, is the reason why sorrow makes you still more beautiful and too touching *this*, that it so often overtakes you, or is it because sorrow borrows the dress of joy? Why must I here confess so passingly my pleasure at your endurance and veiling of sorrows, when at this moment before my fancy so many hearts full of tears sweep by with open countenances full of smiles, and win for your sex the praise of opening its heart as gladly to sorrow as to joy, as flowers, although they *unclose only before the sun, yet also burst open when it is overcast by a cloudy heaven?

Victor, without being led off his track by her answer, continued: "Perhaps you cannot wean yourself from fair nature and from exercise,—these late hours, which I myself feel"—She prevented his finishing the sentence, to remind him that she had, he must remember, brought her present complexion with her from home. One sees, however, in this reminder more forbearance than truth; for she would not complain of her court office before the very one who had helped her gain it.—Victor, who saw her sickliness so clearly, and yet knew not how to propound another question, stood there dumfounded. Their own silence loosens reserved people's tongues: Clotilda began of herself, "As I do not know what harms me here, except the rouge, I beg my physician to prohibit me this dietetic fault," i. e. to persuade the Princess into a revocation of her rouge-edict. "I should be glad," she continued, "to gain some resemblance at least to two such good friends as Giulia and Emanuel,"—i. e. a pale color, or else the notion of a speedy death. Victor threw out a hasty "Yes," and turned his smarting eye toward the rising curtain.

Never, haply, were the scenes of players and hearers more like each other. Iphigenia was Clotilda; the wild Orestes, her brother, was her brother Flamin; the soft, radiant Pylades was his friend Victor. And as Flamin stood below in the pit with his cloudy face,—(he came only for the sake of seeing his sister more conveniently,)—then did it seem to our and his friend as if he were addressed by him, when Orestes said to Pylades:—

"Remind me not of those enchanting days,
When a free room thy house afforded me:
Thy noble father wisely, tenderly,
Nursed the half-stiffened blossoms of my youth;
When thou, an ever-gay associate,
Even as a motley, light-winged butterfly
Plays round a dark-hued flower, day after day
Didst dance and hover round me with new life,
And win thy bliss a way into my soul."

Clotilda felt quite as painfully that they were playing her life on the stage, and struggled against her eyes.... But when Iphigenia said to her brother Orestes,—

"O hear me! Look on me! See how my heart
Opens at last, after so long a time,
To the sweet bliss of kissing that dear brow,
Most precious treasure earth yet holds for me, ...
O let me,—let me—for in brighter waves
Not from Parnassus leaps the eternal stream
From rock to rock down to the golden vale,
Than from my bosom joy outgushing flows
And like a sea of bliss enclasps me round";—

and when Clotilda mournfully surveyed the greater interval of sorrows and days between herself and her brother; then gushed up the inner fountains and filled her large eyes, so often fixed upon the heavens, and a quick bending forward hid the sisterly tear from all eyes untouched by emotion. But it did not escape the feeling eyes with which her friend beside her imitated her.... And here a virtuous voice said within Victor: "Disclose to her that thou knowest the secret of her relationship,—lift off from this sorely oppressed heart the load of silence: perhaps she is withering under a grief which a confidant may cool and take away!" Ah, to listen to this voice was indeed the least with which he could content his infinite sympathy! He said in an extremely low tone, and which emotion rendered almost unintelligible to her: "My father has long since disclosed to me, that Iphigenia knows the presence of her brother and of my friend." Clotilda turned suddenly and blushingly towards him; for a more minute explanation he let his eyes glide down to Flamin; turning pale; she looked away and said nothing; but during the whole play her heart seemed to be far more compressed, and she was compelled now to stifle still more tears and sighs than before. At last in the midst of her sadness she gave gratitude its rights, and whispered to him for his sympathy and his confidence, as if with a dying smile, her thanks. He laid upon the distaff of the conversation entirely new and foreign material, because he would fain, during the spinning, get a clearer and more certain light upon the sad impression which his confession seemed to have produced. He inquired after the latest letters from Emanuel. She replied: "I only wrote to him yesterday all through the eclipse of the moon; he cannot answer me often, because writing pains his breast." Now, as the eclipse of the 25th of February began at twenty minutes after ten in the evening, at eleven o'clock and forty-one minutes was at its climax, and at one o'clock and two minutes was over: accordingly Victor, as physician, could fall upon the medical sinner with sermons and hammers of the law and pronounce the verdict; now, it was no wonder. Pass it by, Doctor! These dear creatures can more easily obey a man—the Ten Commandments,—books,—Virtue,—the Devil himself more easily, than the Dietician. Clotilda said: "The midnight hours are simply my only free hours,—and Maienthal, indeed, I can never forget."

"Ah, how could one?" said he.

The music before the last act, and the tragic tone, and the sorrows inspired her, and she continued: "Did not one drink of *Lethe*, when one trod the shores of Elysium and when one left it?" ... She paused. "I would drink of no Lethe, not in the first case, still less in the *last*,—no!" And never was "No" said in a lower, softer, more slow-drawn tone. In Victor's heart a three-edged compassion passed painfully to and fro, as he imagined to himself Clotilda mocked by fate, writing and weeping in the midnight under a moon dismembered and beclouded by earth's shadow; he said nothing, he stared rigidly into the mournful scenes of the stage, and still wept on when the joyous ones had, there, already evolved themselves in their place.

At home he made his brain-fibres Ariadne's threads to extricate himself from the labyrinth of the causes of her trouble, and particularly of the *new* one which had seemed to come upon her at his disclosure. But he remained in the labyrinth; undoubtedly grief begat the sickness, but who begat the grief? It would be hard for these poor, tender butterflies, if there were more than one mortal affliction; in every lane, in every house, thou wilt find a wife or a daughter who has to go to church or to the Tragedy to sigh, and who must go up into the upper story to weep; but this aggregated trouble is worried away with smiles, and years increase for a long time side by side with the tears. On the contrary, there is a grief which breaks them off,— think of that, dear Victor, in the joyful hours of thy general love,[279] and think of it, all ye who with warm, loving hands draw the throbbing heart of such a delicate creature out of its breast, to take it into your own by the side of your own heart, and warm it forever! When you then throw away this hot heart, which you have torn out like a butterfly's honey-proboscis: still, like that, it continues to quiver, but then it grows cold, and erelong beats no more.

Unhappy love, then, was the gnawing honey-dew on this flower, Sebastian concluded. Naturally he thought of himself first; but all his nicest observations, his now so familiar *ricochet-glances* out of the *corner of his eye* had long since convinced him that he had to ascribe the distinction, which she did not deny him, more to her impartiality than to her inclination. Who else it could be at Court,—that was a thing which he in vain applied one electrometer after another to draw out. And he knew beforehand that he should experiment in vain, since Clotilda would baffle all auscultation of her inner state, if she had an unreciprocated inclination; reason was with her the wax, which they stick to one end of the magnetic needle, in order to obviate or conceal the sinking (*inclination*) of the other. Nevertheless, he made up his mind the next time to hold some divining-rods to her soul.—

I must here utter a thought, which may discover some sense and my general speculation in the matter. My Dog-Post-Master Knef did not probably foresee that I should calculate the year and the duration of this whole story merely from the lunar eclipse of the 25th of February, which he announced, just as, in fact, great astronomers, by means of the moon's phases, found out so much about the earth's geographical longitude. 1793 was the year in which what is related in this chapter occurred: I am good for that; for as, at all events, the whole story, as is well known, takes place in the ninth decade of the eighteenth century, and as no lunar eclipse of a 25th of February is to be found there at all, except in the year 1793, i. e. the present year, my proposition is made out. To make assurance doubly sure, I have compared all the changes of moon and weather occurring in this book with those of 1792 and 1793; and all fitted together beautifully;—the reader should also reckon it after me. It is uncommonly gratifying to me, that, consequently, as I write in July, the history follows in a half-year from my description.—

Victor delayed not his visit to the Princess's, that he might there announce the reserved Clotilda as a complete nervous patient. He himself laughed inwardly at the expression,—and at the Doctors,—and at their nervous cures,—and said, that, as formerly the French kings in their treatment of the goitre had to say, "The King touches thee, but God heals thee," so should physicians say, The city and country physician feels thy pulse, but God works the cure. Here, however, he had three good intentions in giving out that she was a nervous sufferer: first, that of gaining for her the abolition of her Court-vassalage,—at least her deliverance from the precise office of maid of honor, because the splinter of the reproach was continually festering in his heart, "It is my fault that she is obliged to be here"; further, of securing for her in advance permission to take the spring and country air, in case she should by and by sue for it; finally, of releasing her from her compulsory resemblance to those ladies on whose lead-colored faces, as on the leaden soldiers of children, the red daily wears off and is daily renewed. But as Agnola herself painted, he was obliged, out of courtesy, as physician, to forbid it to both at once. The Princess countersigned all his petitions very graciously: only as to the rouge-article she gave, in regard to herself, no resolution at all, and in regard to Clotilda the following: she had nothing to say against her appearing in her presence, except on court days and at the play, without rouge; and she would willingly grant her a dispensation from both, unless her health was restored.

He could hardly wait for the moment of taking leave, so impatient was he to carry this imperial-recess or resolution to the beloved patient. He himself wondered at this complaisance of the Princess, with whom, generally, petitions were sins, and who refused nothing—except what was asked. His perplexity was now only this,—how to communicate to Clotilda the indulgences of the Princess, without the offensive confession of having made a plea of her illness. But out of this slight evil a great one extricated him: when he came into her presence, she looked ten times as sick as she had day before yesterday, at the disclosure of her relationship: her blossoms, heavy with cold dew, drooped to the earth.

Gait and posture were unchanged; there was the same external joyousness, but the glance was often too fluttering, often too fixed; across the lily-cheeks darted often a hectic flush, through the lower lip at one moment a subdued convulsion.... At this point sympathy frightened her friend out of the bounds of courtesy, and he told her outright the consent of the Princess. He summoned to the aid of his burdened heart his previous court-boldness, and commanded her to make the coming spring her apothecary's shop, and the flowers her medicinal herbs, and her—fancy her pharmacy. "You seem," said she, smiling, "to count me among the larks, who must always have *green turf* in their cage. However, that my Princess and you may not have had your kindness for nothing, I will, finally, do it. I confess to you, I am at least a *valide imaginaire*.[280] I feel myself well." ... She interrupted herself to question him, with the frankness of virtue and with an eye swimming in sisterly love, about her brother, whether he was happy and contented, how he worked, how he filled his position? She told him how sad a burden these questions, hitherto locked up so deeply in her soul, had been to her and she thanked him for the gift of his confidence with a warmth which he took as a delicate reproof of his previous silence. Of old she always loved to stand in a flower-garland of children; but in

Flachsenfingen she had gathered still more of these little nebulous stars about her brightness, and indeed for a peculiar reason, namely, to cover the fact, that she drew to herself Giulia, a little five-years-old grandchild of the city Senior, with whom her brother resided, as his unwitting biographer and news-carrier. More than three times he felt as if he must fall at the feet of this lily-white angel, borne higher and higher by her cloud, and say with outspread arms: "Clotilda, be my friend, before thy death,—my old love for thee is long since crushed out, for thou art too good for me and for all of us; but I will be thy friend; my heart will I conquer for thee; for thee will I resign my heaven. O, thou wilt, besides, not live to see the evening dew of age, thou wilt soon close thy eyes, and the morning dew still hangs therein!" For he held her soul to be a pearl, whose mussel-body lies open in the dissolving sun, that the pearl may the earlier be dislodged. On leaving, he could with the frankness of the friend, which had taken the place of the lover's reserve, offer a repetition of his visits. Altogether he treated her now more warmly and unconstrainedly; first, because he had so utterly renounced her noble heart, that he wondered at his former bold claims to it; secondly, because the feeling of his disinterested, self-sacrificing honesty towards her poured balm on his previous stings of remorse.

To this sickness was added an evening or an event, which the reader, I think, will not know how to understand. Victor was to take Joachime to the play, and her brother, was to come and fetch him first. I have already twice set it down, that for some weeks Matthieu had no longer been so repulsive to him as a mouse is to an elephant: he had, after all, found out a single good side, dug out some moral yellow mica attaching to him,—namely, the greatest attachment to his sister Joachime, who alone had the key to his whole heart, closed to his parents, the sole claim on his secrets and his services; secondly, he loved in Matthieu what the Minister condemned,—the spirit-of-salt of freedom; thirdly, it is so with us all: when he have heated our heart for some female one out of a family, we afterwards extend the stove-warmth to the whole kin and trenchership,—brothers, nephews, fathers; fourthly, Matthieu was continually praised and excused by his sister. When Victor arrived at Joachime's, she had with her headache and dressing-maids,— finery and pain were increasing; at last she sent off the live fitting-machines, and so soon as she was hardened into a Venus out of the foam of powder and jewel boxes, rouge-rags and *mouchoirs de Vénus, poudres d'odeur* and lip-pomades, then she sat down and said she should stay at home on account of headache. Victor stayed too, and very gladly. Whoso knows not the framework and cellular work of the human heart will wonder that Victor's friendship for Clotilda brought a whole honey-comb of love for Joachime into his cells; it was delightful to him when they visited and embraced each other; he sought not in the blessing-fingers of the Pope so much healing virtue as in Clotilda's; her friendship seemed to him an excuse for his, and to set Joachime on the pedestal of esteem, to which with all his windlasses he had not been able to raise her. Even the sense of his increasing worth gave him new right to love; and to-day even Clotilda's crape and princely hat would have asserted its helmet ornaments on Joachime's aching and more than commonly patient head. To her continued flirtation with the pair of fools he had long since adapted himself, because he knew very well *which one* among the three wise men from the East she had not for a fool, but for an adorer. But to return!

Matthieu, who also stayed at home to please his sister,—he and Victor and she made the entire band of this *concert spirituel.* Joachime on the sofa leaned back her delicate, sick head against the wall and looked at the inlaid floor, and her drooping eyelids made her more beautiful. The Evangelist went out and came in. Victor, as he always did, dashed round the chamber. It was a very fine evening, and I wish this of mine were so. The conversation turned upon love; and Victor asserted the existence of two kinds,—the citizenly, and the *distingué* or French. He loved the French in books and as a general love, but he hated it the moment it was to be the only love; he described it to-day thus: "Take a little ice,—a little heart,—a little wit,—a little paper,—a little time,—a little incense; pour together and put into two persons of rank; in that way you have a good, true French Fontenellian love." "You forgot," added Mat, "one ingredient,—a small amount of senses, at least a *fifth* or *sixth* part, which must be added to the medicine as *adjuvans* or *constituens*.[281] Meanwhile, it has at least the merit of shortness; love, like a tragedy, should be restricted to unity of time, namely, to the space of one day, that it may not take still more resemblance to the tragic. But describe now common love!"

Victor: "That I prefer."

Matthieu: "Not I. It is merely a longer madness than anger. *On y pleure, on y crie, on y soupire, on y ment, on y enrage, on y tue, on y meurt,—enfin, on se donne à tous les diables, pour avoir son ange.*[282] Our talks are to-day for once full of arabesques and *à la grecque*: I will make you a cookery-book receipt for a good citizenly love: take two young and large hearts,—wash them clean in baptismal water or printer's ink of German romances,—pour on them warm blood and tears,—set them on the fire and under the full moon, and let them boil,—stir them briskly with a dagger,—take them out and garnish them, like crabs, with forget-me-not or other wild-flowers, and serve them up warm: in that way you have a savory citizenly heart-soup."[283]

Matthieu further added, that "in the ardent commonalty-love there was more agony than amusement; in it, as in Dante's poem, the Hell was worked out best, and the Heaven worst. The older a maiden or a pickled herring was, so much the darker was the eye in both, and the eye was made dark by love. Every lady in one of the higher circles ought to be glad that she needs to retain nothing of the man's to whom she is chained but his portrait in the ring, as Prometheus, when Jupiter had once sworn to leave him soldered for thirty thousand years to Caucasus, wore during the whole period only a small bit of this Bastille on his hand in the shape of a finger-ring." Whereupon Matthieu darted out, as he always did after witty explosions. Victor loved the bitterest and most unjust satire in another's mouth, as a work of art; he forgave all, and continued cheerful.

Joachime then said, jestingly: "If, then, no style of love is good for anything, as you two have proved, there is nothing left for us but to hate."

"Surely not," said he, "your respected brother has simply not said a true word. Imagine to yourself, that I were the poor people's catechist[284] and in love. I am in love with the second daughter of the *pastor primarius*; her part is that of a listening-sister;[285] for maidens in citizenly life know not how to talk, at least they can do it better in hatred than in love. The poor's catechist has little *bel esprit*, but much *saint esprit*, much honesty, much truth, too much soft-heartedness, and infinite love. The catechist cannot spin out any gallant intrigue for several weeks or months, still less can he dispute the Pastor's second daughter into love, like a *roué*;—he holds his peace to keep up his hope, but with a heart full of eternal love, full of devoted wishes, trembling and silent, he follows every step of the loved and—loving one; but she guesses not his feelings, nor he hers. And then she dies.... But before she dies, comes the pale catechist disconsolate to the side of her dying bed, and presses her trembling hand ere it relaxes, and gives the cold eye one more tear of joy ere it stiffens, and breaks in even upon the pangs of the wrestling soul with the soft spring sound, 'I love thee.' When he has said it, she dies of the last joy, and then he loves no one on earth any more." ...

The past had come over his soul. Tears hung in his eyes, and confounded in a singular obscurity the image of the sick Clotilda with that of Joachime;—he saw and conceived a form which was not present;—he pressed the hand of the one that looked on him, and thought not that she might refer all to herself.

Suddenly Matthieu entered, smiling, and his sister smiled with him, in order to explain everything, and said, "The court-physician has been taking the trouble to refute thee."

Victor, suddenly chilled, replied ambiguously and bitterly: "You will comprehend, Herr von Schleunes, that it is easiest for me to put you to flight when you are not in the field."

Mat transfixed him with his eyes; but Victor cast his down and repented his bitterness. The sister continued indifferently: "I think my brother is often in the condition of changing with the fashion." He received it with a sunny smile, and thought, as did Victor, that she alluded to his gallant adventures and sham-fights with women of all ranks that sit at the Diet. But when she had sent him off to inquire of her mother who was coming to the *cercle* this evening, she said to the Medicus: "You do not know what I meant. We have at court a sick lady, who is the very incarnation of *your* Pastor's daughter, — and my brother has not so much nor so little spirit as to act the poor's catechist." Victor started back, broke off and took his leave.

Why? How so? On what account? But does not the reader perceive, then, that the sick lady must be Clotilda, who seeks to escape Mat's fine approaches within ear-shot and bow-shot of her heart? In fact, Victor had seen well enough that the Evangelist had been hitherto playing a more devoted part towards Clotilda than before her entrance into his Escurial and robber's castle he could carry on; but Victor had ascribed this politeness simply to the fact of her having there her quarters. But now the map of his plan lay open there: he had intentionally met a person who was indifferent towards him with the show of contempt (which, however, he finely directed more at her future small income than at her personal attractions), in order thereby to win her attention, — that next-door neighbor of love, — and afterward, by a sudden change to complaisance, to win something more than attention. "O, thou canst win nothing!" every sigh in Victor exclaimed. And yet it gave him pain, that this noble woman, this angel, must strike such an adversary with her wings. Now there were thirty things at once suspicious to him. Joachime's disclosure and coldness, Matthieu's smile, and — everything.

So far this chapter, to which I have nothing more to append than some mature thoughts. Of course, one sees plainly, that poor Victor mutilates his soul to the size of every female one, as that tyrant did the bedfellows to the length of their bed.[286] To be sure, respect is the mother of love; but the daughter is often some years older than the mother. He takes back one hope of female worth after another. Latest of all, indeed, did he give up his demand or expectation of that sublime *Indian* sense of eternity, which imparts to us, shadowy figures hanging in the magic smoke of life, an inextinguishable luminous point for self-consciousness, and which lifts us above more than *one* earth; but as he saw that women, among all resemblances to Clotilda, acquired this last, and as he bethought himself that a worldly life grinds down all the greatness in man, as the weather gnaws away from statues and gravestones precisely the *relieved parts*, there wanted nothing to his handing over to Joachime the declaration of love which had long been fairly written out, nothing except, on her part, a misfortune,—a wet eye, a storm of the soul, a buskin. In more perspicuous words, he said to himself: "I wish she were a sentimental ninny and absolutely intolerable. Then when, some time or other, she had her eyes right full, and her heart too, and then, when I could not tell, for emotion, where my head was standing,—then I could advance and take out my heart and reach it to her and say, It is poor Bastian's, only keep it." It seems to me as if I heard him in thought softly add, "To whom else could I give it?"

That he really had the first thought, we see from the fact that he inserted it in his diary, from which my correspondent draws everything, and which he, with the sincerity of the freest soul, made for his father, in order as it were to atone for his faults by protocolling them. His Italian lackey did hardly anything but engross it.—-Did it not depend on the dog and his news-box, his declaration of love should take place this very day: I would break an arm of Joachime's,—or lay her in the sick-bed,—or blow out the Minister's lamp of life, or bring on some disaster or other in her house,—and then I would conduct my hero to the suffering heroine, and say: "When I have gone, kneel down and hand her thy heart." But in this way the chemical process of his love-making may last full as long as a process at law, and I am prepared for three quires.

But here I will confess something which the reader's pride conceals: that he and I, at the entrance of every lady in these Dog-Post-Days, have made a *mis-shot* of *salute*,—every one of them we have taken for the heroine of the hero,—at first Agatha,—then Clotilda,—then, when he enclosed his declaration of love in the watch of the Princess, said, "I see now beforehand through the whole business." Then we both said, "After all, we were right about Clotilda." Then in distress I laid hold on Marie, and said, "I shall not reveal anything further." At last it turns out to be one whom none of us had thought of (at least not I),—Joachime.—So it may fare with myself, when I marry....

Before passing from the Post-Day to the intercalary day, the following additional minutes are to be passed: Clotilda put off her illegitimate cheeks, her *joues* [287] *de Paris*, her rouge, and seldomer exposed now her withering heart to the shaping of the court napkin-press. The Prince, who for her sake had attended as a transient hearer in the lecture-hall of his consort, stayed away somewhat often, and then called at Schleunes's: nevertheless, the Princess had magnanimity enough not to make our Victor atone, by the taking back of her gratitude, for the withdrawal of January's favor.—In Victor there was a long war, whether he should impart to Clotilda's brother the new proofs of her sisterly love:—at last,—moved by Flamin's suffering, impoverished heart, stung by reports and rascals and suspicion, and by the thought that he had been able hitherto to give so little pleasure to this ingenuous friend,—he told him almost everything (*except* the relationship).

P. S.—The undersigned testifies, by request, that the undersigned has completed his 24th Post-Day in due order on the last day of July, or Messidor. On the island of St. John's, 1793.

Jean Paul,

Mining-Superintendent of Scheerau.

SIXTH INTERCALARY DAY

Concerning the Wilderness and the Promised Land of Humanity

There are vegetable men, animal men, and divine men.—

When we were to be dreamed, an angel grew drowsy and fell asleep and dreamed. Then came *Phantasus*,[288] and swept broken meteorological, phenomena, things like nights, fragments of chaos, conglomerated plants, before him, and disappeared with them.

Then came *Phobetor*, who drove herds of beasts along before him, that murdered and grazed as they passed, and disappeared with them.

Then came *Morpheus* and played before him with happy children, with crowned mothers, with shapes that kissed each other, and with fleeting mortals, and when the angel awoke with ecstasy, Morpheus and the human race and the world's history had disappeared....

—At present the angel still sleeps and dreams,—we are still in his dream,—only *Phobetor* is with him, and Morpheus still waits for Phobetor with his beasts to disappear....

But let us, instead of dreaming, think and hope; and for the present ask: will *vegetable* men, *animal* men, at last be succeeded by *divine* men? Does the *going* of the world-clock betray as much design as the building of it, and has it a *dial-plate* wheel and an *index hand*?

One cannot (with a well-known philosopher) reason directly from final causes in *Physics* to final causes in *History*, any more than I, in the individual, can deduce from the teleological (intentional) structure of a man a teleological biography of the same, or any more than, from the ingenious structure of animals, I call infer a continuous plan in their universal history. Nature is iron, always the same, and the wisdom shown in her framework is never obscured; the human race is free, and, like the infusorial animal, the multiform Vorticelle, assumes every moment, now regular, now anomalous shapes. Every physical disorder is only the hull of an order, every foul spring is the hull of a fair autumn; but are, then, our vices the buds of our virtues, and is the earthly fall of a continually sinking villain nothing but a disguised ascension of his to heaven?—And is there an object in the life of a Nero? Then I could just as well take back and reverse all and make out virtues to be the heart-leaves of disguised vices. But if, as many a one does, we carry the abuse of language so far as to reverse *moral* height and depth, like *geometrical*, according to the *point of view*, as *positive* and *negative* magnitudes; if, therefore, all gouty knobs, spotted fevers, and *lead*-[289] or *silver*-colics of the human race are nothing but a different kind of healthiness: then we certainly need not ask whether man will ever get well; in that case he could never in any possible maladies be anything but well.

If a monk of the tenth century had shut himself up in a fit of melancholy, and meditated on the earth, not however on its end, but on its future: would not, in his dreams, the thirteenth century have been already a brighter one, and the eighteenth merely a glorified tenth?

Our weather-prophesyings from *present* temperature are logically correct and historically false, because new casualties, an earthquake, a comet, reverse the currents of the whole atmosphere. Can the above-imagined monk correctly calculate, if he does not assume such future magnitudes as America, Gunpowder, and Printer's ink?—A new religion, a new Alexander, a new disease, a new Franklin, can break, swallow up, dam, turn back the forest stream whose course and contents we propose to reduce on our parchment. There lie still four quarters of the globe full of enchained savage races;—their chain daily grows thinner,—time unlooses it;—what desolation, at least what changes, must they not bring about on the little *bowling-green* of our cultivated countries? Nevertheless, all nations of the earth must one day be fused together and be purified in a common fermentation, if ever this atmosphere of life is to be cleared up.

Can we draw from some miniature earthquakes and volcanoes, which we ourselves have produced with iron-filings and aquafortis, (in this case, types and printer's ink,) conclusions as to the Ætna eruptions, i. e. from the revolutions of the few cultivated peoples as to those of the uncultivated? Since we may assume that the human race lives as many thousands of years as the individual does years, may we venture from the sixth year to set the horoscope of youth and manhood? Add to this that the biography of this childish period is precisely the most meagre, and that awakened nations — almost all quarters of the globe are as yet full of sleeping ones—in *one* year produce more historical material, and *consequently* more historians, than a sleep-buried Africa in a century. We shall, therefore, *then* be best able to prophesy from universal history, when the awaking nations shall have appended to it their million or two supplementary volumes.—All savage nations seem to have been under *one* stamp; on the contrary, the mint of culture coins each one differently. The North American and the old German resemble each other more strongly than Germans do Germans of neighboring centuries. Neither the Golden Bull, nor the *Magna Charta*, nor the *Code Noir*, could Aristotle inlay into his forms of government and obedience; else he would have extended them; but are we then confident of foreseeing any better the future national convention in Mongolia, or the Decretal Letters and Extravagants of the enlightened Dalai-Lama, or the Recesses of the Arab Imperial Bench of Knights? Since Nature coins no people with *one* mint-stamp or one hand alone, but with thousands at once,—hence on the German race is there a greater multitude of impressions than on the shield of Achilles,—how do we, who cannot even calculate the past, but simpler, revolutions of the globe, expect to look into the moral ones of its inhabitants?

Of all that follows from these premises I believe the opposite, excepting the necessity of prophetic modesty. Scepticism, which makes us, instead of slow to believe, unbelieving, and instead of the *eyes* proposes to purge the *light*, becomes nonsense and the most fearful philosophical impotence and atony.

Man regards his century or his half-century as the culmination of light, as a festal-day, to which all other centuries lead only as week-days. He knows only two golden ages,—the one at the beginning of the world, and the one at the end of it,—by which he understands only his own; he finds history to be like great woods, in the middle of which are silence, night-birds, and birds of prey, and whose borders only are filled with light and song.—Certainly all things serve me; but I too serve all. As Nature, who in her eternity knows no loss of time, in her inexhaustibleness no loss of power, has no other law of frugality assigned her than that of prodigality,—as she, with *eggs* and *seed-corns*, ministers equally well to *nourishment* and to *propagation*,[290] and with an undeveloped germ-world sustains half a developed one,—as her way leads over no smooth bowling-alley, but over alps and seas;—our little heart must needs misunderstand her, whether in its hopes or in its fears; it must, as it becomes enlightened, reciprocally interchange *morning* and *evening red*; it must, in its contentment, now regard after-summer as *spring*, and now *after-winter* as *autumn*. *Moral* revolutions mislead us more than *physical*, because the former according to their nature occupy a *greater* play-room and space of time than the latter,—and yet the Dark Ages are nothing but a dipping into the shadow of *Saturn*, or an eclipse of the sun of short duration. A man who should be six thousand years old, would say to the six creation-days of the world's history, They are very good.

But one should never set *moral* and *physical* revolutions and developments too near to each other. All Nature has no other motions than *former* ones; the circle is her path, she has no other years than Platonic,—but man alone is *changeable*, and the straight line or the zigzag describes his course. A sun has its eclipses as well as the moon, has its bloom and decay like a flower, but also its *palingenesia* and renovation. But there lies in the human race the necessity of an everlasting mutation; yet here there are only *ascending* and *descending* signs, no culmination; they do not necessarily draw one another after them, as in physics, and have no extreme limit. No people, no period returns; in physics, all must come back again. It is only accidental, not necessary, that nations, at a certain age and stage of progress, and on a certain rotten round of the ladder, fall again,—one only confounds the *last* step, from which nations fall, with the *highest*; the Romans, with whom not single rounds, but the whole ladder broke, were not necessitated to sink by a culture which does not equal even our own.[291] Nations have no age, or old age with them often precedes youth. Even with individuals the crab's-walk of the mind in old age is only accidental; still less has virtue in them a summer-solstice. Humanity has then the capacity of an endless improvement; but has it the hope also?—

The disturbance of the *equipoise* of his own faculties makes the individual man miserable; the *inequality* of citizens, the *inequality* of nations, makes the earth miserable; just as lightnings arise from the neighborhood of the ebb and flow of the ether, and all storms from unequal distributions of air. But fortunately it lies in the nature of mountains to fill the valleys.

Not inequality of goods,—for the majority of voices and fists on the part of the poor balances in the scale the power of the rich,—but inequality of culture, does most to create and distribute the political fly-presses and forcing-pumps. The *Lex agraria* in the fields of science passes over at last into the physical fields. Since the tree of knowledge has thrust out its branches from the school windows of philosophy and the church windows of the priesthood into the common garden, all nations have become stronger. — Unequal cultivation chains the West Indies to the feet of Europe, Helots to Spartans, and the iron hollow-head[292] with the trigger on the negro's tongue presupposes a hollow-head of another kind.

With such a frightful disparity among nations in power, wealth, culture, only a universal rush of storms from all points of the compass can terminate in a lasting calm. A perpetual balance of Europe presuppose a balance of the four remaining parts of the world, which one may, deducting small librations, promise our globe. In future men will quite as little discover a salvage as an island. One people must draw another out of pits blundering years. A more equal culture will conclude commercial treaties with more equal advantages. The longest rainy months of humanity—which always fell upon the time of national transplantations, just as one always sets out flowers on cloudy days—have spent themselves.

One spectre still remains from the midnight, which reaches far into the hours of light, — War. But the claws and bill of the armorial eagle grow on, till, like the boar's tusks, they crook up and make themselves useless. As it was calculated in regard to Vesuvius, that it contained material for only forty-three eruptions more, — so might one also reckon the number of future wars. This long tempest, which already for six thousand years has been standing over our planet, will continue to storm till clouds and earth have charged each other full with an *equal* measure of electric matter.

All nations become illuminated only in joint fermentation; and the precipitate is blood and dead men's bones. Were the earth narrowed to one half of its size, then would the time of its moral—and physical—development be shortened one half.

With wars the strongest drag-chains of the sciences are cut off. Once war-machines were the sowing-machines of new knowledges, while they crushed old harvests; now it is the press which scatters the pollen more widely and gently. Instead of an Alexander, Greece would need now to send to Asia nothing but a—compositor; the conqueror grafts, the author sows.

It is a characteristic of enlightenment that, although it still leaves to individuals the possibility of the illusion and weakening of vice, nevertheless it releases nations from company-vices and national deceptions, —e. g.

from wrecking, piracy. The best and worst deeds we do in company; war is an example. The slave-trade must in our days, unless indeed the trade in subjects begins, come to an end.[293]

The highest and steepest thrones stand, like the highest mountains, in the warmest lands. The political mountains, like the physical, daily grow lower (especially when they spout fire), and must at last be with the valleys in a common plain.

From all this follows:—

There comes one day a golden age, which every wise and virtuous man even now enjoys, and when men will find it easier to live well because they will find it easier to live indeed,—when men will have, not more pleasure (for this honey they draw from every flower and leaf-louse), but more virtue,—when the people Will take part in thinking, and the thinker—in working,[294] in order that he may save himself the need of Helots,—when military and judicial murder shall be condemned, and only occasionally cannon-balls shall be turned up with the plough. When that time comes, then will a preponderance of good no more stop the machine by frictions. When it comes, then will the necessity no longer lie in human nature of degenerating again and again breeding tempests (for heretofore the noble element has merely kept up a flying fight with the overpowering evil), just as, according to Forster, even on the hot island of St. Helena[295] there are no storms.

When this festal day comes, then will our children's children be—no more. We stand now in the evening and see at the close of our dark day the sun go down with a red-hot glory, and promise us behind the last cloud the still, serene sabbath-day of humanity; but our posterity have yet to travel through a night full of wind, and through a cloud full of poison, till at last over a happier earth an eternal morning-wind full of blossom-spirits, moving on before the sun, expelling all clouds, shall breathe on men without a sigh. Astronomy promises the earth an eternal vernal equinox;[296] and history promises it a higher one; perhaps the two eternal springs may coincide.—

Since man disappears among men, we downcast ones must erect ourselves before humanity. When I think of the Greeks, I see that our hopes move faster than fate.—As one travels by night with lights over the icy Alps, in order not to be terrified at the abysses and at the long road, so does fate spread night around us, and hands us only torches for the way immediately before us, that we may not worry ourselves about the chasms of the future, and the distance of the goal.—There were centuries when humanity was led with bandaged eyes—from one prison to another;—there were other centuries when spectres rattled and overturned all night long, and in the morning nothing was disturbed; there can be no other centuries except those in which individuals die, but nations rise, and in which nations decay, but mankind rises: when mankind itself sinks and falls to ruins, and ends with the scattering of the globe in a dust-cloud ... what shall console us?—

A veiled eye behind the bounds of time, an infinite heart beyond the world. There is a higher order of things than we can demonstrate,—there is a Providence in the world's history and in every one's life which reason has the boldness to deny, and which the heart has the boldness to believe;—there must be a Providence, which, according to other rules than we have hitherto assumed, links this confused earth as daughter-land to a higher city of God,—there must be a God, a Virtue, and an Eternity.

FOOTNOTES:

Footnote 1: His collected works, Vol. III. p. 68.

2: In Faust,—Scene of the Easter Holidays.—Tr.

3: A Jew once separated from his wife when she appeared with bare arms; but it is difficult to ascribe the present frequent divorces in Paris to that cause.

4: It is amusing to hear Jean Paul call it so, but the German diminutive, "Werk*lein*," also expresses attachment to the thing in question. Thus children say *Väter-chen*, "Little Papa; Daddy."—Tr.

5: Descriptive of Venus, or written under her influence.—Tr.

6: The stick on which a painter rests his arm.—Tr.

7: Similarity of the parts to the whole.—Tr.

8: *Fliegende Blätter.*—Tr.

9: Of course, "Forgive us our debts."—Tr.

10: A city of the Tauric Chersonesus, the modern Crimea.—Tr.

11: A Jesuit astronomer, A. D. 1598-1671, who named the moon's spots Tycho, Plato, Hercules, St. Catharine, &c.—Tr.

12: He alludes to the chimney-sweeper of his perukes.

13: The name the Germans give to Death. *Hein* would seem to mean Hal.—Tr.

14: Probably peas, which the children, as now, blew through long tubes with great force.—Tr.

15: In Upper Alsace, where every three years only the best youth receives the crown and medal, and the jurisdiction of the pastures.

16: A sort of fire-ball, which, as it goes, emits smoke to blind the enemy.—Tr.

17: Small balls invented by him to put into a horse's ear, and act as a spur.—Tr.

18: An island of the Malay Archipelago, wooded, volcanic, and spicy.—Tr.

19: It is notorious how little I know of mining operations; I therefore thought I had reason to apply to my superiors for a spur which might stimulate me to do something in such a weighty science,—and such a spur is certainly the office of mining-superintendent.

20: Except the two emperors Silluck and Athnac, and the four kings Sgolta, Sakeph-Katon, etc., I never had intercourse with any; and that only as upper-class scholar, because we jurists, with the Devil's help, had to learn Hebrew, wherein just the above-mentioned six potentates appear as the names of the accents on words. Perhaps, however, my correspondent means the great, acute, crowned accents of nations. [*Sakeph-Katon* is the only one the translator has not been able to verify of these interesting names. *Kauton* is given among the Hebrew accents, but not Sakeph.—Tr.]

21: Justus Möser, author of the "Patriotic Fantasies," one of Germany's dearest memories, in many respects a Franklin.—Tr.

22: Lane of the mine.—Tr.

23: Ass's Post.—Tr.

24: Instrument for taking the distance of a star north or south from the equator.—Tr.

25: Instrument for reckoning the deviation of the hour-circle from the meridian.—Tr.

26: Jean Paul seems to indulge here in an hexameter himself: "Welches sie auch mehr bedarf, als der harmonische Gessner."—Tr.

27: *Bewähren* and *bewahren* are the two German words.—Tr.

28: E. g. their honor suffers, if their carriage does not pass ahead of another carriage of rank.

29: Such letters as David sent by Uriah to Joab. (See 2 Samuel xi. 14, 15.)—Tr.

30: *Kleeblatt* (*trefoil*) in the German.—Tr.

31: After an operation for the cataract, the sensitive retina represents everything magnified.

32: A piece of charred bone or horn used by natives of the East to absorb the blood from wounds made by the bite of a snake. See Tennent's Natural History of Ceylon, p. 312.—Tr.

33: The *Psalter* in the ox's stomach is the *Blättermagen* (lit. *leaf-stomach*), the third stomach of ruminant animals, the tripe. So we speak of the *leaves* of fat.—Tr.

34:

> "My spirit flew in feathers then,
> That is so heavy now."—Hood.

35: Joint-reporter.—Tr.

36: A kind that heads in the form of a capuchin's hood.—Tr.

37: When one's five numbers are all drawn in their order, it is a quinterne.—Tr.

38: *Aufgebunden* may mean either tied up or untied.—Tr.

39: Burlesque and serious operas.—Tr.

41: The ideal of the beautiful.

42: As the Rabbins believe, according to Eisenmenger's Judaism, Part II. 7.

43: *Usance* means the month's grace allowed for the payment of a bill of exchange; double usance, of course, allows two months.—Tr.

44: Petrarch, like German reviewers, avoided nightingales, and sought frogs.

45: "Schatten*riss* oder Schatten*schnitt*" is the German.—Tr.

46: The literal rendering would be *"cut out of the eyes*, or, rather, out of the face."* The phrase in Italics is a German idiom for expressing an exact likeness.—Tr.

47: The readers of Boswell's Johnson will remember that interesting native of the South-Sea Islands.—Tr.

48: Matthieu being the French for *Matthew.*—Tr.

49: *Zeusel* was a court-apothecary, mentioned on page 7, of whom we shall hear more.—Tr.

50: An Italian word, meaning literally gallant, applied to those Platonic lovers who, with the connivance of the husbands, attended married ladies, and were everywhere seen in confidential chat with them.—Tr.

51: La Mettrie was a noted medical man and materialist in his day, b. 1709.—Tr.

52: Remember the beautiful passage in Bede's History, where the Northumbrian prince compares man's life to the flight of the swallow through the lighted hall out of darkness into darkness.—Tr.

53: An allusion, perhaps, to the legend, so lovely to the fancy, that a crucifix in Naples, when Alphonso was besieged there, in 1439, bowed its head before a cannon-ball, which consequently took off only the crown of thorns!—*Voyage d'un François*, Tom. VI. p. 303.

54: This clover insures him who accidentally finds it against future deception. Hitherto it has been found only by—princes and philosophers.

55: *Matz*, in German, means also both a starling and a blockhead.—Tr.

56: Elegant paper for the upper classes.—Tr.

57: In the original, "hang hares' tails on us," i. e. "make fools of us."—Tr.

58: Literally, spit-devils,—a sort of firework.—Tr.

59: I. e. Birthday-festival.—Tr.

60: Not one of the commonplace souls that jog steadily on like the hexameter.—Tr.

61: This was a common practice of our old New England Puritan parsons.—Tr.

62: Disciples of Kennicott, the well-known English verifier of the general accuracy of the Sacred Text.—Tr.

63: A trap extemporized by setting up a heavy book obliquely, with one end resting on a stick, and the cheese attached.—Tr.

64: Christina, daughter of Charles XII., abdicated in May, 1654, at the age of twenty-eight.—Tr.

65: A famous and popular old volume delineating the world of nature and life in pictures, with numbers referring to the different parts of each picture.—Tr.

66: That is, threw into them, as into scrap-baskets, the bits of paper on which he had written his thoughts.—Tr.

67: Allusion to Ezekiel.—Tr.

68: Literally, *God's-box.*—Tr.

69: *Gesprungen* seems to mean both *vibrated* and *snapped.*

70: *Haupt-* und *Staat-actionen*, the phrase used by Faust in his first dialogue with Wagner. Schlegel says the title was affixed to dramas designed for marionettes when they treated heroic and historical subjects.—Tr.

71: Epiglottis.—Tr.

72: What has come into the world feet foremost.—Tr.

73: Basselisse (French).—Tr.

74: *Ladenhüter* (shop-keeper) is the German word, meaning goods that keep the store as a sick man keeps his bed,—*shop-ridden.*—Tr.

75: A court that decided matters in dispute among the sovereigns of the German Confederation.—Tr.

76: A selection of choice learning.—Tr.

77: Midsummer-day.—Tr.

78: A name given by the Greeks to the Hebrew word Jehovah, which consists, in the original, of *four letters.*—Tr.

79: The thumb of a hanged thief was considered as a lucky-bone.—Tr.

80: Full.—Tr.

81: Or it *went a begging,* as we say.—Tr.

82: "Rara avis."—Tr.

84: It is precisely the possession of *heterogeneous* faculties in *similar* degree that makes one inconsequent and inconsistent; men with one predominant faculty act by it with more equableness. In despotisms there is more quiet than in republics; at the hot equator there is a more even rate of the barometer than in the zones of four seasons.

85: One of Burns's words.—Tr.

86: The bust of the Vatican Apollo, by which he would learn to model no other figure than his own.

87: There is something in the use and application of the word *Wissenschaft* which requires for its appreciation an understanding of the peculiar genius of the German mind.—Tr.

88: Bacon's remark will recur to the reader.—Tr.

89: A solar system is only a dotted profile of the genius of the world, but a human eye is his miniature. The *mechanics* of the bodies of the universe the mathematical masters of reckoning may calculate, but the *dioptrics* of the eye, growing bright amidst nothing but dull moistures, transcends our algebraic audit-offices, which therefore cannot reckon away from the imitated eyes (the glasses) the space of diffusion and the narrow field.

90: Jean Paul would probably have said Rubicon if he had not been going to say it elsewhere,—e. g. p. 199.

91: Hieronym. cont. Jov. L 2.

92: *Hof* means in German *both* court—and yard.—Tr.

93: Bayle's Dictionary, Art. *François d'Assise*, Note C.

94: A half-way house.—Tr.

95: Jean Paul probably means, that such noble hearts as Victor's Le Baut might shut up into silence, but could not with his Chamberlain's master-key open and find out their secrets.—Tr.

96: In a later edition Jean Paul substitutes for *Schein-tod* (sham death) a half French word, *Postiche-tod* (supposititious death).—Tr.

97: "On whose board he had a *stone*," literally,—a proverb for being in one's good graces.—Tr.

98: There is an inconsistency in date of month here with p. 135.—Tr.

99: The dog as well as myself know what island that is, but no more.

100: "Burning-chambers," a name originally given to the place for judging criminals of state belonging to illustrious families. The room was lined with black, and lighted with flambeaux. Originated with Francis I. in 1535, in his persecution of heretics.—Tr.

101: Plebeian.—Tr.

102: One at hearing from Emanuel, the other at seeing Clotilda.—Tr.

103: Red drops fall from butterflies in their last transformation, which they used to call bloody rain.

104: When one looks a long time into the blue of heaven, it begins to undulate, and these waves in the air one imagines in childhood to be angels at play.

105: This monologue is a fragment from an earlier dark hour, such as every heart of sensibility once suffers.

106: *Noth-münzen* means originally coin containing alloy, struck off in hard times.—Tr.

107: The Hebrew language has but three vowels ("vowel-points") which, from the assistance they gave in enunciating a vast variety of words, were called *matres lectionis*, or mothers of the reading.—Tr.

108: I. e. bowing so low.—Tr.

109: Herkommen, as a common noun, means *tradition* or *custom.*—Tr.

110: An infusorial or minute animal, called in natural history *rotifera* (wheel-bearer).—Tr.

111: *Famulus* is the Latin name in the German. Wagner was one in Faust.—Tr.

112: So called in allusion to the *shaking* they were giving it.—Tr.

113: *Kopfstück* (lit. *head-piece*), a coin bearing the head of the regent.—Tr.

114: The billiard-pockets (like the contribution-bags) used to have bells to them.—Tr.

115: Who felt himself to be "a child picking up pebbles on the shore of the great ocean of truth."—Tr.

116: A conventual term,—a six.—Tr.

117: God bless you!—Tr.

118: Many thanks!—Tr.

119: Of course a parody on "Verbum sat *sapienti*,"—"A word for the *fool*," &c.—Tr.

120: Or reading-*easel* (the latter word seeming to be an English corruption of the German *Esel*, ass),—any book-rest. *Maler-esel* means a painter's easel.—Tr.

121: When they occur in actual life.—Tr.

122: Eclectic or miscellaneous science, not confined to one department.—Tr.

123: A King of France once sent a vassal *illum baculum, quo se sustentabat, in symbolum traditionis*. (Du Fresne's Glossary.) So far as I know, there has never been made a good and serviceable—abridgment of this *glossarium* for ladies.

124: Just as there are *listening sisters* (*les Tourières* or *Sœurs écoutés*) who go with the nuns into the conversing room, to overhear their talk.

125: Or absentee-curates.—Tr.

126: Literally *looker-on,*—one admitted to behold the secret ceremonies in the Eleusinian mysteries.—Tr.

127: To know how to obey is a glory equal to that of commanding.—Tr.

128: "Slaves are accounted nobodies."—Tr.

129: In real life.—Tr.

130: *To make one a queue* is a proverb for imposing on him (like pinning a rag to one's coat-tail?).—Tr.

131: *Diet* (from *dies*) *implies* the idea of *day*, but the German "Reichs*tag*" makes the pun more palpable in the original.—Tr.

132: A lady's watch, as is well known, shaped like a heart, provided on the back with a dial-gnomon and magnetic needle. The latter points out to the ladies (who hate *cold*) the *south* also, in fact, and the sun-dial-index serves as a moon-dial-index.

133: "Rome concealed the name of her god, and she was wrong; I conceal the name of my goddess, and I am right."

134: Or *Tensa*, the carriage on which they bore the images of the gods in the Circensian games.—Tr.

135: A shrine.—Tr.

136: Properly, a pitcher, or urn.—Tr.

137: Here Jean Paul inserts, after "in die Federn," "(*nicht in die Feder*)," —i. e. *not into the pen* (a German phrase for *dictating*). The pun could not be kept.—Tr.

138: A watch that tells only the hours.—Tr.

139: The reference is to Laurence Sterne, and the snuff-box he mentions in the early part of the "Sentimental Journey," as given him by a monk, and carried ever after as an amulet.—Tr.

140: Ignatius's-plate means probably a breastplate, or medallion, consecrated by Ignatius Loyola.—Tr.

141: I. e. to throw light upon it.—Tr.

142: Like John Buncle, who went round, as was said, to propagate his faith and his species.—Tr.

143: A fourth reason would be, that now, every time be loves another than Clotilda, he seems to earn a new claim to the gratitude of his friend.

144: Italian for everybody.—Tr.

145: May there be a sly allusion—here to the possibility of their putting their hair up in papers torn from the leaves of Jean Paul's works?—Tr.

146: Schickaneder was the Director of a Theatre in Vienna in the time of Mozart, and wrote the text for the *Magic Flute*.—Tr.

147: A wreath given in derision to brides who before marriage had been unchaste.—Tr.

148: And then are ready to verify the proverb: *Curses, like chickens, come home to roost*.—Tr.

149: Musical interval.—Tr.

150: Old scholastic term for a *past* eternity, in contradiction to a coming eternity, *a parte post*.—Tr.

151: The Invisible Lodge; a Biography in Two Parts. [A work of Jean Paul's.—Tr.]

152: Such was the name of his Lordship's wife, who in her twenty-third year sank to rest in the eternal arms.

153: In the original, *Semper-freie* (always free,—eligible to office).—Tr.

154: Hence too it was, that, so long as Victor was at the Parsonage, she avoided Flamin's society.

155: The reader will remember this same remark, in so many words, on p. 223.—Tr.

156: It turned out more fortunately, and without loss of the stones, and I had the satisfaction to find that no woman who read the first edition of this work has, in her womanlike *castling* or *rotation in office*, at all interchanged the two *thats*. Nay, even the female readers of the second edition have remained consistent with themselves.

157: Demoralization.—Tr.

158: The German word *kleiden*; it has a corresponding double meaning of *dressing*, and also of *suiting*.—Tr.

159: Science,—Mathematics.—Tr.

160: Step-measurers.—Tr.

161: Men entitled to lecture in three branches.—Tr.

162: Or disciple of the indifferential calculus.—Tr.

163: Or, in prose, fiery water-wheel.—Tr.

164:

> "And what if all of animated nature
> Be but organic harps diversely framed,
> That tremble into thought, as o'er them sweeps,
> Plastic and vast, one intellectual breeze,
> At once the soul of each and God of all?"

Coleridge, *The Æolian Harp*.

165: *Fromm* is the German. It is time the words *religious* and *pious* were redeemed from the base uses of sectarianism and bigotry.—Tr.

166: *Enlightenment* in an *empty* heart is mere memory-work, let it strain the faculty of acumen ever so much. Most men of our day resemble the new houses in Potsdam, in which (according to Reichard) Frederick the Second caused *lights* to be placed at night, that every one, including Reichard himself, might think they were—*occupied.*

167: Most men have, perhaps, only an equal number of good *thoughts* and *actions*; but it is still an open question how long the virtuous man may interrupt his good thoughts (which have less need than good actions of the outer world) by indifferent ones.

168: For the noblest leans just the most on loving souls, or at least on his ideals of them, with which, however, he is only in so far satisfied as he regards them as pledges of future prototypes. I do not except either the Stoic (that Epicurean God) or the Mystic: both love in the Creator only the sum total of his creatures; we the former in the latter.

169: The German *Vorwand* means literally front wall (not far from the etymological meaning of *pretext*); so that there may be a figurative element here beyond what appears to the casual reader.—Tr.

170: The reader of this letter will readily presuppose that Clotilda, as she does not know into whose hands it may fall,—in fact, it is actually in ours,—will have to hurry over her relations and mysteries (e. g. respecting Flamin, Victor, &c.) with an obscurity which to her proper reader was clear enough.

171: Let the reader remember that she is master of as much of this biography as he, if not more.

172: She means Giulia, from whose corpse grief had hurried her away.

173:

"Now spring returns, but not to me returns
The vernal joy my better years have known," &c.

Michael Bruce.

174: "Fly not from me, because I am always encompassed by a great shadow, which increases till at last it shall wall me up."

175: Every seven years of human life.—Tr.

176:

"Or had it drizzled *needle-points of ice*
Upon a feverish head made suddenly bald."

Coleridge's *Remorse.*

177: As the spots in the moon are fields of flowers and plants.

178: Here ended (in the original) the first volume.—Tr.

179: So called, as it was made to answer for both bed and board. See the next sentence but one.—Tr.

180: The rudiments of printing.—Tr.

181: He is indignant, it is true, only at the *typographical* history of learned works, and despises only the anxious search after the birthdays, &c., of deceased and stupid books in the midst of a world full of wonders; but here, too, he must needs consider that brains which can let nothing *press* upon them more than operations of the *press* still do better this little something, which saves and accumulates most for the better ones, than nothing at all, or anything beyond their ability.

182: A name given to screens used for partitions.—Tr.

183: A well-known good writer on the eyes.

184: Or crystalline lens?—Tr.

185: Glands in the eyelids, discovered by Meibom in 1673.—Tr.

186: A glandule at the corner of the eye, which secretes moisture.—Tr.

187: Honeymoon. One of Jean Paul's variations on the phrase.—Tr.

188: The Germans are peculiarly rich in synonymes for the honeymoon. The word used here is *Flitterwochen* (Spangle-weeks).—Tr.

189: Moldavian or Wallachian governor.—Tr.

190: Some of the German written letters are like the Greek. *Alphabet* (at the end of the sentence) is a printer's term for 23 sheets.—Tr.

191: The Fetzpopel, or *ragged ninny,* was a sort of scarecrow or bugbear.—Tr.

192: A fistful.—Tr.

193: An Indian moss used for the gout.—Tr.

194: An allusion to a scandalous Scotch imposture of 1780.—Tr.

195: Sledges for riding astraddle.—Tr.

196: The Britons found out that whalebone shavings made the softest kind of bed.

197: The English of this seems to be:—

"Turkey rhubarb powdered.
Starred anise-seed.

Fennel do.

Peel of green orange.

Carbonate of potash,—equal parts,—1 drachm.

Leaves of Alexandrian senna without stalks,—2 drachms.

Half an ounce of white sugar."

And the final direction may read, "Of which let him take a mixture, finely pulverized, given in sufficient quantity to produce ejection. Mark [i. e. on the paper], Wind-powders," &c.—Tr.

198: The name given to the halo about the head, when one is electrized.

199: An allusion, perhaps, to the pasteboard images carried about on the heads of Italian peddlers, in which the loose-hung head bobs right and left to the spectators.—Tr.

200: The German expression for all this is too elliptical to be literally rendered. It is simply "Meinetwegen!" (For all me!)—Tr.

201: Fancy-man.—Tr.

202: Their good works are good words.—Tr.

203: The horse referred to on page 91.—Tr.

204: That is, he would be, when this letter arrived, for he was going to carry it.—Tr.

205: Culpepper never did him the pleasure, for which he had so often begged him, of prescribing for the Prince a clyster, which then the apothecary himself would have administered, in order just for once to *get at* the ruler, and transform *his* weak side into his own sunny side.

206: When those twins chipped the shell of Leda's egg, out of which they were born.—Tr.

207: Literally, "Knapsack."—Tr.

208: French for clyster.—Tr.

209: A Greek jurist, compared by Gibbon to Bacon, of great influence in the first half of the sixth century,—dishonest, but able.—Tr.

210: The red-deer, and the wild-boar, bear, badger, &c.—Tr.

211: i. e. about two kreutzers.—Tr.

212: Entity.—Tr.

213: "*Gesegnete Mahlzeit*" is the familiar phrase Richter uses; it was formerly common, at the close of dinner, to shake hands and wish "a blessing on the meal."—Tr.

214:

> "Hast thou a friend, take care to keep him,
> And often to his threshold wend:
> Briers and thorns o'ergrow the path
> On which a man neglects to walk." —*Old Saying*.

Tr.

215; Little Britain.—Tr.

216: He with the long shoes, in his "Education of a Young Prince, 1705."

217: Thus did merely the first edition, in 1797, speak of the Viennese; a third, improved one, in 1819, acknowledges also an improved edition of them, although it retains lively *shadows* of their former times.

218: A coarse writer no longer known.—Tr.

219: Author of the Burlesque Virgil.—Tr.

220: The author appears to have had in his mind a reminiscence of a passage in Bürger's "Lenore":—

> "Like croak of frogs in marshy plain,
> Swelled on the breeze that dismal strain," &c.—Tr.

221: Sacred musical composition of a stylish character.—Tr.

222: The Jewish name for Sabbath in the Middle Ages. See Auerbach's Spinoza.—Tr.

223: Latin for ruins, fragments of old buildings, &c.—Tr.

224: "He toucheth the hills, and they smoke."—Tr.

225: December is most favorable to astronomical observations.

226: A musical direction: Go back to the sign; Begin again.—Tr.

227: The German word is *Kälte*, which explains the incongruity of our English heading.—Tr.

228: A word copied exactly from the German, and well enough justified by the analogy of *rookery*, for instance.—Tr.

229: See that noble passage of Milton, beginning

> "I cannot praise a fugitive and cloistered virtue."—Tr.

230: I have wholly recast the letter N, because in the first edition I unfortunately had a good idea, which, without recollecting its first publication, I gave the world a second time, as a learned thief of my own property, in the commentary on the woodcuts. [Probably the ones illustrating the Ten Commandments, in the *Campaner Thal*, Jean Paul's work on Immortality.—Tr.]

231: The royal band (of twenty-four).—Tr.

232: A freethinker and Freemason, in the latter half of the eighteenth century imprisoned, for a certain comedy, in Magdeburg fortress.—Tr.

233: The highway.—Tr.

234: As an example, we have now the First Principle of Morals, and that of the Forms of Government.

235: Self-government.—Tr.

236: See his *Amœn. Acad.*, the treatise on the habitable globe.

237: The hysterical ball, i. e. the hysteric morbid feeling, as if a ball were rolling up into the throat.

238: Used here by Jean Paul evidently, with figurative freedom, for a Russian swing, but meaning originally a *chariot-race* (afterward tournament), and derived from *currus solis* (chariot of the sun).—Tr.

239: Conjurer's jargon.—Tr.

240: "The *Litones* were slaves among the old Saxons, who still possessed a third of their property, and could make contracts for it." *Flegeljahre*, No. 8.—Tr.

241: An instrument for determining the blueness of the sky.

242: French for a male flirt.—Tr.

243: Differing laws.—Tr.

244: Axiom in law; named from Brocard, a Bishop of Worms, who made a collection of canons called "Brocardica Juris."—Tr.

245: Proculus and Sabinus were the founders of two rival schools of jurisprudence in Rome (Proculians and Sabinians) in the first century of our era.—Tr.

246: A term from the Pandects of Justinian, meaning liabilities to burdens or duties.—Tr.

247: Alluding to the consolidating of stocks, debts, &c.—Tr.

248: An Italian astronomer and anatomist, born in 1602.—Tr.

249: Faust (meaning both fist and the Faust of story) is the word in the original.—Tr.

250: Or journey.—Tr.

251: There is a play on words in the original, *Hof* meaning *court*, and also, when applied to the sun or moon, a *circle* round the luminary.—Tr.

252: The original has a slight pun; *über die Tafel* meaning both *on the subject* of the table and *during* the table (or dinner).—Tr.

253: A name given to different groups of delicate muscles in certain sensitive parts of the human body.—Tr.

254:

"But where of ye, O tempests, is the goal!
Are ye like those within the human breast,
Or do ye find, like eagles, some high nest?"

Childe Harold.

255: The snake-stone sucks at the wound till it has sucked out all the poison.

256: In a nutshell.—Tr.

257: The conservative or court party in the French Revolution were called the *noirs* (blacks), from the fact of the emigrant nobles wearing black velvet. The *Ensragés* was the name of a radical club.—Tr.

258: Literally, the game of *man* (*ombre*, Spanish).—Tr.

259: Joachime, Clotilda, Victor, and the Devil.

260: *Mort* (French) in the original.—Tr.

261: Manager of the game.—Tr.

262: Or face-card.—Tr.

263: No pun in the original.—Tr.]

264: A Parisian anatomiste (b. 1719) persecuted by the profession to London, where she exhibited her wax-skeleton with success.—Tr.

265: Described on Another pages

266: Entertainments for the gods, at which their images were laid on couches (*lecti*), and food was served up to them in public.—Tr.

267: *Panist* from the Latin *panis*,—an allusion to an old class of charity scholars. It might be rendered, *loafer*.—Tr.

268: Alluding to the long attempts in Germany to fuse the Calvinistie and Lutheran Churches.—Tr.

269: *Musicus* here, not *musicant*, which latter means the more common performer, fiddler, or whatever else.—Tr.

270: Father confessor.—Tr.

271: Plutarch mentions how vain Pompey's cavaliers were of their personal appearance, and that Cæsar accordingly directed his soldiers to aim at their faces; "for Cæsar hoped that those young cavaliers who had not been used to wars and wounds, and who set a great value on their beauty, would avoid above all things a stroke in that part, and immediately give way, as well on account of the present danger as the future deformity. The event answered his expectation."—Tr.

272: To save the external decencies of virtue.—Tr.

273: I. e., O Clarissa! behold your Lovelace; let us skip the first four volumes, and, like the makers of Epics, begin with the rest!

274: A kind of fire-alarm.—Tr.

276: He mistakes; Leibnitz only said, everything difficult was light to him, and everything light difficult.

277: As the old fellow who carried his pipe in his boot, when his leg was shot off at the battle of Prague, grabbed at his pipe first and then at his leg. (See Old Song.)—Tr.

278: "Colors produced on ores by the action of the air."—Adler.

279: *Viel-Liebe* is Jean Paul's word, to match which, after the analogy of Polygamy (marriage to many), we might coin the word *Polyagapy* (love to many).—Tr.

280: Instead of *malade imaginaire*, an imaginary invalid, she was an imaginary *convalescent*.—Tr.

281: *Adjuvans* is the ingredient which strengthens the powers of the main ingredients; *constituens* is what gives the medicine the form of pill, electuary or mixture.

282: One weeps, one cries, one sighs, one lies, one raves, one kills, one dies,—in fine, one gives himself to all the devils, in order to have his angel.—Tr.

283: As we say *pea-soup, vermicelli-soup*.

284: Referring to the one whose marriage to the Senior Parson's daughter Victor witnessed that night from his window.—Tr.

285: See note

286: Of course, Procrustes.—Tr.

287: Cheeks.—Tr.

288: The God of sleep was attended by three beings: *Phantasus,* who could change himself only into lifeless things; *Phobetor,* who could assume and conjure up all animal forms; and *Moropheus,* who could, all human forms. Metamorph. Lib. II. Fab. 10.

289: Painter's colics.—Tr.

290: "Seed to the sower and bread to the eater." (Isaiah.)—Tr.

291: Nor yet by a luxury, whose magnitude one exaggerates in comparing their outlays with our income, and which injured them only in this way, that they inherited the nations like East Indian cousins. It was that of a cobbler who has won the highest prize in the lottery; it was the squandering of a soldier after the plundering. Hence they had luxury without refinement. It could maintain its greatness only by growing greater. Had one thrown to them America with its gold bars, they might, with greater luxury, have gone on this crutch some centuries longer.

292: It is well known that the head of the poor negro is shut up in a hollow one of iron, which presses down his tongue.

293: Written in the year 1792.

294: The millionnaire presupposes the beggar, the scholar, the Helot; the higher culture of individuals is purchased by the degradation of the mass.

295: Written in 1792. At present the tempest which once stood in the heavens over all Europe lies out there in the level earth.

296: For after 400,000 years the earth's axis, as Jupiter's is now, will be perpendicular to the plane of its orbit.